THE SCENT OF FRANGIPANI

Anjana Rai Chaudhuri grew up in India and studied and worked in India, America and the UK, before settling in Singapore. A retired scientist, Anjana divides her time between writing, reading and social work.

Learn more about the author at www.anjanaraichaudhuri.com and follow her on Twitter: @ChaudhuriAnjana and on Facebook: Anjana Rai Chaudhuri Author.

THE SCENT OF FRANGIPANI

ANJANA RAI CHAUDHURI

Dollarbird

 Dollarbird

First published in 2019
by Dollarbird, an imprint of Monsoon Books Ltd
www.dollarbird.co.uk
www.monsoonbooks.co.uk

No.1 The Lodge, Burrough Court,
Burrough on the Hill, LE14 2QS, UK.

ISBN (paperback): 978-1-912049-54-7
ISBN (ebook): 978-1-912049-55-4

Cover design by Cover Kitchen.

A Cataloguing-in-Publication data record is available from the British
Library.

Printed and bound in Great Britain by Clays Ltd, Elcograf S.p.A.
21 20 19   1 2 3

For my husband, Royston,

and

Uma and Dilip Rai Chaudhuri
(my late parents)

PART ONE

Childhood

1915–1926

"There is always one moment in childhood
when the door opens and lets the future in."
Graham Greene

1

Singapore, 1915

On a brooding August day, a small village in the eastern part of the island slumbered uneasily under the oppressive heat. The leaves of the trees were motionless; the voices of washerwomen lifted joyously into the air, pure and true, in rhythm with their activities on the riverbank, the hint of urgency in their movements heralding the approaching storm. The farmers in the fields had taken off their conical straw hats, their bare, sweating backs glistening like mirrors. It was late afternoon, but some fishermen were already making their way back to their huts, unwilling to risk being caught at sea in a storm. Black clouds hung like stalactites from the sky, and the village waited anxiously.

In one farm hut, a Chinese woman writhed on her bed like an animal in pain, emitting fresh moans from paper-white lips as contractions stabbed at her body. Beads of sweat trickled down her face to wet her *kebaya,* and her bosom heaved as she gasped for the air that would ease her child into the world. The sound of a door opening penetrated the thick mist of suffering in the confinement room, and the woman looked up to see the face of Old Lingling, the village sorceress.

The crone uttered a soft expletive in Bazaar Malay before

switching to Hokkien, the common Chinese dialect spoken in the village. "What can you expect but calamity if you give birth in the month of the hungry ghosts? Today is the seventh day of the seventh moon, when ghosts are clamouring to be let out of the gates of hell. Some ghosts are souls without descendants, and they want your child."

"No! Do not utter inauspicious words, Old Mother," the woman, Chingching, pleaded, her arms flailing weakly in the air before falling to the oilcloth draping the bed. Her swollen body twisted with effort, and she continued in a whisper, "I know today is the double seventh, when we celebrate the love of the cowherd and the weaver maiden. The ghosts do not visit us until the fifteenth day, Old Mother."

Old Lingling was incensed. "You dare to correct me, Chingching? The double seventh day is a day of sorrow, when we recall the tragic love story of the cowherd and the weaver maiden. If we do not appease the gods and ghosts today, your baby, if lucky enough to live, will be unlucky in love, and have a doomed marriage."

"But I was told that this day is auspicious for marriages! If one is married on the double seventh, one will have the faithful love of the cowherd and the weaver maiden of folklore," Chingching whispered desperately. "No matter. Midwife, please place the *T'ung Shu* on my abdomen. The holy book will shield my womb from evil spirits."

Old Lingling snorted. "The almanac cannot save you, girl. We need stronger measures."

Chingching sank back on the bed, drained. "I defer to your

judgement. Oh, please do as you see fit, Old Mistress. We must protect my baby."

"Dan Long!" Old Lingling cried. "Come here, boy!"

A thin boy of eight rushed in from the next room, eyes round with fright. Old Lingling thrust out a piece of yellow paper and instructed him to fetch red ink to write down a charm from the holy book, one which would protect the baby from evil spirits.

"Where is Liao Wei?" The old woman muttered in irritation as Dan Long dropped the yellow paper on the floor.

"Pa has gone for the Chinese medicine man," Dan Long replied.

The pain was intense now. Chingching gripped the sides of the bed and bit her lip so hard that blood, fresh and red, spurted forth. From far away, she heard the old woman's voice prescribe an ancient charm, and the lilting intonation lulled her senses. She could feel the child inside her yearning to escape the velvety darkness of her womb, eager to blink its eyes in the harsh glare of the world.

"We have burnt the charm and mixed the ashes with water, Chingching. Drink up the ashes and you will be saved yet." Old Lingling thrust her face near the eyes that were beginning to glaze over.

Thunder rumbled nearby and Chingching, tottering on the brink of unconsciousness, parted her lips reluctantly. The water trickled down her throat and her midriff exploded in agony. Her limbs thrashed wildly, and the Chinese almanac shot into the air and dropped to the floor.

"Get Liao Wei!" The midwife screamed at Dan Long. "We

may not be able to save either mother or baby!"

The thunderstorm broke. Lanterns were hurriedly lit but failed to penetrate the curtain of darkness drawing slowly over the mind and eyes of the young woman. And an eight-year-old boy raced down the dirt road of the *kampong*, his heart pounding, feet slithering and sliding, the rain lashing his face, his mind clouded with worry about his mother.

When Chingching's husband, Liao Wei, rushed into his house, his neighbours had gathered in the front room, their heads shaking and their faces grave.

Her husband's comforting presence gave Chingching the strength to fight, and she thrust out her legs with renewed vigour. She heard the midwife cry out joyfully, and dimly she registered the wail of her newborn baby.

Chingching lay back spent, her face and neck bathed in moisture, no energy left in her to combat the mist veiling her mind, the paralysis stealing through her limbs. Her mouth formed words not destined for human ears, and her open eyes saw little of the world she was leaving. A sob escaped her throat on realizing that she would become a memory to her family.

Liao Wei placed their baby in her arms. The mother looked at her child through tears, and blessed it with her failing heart and slipping mind.

"Wife, fortune has smiled on us, we have a daughter," Liao Wei said.

"I am not destined to enjoy our daughter's childhood." Liao Wei and Dan Long had to strain their ears to hear Chingching's tired whisper. "Please name our daughter—Mei Mei. It means younger sister. That way, Dan Long will always remember to take care of her for his mother."

Anxiety pricked Chingching's dimming mind. She had one last duty to perform before she crossed the river to go home.

Her voice rose. "Husband, if you remarry, please allow my cousin, Ai Lin, to take care of my daughter. Ai Lin is not blessed with children, and my daughter will be motherless. Unite them, dear husband. This is my last wish." She folded her son's hand in her own. "And if that comes to pass, Dan Long, follow Mei Mei to Aunt Ai Lin's house. Never be parted from your sister." Chingching smiled faintly at her son before closing her eyes.

Liao Wei passed the baby to one of the village women who crooned, "This child will grow up to be as beautiful as her mother."

The evening lay suspended in time until the pendulum of life stilled in the body lying on the bed.

Old Lingling wiped a solitary tear from her eye. "Chingching was only thirty years old. She was taken too young." The old crone looked at the villagers. "Come, let us prepare for her wake."

So it was, that on the seventh day of the seventh lunar month of 1915, the Year of the Rabbit, Liao Mei Mei was born; and to save her from the clutches of the hungry ghosts, so the story went, her mother sacrificed her own life. Later, when Mei Mei had grown up, the villagers would shake their heads and wonder whether Chingching's death had been in vain, and whether an inauspicious birth hour forever doomed one's destiny.

2

England, 1923

Clementine was in the wild Cornish countryside, where the sound of the sea was a distant murmur. Out of a white smoky mist rose a steep black rock, a ruined building with crumbling walls and broken windows perched on its summit like a skullcap. She knew she had to reach the rock and the room at the top, or someone would die. Her heart hammered as tendrils of yellow fog coalesced to form an opaque blanket, hiding the ruin on the rock from view. Strange whispers from pixie creatures swirled around her, and she knew they would lead her astray. The whispers grew louder, and a sharp cry rent the air.

Ten-year-old Clementine's eyes flew open and stared at the whitewashed ceiling of her bedroom in her father's manor house. Her heartbeat slowed, but her blue eyes held traces of the panic from her nightmare. She ran her hands through her golden curls and stiffened as the whispers started again. Now she could hear the faint murmur of voices, and her hands relaxed around the bed sheet she had been clutching. Her parents occupied the room below: it was their voices she could hear coming up through the fireplace, not those of pixies.

She could hear her mother's hysterical crying, interspersed

with her father's rough baritone. Clem pulled the quilt over her head and buried her head into her pillow to drown out the sound of her mother's tears and pleadings. The terror of the nightmare was replaced by fear for her mother. Mama was so beautiful, with her golden ringlets piled high on her head, her blue eyes luminous with a wild light, strangely attractive and frightening at the same time. Clem caught her breath every time she looked at Muriel Arbuthnot, and her world filled with happiness when Muriel folded her into her arms in a tight embrace.

Clem shifted uneasily under the bedclothes. The instances of intimacy with her mother were growing fewer, as a mysterious disease laid hold of Muriel's body and mind. Clementine frowned. She caught whispers of "Neurotic, that's what's wrong," and "Gone in the 'ead" from the servants; but Muriel had taught her daughter not to listen to servants' gossip.

"Let nobody stand in the way of your dreams and you will know happiness," her mother had whispered to Clem. That had been two months ago, when they had had their last long talk together in Muriel's bedroom. Muriel's eyes had widened with a wistful look, and she had buried her face in her daughter's soft golden hair.

"What are you thinking, Mama?" Clem burrowed out of her mother's embrace.

Muriel sighed. "I always wanted to see the Continent and the Far East. I am not sure I ever will. I have a childhood friend, Eleanor Harrison, who lives in Singapore, a land far from us. We were inseparable when we were young, and I would have dearly liked to visit her one day. She has invited me countless times. She says Singapore has bright sunshine every day, clear blue skies, and huge rubber trees. She says birdsong greets her every morning when she opens her eyes, and the ocean has so many liners. Here in Cornwall, we are greeted by the squawk of gulls, grey skies and rain."

"Maybe you will go to this foreign land one day, Mama," Clem said, alarmed at the sad light in her mother's eyes.

"I don't think so, darling," Muriel said and laughed, the sound becoming shrill.

Clem jumped and looked uneasily at her mother. Why was Mama laughing and crying at the same time?

Muriel's hysterics brought Nurse Watkins from the next room, a bottle of soothing syrup in her hands. The nurse told Clem to go out and play.

Clem burrowed deeper underneath the blanket. Thoughts of her mother worried her, and she turned her mind to her nanny, thinking of the picnic they had planned for tomorrow, after Sunday church.

Nanny Pengelly was Cornish and prone to what her mother described as "telling tall tales". Nanny firmly believed in pixies, the mythical and mischievous little people of Cornwall. She warned Clem never to be out on Bodmin moor alone, for pixies were good at stealing children. Clem had laughed, but when darkness fell over the sea, and the only sound was the waves thundering on the Newquay shore, she felt that pixies were prowling around the garden outside. Clem's isolated existence was relieved by Nanny's tales, her picnics, and her cheerful demeanour that was a sharp contrast to Muriel's oscillating moods.

The house was silent. Muriel had stopped crying in the room downstairs, and slowly Clem eased herself out from under the duvet. The fire had been lit and the room was warm. Soon the child's eyes grew heavy as the clouds in the sky outside lightened with the breaking of dawn. Clementine slept.

The next day emerged bright and sunny, with the sea a clear blue and the waters calm. Nanny and Clem took the bus to Bodmin, carrying baskets of food and drink. In the bus, Clem looked at Nanny gazing out of the window and smiled. Clem knew that once they spread out the quilt over the grassland and started their picnic, Nanny would embark on one of her tales that would hold Clem spellbound, for Clem's gothic imagination found a ready home in Nanny Pengelly's tales of Camelot, King Arthur's bravery and Merlin's magic. Muriel often said that Clem dwelt in a dark world of her own, where magic weaved fairy-tales from malevolent deeds.

Soon the sea was left behind, and the bus began to climb a narrow road amid brown and green moorland vegetation. Not a house or farm was in sight, and the inland air was cooler than near the sea. Clem, attuned to atmosphere, felt a chill travel down her spine—the landscape seemed vaguely familiar.

Suddenly, in the distance, a menacing black shape rose from the thin mist. It seemed to come out of nowhere, looming and leering over the landscape like a gigantic bird of prey.

"What is that thing?" Clem croaked.

"Sakes alive, Miss, that be Roche Rock. Just a slab of stone from ancient times, nothing more." Nanny Pengelly turned to face Clem.

"Does it have a ruined building on the top?" Clem's voice was suddenly clear.

"Yes, that it does," Nanny smiled. "That be the ruined chapel on top of Roche Rock. We be having our picnic nearby and you be welcome to explore the rock, Miss. Just be careful of them iron ladders leading to the top floor."

She rose from her seat, ready to disembark, the picnic basket clutched in one hand and Clem's hand in the other. With a cacophony of screeching brakes and grinding gears, the country bus drew to a shuddering halt.

Roche Rock looked even more forbidding up close. Rising out of the flat moorland, the steep rock stood in solitary splendour, a silent sentinel towering over the windswept landscape. The chapel crowning it was at once magnificent and bleak, a sanctuary for travellers and hermits of old, Nanny said, a place where star-crossed lovers took shelter.

Sitting on a quilt with a plate of sandwiches in her hands, Nanny told the centuries-old tale of Tristan and Iseult, who had fallen passionately in love after drinking love potions. Iseult was married to King Mark, Tristan's beloved uncle, who had sent his men to kill the lovers.

"They escaped to Roche Rock, they did." Nanny's eyes were fixed dreamily on the chapel. "A hermit was living in the chapel and he gave the lovers sanctuary. Many a time, through the ages, men and women have sought shelter in that chapel. Come, Miss, we will go and explore it, shall we?"

They climbed the iron ladder to the chapel and stood framed in the window. The view was spectacular, the moors stretching out on either side, the sun shining brightly, lighting up the landscape with colour like a bright painting on canvas, fluffy white clouds placidly rolling over the blue expanse of sky.

Clem wandered around the chamber, pulling at the rusty iron hooks protruding from the mossy walls to see if they crumbled to dust. She looked at the window—a figure in black was crouching on the sill.

"Nanny!" Clem's voice rose in panic, her blue eyes pinpricks of terror. "Where are you?"

Nanny Pengelly clambered down a flight of iron stairs from the top floor. "What's the matter, my baby?"

"There's someone at the window," Clem whispered.

Nanny looked across the room and said, "Oh, Miss. This place is playing tricks on you. There be no one there."

Clem rushed to where she had glimpsed the figure, leaned over the sill, and stared down. There was a black body lying on the grass below. Clem screamed again and beckoned urgently to Nanny.

Nanny Pengelly came to the window and looked down to where Clem was pointing with a shaking finger. "Miss, that is just a rock." Nanny gave Clem a gentle shake. "It is a misshapen black rock, nothing more. Come, let us climb down. Be careful, Miss."

She shepherded Clem down the narrow iron stairs and took her to the long black boulder they had glimpsed from the window.

"See, it's only a rock." Nanny said reassuringly.

Clem edged away from it and said softly, "I want to go home, Nanny."

As the bus made its way down the curving road, Clem looked back at the chapel and shivered. Black clouds had gathered, and the granite rock brooded over the land like a sulky visage, with two windows for its eyes. She turned away as the first drops of rain began to fall.

When she entered her house, Clem stopped in surprise. Her father was standing in the hall beside a tall, dark woman with a plain face and luxuriant brown hair held in place by pins. Roger Arbuthnot was 35 years old, florid and cheery, with a tousled head of brown hair. His moustache bristled with affection as he folded his daughter in his arms.

"Clementine," he said in his deep voice, "your mother has decided that the local school is inept at teaching you the piano and other social skills, and that you are too old to have a nanny. She has hired Governess Clara Higgins to teach you music, singing and dancing."

"But I want Nanny Pengelly to stay." Clem's thin lips set in a disgruntled pout, and she turned stormy eyes on her father.

"Now then, Nanny has her life to lead, too, eh?" Roger grinned. "Nanny Pengelly is to be married soon, and we will lose her to our chauffeur, Albert. Albert and Nanny are to run a small inn in Dorset, child." He released Clem and turned to the woman beside him. "Miss Higgins, let me introduce your charge—Clementine. She has a heightened imagination, but she manages to overcome her sudden bleak fancies."

Clem looked sullenly into the cool brown eyes of her governess.

Clementine sat on the window seat in her bedroom and gazed at the grey landscape beyond. The morning's incessant rain had stopped, but the afternoon remained bitterly cold, and the stormy sea crashed fiercely to the shore, stirring up angry white foam. Lunch was bread and water in her bedroom, as punishment for not having learnt a new piano tune to Governess Clara's satisfaction. At first, Clem had fiercely rebelled against Governess Clara's penchant for harsh punishments for the slightest mistakes—but with Muriel having taken permanently to her bed, the governess had a free hand in Clem's upbringing, and so Clem kept her peace.

Clem looked down into the garden and frowned. Her father was showing her governess the roses in his garden. He looked young and carefree, laughing at Clara Higgins' words, his face bent to hers. Clementine crept away from the window and marched to the schoolroom. From the window there she shouted, "I have finished my sums, Miss Higgins! Aren't we going to have that geography lesson this afternoon?"

Roger glanced up, his guilty face satisfying Clem; but she was unprepared for the look of cold anger in her governess's eyes as Clara strode into the schoolroom.

"Speaking when you are spoken to is a lesson worth learning, Clementine," Clara said, taking a seat at the study table. "Wait for me in the schoolroom in the future, and do not shout from the window like a hooligan."

Clem's look of pure hatred mirrored that of her governess.

3

Singapore, 1923

Mei Mei sat happily on the wooden floor of her father's portico, eating *goreng pisang* bought from the seller hawking his wares on the dirt road outside. The warmth of the setting sun left a sheen of moisture on Mei Mei's aquiline nose and above her full red lips, and as she flicked back her braided hair, she looked beautiful. She bit into the banana fritters and looked across the narrow dirt road to the stream, a hive of activity at this time of the evening. Several huts erected on stilts floated on the stream like squat ships at anchor, with women sitting on their porches preparing dinner. Mei Mei's face lit up as she spied her brother coming along the dirt road, tired after a hard day's work at their father's farm. She ran and fetched a pitcher of water for him to wash his face and take a drink.

Soon after, Liao Wei and his two children sat down to their meagre meal. Liao Wei's head of thick white hair and stoop made him look older than his thirty-eight years. He looked suspiciously at his son's glowing face and snorted.

"Dan Long, you think I don't know that you slunk away from the farm this afternoon? Where were you?"

Dan Long smiled, a dreamy look in his eyes. He was a

handsome, strapping lad of sixteen, with large eyes hid behind thick spectacles.

"I went to attend Dr Sun Yat-Sen's rally, Pa! My night schoolteachers speak highly of him, and I was filled with admiration on hearing his speech," Dan Long said. "He is fearless, fighting the Qing emperor in a bid to end imperialism in China. He is forming Kuomintang Party branches in Singapore, and I am going to sign up as a member. Down with the Qing!" Dan Long held up his hand dramatically.

Liao Wei dropped his chopsticks with a clatter and stopped Mei Mei's giggles with a glare. "You will do no such thing, Dan Long. What have China's politics got to do with us here?"

"Pa, have you forgotten that you were born and bred in China? Dr Sun is trying to better the lot of our relatives there! We should support him. Many clan leaders donated funds today for the Kuomintang movement."

"I have a good mind to stop you from attending night school, Son. Education is one thing, it will help you procure a good job; but if it is making you follow foolish ideologies, recited by your mainland China teachers, it will do more harm than good. Do not join the Kuomintang Party! Who knows when they will incite violence against British imperialism? Then we are done for. We eat British salt, don't forget."

Dan Long did not reply and returned to his food.

Singapore, 1925
The early morning air of the market near Mei Mei's village resounded with the shouts of fishmongers proclaiming the

freshness of the shoals of glistening, silvery fish laid out side by side in wicker baskets. Bullock carts rolled down the road with logs of wood or barrels of produce, while rickshaw pullers traversed the street edges, ferrying children to school and women to the markets. Three food vendors, bamboo poles with baskets of ingredients and kitchen tools balanced on their shoulders, ran along the road towards the bigger market a mile away.

Ten-year-old Mei Mei sat on an upturned bucket in front of a pushcart hawker, eating *kaya* toast. She loved coconut jam. Dan Long stood nearby, eating barbecued pork buns, while Liao Wei, dressed in his best clothes, drank tea from a cracked cup. Mei Mei's doe-like eyes held traces of fear, and a nervous tic twitched at the corner of her mouth.

Her life had changed two years earlier, when her father had married Old Lingling's granddaughter, nineteen-year-old Shu Lan. Mei Mei shuddered as her thoughts returned to the tragic day she feared would haunt her all her life.

She had been overjoyed when Shu Lan had given birth to her stepbrother, Wen Long, and Mei Mei had doted on her young brother, always by his side from the moment she came home from school. One day, when Wen Long was seven months old, Mei Mei was caring for him while his mother attended a *wayang*. It was a Sunday, and the village men were fishing by the stream while their children played in the fields surrounding the village. Without warning, Wen Long's eyes had rolled up revealing the whites, and he had begun to shake and kick his legs, all the while foaming at the mouth. Mei Mei had lain him in her lap and vainly tried to rock him back to sleep. An hour later, Shu Lan had returned from the street opera to find Mei Mei singing a lullaby as she rocked her brother's lifeless body.

Mei Mei's heartbeat had filled her chest on hearing Shu Lan's keening wail. Villagers had rushed into the room and the *sinseh*, after noticing a milk stain on the baby's vest, had pronounced that the contaminated milk that had already taken two young lives in the village had now claimed Wen Long's.

Mei Mei's eyes flashed as she remembered the harsh, grating voice of Old Lingling. The village crone had wiped a solitary tear from her eye and said, "Whatever the medicine man says, this death was caused by Chingching's spirit working through her daughter, Mei Mei. Wen Long died in the arms of a cursed child." Old Lingling looked at her granddaughter, who was glaring at Mei Mei. "You would do well to turn Mei Mei out of this house if you want to start a family, Shu Lan."

Overcome with grief by her child's death, and jealous of Liao Wei's love for his daughter, Shu Lan had lost her head and screamed, "I curse you, Liao Mei Mei! May you never enjoy the joys of motherhood, and die an early death."

Ignoring the uneasy murmurings of the villagers, she rounded on Liao Wei, who was gazing at her, stunned. "Old Man, I married you to beget children, not to take care of your precious daughter. She is a jinx and has taken my son's life. Get her out of my house or I will jump into the well."

Dan Long had watched the light of hope in his sister's eyes die as she gazed at their father. He went to her and enveloped her in a tight embrace. "Wherever you go, Mei Mei, I will follow you, for you are my younger sister, my Mei Mei. I will uphold my promise to Ma."

Two nights later, Mei Mei had been crying into her pillow, remembering Wen Long's sweet face, when she had heard her father rise from his creaking bed in the next room. She followed his lantern light to the kitchen and saw him rummage inside a small cupboard. Mei Mei watched in silence as Liao Wei then entered the back garden, 'Bank of Hell' notes clutched in his hands.

The stream beyond the dirt road glittered in the moonlight, and as she gazed into the night sky, Mei Mei saw that the stars were out. Liao Wei struck a match to the papers and watched them light up. His face glowed in the firelight, and he began to chant slowly, his voice piercing the silence of the night.

"Chingching, my wife, now a benevolent spirit, I am sending Mei Mei to Ai Lin like you said, but please forgive me for selling her as a *mui-tsai* to the House of Toh. Ai Lin's mother-in-law is the matriarch of the house and will not have it otherwise, and Shu Lan will mistreat our daughter if she stays with me. I know you are angry at my failure to discipline Shu Lan, and I therefore burn these papers to appease you. They represent my meagre fortune."

"No!" Mei Mei had rushed out of the kitchen door and fallen at her father's feet. "Pa, please do not sell me as a bondmaid! I have heard such horror stories from other bondmaids. They are beaten black and blue by their employers. I beg of you, dear Father, please do not send me away. I promise to stay out of Stepma's way and be a good girl. Please, Pa, have mercy on your poor daughter."

Tears trickled down Liao Wei's face. The firelight danced,

the papers crackled, and a dog began to bark obsessively in the distance. The birds on the branches of the trees watched the apparitions by the fire in surprise. When the papers had burned to ashes, Liao Wei rose from the ground, his face bathed in sweat and tears. Dreams for his beautiful daughter lay scattered in the ashes, and Chingching's essence was everywhere, in the crevices of the trees, in the murmur of the river.

Her father had taken Mei Mei in his arms and said in a shaking voice, "You are a sweet angel and deserve better than your poor father can provide. The *mui-tsai* system is a part of our culture, little one. Poor fathers who wish to give a better life to our daughters send them as bondmaids to affluent homes. That is all it is, eh? You will never have to fear poverty or hunger in your life. When she sees your beautiful face, Ai Lin's mother-in-law will ask me to sign the red adoption papers, and not the white contract of servitude. Do not fret!"

Now, Mei Mei shook her head to clear away the memories, and finished her *kaya* toast. Today, she would set out from her father's house to live with her aunt. Her eyes glimmered with tears at the thought of leaving the place of her birth.

Moved by her sorrow, Liao Wei said gruffly, "You will be living in the lap of luxury, with servants taking care of all your needs, daughter. It was a lucky day when your Aunt Ai Lin married your Uncle Toh. He is called Towkay Toh, you know, and is a very wealthy businessman. Your aunt has promised that you will go to school, my child. Besides, your brother will be residing with you. You will not be lonely."

He turned to his son. "Dan Long, you are lucky to procure

the job of accountant at your Uncle Toh's office; this is your only chance of making something of your life." Liao Wei added sternly, "Let us not hear anything more of the Kuomintang Party, and I want good reports from Uncle Toh on your performance in his warehouse."

Mei Mei gave a tremulous smile—whatever the future held, her brother was going to be by her side. The sweet, lingering scent of frangipani drifted over her, a fragrance that would always remind her of the beloved *kampong* of her birth.

After the family had finished breakfast at the hawker stall—a farewell meal for Mei Mei that Liao Wei had arranged behind Shu Lan's back—a rickshaw was hailed to take the family to Towkay Toh's mansion. The rickshaw stopped in front of a house on a tree-lined avenue called Waterloo Street, near enough to the sea to smell the salty air.

Mei Mei gazed in awe at the splendour of her new home. Eight steps from the well-paved road led up to a wrought iron gate, which opened onto a tiled portico. The two-storey bungalow rose up a few yards beyond, with numerous ornate windows covered by colourful shutters for ventilation, and a stone wall separating the house from the road for privacy. Affluence breathed from every corner of the neighbourhood, a far cry from the humble *kampong* of Mei Mei's birth.

"Mei Mei! Welcome to the House of Toh!" A woman in her mid-thirties, dressed in a yellow silk cheongsam embroidered with black flowers, rushed out of the front door of the mansion. Coloured pins held her stiffly coifed hair in place, and silk slippers adorned her tiny feet.

Mei Mei submitted to Aunt Ai Lin's warm embrace, and inhaled the perfume from her clothes appreciatively. After a moment her aunt released her and led the way to a big hall, with rooms opening from it on either side. In the middle, on a huge, ornate chair, sat the fiercest looking old woman Mei Mei had ever seen. She had braided white hair piled high on her head, and thick eyebrows jutting over burning, coal-black eyes that raked Mei Mei from head to toe.

"This is Grandma Sim, Mei Mei," Aunt Ai Lin whispered in Hokkien, her big eyes wide with trepidation, "my mother-in-law. Please pay your respects."

Mei Mei bowed to Grandma Sim, who continued to gaze at her with piercing eyes. The old woman said in Hokkien: "Walk down the hall for me. It will never do to buy a maid who cannot walk gracefully." After pronouncing satisfaction at her gait, the old lady pulled Mei Mei towards her and pinched her hands.

The child screamed in rage and backed away. "Learn to endure pain, child," Grandma Sim scolded Mei Mei, a malicious smile lighting her leathery face. "Men are born to labour, while women are born to pain. How will you give birth, eh, if you cannot tolerate discomfort?"

Grandma Sim's sharp eyes fixed brightly on Liao Wei, like a vulture viewing a bloodied corpse. "Your girl has a flat stomach and soft hands, and there is promise of beauty to come. We need that, eh, to marry her off at eighteen. Liao, your daughter was born in the calamitous month of the hungry ghosts. I cannot pay you more than fifty dollars for her."

Liao Wei looked with disappointment at the sheet of white

paper the Toh matriarch, Grandma Sim, was holding forth for his signature.

"Liao Wei," the old woman jeered on seeing his stricken face, "come on! Your daughter was born in the most inauspicious month in the Chinese calendar! How can I adopt her as a daughter of this house? She will be a *mui-tsai* and no more! Take it or leave it," the old woman added for good measure.

Liao Wei overcame his hesitation at the thought of Shu Lan's wrathful face if he returned home with Mei Mei. Slowly and laboriously, his pen moved over the contract. He sold his daughter as a domestic servant to the House of Toh.

"Pa, you are selling me?" Mei Mei cried, her eyes pools of horror. She had thought her father would take her home unless she was adopted.

Liao Wei cringed from Mei Mei. As she grasped the reason for her father's discomfiture, a change came over Mei Mei's face. Nostrils flared, she looked directly into his eyes and whispered in Hokkien, "To my father, I am no better than the crops he grows on his farm."

The colour drained from Liao Wei's face. His daughter's accusing eyes ignited a flame of guilt within him, which spread to consume him on a funeral pyre of deep remorse. He turned on his heel and ran from the house, his face red with shame.

That night, lying between embroidered satin sheets on a grand four-poster bed, Mei Mei desperately longed for the torn mattress of her father's house and his comforting presence. Outside, an owl gave a heart-wrenching cry. Mei Mei saw its dancing shadow on the iron bars of the window, as it searched vainly for its nest.

* * *

The uncertainty and fear that had accompanied her to the House of Toh abated when Mei Mei realised that she was treated as Ai Lin's niece by the household, rather than as a bondmaid. Aunt Ai Lin's husband, Uncle Toh, a stout, dark-skinned man of forty, with sleepy eyes, appeared at the house only at nights and on Sundays. He spent the rest of his time supervising the unloading of rice at his warehouse on Boat Quay, and its sale from his shop on Rochor Road. He owned a side business distributing rubber for plantation owners, and it was in his rubber distribution warehouse that Dan Long worked as an accountant. Towkay Toh spoke little, but treated Mei Mei with a quiet affection that lit a spark of joy in the little girl. He enrolled her in the English-medium Methodist Girls' School, determined to give his wife's niece a good education.

Mei Mei approached her first day at school with trepidation. She nervously clutched her aunt's hand as she was led to the gharry to take her to school. The gharry was a two-seater carriage drawn by a sleepy-looking black pony and presided over by the Toh coachman, Sulaiman, an old Malay, with a bald head and merry, twinkling eyes. Mei Mei looked questioningly at the black curtains piled behind the seats.

"Girls are not to be seen when travelling on the open road, little one," Ai Lin said softly. "When we are seated, Sulaiman will draw the curtains."

"Then I won't be able to see the road and shops!" Mei Mei cried in dismay.

"Now, little one," said Ai Lin, patting Mei Mei's head, "we have to follow custom. Don't be afraid of school; I will soon be there to bring you home again."

Sulaiman jerked the reins, the horse set off, and after a bumpy ten minutes, the dark gharry finally drew to a stop. Sulaiman flung back the curtains and Mei Mei blinked in the sudden sunlight. Her vision cleared to see that they had joined the end of a line of carts and rickshaws in front of an imposing white building with a pyramid-shaped roof and huge white pillars.

At the gate, a tall schoolmistress was greeting the new girls and dispatching them to their classrooms with the help of older students. Mei Mei bade goodbye to Ai Lin and followed a senior girl into the school building. Soon she was installed in a classroom, and her heartbeat quickened as thirty strange girls created bedlam all around her. It wasn't long, however, before she was engrossed in her lessons, and she felt elated when the teacher praised her in needlework class.

When school finished for the day, Mei Mei ran to Ai Lin at the school gates and hugged her.

"There now, little one, it wasn't so bad, was it?" Her aunt's voice was comforting. "Today Sulaiman is busy taking your uncle to the shops, and we will have to walk home. Instead of going through Middle Road to Waterloo Street, we will take a detour and visit Queen Street. My dear friend lost her grandniece in China, and I promised to meet her at a food stall in Queen Street, just for a few moments."

Queen Street was a narrow road, lined with dilapidated terraced houses. Food stalls occupied some of the lower floors, with tables set up along the wide, sheltered corridor that formed the five foot pedestrian walkway outside the houses. Children played in the middle of the street, and a game of hopscotch proceeded in one corner, with young girls dexterously negotiating the chalk-marked squares they had drawn on the pavement.

Mei Mei came to a halt as she spied a tall girl, with a smooth white complexion and brown pigtails, talking to a Malay satay-seller whose mobile cart was parked next to the pavement. She recognised the girl as one of her schoolmates who had sat at the back of the class. The seller had unloaded the barbecue pit from his cart onto the road and had lit the coals inside. He squatted down beside the brazier and began to fan the embers with his straw hat. Mei Mei watched, fascinated. Soon the coals were glowing red, and the seller placed four beef skewers on the barbecue grate. The burning coals sent up a spiral of smoke, carrying the enticing aroma of roasting meat into the evening air.

"Can I have some satay, Aunt Ai Lin?" Mei Mei pleaded.

Ai Lin smiled and nodded. She gave her niece a handful of coins and said, "Go on with you then. I can see my friend waiting for me. I will collect you later. Don't wander off, little one."

Mei Mei ran to the seller and asked for two sticks of grilled chicken. She glanced shyly at the tall girl waiting for the beef sticks that were already sizzling on the grate.

"Wait! Aren't you in my class?" the girl asked; and when Mei Mei nodded smiling, they solemnly shook hands. "What's your name?"

"I am Liao Mei Mei. What's yours?"

"I'm Winnie Pereira. Why, Mei Mei is a pretty name, and

you're a pretty girl."

The satay-seller came over with two cracked plates containing four skewers of grilled meat, ample peanut sauce, pickles and rice cakes.

"My house is just here," Winnie called gaily. "We can sit on the front steps and eat. Come along, Mei Mei."

The two girls took their plates and sat on the top steps of a narrow two-storey house with a green door. Munching the delicious satay and watching the pedestrians walk by, the two girls exchanged their family histories. Soon they were fast friends.

Winnie was tall for her age, had a pleasant face with a pert nose, a generous mouth, and long brown hair tied severely into pigtails. Winnie's mother had died of tuberculosis when Winnie was five years old. She lived with her father and her paternal grandmother.

"My father is of mixed Portuguese and Indian blood. We call ourselves 'Eurasians'," Winnie said, between mouthfuls of grilled meat and rice cakes. "Gran is from Calcutta. She calls herself an Anglo-Indian, and you should hear the tales she tells of colonial India! Gramps was a Portuguese seaman, and he met Gran while on shore leave in Calcutta. They married there, and Gramps brought Gran back to Singapore. He died before I was born. Pa has a mistress in Malabar Street, a Chinese *ah ku* he calls Mona, but Gran will never allow him to marry a prostitute. I have two half-sisters." Winnie laughed, her clear brown eyes merry and the sides of her nose crinkling becomingly. "My father got a good job in a bank three years ago. That's why he could afford to send me to the Methodist Girls' School. Gran home-schooled me before that. So now you know why I'm older than you but in the same class." She gave an attractive gap-toothed grin.

Later that week, the girls went to a *pasar malam* in Chinatown and bought two gold-plated pendants held by thick black threads. In the bright lights of the night market, they cut a lock from each other's hair, slid the pendants open, and placed the intertwined brown and black locks in the tiny spaces. Mei Mei and Winnie proudly wore their 'best friend' necklaces every day, taking them off only when they went to bed.

Whenever Mei Mei visited Winnie's home, Winnie's grandmother, a smiling woman with snow-white hair known to everyone as "Gran", would send the girls to Ah Teng's Bakery for curry puffs and cakes. The children ate them with tea in the small room off the kitchen that served as a dining room.

While the girls did their school homework together at the dining table, Gran would sometimes bake her delicious *sugee* cake. The house would fill with an aroma that made the girls' mouths water. After a delicious meal of rice, devilled eggs and Babi Assam curry—pork cooked with tamarind pulp—Gran would place a plate of the moist semolina-and-almond cake slices on the dining table for dessert. After they had eaten, the two girls would go onto the walkway to play with other children of their age. With time, Mei Mei began to miss her *kampong* less and less.

As the years passed, the bond of camaraderie established between Mei Mei and Winnie in their youth evolved into a deep attachment of love and loyalty. And for Mei Mei, the time would come when it would be responsible for a decision that would turn her life upside down.

4

Singapore, Summer, 1926

Thirteen-year-old Clementine opened her blue eyes at the sound of the foghorn. The tiny cabin of the ship that had ferried her from England to the Crown Colony of Singapore was filled with bright sunlight that streamed through the porthole. A sickly-sweet smell drifted in with the hot breeze, and Clem found herself bathed in tropical humidity. Easing herself off the tiny bunk, she peered through the porthole.

A picturesque sight met her eyes. Huge, brightly painted *tongkangs* were bobbing on the grey sea, and the raucous shouts of Chinese coolies filled the air. Clem hurriedly dressed and performed her toilette before running onto the deck. The breeze blew her golden curls over her face as she hung over the railing.

There was a riot of colour wherever she turned. Red Chinese junks and green Malay prows carried half-naked coolies and natives, who laughed as they counted their produce. Nearby, where the water swished against the Quay wall, a junk was unloading baskets of fruit that exuded the sickly sweet scent that had filled her cabin. As Clem watched, one of the fruits rolled into the sea.

She turned and looked out to the horizon, and her breath

caught in wonder. Huge vessels with majestic masts and sails were approaching and retreating, their dark silhouettes framed against the sky, colourful boats revolving around them like planets circling the sun. Beneath her feet, Clem felt the engines judder as the ship slowed down before dropping anchor.

She looked at the approaching shore and felt a thrill. The green vegetation was dense and unruly, like a primitive beast of nature, evoking mystique and adventure. Clem saw with delight a profusion of orange, yellow, red and purple flowers in the trees lining the harbour. They lit a flame of hope in her heart: perhaps one day she could be happy again.

But the memory of her departure from England surfaced in Clem's mind, making her hands clench tightly. Only Nanny Pengelly and her husband, along with her father's friend, Tom Whitehead, who lived in Liverpool, had stood on the docks to see her off. Roger had been too immersed in his own affairs to take the trouble to make the journey. Clem's face clouded and a haunted look flitted into her eyes as she remembered the past year.

The dreams of Roche Rock had begun occurring with alarming frequency, interrupting Clem's sleep at night as Muriel Arbuthnot slid further and further into decay. Finally, on a bleak August day, thirty-two-year-old Muriel's broken spirit had parted from her tired body. The Cornish sea, land and sky had seemed at war with each other. From her bedroom window, Clem had watched the angry waves batter the unyielding shore, while a grey sky poured out its dissatisfaction in incessant, driving rain.

A week after her mother's funeral, Clem had her most vivid nightmare of Roche Rock. This time there were two figures in her dream. Her mother was running towards the rock with Clem following her. Clem's short legs could not keep up, and her mother disappeared up the iron ladder to the chapel. A moment later, Clem spotted her mother's figure at the first-floor window, and she cried out, "Mama!"

In horror, Clem watched Muriel perch on the ledge outside the window and hang there precariously, before falling to the rocks below like a rag doll. Clem screamed and woke drenched in sweat. She badly needed the comfort of her father's strong embrace.

She put on her dressing gown, stepped out into the corridor, and paused outside her father's bedroom door. From inside came the sound of moaning: poor Papa must be crying for Mama. Clem flung open the door and rushed in.

A lamp encased the bed in a dim glow, outlining clearly the naked, intertwined figures of Roger and Governess Clara. Roger's sweaty face paled as he beheld his daughter gaping at him.

"What are you doing here?" Clementine froze as she heard anger for the first time in her gentle father's voice.

Roger rushed for his dressing gown while Clara slipped under a blanket. "Go back to your room at once!" Roger ordered, and Clementine fled.

Roger and Clara had come into the schoolroom together the next morning.

"Clementine," Roger's voice had been firm, "I loved your mother dearly, but most of our married life, she was very ill. I was very lonely, my child. Clara has brought me much joy. Clem, I have asked Clara to marry me, and she has agreed."

The colour had rushed to Clem's face. Her eyes stormy, she had cried, "I will never accept Governess Higgins as my stepmother! She is harsh and unkind. Papa, how could you do this so soon after Mama's death?"

Roger looked away.

Clara said, "Don't be melodramatic, Clementine. Your father and I have been in love for some time. Due to your mother's prolonged illness, your father has been all alone. You should be happy for him now." She turned to Roger. "I have told you many times, Roger, that Clementine should be at boarding school. She is wild and arrogant. Boarding school will shape her into a humble young lady."

Clem's eyes had been shards of blue ice, and cold anger had contorted her delicate features as she looked at her governess. "I will never go to boarding school, and I will never accept you as my stepmother."

Clem's lips thinned to a hard line as she remembered her flight to Roche Rock to escape boarding school. She had packed enough tins of food for a week, and had settled into the lonely chapel with only a pillow and sheet for her bed. It had been two days before the police, alerted by a frantic Roger, had found her. After a search in Newquay for Clem had proven fruitless, Roger had driven to Nanny Pengelly's house in Dorset. It was Nanny who had told him that the child liked visiting Roche Rock.

Roger had sat in Clem's bedroom with his head in his hands.

"Clementine, do you know what you put me through by running away? I went through hell thinking you had been kidnapped or run over, or that you were lying injured and dying in a hospital." His brown eyes moist, Roger had continued to plead. "Clem, does my happiness mean nothing to you? Clara and I are to be married. The sooner you accept that, the better it will be for everyone. I have persuaded Clara not to send you to boarding school. You will live with us in this house, my child. Is that not enough?"

Clem had looked at him with eyes full of hate. "No. I will never accept Governess Higgins as my stepmother." Roger flinched. "She has taken you away from me, and I will never forgive her for that. I will always hate her for coming into our house and breaking up our family."

Roger's eyes had cooled, and he had said, "It is obvious that you do not want to reach a compromise with us. Regardless of your attitude, Clara and I are getting married. I have no option but to send you abroad, Clementine. You may remember your Mama talking of her friend, Eleanor Harrison, living in the tropics. She lives in a place called Singapore. She was very close to Muriel and has invited you to spend a year with her and her family. I have purchased your ticket on the ship, and you will be leaving England in a month's time."

Now, as she watched Singapore's shores approaching, a sliver of fear stabbed at Clem's heart. Had her father sent her away for good, so that he could start a new family?

The ship was docking now, and Clem looked at the crowd on the shore. Would someone be there to receive her? Her Aunt Eleanor had written to her, telling Clem that she lived with her husband, John, a rubber planter, and their son, Richard, who was a year older than Clem. Clem wondered about Richard. She did not like raucous, unruly boys. Their rudeness grated on her nerves.

She went below deck to gather her belongings, and when she emerged again, the gangway was in place. The ship's passengers had started walking down the gangplank to the shore. Clem followed them, a babble of noise greeting her as she stepped onto the harbour. She looked around, feeling lost.

"You must be Clementine."

Clem turned. A tall English boy was standing next to her. He had dancing green eyes, a shock of bright auburn hair, and many freckles on his round face. The boy held out his hand.

"I am Richard Harrison. You are staying with us, you know. Come now, shake hands."

Some of the ice floating in Clem's heart began to melt, although her eyes remained suspicious. She reluctantly shook the boy's hand.

"Please come with me, Clementine," Richard said, his voice warm and friendly. "Papa is waiting in the car and we can go home. I'm sure you're starving. I've heard the grub they serve on the boat is terrible."

Clementine melted some more. "The food is horrible," she conceded, keeping close to Richard as they made their way through the crowds. "Did you know they gave us boiled mutton and cabbage for one whole week?"

"No!" Richard cried in mock horror before asking engagingly, "I say, do you play tennis?"

"No," Clementine replied, "but I can learn, and then I would probably beat you."

"Splendid!" Richard threw back his head and laughed, and Clementine turned away from him to hide a smile. They arrived on a road where carriages and cars were parked.

"I think we're going to be very good friends," Richard continued. His face became sombre and he said softly, "I'm very sorry about Aunt Muriel's death. It must have been rum watching your mother being buried and learning that your father is going to marry your governess."

Clementine whirled around, her face transformed to a cold mask. She said frigidly, "Don't ever talk to me about my father again."

"Ahem," a deep voice interrupted before a startled Richard could reply.

Clementine looked up into the warm, twinkling blue eyes of a burly Englishman in his early forties, wearing a hat and white suit.

"Clementine, I presume?" he asked in a deep voice, and gave a bow. "I'm John Harrison. You can call me Uncle John. Did you have a good voyage?"

A Malay man in a driver's uniform and cap sidled up. "*Tuan Besar*, Memsahib said to bring little Missie pronto. Lunch, it waits."

Clem hung out of the car window as it sped along the road, drinking in the sights of the city. The esplanade, called Connaught Drive, was filled with English ladies in their broughams leaning across to speak to their friends in neighbouring gigs. Clem felt immediately at home. Some of the flame coloured flowers she had glimpsed at the harbour had fallen onto the road, and she yearned to walk barefoot on the natural floral carpet. Soon the harbour was left behind, and the car snaked through a narrow road crowded with native dwellings.

An intense fragrance wafted into the car, and Clem felt nauseated. "What *is* that smell?" she asked.

"That is the scent of the frangipani flowers you were admiring, the flowers that were scattered on the road." Richard smiled. "Isn't it wonderful?"

"I don't like it," Clem announced. "It is too cloying and overpowering." She glanced outside again.

The native houses were painted bluish-white, and they had wavy, red-tiled roofs. Some had colourful shutters, and through them Clem heard women calling to their children in a curious, lilting lingo. Bullock carts rumbled past laden with cargo, and a pony trotted by pulling a cart full of laughing native girls. The girls saw Clem hanging out of the car window with her mouth open and waved, but Clem turned hastily away. In contrast, when they reached the colonial section along Tanglin Road, with its large compounds and bungalows, the street was quiet, and Clem missed the chatter and colour of the native quarters.

John Harrison's white and black bungalow was far grander than Clementine's Cornwall home, and the little girl gazed at the house with delight.

A large woman in her late thirties, with untidy brown hair and a big bosom, dressed in a tweed skirt and white blouse, rushed to Clementine and folded her in her ample arms. Richard's mother was large and florid, with a weather-beaten face, a hearty laugh, boiled gooseberry eyes, and a very large nose.

Clem extricated herself with difficulty from the woman's tight embrace. Eleanor Harrison gushed, "You don't know me, Clem, but Muriel and I grew up together in a small Yorkshire town, and we were great friends. I have so many memories of your mother! She was adventurous, and such a skilled musician and artist!" Tears trickled down Eleanor Harrison's cheeks. "I was devastated to hear of her death. She was taken too young."

She went to stand by her husband's side. "Welcome to Singapore, Clementine. You must stay as long as you like. It's the least I can do for Muriel." She looked affectionately at her son and rumpled his hair. "Richard will be good company for you."

For the first time, Clem smiled. "Thank you, Aunt Eleanor."

"We have a gift for you." There was a grin on Richard's face. He rushed into the house and emerged with a wooden basket. He offered it to Clem and said, "Look inside."

Clem opened the lid of the basket and gazed into the loving eyes of a golden spaniel puppy. The last pieces of ice around Clem's heart melted as she hugged the puppy to her chest and buried her head in its fur.

Part Two

Falling in Love

Singapore 1926–1933

"Nothing can bring back the hour
of splendour in the grass, of glory in the flower."
William Wordsworth

5

December 1926

The wooden huts of the village basked in the dappled sunlight that filtered through trees sagging with fruit, as Dan Long strode along the dirt road to his father's house. Women were washing clothes and utensils in the stream that ran parallel to the road, and they shouted greetings as he passed by. Village girls talking under the trees tried to catch the eye of the tall, bespectacled, well-built young man; but Dan Long was impervious to coquettish glances. He was intent on reaching his father before Liao Wei, who was critically ill, drew his last breath.

When word had reached him that his father was on his death bed, Dan Long had prepared to go to him immediately, pausing only to plead with Mei Mei to join him in paying their last respects. Mei Mei's eyes had flashed with anger, the tic near her mouth pulsing violently. Shaking her head, she had run away from him.

Dan Long awoke from his reverie to find himself in front of his father's house. He followed the sound of Shu Lan's whimpers to his father's bedroom.

"Dan Long!" Liao Wei whispered urgently, his eyes rolling as he fought to focus on his first-born. "Beneath my pillow is the yellow jade bangle that I gave your mother on our wedding day. Place it around Mei Mei's wrist, and we will both be with her in spirit all her life. Please tell her to forgive her errant father. To you, my son, I bequeath my farm, and I depend on you to take care of your stepmother."

The man on the bed shivered against the cold wind stealing its way through the house, its hungry breath seeking to envelop him like a shroud. Tears welled up in his eyes and trickled down his cheeks. Dan Long knew what his father was thinking. He was not dying a dignified five blossom death—he would not live to see his grandchildren being born, and he would not have the leverage of old age and good deeds to ensure entry through the gate of heaven. He was despised by his daughter and disrespected by his community for listening to a selfish second wife and selling his own child for gold coins. The courts of hell would be his destiny, and Dan Long heard Liao Wei whimper at the prospect of doing penance there.

"Mei Mei!" The man on the bed jerked up, his eyes wildly searching the dark corners of the room. The arctic wind drew closer and the cold crept up his thin legs. He emerged from his dreams to see his son sobbing by his bedside.

Liao Wei said with sudden coherence, "Dan Long, I am about to enter the courts of hell for my heinous crime of selling my daughter. The *mui-tsai* system is part of our culture, and I convinced myself that I was selling Mei Mei to give her a better life. But I understood what a villain I was when she berated me for treating her no better than my crops. Please take care of me in my afterlife with regular prayers. You are earning well, my son. On the anniversary of my death, feed the poor and needy. Let everyone in the village know that Liao Wei's son is kind and good, and release me from hell, my son. My last wish was to see my beautiful daughter one more time and see forgiveness in her eyes—but it is not to be. No matter, my son. I am very tired and ready for my rest."

Liao Wei's weary eyes began to droop, and his chest heaved. Shu Lan uttered a fearful scream and lunged at her husband, but Dan Long said, "Sleep, dear Father. Your travail was long and arduous, but now it is over." He smoothed back his father's hair and tenderly kissed his forehead. "It is time to rest."

When Dan Long returned home, he quietly entered his sister's bedchamber. Mei Mei lay on her bed, weeping tears for the father she had spurned. Dan Long gently took her right hand and slipped the jade bangle over her fingers. It was too large for her thin wrist, but Mei Mei clung to it like a drowning girl clutching at a log of wood.

"Mei Mei," Dan Long spoke softly, wiping away his sister's tears with his large white handkerchief. "Pa gave this bangle to Ma on their wedding day, but it has a lot of significance for you. Let me explain. The yellow colour of the jade symbolizes happiness and prosperity, but do you see the way it is made?" He pointed to the intricate design of an entwined dragon and phoenix, with a pearl gracing the centre. "The dragon represents yang, the male protector—Pa's spirit. The phoenix represents the nurturing and compassionate female—Ma's spirit. The pearl represents the human—yourself. Our parents' spirits will protect and nurture you all your life, little sister."

"I will never be parted from this bangle. I will wear it till my dying day," Mei Mei vowed before beginning to weep again. She continued in Hokkien, "I searched for a feeling of retribution when Aunt told me Pa had died, but I feel nothing. I am dead inside, Brother, filled with a burning regret that I never visited Pa on his deathbed."

Dan Long gathered Mei Mei into his arms. He remembered vividly the day of her birth and the death of his mother. With tears glistening in his eyes, he said, "We are bereaved, my sister, orphaned now. All we have is each other."

Brother and sister clung to each other, mourning their father.

January 1927

Dan Long walked into the Tanjong Pagar Docks with his trusted friend and Kuomintang Party comrade, Poh Tek Siong. Poh was tall and gangly, with a pockmarked face and intelligent eyes hidden behind black-framed spectacles. Not as old as Dan Long, at seventeen Poh was proficient in Chinese languages and cultural studies. He had graduated from a renowned Chinese school in Peking before poverty had forced him to come to the *Nanyang* as a coolie in the docks. Since arriving two years ago, he had paid off his loan to the *kheh-tau*, and progressed from coolie to teacher at a night school. Poh had left behind a younger sister in Peking, and when Dan Long had asked him to tutor Mei Mei in Chinese dialects, religions and culture, he had agreed with alacrity and embraced Mei Mei as his sister. An easy camaraderie had soon developed between Mei Mei and *Kor* Poh.

With Liao Wei's farm relinquished as the dowry for Shu Lan's second marriage to a fishmonger, Dan Long knew that both he and Mei Mei had to be gainfully employed to make something of their lives. To that end, he had successfully appealed to Uncle Toh to hire Poh as Mei Mei's tutor so that she would pass her Chinese subjects with ease; good results in the Senior Cambridge Examinations would enable her to train as a teacher.

But while he admired his friend's knowledge of Chinese, Dan Long was less certain about his grasp of politics. He sighed as he listened to Poh's questions.

"Dan Long, are you certain that asking the dock workers to strike against their British masters is totally in line with Dr Sun's principles? Our revered leader was fighting imperialism in China, where the Qing dynasty had destroyed the lives of the Chinese farmers; our British masters pay the dock workers a good wage. If the workers revolt, their employment will be terminated, and how will they feed their children?"

Impervious to his friend's wise words, Dan Long strode on and was soon delivering a short speech to the workers on the dock. Soon more and more men left their duties to gather around Dan Long, forming concentric circles of unrest around his militant focal point.

February 1927

The Toh gharry rolled to the entrance of the New World amusement park, where garish neon lights spelling out its name in English twinkled merrily above the wrought iron gates. Courting couples munching satay milled around with the street vendors outside. The air was filled with delicious aromas and the heady excitement of romance.

Dan Long and Poh jumped down from the gharry and helped fifteen-year-old Winnie and twelve-year-old Mei Mei alight. Both girls were dressed in long frocks and were giggling. Dan Long and Poh had good-naturedly acceded to young Mei Mei's request that they all periodically go to the cinema. Winnie and Mei Mei loved watching English cinema and Chinese opera, but were apprehensive of visiting New World without male escorts.

The four youngsters bought tickets to the film, *Dr Jekyll and Mr Hyde*, and settled themselves on wooden chairs in the stalls. Winnie sat between Dan Long and Mei Mei, with Poh on Mei Mei's other side. The lights dimmed, and the screen came alive, the silent movie whirring into action.

Winnie was transfixed with terror every time Dr Jekyll became Mr Hyde, and when Mr Hyde was transforming back to Dr Jekyll and his prosthetic finger flew from his hand, Winnie uttered a small scream and clutched Dan Long's arm.

Dan Long smiled and allowed Winnie to hold onto him. He found himself sneaking glances at her, thinking how pretty she was, and noticing how her short, wavy hair swayed fetchingly as she shook her head in horror. He was fascinated by the way her pert nose crinkled when she became emotional. When the film ended, Dan Long gently disengaged his arm from Winnie's grasp and smiled when she blushed furiously.

Dan Long and Poh took the girls to a noodle stall in Queen Street, where they wolfed down steaming *char kway teow*, a delicious deep-fried noodle dish made with dark soy sauce, sliced beef, cockles, eggs, bean sprouts and red chilli paste. Animated by the movie and Dan Long's company, Winnie's eyes sparkled with exhilaration.

Later, Mei Mei entered Dan Long's bedroom at the House of Toh to find her brother sitting on his bed, poring over Kuomintang pamphlets. She sat beside him and swept the papers away.

"What are you doing, Mei Mei?" Dan Long asked in irritation. "I need to prepare for the rally! We are marking the occasion of Dr Sun's death anniversary with speeches and songs."

"That can wait," Mei Mei said, mischief dancing in her eyes. "I saw the way you were looking at Winnie."

Dan Long blushed and began to rummage among the scattered papers on his bed. "Don't be silly," he said in a muffled voice.

"You like Winnie," Mei Mei persisted, plucking the paper from Dan Long's hand.

Dan Long sighed and looked up. "Mei Mei, Winnie is a Eurasian, and she is only fifteen years old. Of course, I like her. She is a nice girl. But that's all there is to it." He looked sadly at Mei Mei. "You know me, Sister. I revere our Chinese culture. If I ever get married, it will be to a Chinese girl."

Mei Mei made a face at him and left the room. She returned an hour later with his glass of milk to find him in the same position, his papers forgotten on the bed, his dreamy eyes gazing through the window at the night sky. Mei Mei deposited the glass of milk on the bedside table, burst into giggles, and exited her brother's bedroom.

March 1927

Crowds of people were gathering at the Happy Valley grounds. In front of a huge poster of Dr Sun Yat-Sen, joss sticks burned brightly. The Chinese revolutionary leader had succumbed to cancer two years earlier.

Suddenly a voice shouted out: "Down with the British! End all imperialism!"

Horrified, Mei Mei and Winnie saw Dan Long, his face alight with revolutionary fervour, waving a huge banner with 'Equality' written on it in bold Chinese characters. Hundreds of men punched their fists in the air, taking up Dan Long's cry as the radical branch of the Kuomintang Party assumed control of the memorial service. Pandemonium raged as the leftist group began shouting slogans and marching through the crowd. The rally organizers from the moderate faction of the party watched nonplussed, unable to stem the outpouring of pro-communist sentiment.

Growing in confidence and size, the group of marchers strode down the road to the Kreta Ayer police station, holding up traffic on the way. Mei Mei and Winnie trailed behind the marchers, dread in their hearts. When they reached the police station, the marchers stopped. Patriotic slogans rent the air, along with derisive shouts of "Go home, Imperialist dogs!"

Several British police officers took up position in front of the station, rifles at the ready. A sudden hush descended on the marchers. Seizing his opportunity, the commanding officer addressed the crowd: "You are breaking the law! China's politics have no place here. The British are in charge. Disperse at once!"

At these inflammatory words, the crowd roared its disapproval and surged forward. Gunfire filled the air, and chaos erupted as the crowd scattered amidst screams of fear and pain.

Faces tight with tension and hearts racing with fear, Mei Mei and Winnie ran towards the police station; but the panic-stricken crowd pushed them back. When they finally made their way through, an uncanny silence reigned over the street. The acrid smell of gunpowder hung in the air, and blood-splattered corpses lay scattered on the ground.

Battling the nausea rising in their throats, Mei Mei and Winnie bent to look at the faces of the corpses. They cried with relief when they found Dan Long was not among them.

"He must have escaped." Winnie ran her hands agitatedly through her hair. "But the police have informers. They will find him in no time."

That night, while Winnie was drinking warm milk in her bedroom, gravel rained on her closed window. Winnie ran to investigate and found Dan Long looking up at her from the street, gesticulating wildly.

The young girl ran down the stairs, unlocked the front door and crept out to where Dan Long waited, his face frightened and his clothes dishevelled.

"The police know where I live," Dan Long whispered. "Aunt Ai Lin and Uncle Toh have treated me and Mei Mei well. I cannot bring trouble on them by returning to the House of Toh."

Winnie's heart melted, while her mind worked furiously to formulate a plan. Her voice came in an excited whisper. "Mona Ma can hide you for a few months. She lives in Lim Chu Kang *kampong*."

"Who is Mona Ma?"

Winnie looked down and plucked at her dress. "Remember I told you that my father had a Chinese mistress and I have two half-siblings? I went to see them and well—I liked them very much." She glanced up defiantly. "I don't remember my own mother, and Mona Ma took me under her wing. She is married to a Chinese pig farmer now, and they have a farm in Lim Chu Kang. I visit them often and they look on me as family. I'm sure they will shelter you for a while."

Dan Long gazed at Winnie, his eyes filled with love, longing and gratitude.

January 1929

To escape the vigilant eyes of the British police, Dan Long could only visit the cinema late at night, so Mei Mei, Winnie and Poh would meet him at New World after dark. On one such night, after watching a Chinese opera, Dan Long and Poh accompanied Mei Mei and Winnie in the gharry to see them safely home.

Arriving at the Queen Street house to drop Winnie off, the quartet were puzzled to find the residence in darkness. A neighbour informed a horrified Winnie that her grandmother had suffered a massive heart attack and had been admitted to hospital. The Toh coachman rushed the four youngsters there immediately.

When they arrived, Gran was unconscious and Winnie's father stood miserably in the waiting room with his head in his hands. His British bank had collapsed, and he had lost his job—the latest victim of the Great Depression that was sweeping Singapore, bringing food shortages and upheavals in its wake. When he had told Gran the ill tidings, she had suffered a massive heart attack.

Gran died later that night. Attending her wake at the family home in Queen Street, Mei Mei wept bitterly as she gazed at the kind face of Gran, lying still in her coffin. Winnie was inconsolable: Gran had been the only mother she had known. At Winnie's father's request, Ai Lin agreed to allow Mei Mei to stay with Winnie for a few days until the funeral.

In the privacy of her bedroom, Winnie looked at Mei Mei piteously. "I can't imagine life without Gran, Mei Mei! She brought me up single-handedly while my mother was sick. Gran was the one who told me stories. She smoothed my brow when I burnt with fever. My greatest wish was to take care of her in her old age. That's not going to happen now."

Mei Mei embraced her friend. "I know how you feel, Winnie. At least you did not part from Gran on bitter terms. I never forgave my Pa before he died. I will miss Gran, too. She was always there for us when we were sad. Uncle Gerard is distraught! Winnie, you need to comfort him."

"Papa is bankrupt," Winnie said sadly. "He told me he has no choice but to sell this house."

Mei Mei's face paled, and she brushed the tears away from her eyes. "Where will you live, Winnie?"

"Papa is thinking of migrating to Australia to make his fortune." Winnie burst into fresh sobs.

"No, Winnie! I won't let you go!"

Winnie nodded. "I don't want to go to Australia, and I told Papa that. He has agreed to arrange for me to board at the Methodist Girls' School Hostel. But I will miss him, Mei Mei!

Life is so hard."

Gran was buried at Bukit Brown Cemetery. Gran's many Eurasian friends, Gerard, Winnie, Mei Mei, Dan Long, Poh, Uncle Toh and Aunt Ai Lin attended the funeral. On a day bright with sunshine, Gran was laid to rest in the country where she had arrived as a bride.

Standing in the graveyard, Dan Long's eyes were moist as he watched Winnie sobbing as she knelt beside her grandmother's coffin. How he yearned to take her in his arms and wipe away her tears. He looked down at the ground and acknowledged to himself that he loved the Eurasian girl who was his sister's best friend.

January 1930

Dan Long glanced up wearily from feeding the pigs their dinner. Eighteen-year-old Winnie, wearing a lovely frock and high heels, was walking down the track towards him. Dan Long had to strain his ears to hear her voice above the contented grunting of the pigs as they chomped their evening meal.

"I asked how you were," Winnie shouted, her nose crinkling and her eyes laughing as Dan Long glared at her.

"How do you think I am?" Dan Long's voice was petulant. "I am a twenty-three-year-old scholar, and here I am feeding pigs! My body hurts and my bones ache. I don't know how long I can stand this. I was not born for this kind of life, Winnie."

Winnie's eyes flashed. "You are a farmer's son! And who told you to get mixed up with a political party?"

Dan Long softened, and he said in a tender voice, "I just want to earn more than I do now. If I can't save any money, we won't have a happy life together, Winnie."

A flush crept up Winnie's neck and face, and she lowered her eyes. "What do you mean?" she whispered.

"I love you, Winifred," Dan Long said, his voice strong. "I wish to make you my wife."

Winnie peered at him from behind thick eyelashes. A soft smile tugged at her lips.

"Well?" Dan Long demanded, his eyes anxious despite the bravado in his voice.

"What do you want to know?" Winnie turned to Dan Long, her smile mischievous.

Dan Long sighed and Winnie collapsed in a paroxysm of giggles. When she had recovered from her mirth, she said softly, "I love you too, Dan Long. I hope to pass my examinations and become a teacher. Then we can get married." She gave him her gap-toothed grin and added, "Papa has asked me to join him in Perth. He is making money mining coal. But I have no desire to go to Australia. Singapore is my home, and it is where Gran is buried." Winnie's lips trembled.

"Don't cry, sweetheart. I won't marry you until I earn well enough to keep both of us," Dan Long said. His voice became a whisper. "One of my old night-school teachers was telling me of job vacancies for teachers in China."

"China!" Winnie screamed, before clapping a hand over her mouth. "How can you even think of leaving Mei Mei and me alone in Singapore? You promised your dying mother you would never leave your sister's side!"

Dan Long expostulated, "Aunt Ai Lin is a second mother to Mei Mei, and I will return as soon as I have made some money. I am a hunted criminal in Singapore, you know that." Dan Long stepped towards Winnie and clasped her hands. "Winifred, I know that you will treat our separation as a necessary measure to secure our future."

Winnie looked at Dan Long's thin figure and hollow cheeks, and nodded miserably. Dan Long folded her in his arms and Mona Ma, who had come to call him to dinner, stepped back behind a tree to allow the lovers solitude.

Two months later, on a cold and rainy night, Winnie and Mei Mei stood at the docks to see Dan Long set off to China. At night, the Old Harbour of Singapore looked surreal with the silhouettes of huge ships looming out of the mist, and the sound of foghorns mingling with the quayside chatter as people waited to set sail for distant lands. The lights from the ships cast a dim glow over the dark, swirling waters, and coolie porters ran along gangplanks carrying suitcases and bundles on their heads.

Dan Long looked with suppressed excitement at the ship that would take him to China. After embracing Mei Mei and Winnie, he went cheerfully up the gangplank, keen to see the land where his parents had been born and raised. After fighting for China's ideals from a young age, here at last was his chance to witness at first-hand the country's transformation to Communist China. But as he stood at the rail watching Singapore's shores recede into the horizon, Dan Long little imagined the price he and his family would have to pay for his idealism about a country that was not his own.

6

Seventeen-year-old Clementine walked through John Harrison's rubber plantation, her golden hair shining under the climbing sun, her blue eyes dreamy and unfocussed. Her spaniel, Jasper, panted at her heels. The rubber trees, some forty feet tall, bloomed with pale yellow flowers. Through the canopy of their shiny leaves, she could glimpse the white contours of the bungalow the rubber planter had built for his family. She stopped at a tree to watch the tapper scrape the bark diagonally with his knife and release the milky latex into a tin cup tied to the trunk. The sap would be processed into bales of rubber in the Harrison factory, and exported to distant countries to be used as motorcar and bicycle tyres.

Clem knew that Richard would one day rule as king of this domain. He was learning the rudiments of rubber planting whenever he could escape from Raffles College, but his dreams were centred on being a painter, not a planter. Herself an accomplished musician, she understood Richard's craving to disappear from both college and plantation, to set up his easel on the banks of the Singapore River and to capture the activity there on canvas.

She frowned as she recalled the conversation she'd had with Richard one sunny morning, as he sat painting in the garden. She had rushed in from school and demanded to be taken to the upcoming Raffles Hotel Summer Ball. Clem shivered as she remembered the pity she had seen in Richard's green eyes.

He had said in a soft voice, "We are friends, Clem, but I do not have romantic feelings for you."

Eleanor had stepped forward from behind the hedge where she had been cutting flowers for the dining table.

"Nonsense, Richard!" his mother had said blithely, her arms around Clem, whose blue eyes were swimming with tears. "You are only eighteen—too young to know your own mind. Of course you must take Clem to balls and be her escort! That is the way to get to know each other and fall in love." She had given a booming laugh. "Why, your father and I courted for three years before he proposed marriage! He took me dancing and to the theatre. We had intimate dinners together, and finally we realised that we were in love. Don't tell me, Richard, that you look upon Clem as a sister?"

Richard had blushed and muttered, "No."

"Well then." Eleanor had nodded encouragingly at Clem and walked away.

A small smile tugged now at Clem's mouth, and suddenly her eyes were luminous with the excitement of first love. Eleanor's words were coming true; she sighed as she remembered what had happened the previous night.

Richard liked moonlight picnics and he had escorted Clem to the Botanic Gardens to attend a midnight orchestral concert under the stars. The two of them had spread a quilt on the grass mound overlooking the outdoor stage and sat with a picnic basket between them, enjoying the music and the balmy air of a tropical night.

Clem was wearing a white organza frock with an abundance of lace. From time to time she caught Richard flicking her admiring glances, and her lips grew soft and moist. After feasting on roasted chicken legs, salad, fish fingers and cake, Richard stretched out on the quilt and gazed up at the night sky. The music echoed around them, haunting tunes that spoke of melancholy and longing. It felt entirely natural when he sat up, leaned over and kissed Clem lightly on the lips. She had blushed prettily, her heart pounding, and through half-closed eyes, she had seen Richard smiling at her tenderly.

Clem sighed. Her first kiss had been all that she had imagined it would be. Fanned by Eleanor's desire to see her married to Richard, and her own tender feelings for her childhood friend, the flames of first love burned in Clem's heart with fiery intensity.

She had heard that Roger and Clara were now the proud parents of twin girls, with another baby on the way. It was obvious her father had cut her from his life and was forming a new family. When Eleanor had proposed that Clem make a permanent home with the Harrisons in Singapore, Clem had agreed with alacrity.

Now she saw that Richard was absent from the rubber factory on the far side of the plantation, and Clem slowly walked back to the house. As she passed Eleanor's boudoir, the older woman called out to her.

"Sit beside me, Clem." When the young girl had seated

herself, Eleanor said in a serious tone, "John received a telegram this morning from Roger. I have some bad news. Roger is in the terminal stages of blood cancer, and he is not expected to last two months."

The colour left Clem's face and there was a sheen of moisture in her blue eyes.

Eleanor clasped Clem's cold hands in hers and said, "John has asked his overseer, Lim, to purchase you a ticket on a ship that sails tomorrow for England. We hope you will arrive in time to see Roger alive."

Clem extricated her hands from Eleanor's grasp and said formally, "Thank you for telling me of my father's illness, Aunt Eleanor, but I won't be going to England. My father made his wishes clear when he sent me away."

Eleanor blanched at Clem's icy tone but said briskly, "I would go if I were you, Clementine. There is the issue of the Newquay house. It belonged to Muriel, you know, bequeathed to her by her aunt. Clara Higgins should not have any part of it. It is an inheritance worth fighting for, my child." Eleanor cleared her throat. "Nothing would please me more than to see you as Richard's bride, but John and I had always hoped that Richard would marry a girl who would bring a fortune with her."

A blue fire had been lit in Clem's eyes at the mention of her stepmother. "Very well, Aunt Eleanor," she said. "I will leave for England tomorrow."

The room grew suddenly cold, and Eleanor glanced uneasily at the windows. A black cloud had obscured the sun, and a chill wind was blowing the green brocade curtains outward. Eleanor rose to shut the windows, and when she returned to the sofa, Clem was gone.

England, June 1930

Clementine sat by her father's bedside in Truro's hospital, staring stonily at his waxen face and closed eyes. His form was skeletal, and he had lost most of his hair from the radiation treatment used to battle his leukaemia.

Roger's eyelids flickered, and his eyes opened. He gazed directly at Clem and his lips formed a grotesque grin.

"I'm dying, Clem," Roger Arbuthnot whispered. "I now understand Muriel's pain those last months before she passed." Roger's eyes searched Clem's frantically. "Are you happy in Singapore, Clementine? Are John and Eleanor kind to you?"

Clem said in a cool voice, "I am very happy in Singapore, Papa. Aunt Eleanor and Uncle John are like the parents I never had." She was happy to see Roger flinch with pain at her words.

"You had Muriel, my child," Roger whispered. "She loved you very much before she became ill. Muriel's illness was in her mind, though later she suffered physically as well." Tears welled in his eyes.

Clem said, "I need to know something, Papa. Did the Newquay manor belong to Mama?"

Roger's face paled but he nodded. "Yes, it did. She left the house to me during my lifetime with the provision in her will that it goes to you after my death. You can complete the legal formalities with Jacobson and Sons in Truro; they were your mother's solicitors." There was fear in his face as he said, "In the last few years, I have incurred debts, what with the children arriving, and my employers filing for bankruptcy. Clara miscarried our third child, and there were her hospital bills to pay. Now my own illness is incurring expense. I have little money to leave Clara." His voice faltered. "This is my last wish: please give Clara and your sisters shelter in your house, Clem."

Clementine's voice was deceptively gentle as she said, "Why of course, Papa. I will be returning to Singapore, so Clara can continue living at the Newquay house."

She avoided Roger's hands stretched towards her, rose from the stool by his bed and made for the door. Her eyes narrowed into slits, but the smile that played on her mouth yearned to burst forth like the sun from behind clouds.

That afternoon, Clementine stood in the chapel at Roche Rock, framed in a window, gazing at the sun-drenched countryside stretching out to sea. In Singapore, the image of Roche Rock had been steeped in the mists of the past and had remained on the fringes of her memory like the gauzy fabric of a dream. Now as she stood on the rock, a lone, desolate figure in the window of a ruined chapel, memories rushed back, overpowering her with unwanted images.

She remembered Clara and Roger making love, with her mother not cold in her grave. She thought of the day she had been threatened with being packed off to boarding school. Clara had been too eager to rid herself of her stepdaughter for Clem to feel anything now but resentment and loathing for her former governess.

A week later, Clem stood at the window of the room she had

occupied as a child and watched the waves crash on the shore. Roger Arbuthnot's funeral was over, and she had purchased her return ticket to Singapore. She had visited Jacobson and Sons at Truro and had enjoyed a long and fruitful conversation with them.

A knock on the door made her turn from the window. Clara entered, followed by two little girls who gazed at Clem with intense curiosity. Grief and penury had taken their toll on Clara. Her hair was grey, and her face was creased with fatigue and worry.

"I expect you to leave these premises by the morning." Clara cringed at the anger and dislike blazing out of her stepdaughter's eyes.

"But you promised Roger on his deathbed that you would allow us to live here, Clem." Clara's voice shook.

"I did no such thing," Clementine lied glibly. "I have already talked to my solicitors, and they will lease the house out and pay the rent into my bank account in England." Her eyes flashing, Clem finally allowed her pent-up emotions to escape. "This was my mother's house, Clara. Do you remember my mother? She was sick in bed when you were seducing my father. I am certain she would not have wanted you to live in her house."

"We have nowhere to go, Clem." Tears trickled down Clara's cheeks. She pushed her two girls towards Clementine. "They are your sisters, Clementine, please have mercy. They are so young! Where will they go?"

"Don't you dare come near me!" Clementine shouted at her two frightened stepsisters, who burst into tears. "Clara, you've got your just deserts. You thought nothing of breaking up my home and taking my father away from me. Go and pack your bags."

The next morning, Clementine watched with satisfaction as Clara and her two children trudged miserably from the house in the bitter cold and rain. Clara deserved no pity and Clem refused to think of her two young stepsisters. Eleanor would be pleased that Clem was bringing in a fortune.

Clementine smiled and dreamed—of living with Richard in her beloved Cornwall manor, chasing their children in the garden, having picnics at Roche Rock. She conjured up Richard's image in her mind and her heart beat fast. If love was feeling short of breath whenever you saw someone, if it meant wanting to own a person, body and soul—why, then, she was madly in love with Richard Harrison.

A raven cawed at the window. Clem gazed at its black form and beady eyes and suddenly shivered.

7

The Great Depression cast its long shadow over the House of Toh. Rubber prices fell and Towkay Toh was forced to close his failing rubber distribution plant and pour all his savings into the rice business. The result was a need for cost-cutting measures at home. The proud and venerated House of Toh was forced to lose face as Sulaiman, the cook's assistant, the maids, and the gardener left, with only the Hainanese cook and Aunt Ai Lin's bondmaid, Li Jun, kept on with full wages. Mei Mei abandoned her studies with Poh and spent evenings with Winnie, studying hard for their examinations. Both girls wanted to be financially independent, and competition was fierce for the few available teaching vacancies.

The winds of misfortune grew stronger, carrying clouds of scandal toward the House of Toh. The grapevine snaking from the affluent Chinese residential homes of Waterloo Street into the heart of Chinatown, reported Uncle Toh frequenting an opium brothel in Malabar Street, and in the deadly embrace of the fatal habit.

On a hot clear afternoon, Second Mistress Meisheng entered Mei Mei's life. When a shadow darkened the main door, Mei

Mei looked up from reading a book in the hall to see a beautiful woman, in her late twenties, dressed in a white silk gown embroidered with golden dragons, standing in the doorway. Hair the colour of night, dressed with jasmine flowers, framed an oval face. The woman held the hands of a chubby little boy, and Uncle Toh came to stand next to her, a protective arm around her waist.

When Grandmother Sim hobbled into the hall, her son looked at her sheepishly. "Ma, this is my second wife, Meisheng, and my baby boy, Chu Meng. Pay your respects, Wife!"

Grandmother Sim held up her hand. "Wait a minute! I know this woman. She is a prostitute from Mainland China. Until recently, she resided in an opium brothel in Malabar Street. The little boy looks at least five years old, Toh, and you have been visiting this woman for six months. How can the boy be born from your loins? This witch has brainwashed you, Son!"

Mei Mei, gaping from the hallway, glanced up the staircase and froze. Aunt Ai Lin tottered precariously on the top step, aghast at Uncle Toh's proclamation. Her bondmaid rushed to her, and Ai Lin quietly fainted into her arms.

"Very well, I admit my wife was a former whore," Towkay Toh mumbled with a mad light in his eyes. "I paid the *kwai-po* a large amount of money to procure her. But there is nothing unusual in taking a second wife, especially for procreation." Towkay Toh looked guiltily up the stairs to where an unconscious Ai Lin was being borne away to her bedroom by her bondmaid.

Grandmother Sim's calculating eyes glittered like black jewels. "If this woman resides here and gives birth to another son, I will personally arrange for your second wedding celebrations.

Go, Toh, warm your concubine's bed until then."

Towkay Toh heaved a sigh of relief. "Ai Lin will be addressed as First Mistress, while Meisheng will be called Second Mistress, as befitting their positions."

Like an evil westerly wind, Second Mistress Meisheng blew into the Toh household accompanied by scandal and drama. Mei Mei soon began to understand the reason for Aunt Ai Lin's wistful eyes and the muffled sobs that emerged from her bedroom at night.

* * *

Second Mistress Meisheng soon assumed control of the House of Toh. She wormed her way into Grandma Sim's favours by giving her invigorating massages, singing to her in her bedroom, and helping her with her toilette.

One evening, as she massaged the old woman's feet with fragrant oils, Meisheng stole a glance at Grandma Sim's face, serene and contented from her ministrations.

Second Mistress Meisheng said softly in Mandarin, "Ma, we have so few servants in the house, and First Mistress Ai Lin seldom leaves her bedroom. I have tried to manage the household as best I can, but it is truly becoming difficult to keep the house clean."

Grandma Sim's sleepy eyes suddenly sharpened. She sighed and said, "Times are bad, Meisheng, my girl. What can poor Toh do in this climate?"

"True, true." Meisheng smiled before her tone sharpened.

"And a *mui-tsai* sitting in this house, shaking her legs!"

Grandma Sim rose up, and Meisheng quickly placed fluffed pillows behind the old woman's back.

"Ma, Mei Mei is a *mui-tsai*. You paid her father money, now is the time to reap the harvest," Second Mistress Meisheng said, her eyes flicking over Grandma Sim like an artful lizard over its prey. "Why, the tin merchant's wife, who visited us yesterday, was surprised that our house is grimy and the furniture dusty with a *mui-tsai* in attendance. I was too ashamed to tell her that our *mui-tsai* is a little lady attending school and would turn up her nose in disdain if asked to dust furniture. A cursed *mui-tsai* at that, born on the double seventh. The ill-luck she carries with her may be responsible for the state of Toh's finances. Put that lazy chit of a girl to work, Ma. Leave it to me to get Toh's approval."

Grandma Sim rose angrily from the bed. "Ai Lin will complain to Toh if I set her niece to work, so you see to it that Toh backs me up. I have never looked upon that child as anything but a servant," Grandma Sim said decisively. With that, she went to the door, leaving Meisheng smiling after her.

* * *

Second Mistress Meisheng entered her bedchamber to find Towkay Toh poring over some red papers on the bed. She sat at her dressing table and arranged her hair. While applying kohl to her eyes, she said softly: "Towkay, after a long time, I see you absorbed in your work. I am happy that you have abstained from *chandu* today."

Towkay Toh looked up and grinned. "I have asked my lawyer to come in a few days to draw up the red adoption papers. My legal adoption of Mei Mei has been left undone too long."

Meisheng's face paled but she recovered well, smiling brightly. "Of course, Towkay. Little Mei Mei is a sweet flower that blooms brightly in this house. May the line of Toh be forever preserved through her." She turned her face away to hide a tear.

Towkay Toh got up from the bed and came towards his concubine. "Meisheng, do not be afraid. Chu Meng is not my son, but rest assured that I will make good provision for him in my will."

Second Mistress Meisheng turned to Towkay Toh and seductively put up her face to be kissed. She looked hauntingly lovely in her frilly nightgown, the swell of her breasts visible above the neckline. Towkay Toh felt himself harden pleasurably.

When he murmured endearments in her ear, she gently led him to the bed. He was spent after their lovemaking and eagerly snatched the opium pipe she offered. Soon he was as docile as a child, gazing at her with vacant eyes, his mouth stupid and drooling. She wiped his lips tenderly and removed the red adoption papers from the bed. She tore them up in front of his uncomprehending eyes, all the while smiling dazzlingly.

* * *

November was a month of grey skies, singing bullfrogs in monsoon drains, the sea swollen and rolling with boats precariously balanced on the crests of waves, roads shining after a sharp downpour, children running amok in dirty puddles—and destinies lying at crossroads.

Mei Mei was on her hands and knees on the marble steps connecting the road to the portico of the House of Toh. Her hands ached from scrubbing the steps from seven in the morning, and her knees pulsated with pain from kneeling on the hard stone. But nothing could match the pain resonating through her heart, a sharp knife that punctured her very soul. The tic at the corner of her mouth pulsed erratically.

Such was her confidence in her aunt and uncle's love for her, that she had smiled incredulously at Second Mistress Meisheng when she was told that she had been removed from the Methodist School's register and would now have to earn her *mui-tsai* wages. Mei Mei had run to Ai Lin's bedchamber, but Grandma Sim had barred her way, and Mei Mei had stared with shock at the sturdy cane in the old woman's hand.

"You are a *mui-tsai* in my house, Liao Mei Mei," the old woman taunted. "I paid your father fifty dollars for your services, and I want reimbursement for my money. Times are bad, your uncle's business is floundering, and we cannot afford to hire servants. You will now earn your keep by sweeping and mopping the house. Get going!"

Second Mistress Meisheng was waiting by the stairs for Mei Mei. Her lips stretched into a thin smile in her parchment-white face as she said in Mandarin, "Little sister of our house, go to the scullery and you will find scrubbing materials, mops, buckets and brooms. Your uncle is a member of the Chinese Chamber of Commerce and has many visitors. This house needs to be sparkling clean. We have an image to uphold in our community. And ask Ai Lin's bondmaid for trousers and *kebaya*. There will be no more parading around in frocks, Missy!"

Her face white, Mei Mei found her voice. "I wish to see my uncle. I want to hear from him that he wants me to work as a *mui-tsai* in his house."

Nodding impatiently, Meisheng led the way to her bedchamber. Mei Mei flinched on seeing her uncle's emaciated form reclining on the bed, a pipe to his lips. He looked blearily at Mei Mei.

"Toh, we are short-handed in this house," Meisheng said in a brisk voice. "Your rice business is failing, but we must keep face in the community, eh?"

Towkay Toh nodded. "Must keep face," he intoned, a stupid smile tugging at lips caked with white crust.

"Mei Mei is a *mui-tsai* in your household. She needs to do household chores. You agree or not?" Suddenly, Meisheng snatched the opium pipe from Uncle Toh's grasp. "Are you listening to me, Towkay? Mei Mei needs to mop and clean the house."

Towkay Toh's eyes fixed on the opium pipe longingly. He focussed on Meisheng's words and whined, "Do as your step-aunt says, Mei Mei. Times are bad. I cannot afford servants, and I paid money for your services as a domestic helper in my house."

He was unprepared for the anger radiating from Mei Mei's eyes. "Yes, you bought me from my father, Towkay. You also promised him that I would go to school and be treated as your niece and not as a bondmaid."

Meisheng made as if to leave and Towkay Toh shouted,

"Meisheng, don't take away my *chandu* pipe, there's a dear." Towkay Toh looked with annoyance at Mei Mei. "Mei Mei, you will do your step-aunt's bidding if you want to eat rice out of my bowl."

Mei Mei sighed and sat on the steps of her uncle's portico, her hands too tired to scrub any longer. She stiffened as the bushes near the steps rustled.

"Mei Mei!" A whisper floated in the air.

Mei Mei moved tentatively towards the wild undergrowth, and was startled to see Winnie's face peeping out from behind nettles and brambles.

"Mei Mei, why are you not attending school?" Winnie's eyes rounded as she took in Mei Mei's appearance and occupation. "No!" she whispered in horror. "You are working in your uncle's house as a bondmaid?"

Tears glistened in Mei Mei's eyes, but she said in a stoic voice, "Second Mistress Meisheng has convinced Grandma Sim and Towkay Toh to remove me from school and put me to work as a domestic servant in their house."

Winnie scrambled indignantly out of the hedge and dusted off the nettles clinging to her frock. "How dare they remove you from school? The Senior Cambridge examinations are around the corner. Have you spoken to your aunt?"

Mei Mei shook her head. "Aunt Ai Lin keeps to her bedchamber and lives in her own world of misery. I am not allowed to see her. When I finish my chores and meals, I am locked in the scullery. I sleep on mattresses on the floor."

"I can write to Dan Long, but he is far away and of little use."

Winnie frowned. Then her face brightened. "I heard that Poh, your former tutor, is living in Chinatown. I am certain he will help you, Mei Mei. He can lodge a complaint with the Chinese Protectorate for *mui-tsai* abuse. I heard his friend is a peon at the Chinese Protectorate Office."

Mei Mei clutched Winnie's hand. "What can the Protectorate do? The *mui-tsai* law cannot be broken." A solitary tear glistened for a moment in Mei Mei's eye, before spilling onto her cheek. "I'm afraid that Second Mistress will manipulate Grandma Sim into selling me to a brothel. I overheard Mistress Meisheng and Grandma Sim discussing the appropriate time to sell me. It seems that I will fetch a good price." Mei Mei's voice shook, and she placed a finger over the tic pulsating at the corner of her mouth. "I can withstand working to the bone from dawn to dusk, but I will kill myself if I am made to sell my body."

"Please try to talk to your aunt, Mei Mei," Winnie whispered urgently. "Surely her room is not guarded by her mother-in-law every hour of the day?"

"Aunt's bondmaid told me that Aunt Ai Lin is sick. The Chinese medicine doctor attends to her every day. Her door is locked from the inside, Winnie."

"Then knock on the door!" Winnie cried, forgetting to whisper.

"Have you finished cleaning the steps, little sister?" Meisheng's shout galvanized Winnie into action, and she ran away down Waterloo Street.

Meisheng appeared in the portico and grabbed Mei Mei's shoulder. "Whom were you talking to on the road?"

"Nobody." Mei Mei squirmed under Meisheng's grip. "I will wash the steps with water now."

Meisheng's eyes narrowed and she peered down the road, looking first left then right. Slowly, she released her hold on Mei Mei's shoulder and said in a cold voice, "Come to my room after you have finished sweeping and mopping the hall."

It was midnight. Mei Mei's back throbbed with such pain from Mistress Meisheng's cane that she lay on the mattress on the floor, unmoving, eyes staring bleakly into the darkness, her mind reliving the blows that had rained on her back in the seclusion of Meisheng's room.

"Let this be a lesson to you not to dawdle in your work, and not to talk to anyone outside this house about your workload or life," Meisheng intoned as Mei Mei trudged out of the door and climbed painfully down the stairs to the scullery.

Mei Mei whimpered into the darkness, and only the kitchen cat heard her. "Oh, I was caned worse than an animal today. What will happen to me? I will never sell my body, never!"

Mei Mei's chaotic mind attempted to reason why destiny played such cruel tricks on her; why every day the sun rose, but never seemed to break through the cloudy skies of her life. She was cursed after all, she thought, a girl born on an inauspicious date, the seventh night of the seventh moon.

* * *

The day was spoiling for a thunderstorm. Armed with a tall

umbrella, her brows puckered, Winnie hailed a rickshaw to take her to Chinatown. Her heart pounded; the part of town she was visiting was infamous for its crime and prostitution. Rows of three-storey houses lined each side of the street, with coolies and workers occupying tiny cubicles inside and sharing toilets. The stench of poverty and sickness hit Winnie's nostrils and made her nauseous.

Disembarking from the rickshaw, she entered a dilapidated house, her eyes searching the dim interior for Poh. She climbed a narrow, dirty stairway strewn with rubbish, and as she reached the top, Poh emerged from his cubicle to light a cigarette. He was thin, his face pinched and white. The upper part of his body was bare, and his trousers were tattered.

Settled on stools in front of a small wooden table, with two steaming coffees from the *sarabat* stall, Winnie related to Poh Mei Mei's predicament at the House of Toh. She watched amazement, horror and rage fly across Poh's face. He sat still for some time after Winnie had finished her story and then rose, his coffee half-consumed.

"Do not worry, Winifred," he said at last. "Tomorrow I will go and ask my peon friend for an audience with the powerful secretary to the Assistant Chinese Protectorate, Lady Matilda Robertson. She will help Mei Mei."

The next day, Winnie arrived at her hostel to find one of Poh's friends waiting for her. He brought terrible news. Assailants had accosted Poh near the docks the previous night and had cracked open his skull. He was in a critical condition at the General Hospital.

The friend said tersely, "Poh heard the gang that was beating him up mention Mistress Meisheng's name. Poh thinks he was attacked by the prostitute's triad thugs."

Her heart heavy, Winnie entered the Cathedral of the Good Shepherd in Queen Street. She and Mei Mei had visited this church so often with Gran during festivals and bad times. The memory of Gran's kindly face and merry eyes brought tears to her eyes. In the silent nave, Winnie kneeled reverentially in a pew and wept—for Gran, who could have counselled them, for Dan Long whom she loved, for Poh, lying critically ill in a hospital bed, and for Mei Mei, her dear friend, now facing a bitter ordeal in her young life.

December 1930

From the gate, Mei Mei watched Grandma Sim and Second Mistress Meisheng hail a rickshaw to take them to the temple of the Goddess Kuan Yin for prayers. Uncle Toh was ill with a cold, and with an outbreak of cholera in the surrounding area, Grandma Sim wanted to pray for protection for her son.

Mei Mei slowly climbed the stairs to the first floor of the House of Toh, her back still painful from Meisheng's caning. To her surprise, Aunt Ai Lin's bedroom door was ajar. She heard the cook shout from the kitchen, "Li Jun, don't forget to bring the condiments from Chinatown on your way back from visiting your friend."

Mei Mei brightened. It was Li Jun's day off from work and Grandma Sim and Meisheng were at the temple. *This is my chance to talk to Aunt*, Mei Mei thought. She went to the door and peeped in.

Ai Lin was lounging on a day bed, looking out of the window. She turned at Mei Mei's entrance, and her niece was shocked to see Ai Lin's thin face, the dark circles under her eyes, and her wan cheeks. Ai Lin seemed to have aged ten years.

"Little one," Ai Lin said listlessly in Hokkien, "why are you not at school?"

Mei Mei ran into the room and fell sobbing at her aunt's feet. "They are making me work as a bondmaid in this house, Aunt!"

Ai Lin sat up and shook Mei Mei's shoulder. Her face shocked, she asked, "Who has dared to do that? Tell me, little one, at once!"

Mei Mei narrated her sad story. When she had finished, she lifted her *kebaya* so that Ai Lin could see the lacerations on her back.

Ai Lin exclaimed in horror and stood up. Her head reeled and she sat back down on the day bed with a thump. "I am ill, little one. Toh and I had a happy marriage. I never imagined that he would betray me with another woman, but here we are. Opium is the devil! And that hussy, she dared to beat you. I won't stand for it!"

"I overheard Grandma Sim and Second Mistress saying they will sell me to a brothel, Aunt!" Mei Mei's eyes shone with terror.

"Over my dead body!" Ai Lin said resolutely. She got to her feet again and took small steps towards her medicine cabinet. "Come to me, little one. I will treat your wounds with soothing ointments. Don't worry, I will fight for your rights as my niece in this house. Toh may be in the grip of opium, but there is more than one way to handle him. I have been an imbecile, sitting here moaning and moping, allowing that hussy to rule the house. No more!"

Mei Mei buried her face in her aunt's bosom and wept.

* * *

Fifty-year-old Lady Matilda Robertson sat in the small office assigned to the secretary to the Assistant Chinese Protectorate. Shelves with files surrounded her, and her small table was strewn with her reports as a voluntary inspector of *mui-tsais* in Chinese households. Lady Matilda's hair was a garish shade of bronze, coiffed and curled over a shapely head. Her large nose and rugged features prevented her from being termed handsome, but her kind grey eyes and full lips gave her face character and warmth.

Matilda Robertson had been Lady Matilda Shillington, widow of a highly decorated First World War British officer, when she had met Clyde Robertson at a dinner party in London. The rubber planter from Singapore had been spending the summer in the English capital, furthering his business interests. He had been entranced by Lady Matilda's sophistication and charm. The adventuress in Lady Matilda had reared its head when he had proposed marriage, and she had readily accepted and set sail for Singapore with her newly acquired husband.

There, she had taken society by storm. A born organizer with a forceful personality, in no time, she was running Clyde Robertson's business and life. Tapping her vast network of contacts, she had been instrumental in furthering her husband's business interests, so much so that he had become the wealthiest rubber planter in Singapore.

Matilda fervently wished to see Clyde enter politics in England. In addition, she possessed a fiery feminist streak that made her a passionate champion of women and children. Taking a keen interest in Chinese society and culture, she spearheaded the movement by the British gentry in Singapore to purge Chinese society of the *mui-tsai* system. Her job as the powerful secretary to the Assistant Chinese Protectorate allowed her to oversee households with 'little sisters', a position she used to clamp down on child abuse. She was also advisor to the committee of Chinese businessmen that ran the Poh Leung Kuk Orphanage, *Home for the Protection of Women and Children*.

Lady Matilda glanced up as her Chinese peon knocked diffidently on her office door.

"Someone to see you, Memsahib, waiting long outside," the peon announced before shepherding Aunt Ai Lin into the dusty room. "Madam Wu Ai Lin to see you, Memsahib." He pointed Ai Lin to a chair and bowed himself out of the room.

Lady Matilda looked with interest at the wan face of the middle-aged Chinese woman facing her. She could see she had once been endowed with homely beauty, traces of which remained in the big eyes, curly lashes and shapely lips. Those lips were twisted now into a grimace of pain.

"What can I do for you?" Lady Matilda asked kindly.

The Chinese woman hesitated before saying in broken English, "This place right place for *mui-tsai* complain?"

"Yes, yes, I am an inspector of *mui-tsai* households. Do you own a *mui-tsai*?" Lady Matilda grimaced as she said the word 'own.'

The Chinese woman's face went white and her lips trembled. "In 1925, my husband, Towkay Toh and my ma-in-law, Madam Sim, pay fifty dollars for my niece, Liao Mei Mei. Mei Mei's ma, my cousin, die giving birth to Mei Mei and she not treated well by Stepma, you understand? I loved Mei Mei's ma as my own sister and I tell my husband we adopt Mei Mei. School her, you know? Treat her like daughter. We are childless." Ai Lin's eyes brimmed with tears.

"Very commendable." Lady Matilda approved whole-heartedly. "Few households are so kind to their bondmaids. Which school does the girl attend?"

"Methodist Girls'," Wu Ai Lin said, her thin arms resting on the table.

Lady Matilda's eyebrows shot up into her hair. She had yet to encounter an employer who sent her *mui-tsai* to an English-medium school for education. "And were the adoption papers signed?" she asked sharply.

Two tears spilled onto Ai Lin's cheeks. "No," she whispered. "It was going well for Mei Mei, she did good at school. Then my husband's business went kaput and he go *chandu* brothel. He take second wife who is a lady of the night, you know? And she make Toh take Mei Mei out from school and set her to sweep and mop our house."

"Your husband is an opium addict?" Lady Matilda's face fell.

"Yes, he not in senses and his concubine take advantage, you know? Refuse *chandu* pipe unless Mei Mei work." Ai Lin's eyes suddenly flashed fire, and her mouth trembled with anger. "I powerless so I come to you, Madam Matilda."

Lady Matilda nodded and shuffled the papers on her desk. "Any beatings?" At Ai Lin's look of incomprehension, Lady Matilda elaborated, "This second wife of your husband's, has she beaten the bondmaid? I need evidence of abuse."

Ai Lin's nostrils flared. "Not only beat but say sell *mui-tsai* to brothel. My own sister's child be made to sell her body for money while I live!"

Ai Lin's voice had risen, and Lady Matilda went to the distraught woman and patted her shoulder. "Selling the little sister to a brothel is abuse, Madam Wu. I will tell you what I will do. This Sunday, I will visit your house as inspector of *mui-tsais*. I will talk to your niece as well as to your husband. Please leave your address with my peon. Do not worry. Your niece will not be sold to a whorehouse."

Ai Lin rose and clung to Lady Matilda's hand, a tremulous smile on her lips. "Thank you, Lady Matilda," she said with dignity.

Lady Matilda hollered for her peon and, bowing to the Englishwoman, Ai Lin hurried out of the office.

Lady Matilda watched her go, noticing that her back was straight and proud.

"I will see to it that this Chinese slavery system is abolished," Lady Matilda vowed to her peon.

The Chinese peon's face was bland as he said, "The little sisters would have died if they were not sold."

Lady Matilda rounded on her hapless peon, and her voice shook with anger as she said, "It is because of misinformed beliefs like yours that the slavery system thrives. Now go and get me some tiffin."

Lady Matilda Robertson entered her office and shut the door in her peon's face.

*　*　*

It was a bright Sunday morning at the House of Toh. The Hainanese cook had prepared enticing pork dumplings, pork *congee* and steamed prawns for breakfast, and Mei Mei scurried between the kitchen and the dining room, carrying the steaming dishes to the oval dining table. Towkay Toh, having abstained from opium for a week, was tucking greedily into his breakfast, appreciating the mild flavours of the rice porridge in front of him. Grandma Sim sat opposite him, delicately spearing the steamed prawns with her chopsticks, her eyes darting with affection to her son. Second Mistress Meisheng stood in attendance behind Grandma Sim's chair, a small smile playing on her lips.

There was a movement at the doorway and Towkay Toh looked up in surprise. "Ai Lin! You are joining us for breakfast today?"

First Mistress Ai Lin, dressed in a bright blue cheongsam and with her hair braided around her head, nodded. Her complexion was wan, but her eyes glittered. She took her place next to her husband, and Mei Mei placed a steaming bowl of *congee* in front of her aunt, her face filled with joy.

"Good, good." Towkay Toh said uneasily as Meisheng's lips hardened into a thin line.

Ai Lin faced her husband with equanimity and said in Hokkien, "I feel well enough to join the family for breakfast. It is fortuitous that you are in your senses today, Towkay."

There was a knock on the dining room door, and Ai Lin's bondmaid, Li Jun, appeared, her eyes round and scared.

"Madam," she addressed Ai Lin in Hokkien, "there is an Englishwoman at our door. She says her name is Lady Robertson and she asks to see the master and mistress of this house. She says that she is a volunteer inspector of *mui-tsais*. I have shown her into the drawing room."

Ai Lin rose gracefully and addressed her husband. "Come, Toh, we have to meet Lady Robertson."

Mei Mei, lurking in the shadows of the dining room, gazed with fascination at Meisheng. She was clutching a chair with clenched hands and her face was white. Grandma Sim looked with surprise at Li Jun.

"Lady Robertson?" she quavered in Hokkien. "A *mui-tsai* inspector? Who informed the Chinese Protectorate that we needed their services?"

"Mei Mei!" Ai Lin commanded. "Follow your uncle and me to the drawing room, and speak the truth about your treatment in this house to the inspector. Understand?"

Lady Matilda rose from the sofa in the ornate drawing room of the Toh mansion as Towkay Toh followed Ai Lin into the room. The Englishwoman's eyes rested with interest on the girl who followed the couple.

Matilda looked at Ai Lin and inclined her head towards Mei Mei. "Is she your *mui-tsai*?"

Ai Lin nodded and said in broken English, "Can ask question. My niece speak good English."

Before Lady Matilda could reply, two more people entered the room.

"Madam Sim, my ma-in-law." Ai Lin did not look at Grandma Sim. Then she said in a hard voice, "And Meisheng, my husband's concubine."

After everyone had seated themselves, Matilda said in booming tones, "Let me introduce myself. I am secretary to the Chinese Protectorate and a volunteer inspector of *mui-tsais*. I work for the Government and make sure that *mui-tsais* are treated kindly."

Meisheng and Grandma Sim looked blank, and Ai Lin's brows were furrowed as she tried to follow Lady Matilda's speech. Only Towkay Toh and Mei Mei nodded their heads in comprehension.

Lady Matilda turned to Mei Mei. "What are your duties in this house, child?" She smiled kindly at the frightened girl. "Don't worry, you can be honest with me. No one will hurt you." She settled herself awkwardly on the sofa.

"I did no work at the Toh household until Second Mistress Meisheng entered this house," Mei Mei said spiritedly, drawing confidence from Aunt Ai Lin's encouraging nods. "I was treated as the daughter of the house."

"And what happened after your uncle's concubine arrived?" Matilda prompted, taking a quick look at Meisheng's bland face and glittering eyes.

Mei Mei hung her head and said in a small voice. "I was ordered by my uncle to sweep and mop the house and the steps by the gate. I was told not to go to school anymore and to sleep on a mattress in the scullery."

Towkay Toh's eyes slunk away from Lady Matilda's measured gaze and Ai Lin's accusing stare. He said weakly, "We had a labour shortage at our house. Times were bad. So I asked Mei Mei to assist with chores." He continued in a stronger voice, "Mei Mei's father was poor, and he sold her to us as a domestic servant. The *mui-tsai* system takes care of girls from poor families, allowing them to lead better lives. When Mei Mei turns eighteen, she will be released from her contract, and we will marry her off to a suitable groom." He smiled winningly.

"Why did you stop her schooling?" Lady Matilda enquired, her grey eyes sceptical. "You have no money to pay her school fees?"

Ai Lin darted forward, pushed her niece towards Lady Matilda, and pulled up her blouse so that the Englishwoman had a full view of the lacerations and scars on her back.

Lady Matilda gasped. Her eyes were stern as she asked Mei Mei, "Were you beaten by someone in this house, child?"

Ai Lin prodded Mei Mei. "Not be afraid, not be afraid. Tell, little one. Tell kind English lady."

Mei Mei's face was pale, but she took a deep breath and said, "I was washing the steps to the gate, and my friend, Winifred, visited me to ask why I was not attending school. Second Mistress Meisheng heard us talking and caned me in her bedroom that night."

Meisheng's eyes glittered like black jewels as Towkay Toh turned a distressed face to his concubine. "Meisheng, why did you beat the child? You should not lay a hand on Mei Mei. She may be a bondmaid, but she is also Ai Lin's blood relative."

Lady Matilda grunted. "This is the reason why we inspectors visit households. Employers can misuse their power over the little sisters with abuse such as this.

"You cannot lay a hand on the child," Lady Matilda told Meisheng. "I will come to this house again in two weeks' time. The scars on the child's back had better be healed, and I don't want to find more. If there are fresh wounds on any part of the child's body, I will recommend to the Chinese Protectorate that Mei Mei be sent to live at the Poh Leung Kuk Orphanage. It is a shelter for abused *mui-tsais*."

Ai Lin had not finished her tirade against her husband's concubine. She pointed at Meisheng and said, "Mei Mei hear Second Mistress and my ma-in-law talk of selling her to Geylang Serai brothel." Her eyes were pinpricks of outrage, and even Towkay Toh cowered under the onslaught of her anger.

"We will arrest you if you sell Mei Mei to a brothel," Lady Matilda told Meisheng, and Mei Mei translated her words into Mandarin. Two spots of colour appeared on Meisheng's face, and without a word, she rose from the couch and walked out of the room.

Towkay Toh rose and stated formally, "Lady Matilda, I was unaware that Mei Mei was beaten, and that a plan had been hatched to sell her to a brothel. I will take steps to ensure that Mei Mei is treated as she was before Meisheng entered our house. I will reinstate her at the Methodist School, and she will do no more domestic chores. You have my word."

Lady Matilda nodded and rose. She looked at Mei Mei, and a kind light glimmered in her eyes. "My child, my door is always open for you. If anyone beats you again, come to my office and report it to me."

Lady Matilda nodded pleasantly at Ai Lin and gave a curt nod in Towkay Toh's direction. He led the way to the gate, all the while offering platitudes to the Englishwoman.

* * *

Mei Mei sat on a bench in the portico of the House of Toh, making a necklace for Winnie. The beads were scarlet seeds from the crab's eye plant growing in the garden. Sunlight spilled over the trees and road, bathing the landscape in a yellow glow, forming a triangular pool of light at Mei Mei's feet. A bird gave a jubilant trill from the nearby frangipani tree. A mild breeze nudged dead leaves around the portico, and Mei Mei decided to sweep them up after she had finished the necklace.

The household had settled into an uneasy truce after Lady Matilda's visit. While Mei Mei had resumed her schooling at the Methodist Girls' School, she was viewed with repressed animosity by both Meisheng and Grandma Sim. Ai Lin disregarded her mother-in-law's attitude and, for the first time in months, welcomed her husband into her bedchamber.

A shadow fell over the seeds in Mei Mei's lap. She looked up to see Meisheng staring at the seeds with an odd expression on her face. Observing Mei Mei's look, the concubine averted her eyes and went inside the house.

Mei Mei had finished half the necklace and was about to go indoors when Ai Lin's bondmaid, Li Jun, only two years older than Mei Mei, accosted her.

"Madam Ai Lin is in bed with a cold and craves beef curry, Miss," Li Jun whispered, her eyes not meeting Mei Mei's surprised gaze. "She asked me to request that you make her favourite curry."

Mei Mei rose with alacrity from the bench. "Of course. Tell Aunt I will bring a bowl to her room at night. I was going to sweep the portico floor and then I will go to the kitchen."

"Oh, I will sweep the portico, Miss, don't you worry," Li Jun said. "You go on to the kitchen, now." She watched Mei Mei gather the necklace and crab's eye seeds and put them into a wooden box.

With painstaking care, Mei Mei single-handedly prepared all the ingredients for the curry. After it had boiled for an hour, she tasted it. The meat was soft and tender and the curry tangy, tasting strongly of aromatic spices. The cook nodded approvingly as Mei Mei ladled some curry into a bowl. Li Jun, standing at the kitchen door, smiled.

"May I take the bowl up to my mistress, Miss?" she asked.

Mei Mei smiled and shook her head. "No, I want to take it to my aunt."

"But Miss," Li Jun objected in Hokkien, as she followed Mei Mei from the kitchen to the dining room, "you have not garnished the curry with coriander leaves. My mistress loves the taste of coriander."

Mei Mei paused. "Cook said he has run out of coriander leaves." Her brows furrowed. It was true that Ai Lin loved the taste of coriander.

"It is only twilight. I could go to the back garden and pick some leaves for you," offered Li Jun. "But my mistress wants me to prepare a hot bath for her." She hesitated.

Mei Mei placed the bowl of curry on the dining table. She smiled and said, "You go on upstairs, Li Jun. I will go to the garden now and pick some leaves."

After picking the leaves, Mei Mei returned to the kitchen to wash them, before taking them into the dining room to garnish the bowl of beef curry. Then she took the bowl upstairs to her aunt's bedroom. Ai Lin was delighted, and promised to try the dish as an evening snack.

At the crack of dawn, frenzied screams from Ai Lin's bondmaid woke the Toh household from slumber.

"My mistress lies dead in her bed! Oh, why do the gods punish me so?" Li Jun shrieked.

Mei Mei entered Ai Lin's bedchamber in disbelief, expecting to see her aunt alive and well. Instead, stretched out on the bed, Ai Lin's unseeing eyes stared at the ceiling from a paper-white face. Overwhelmed by shock, it was some time before Mei Mei noticed the bowl of beef curry standing on the bedside table. It was half-eaten, and malodorous vomit spattered the floor.

A horrible thought entered Mei Mei's head. Had the beef curry poisoned Ai Lin?

8

January 1931

Richard alighted from the car and stepped onto the paved courtyard of the Singapore Assizes, the imposing building by the Singapore River where the criminal courts held trials. The air was filled with the voices of coolies shouting to each other from the colourful bumboats that plied their trade on the Singapore River. The sun was climbing over the horizon, and Richard yearned to capture the frenetic activity on canvas.

Instead, he steeled himself and entered the cool interior of the courthouse. This was his first job as a court artist, a position he had won over four other British and Chinese youths. Intent on exploring portrait painting, he had applied for the post on a whim. The court artists drew pictures of prisoners, law personnel and witnesses as a pictorial record of the proceedings. Only that morning he had learnt that he had been appointed to the trial of a bondmaid, Liao Mei Mei, accused of the murder of one Madam Wu Ai Lin. Richard frowned. He had thought he would be given one of the smaller criminal trials, pig farmers stealing from each other, or moneylenders beating up clients to recover their money. He had not imagined that his first employment at the Assizes would see him assigned to the sensational murder case that was gripping the nation.

Richard took his seat in the court and loosened his collar; the room was stiflingly hot. The soft murmur of human voices rose and fell as the gathered crowd waited with bated breath for the spectacle to unfold. The more generous among them had the anticipatory look of a circus audience, while others wore the masks of predators waiting to pounce.

She was the most beautiful Chinese girl he had ever seen.

The bondmaid in the dock gazed out of the barred window at the frangipani and hibiscus flowers nodding together in a riot of colour, the sky peeping through the branches of the trees. Richard knew what she was thinking: freedom lay outside, so close, yet so far away. She met his eyes, then looked away through the wooden bars of the dock to the faces beyond, to the people who had squeezed into the claustrophobic room, eager to see her humiliated and censured.

Richard looked with interest at the jury trooping in to take their places on special raised seats near the judge's throne. They were seven in number, all educated Chinese, fluent in English. He saw them looking at Mei Mei with undisguised curiosity.

Richard turned his eyes away from them as the judge spoke.

Judge Maurice Weston had a thin face framing a hawk's nose, and colourless lips that suggested a sternness belied by his kindly blue eyes.

"Mr Bagley, you may begin the proceedings," the judge ordered the public prosecutor. "Let us get to the bottom of the mystery surrounding the death of Madam Wu Ai Lin of the House of Toh." Weston's eyes sharpened as he looked at the crowded courtroom. "I don't need to tell you that the prisoner is a minor, a girl only fifteen years of age. When accosted by journalists outside the courtroom, I advise all of you to exercise moderation when discussing the proceedings. We will have a Chinese translator sworn in to aid the questioning of the natives who are not proficient in English. Fortunately, the prisoner is educated and will not need interpretation. The jury will now be sworn in. Have you elected a foreman yet?"

A tall, thin man, with a scholarly bearing, stood and bowed to the judge. "I am the foreman, Your Honour. My name is Lee Han Ching, tin merchant."

Richard felt the prisoner's gaze on him, speculative, measuring. I am not much older than her, he thought. What violent abuse had prompted the bondmaid to kill her employer? Perhaps Mei Mei had been beaten and bruised by cruel masters, until her spark of rebellion had become a roaring fire that had finally consumed her aunt.

The public prosecutor said, "Three weeks ago, Wu Ai Lin, wife of Toh Way Ming, a reputable Chinese businessman, was found dead in her bed by her bondmaid in the early hours of the morning. There was vomit on the floor, and a bowl of beef curry on a small table by the bedside. The beef curry had been prepared the night before by the *mui-tsai* of the House of Toh, Liao Mei Mei, the prisoner in the dock."

Mui-tsai. The eyes of the girl in the dock flashed and her face flushed. Richard's pencil flew over his notepad as he attempted to capture her outrage at the word that demeaned her.

He remained focused on Mei Mei throughout Bagley's

examination of the police surgeon, Michael Sutton. It was only at the end of Sutton's testimony that one sentence roused naked fear in the prisoner's eyes, forcing Richard's attention back to the witness stand.

"I found two crab's eye seeds in the beef curry," Sutton was saying. "While the seeds look harmless, they contain a poison called abrin, which is fatal. According to my tests, the concoction may have contained a few more crab's eye seeds in powder form."

There was an uneasy murmur from the room at Dr Sutton's proclamation, and Richard saw a look of horror in Mei Mei's eyes as she gazed at the jury, no doubt seeing censure on every face. The judge pronounced the court adjourned for lunch, and the crowd of spectators started trooping out. Richard made his way to the dock.

"I say, don't be afraid," he said, smiling encouragingly at Mei Mei. "My name is Richard Harrison. My father is a rubber planter here. I want to wish you good luck. Please have faith in our justice system. It is pretty fair."

Lady Matilda, one of his father's friends, approached with a smile on her face. "I am covering this trial for the Chinese Protectorate, and I have been assigned to write a report for the British Parliament on Chinese *mui-tsais* in Singapore. Child," Matilda's voice was gruff, "I have trouble believing that you poisoned your aunt. I saw with my own eyes the devotion between you. Truth will out, child, do not worry."

Mei Mei gave a shaky smile before the prison warden escorted her towards the door leading to the holding cell.

"Lady Matilda, you know the girl?" Richard asked.

"Yes, dear boy, and Mei Mei was devoted to her aunt. I can't believe she would poison her. There is something fishy going on here."

Deep in thought, Richard went to the door; and the memory of Mei Mei's liquid eyes remained in the fabric of his mind long after he reached home.

* * *

Dusk was falling over the tropical landscape as the Harrison family and their new plantation overseer sat down to dinner on the back porch of their bungalow. Jeffrey Peters, a thin young man of twenty-four, with sandy hair and pale blue eyes, had arrived the previous week from a Nigerian plantation to take up the post of overseer in John Harrison's rubber plantation. Jeff came with impeccable recommendations from his previous employer, with whom he had pioneered an impressive new technique for washing rubber slabs. His intelligent eyes were shy, veering away from Clem's face, leaving Richard in no doubt that he admired her beauty. His hooked nose meant he would never be called handsome, but his pleasant conversation and relaxed bearing had already won him Richard as a friend.

"Ah, chicken from Kedah!" John Harrison rubbed his hands together as the roasted fowl was borne ceremoniously to the dinner table by his Indian butler, Sher Singh. John looked at his son. "Today was the first day of the murder trial of Towkay Toh's bondmaid, eh?" He turned to Jeff. "Toh worked as one of my rubber distributors before his business folded. The Toh family must have ill-treated the poor *mui-tsai*, Mei Mei, to such an extent that she resorted to murder."

Richard made as if to speak, found Clementine's eyes fixed on him and shut his mouth.

John thumped the table with his fist, startling everyone. "*Mui-tsai* means 'little sister' in Cantonese. Little sisters, my foot! They are slaves. I have heard that many of them are violated by their employers. Abominable! The whole system of slavery should be abolished altogether!" he thundered. "We British should civilize the natives, and the first item on the agenda is to rid Chinese society of the *mui-tsai* system. It's time we took a stand! Hmm. I will have a word with Maurice Weston, the judge in Mei Mei's case. He may allow me into the court as an observer."

"There's no need to carry on so, John." Eleanor pursed her lips. "What will Jeffrey think?"

"I hope the poor girl gets off," Richard muttered. "She looked so alone sitting in the dock, listening to that cadaverous Public Prosecutor. But I never saw tears in her eyes. Lady Matilda believes the girl is innocent. Will she get a fair trial, Father? As far as I could see, the jurors are all Chinese traders and merchants. They have bondmaids in their own houses. They are sure to be biased against the poor girl."

A chair grated across the floor as Clementine rose. "May I be excused, Aunt Eleanor? I have heard enough about native slave girls."

"I've heard the Kuomintang Party has a strong base in Singapore." Jeff hurriedly changed the subject. He smiled as Clementine resumed her seat, her face less thunderous than before.

"Not for long!" cried John Harrison. "I heard that Clementi invited the Kuomintang leaders to Government House and gave them a royal ticking off. He told them they could not behave like double-headed snakes."

The dinner table conversation whirled around Richard, but all he could see were Mei Mei's sad eyes and sweet face. Clem's agitated voice woke him from his reverie. He could feel her eyes on him, attempting to analyse his every thought.

"Uncle John, can you make arrangements for me to attend the trial of the bondmaid?"

Eleanor looked scandalized. "Clem, it is not proper for you to sit in a violent crowd in the courtroom. So many natives! You will catch one of those dreadful tropical diseases."

"Oh, tosh," Clem said rudely. She turned to John Harrison. "We are doing a school project on Chinese culture, so it would be educational for me to attend the trial. Richard can escort me to court. I will sit with Lady Matilda."

"I will see what I can do," John said, and bent towards his dessert plate.

The butler drew down reed mats over the veranda, hiding the dusky tropical landscape from view. As the family laughed and joked over coffee with their new overseer, the lamplighters began to climb their ladders, heralding the death of another tropical day.

* * *

Richard took his seat opposite the dock and looked at Mei Mei. She met his gaze fearlessly, but could manage only a tremulous smile. He sketched her downcast, heart-shaped face, aquiline nose, rosebud mouth and curly black lashes. He was aware of Clementine's eyes fixed on him like gimlets from her place next to Lady Matilda in the front row of the British spectators. Her unrelenting regard never ceased to irritate him; he was her prisoner, his unwelcome future rushing towards him like an avalanche, ready to smother him in a marriage of convenience.

Second Mistress Meisheng of the House of Toh was taking the witness stand. Richard looked at her with interest. Meisheng had a regal bearing, pallid complexion and lotus-shaped eyes. Surprised, Richard realised the woman wore the same white makeup he had heard was used by Japanese Geisha girls. The effect was like a mask.

David Bagley was at his genial best. "The Honourable Justice Maurice Weston has allowed an interpreter to be sworn in for our next witness, Second Mistress Meisheng of the House of Toh," he announced.

A petite Chinese woman, dressed in a white sarong and dark blue *kebaya*, scuttled towards the witness box and stood to attention.

Bagley ambled towards the stand and smiled encouragingly at Second Mistress Meisheng.

"Madam, please tell the court what you saw on the day the bondmaid was making the curry," David Bagley urged.

"I was going to Johor to visit my friend who had had a fall. I happened to come to the portico in front of the house, and Mei Mei was sitting there, making a necklace of crab's eye seeds."

When the excited babble in the courtroom had died down,

Bagley asked, "Would you say that Mei Mei was on good terms with her aunt and uncle?"

"What can I say? I was only married to my husband a short time before the murder. Outwardly, the child was very affectionate towards both Ai Lin and Toh. I was not going to mention Mei Mei's former tutor, Poh Tek Siong, who is a member of the Kuomintang Party—but I must tell the truth to unravel the mystery of First Mistress's death. Mei Mei and Poh were lovers."

There was a gasp from the crowd, and Richard saw Mei Mei's mouth drop open in shock.

"Your Honour, I fail to see the relevance of the information being provided by the witness. It is nothing but gossip and scandal. Liao Mei Mei's tutor's life has no bearing on this case." The defence attorney, a Welshman called Herbert Evans, spoke up.

David Bagley turned to the witness and smiled engagingly. "Do you know why Mei Mei would want her aunt dead?"

The interpreter translated Meisheng's words. "First Mistress Ai Lin did not possess any wealth, except for the fine pieces of jewellery that Toh gifted her. I daresay she was killed by the wretched child for the jewellery. Her lover was poor, and he must have incited her to do away with First Mistress and steal the jewellery. I checked First Mistress Ai Lin's jewellery box after the murder, and her jewellery is missing."

With hauteur, Meisheng left the witness stand. There was commotion as Inspector Robert Shipley, a brown-haired man with a jowly face and huge whiskers, made his way to the judge's table. He held a whispered consultation with the judge, after which Maurice Weston cleared his throat.

"Ahem, some new evidence has come to light." The judge looked at the jury. "The police conducted a second search of the chambers of the accused last week. A pouch with some of the missing jewels was found hidden behind the cistern of the bathroom adjoining her bedchamber. I understand that the police had failed to search that place before. Mr Bagley, it would be best if you called Inspector Shipley as your next witness."

After Shipley was seated in the witness stand, Bagley asked, "Were any crab's eye seeds found when your men searched the House of Toh the morning after the murder, Inspector?"

Inspector Shipley's beady brown eyes gleamed. "Yes. My men found a necklace of crab's eye seeds in a wooden box in Liao Mei Mei's room."

"When did you conduct a second search of the premises, Inspector, and what was found?" Bagley barked.

The judge and jurors leaned forward to hear the new evidence, their faces stern.

Shipley cleared his throat. "I must apologise for the ineptitude of my sergeant and constables. The first search was conducted the day after the murder, and no stolen jewellery was found. Mistress Meisheng did, however, lodge a complaint a week ago that First Mistress Ai Lin's jewellery was missing. I then sent my men for a second search of the premises, and they found some of the jewellery hidden behind the cistern of the bathroom adjoining Liao Mei Mei's bedroom."

Richard saw scepticism on the judge's face, and his heart lifted. Judge Weston said, "Please cross-examine, Mr Evans."

Herb Evans got to his feet. "Inspector, what did Liao Mei Mei say when questioned about the crab's eye seed necklace found in her bedroom?"

Shipley raised a brow and said derisively, "She said she was making the necklace for her friend, Winifred, whose birthday was approaching."

"Was the necklace complete or half-done?" Evans asked pleasantly.

Inspector Shipley said, "Half-done. You can see for yourself, Mr Evans. It is Exhibit A."

Herb Evans examined the necklace and the clerk passed it to the judge, who then passed it to the jurors. Mei Mei's eyes were fixed on the jury, as if trying to tell what they were making of the evidence.

Herb Evans asked, "Inspector, this necklace is only half complete. Where are the rest of the seeds? Surely Liao Mei Mei had picked enough for a fully beaded necklace?"

"Why, the rest of the seeds were in the curry!" Shipley said triumphantly, and a faint smile illuminated Second Mistress Meisheng's face.

"But Dr Sutton only found evidence of two crab's eye seeds in the remains of the curry," Evans objected.

"We did not find any loose crab's eye seeds in Liao Mei Mei's bedroom," Shipley asserted. "Nor in any other room in the house. The beef curry was eaten by the master of the house and his mother, as well as by Wu Ai Lin. Since they were not sick, the rest of the crab's eye seeds must have been in the bowl of curry Liao Mei Mei presented to her aunt. Dr Sutton found two loose seeds in the bowl given to Madam Wu, but you've heard him say that he found traces of crab's eye seeds in powder form there too. Obviously, that powder was ground from the loose seeds set aside to complete the necklace. It was a premeditated murder. What a diabolical young lady!" Shipley directed a look of contempt at Mei Mei.

"Control yourself, Inspector!" Judge Weston admonished. "The court will deal with facts, and facts only. Proceed, Mr Evans."

"Let us come now to the search of the premises," Evans said. "Since there was a gap in time before the stolen jewellery was recovered, was it not possible for someone to have planted the jewellery behind the cistern after Liao Mei Mei's arrest? How can you be certain it was she who hid the jewellery, since it was not found on your first search?"

Three jurors leant forward, their faces intent, their eyes on Shipley. Richard felt his heart thumping. There was commotion in the court and the judge asked for silence.

Inspector Shipley frowned. "As I said before, we found no stolen jewellery during our first search, but, unfortunately, my constables did not thoroughly investigate the bathroom adjoining Liao Mei Mei's bedroom. For that, I apologise. That is where the accused had hidden the jewellery, and it was found during the second search."

After two more days of proceedings, Judge Weston addressed the jury and asked for a verdict. The jurors retired to confer in a separate room. When they trooped back into the courtroom, Richard saw Mei Mei anxiously scanning their faces. None would meet her eye.

Judge Weston asked, "Have you reached a majority or unanimous verdict? Foreman, what say you?"

Lee Han Ching rose and said, "We have been unable to reach a unanimous verdict. We have a verdict of 'guilty', four to three."

"That is not a majority, Mr Lee!" Weston said. "We need at least a five-three vote of 'guilty' to convict the accused. Please reconvene, and return with a majority verdict."

But the jury was unable to do so. In the end, Judge Weston declared, "Without a majority verdict, I have no option but to order a retrial with a different jury. The prisoner will be remanded in custody."

Heedless of propriety, Richard rushed to the dock, his green eyes shining with hope.

Lady Matilda joined him, and Mei Mei turned to her, her eyes filled with entreaty. "I don't see my uncle, Lady Matilda. Where is he?"

Lady Matilda sighed. "I have some bad news, Mei Mei. Your uncle has disappeared, and we are afraid he has left Singapore. He has cleaned out his bank accounts. The rumour mills are rife with the story that Toh discovered Second Mistress had taken Inspector Shipley as her lover. I am so ashamed to say this, my child." Tears glimmered in the Englishwoman's eyes, but her voice was brusque as she said, "Toh gave a fat retainer to your defence attorney, Herb Evans, and he will fight for you in the retrial. Do not lose hope, child."

After Mei Mei had been taken back to the holding cell, Richard looked for Clem to escort her home; but there was no sign of her. Clementine had already left.

* * *

The March skies were blue and clear, and the scent of flowers filled the air, as Richard, dressed informally in trousers and a white shirt, walked along the winding path of his father's plantation. He observed with pleasure the flame trees blazing with blossoms as he strode down the dirt road to the *kampong* where his father's workers lived. The pungent scent of prawn paste hung in the air, and he saw village women sitting in front of their houses, sorting stones from rice or shelling peas. They smiled a welcome at him, and he gave a cheery wave.

The sound of a hacking cough came from a nearby hut. Richard paused and noted the hut's location. Muthu, a relatively new Tamil worker come all the way from Madras, resided in the tumbledown building. Richard made a mental note to ask the estate doctor to pay a visit and check out his cough. If Muthu had tuberculosis, he would need to be segregated at Middletown Hospital to keep other workers safe from the disease. John Harrison had lost many workers in a tuberculosis epidemic a few years earlier, and had instituted diligent checks on working conditions and the health of workers ever since. His plantation was one of the few equipped with a makeshift hospital, an estate doctor and a *dressar*.

A child in ragged clothing ran up to Richard, his dirty face filled with delight, and his mouth stretched in a grin.

"Ali, why are you not at school?" Richard demanded in

Bazaar Malay.

"Me sick," Ali grinned, replying in English. He pointed to his stomach. "Tummy pain, *Tuan*."

"Now do not make up lies, boy." Richard said gently. "School is good for you. When you grow up, you can work in an office and not in a plantation, eh? Come on now."

Ali followed Richard to the plantation schoolhouse, a thatched hut with a garden of bright flowers. Here the estate schoolmaster, a Eurasian named Desmond, was conducting a lesson under a banyan tree, his students seated in a circle around him.

The teacher looked over his round spectacles as Richard led Ali into the garden. "Stomach pain again, Ali?"

The boy nodded delightedly while the other children laughed.

Richard chatted briefly to Desmond about buying supplies for the school, before making his way to the estate hospital down the road. This was a bigger hut than the schoolhouse, containing five hospital beds, a clinic and dispensary. The estate doctor, an Indian called Dr Ravi, was doing his rounds, and Richard waited for him to return to the clinic.

"Two Tamil workers have malaria," Dr Ravi told Richard when he had finished with his patients.

"Do you need more quinine?" Richard asked. "I am going into the city and can order supplies, Dr Ravi."

"Thank you, Master Richard, that is good of you."

Dr Ravi frowned when Richard mentioned Muthu's cough. "I will visit Muthu and send him for tests at Middletown. We must prevent a tuberculosis epidemic at all costs, *Tuan*."

Richard nodded and made his way back to the house. After

refreshing himself with a quick drink of lemonade, he asked the chauffeur to take him to Outram Prison. There he asked to see Mei Mei.

"I came to offer you my support," he said, his uneven teeth flashing in an attractive smile as he looked at her across the table in an interview room.

"I did not kill my aunt," Mei Mei said with spirit.

Richard nodded, and steepled his hands on the table. "We need to prove your innocence," he said, his green eyes gentle. "It is probable that someone else placed crab's eye seeds into the bowl of curry, but we need evidence. Let us talk about the day of your aunt's murder. Perhaps we can find something the police failed to uncover."

"Why are you helping me?" Mei Mei asked, a hint of suspicion in her voice.

"Out of humanitarianism." At Mei Mei's look of incomprehension, a flush crept up Richard's face. "I believe the *mui-tsai* system should be abolished. It is too open to abuse by employers. I understand that many little sisters are nothing but concubines to their masters." He blushed painfully as he realised that he was speaking openly of sex to a young native girl.

A quiver of amusement rippled across Mei Mei's face and her eyes were bright with suppressed laughter as she said, "I understand, and I am grateful for your interest. I have been thinking of the day of Aunt Ai Lin's death, and something troubles me. The bondmaid, Li Jun, told me that Aunt wished to eat beef curry, but when I presented it to her, she seemed surprised that I had taken the trouble to cook it."

Richard immediately pounced on the implications of Mei Mei's statement. "So someone could have bribed Li Jun to say that Madam Wu wanted you to cook curry for her? Was the bowl of curry left unattended at any time?"

Mei Mei nodded. "Li Jun observed that I had not garnished the curry with coriander leaves, so I left the bowl on the dining table and walked to the back garden to pick some. I was gone for ten minutes or so. Li Jun had gone to draw Aunt's bath, and Mistress Meisheng was in Johor. But Li Jun could easily have nipped down from upstairs and doctored the curry, Richard."

Richard was animated. "The bondmaid. What is she like? Did your aunt sing her praises?"

Mei Mei knitted her brows and shook her head. "Li Jun is new to our household. Aunt's old bondmaid went home to China, and Aunt hired Li Jun—oh, maybe six months before Second Mistress entered our house." Mei Mei frowned with the strain of dredging up a past she wished to forget. "Aunt Ai Lin complained that Li Jun was lazy and greedy for money. When Uncle went bankrupt and had to rid himself of household staff, Li Jun demanded an extra two dollars a month for tending to Grandma Sim, in addition to her salary for serving Aunt Ai Lin."

Richard asked, "Where was everybody on the day of the murder, Mei Mei?"

"Uncle had gone to his warehouses for business, and Second Mistress Meisheng was in Johor, visiting a friend. However, before she left she saw me in the portico, beading the crab's eye seed necklace. She left at around eleven, and returned at nine in the evening. Madam Sim spent the morning in the temple and the afternoon in her room. I did not see her come downstairs until dinner. Uncle came back for dinner as well, and we all ate the beef curry I had made for our evening meal. The cook was in the kitchen most of the day. Li Jun was hanging about the portico in the morning, and she was the one who told me that Aunt Ai Lin wanted curry. She was in and out of the kitchen when I was making it."

"And you are certain that there was no jewellery hidden behind the cistern in your bathroom when you were arrested?" Richard demanded, no doubt in his mind of Mei Mei's innocence.

Mei Mei shook her head. "The police sergeant searched the bathroom and did not find any jewels. Ask him." Mei Mei's eyes were soft as she added, "He was sympathetic, and very embarrassed to be searching my belongings. He was so different from Inspector Shipley, who was rude and arrogant."

"Shipley is Mistress Meisheng's client. I wonder who his sergeant is?"

"His name is William Doyle."

Richard's eyes widened. "Billy Doyle? I design sets for an amateur British theatre company, and Sergeant Billy Doyle is one of the actors. I will talk to him." He rose and smiled at Mei Mei. "I believe in your innocence, and I will talk to Lady Matilda and your lawyer. I am sure we will gather enough evidence to convince the judge and jury to deliver a verdict of not guilty. Li Jun must have poisoned the curry."

Mei Mei flushed and stammered, "Thank you, Richard, for believing in my innocence." She smiled shyly as he held up his hand in farewell and strode out of the interview room.

* * *

It was a bright, sunny morning with the birds chirruping in the trees, the sky the indigo blue of the tropics, and the frangipani trees flowering with white and pink blossoms. The air was thick with fragrance, and heavy with the promise of hot weather after the rainy months. Richard walked through Lady Matilda's garden, following the path to her bower. There, under the shade of a *tembusu* tree, the servants had set up tables and chairs for elevenses. Lady Matilda was already seated, talking animatedly to Mei Mei's defence lawyer, Herbert Evans, over glasses of pink lemonade. She spoke a cheery greeting to Richard.

Richard took a seat opposite Evans and studied him closely. He had dark brown hair which curled at the nape of his neck, a craggy yet sensitive face, and cornflower blue eyes that shyly avoided Lady Matilda's clear grey ones. His cheeks were hollow, and the Adam's apple in his throat was prominent, bobbing up and down every time he spoke. He displayed a dry sense of humour in his replies to Lady Matilda as they talked politics.

Richard apprised his listeners of his conversation with Mei Mei.

Lady Matilda's eyes sharpened. "Isn't it true that only part of the stolen jewellery was recovered from behind the bathroom cistern?" she demanded, barely able to contain her excitement.

Herb sounded just as elated. "Could it be that part of the jewellery was placed in her bathroom to frame Mei Mei, but the rest was used to bribe Li Jun? The police did search Li Jun's room along with those of the other servants, though."

Lady Matilda snorted. "Maybe Li Jun had already pawned the jewellery. With so many *chettiars* in the neighbourhood, it is easy enough to do. We need to do our own detective work—but how?"

Richard said, "We can forget asking Shipley to help us—his mistress is Meisheng. I know Shipley's deputy, though. Sergeant Billy Doyle acts for the Rambunctious Playhouse—you know, the amateur theatre company. I design sets for them. I have made an appointment with him for a drink at the Raffles Hotel at five today. He is a good chap, Lady Matilda, and I think he will help us."

"If Doyle can interview the *chettiar*s around the area, and we can find one who can identify Li Jun as the girl pawning Madam Ai Lin's jewels, why then, we have a case." Herb Evans got to his feet. "If I can find another person in the household with a motive for killing Madam Wu, Mei Mei will be exonerated. There's no way the jury will be able to find her guilty beyond a reasonable doubt."

Richard made his way back to the plantation, his mind easier now that they had formulated a plan of action. He remembered the mute appeal in Mei Mei's eyes and quickened his step.

9

April 1931

The prison cell was stifling, the air trying to trickle in through a narrow rectangular opening high in the wall, with two iron bars fitted across it. Mei Mei sat on the hard cement floor, next to a hole that stank of her own excrement, and wept. The tears flowed freely for her predicament, her inauspicious birth hour, and the fear of her life being extinguished like the flame of a sputtering candle. A small voice inside her head whispered that the next set of jurors, all Chinese men, and many with bondmaids in their households, would find her guilty of murder. They would convict her, regardless of her innocence, to remind their own bondmaids who provided their rice bowls. Mei Mei shivered.

The scent of frangipani suddenly wafted into the claustrophobic cell, and Mei Mei's chaotic mind conjured up her father's ghost. Liao Wei, she was sure, had come to comfort her; she could feel his essence in her troubled mind.

The dam that had been holding her emotions in check broke, and Mei Mei railed against her destiny. "It is true that I'm a child of the hungry ghosts," she cried, "otherwise, why would I have such a fate? My father sells me off and dies before I can forgive him. I become my aunt's murderer through the actions of a wicked woman. I bring death and despair to those I love!"

She heard her father's ghostly whisper. "No, my child. Your actions and choices in life shape your fate, little one. I chose to sell you, my daughter, so I died an early death and reside in hell. Fight for your freedom, my child. There will be others to help you. You have done naught but loved your dear ones deeply. Your mother and I are with you, little one. Do not give up."

"Oh Father! I pray for you in the seventh lunar month," Mei Mei said through her tears. "I pray that the God of Death does not cut off your tongue, and that you will soon qualify for a higher court in hell. I am sad that being the father of a convicted murderer will bring you no reprieve. But I promise you, Pa, I loved Aunt Ai Lin as a mother. I did no bad deeds, as the gods are my judges."

Mei Mei dried her tears and stroked the mark on her wrist that showed the place where she had worn her father's gift, the yellow jade bangle. The bangle had been removed by the warden, as prisoners had been known to use broken glass to cut their wrists. There was a deep stirring in her heart, and from somewhere Mei Mei found the will to fight for her release. She thought of Richard Harrison and his kindness towards her, of Lady Matilda and her belief in her innocence. The thought of Richard's clear green eyes brought a faint blush to her cheeks. They were beautiful, she thought, like a placid lake strewn with moss. Her heart beat erratically, but she did not know why.

* * *

The morning of Mei Mei's re-trial dawned gloomy and overcast. People stood in a long queue that snaked around the courthouse, and some had camped overnight to be allowed a seat in the crowded courtroom. Bumboats with coolies hugged the shores of the Singapore River, the men standing on the decks and peering at the courthouse, waiting to hear the verdict.

Mei Mei, wearing a blue sarong and *kebaya*, her hair tied in one long braid reaching to her waist, was shepherded in by the warden and took her place in the dock. Due to the inclement weather, the gas lamps inside the courthouse were lit. They threw grotesque shadows on the walls, forming figures that bobbed and danced in frenzied anticipation. Mei Mei spied Richard sitting between Lady Matilda and a beautiful blonde girl. An unwary joy lit up Mei Mei's face as her eyes met Richard's.

As Judge Lawrence Manning entered, the skies opened, and rain pelted down in sheets, drenching the crowd outside and eliciting shouts of disapproval. The bumboats reluctantly began docking at the pier. Mei Mei turned a deaf ear to the cries outside. She drew comfort from the reassuring faces of Richard and Lady Matilda, and settled into her seat as the Public Prosecutor made his speeches and called witnesses, including Inspector Shipley.

It was on the second day of the trial that Mei Mei's lawyer, Herb Evans, delivered his introductory speech. Mei Mei scrutinized the jurors closely but was unable to deduce anything from their impassive faces. Only one juror gave her a faint smile. Evans' first witness was Lady Matilda, and Mei Mei watched the Englishwoman make her way ponderously to the witness stand.

Evans gently took Lady Matilda through her evidence of

Aunt Ai Lin's visit to the Chinese Protectorate's office, and the Englishwoman's subsequent visit to inspect the conditions at the House of Toh.

"Were there any signs of physical abuse on Mei Mei, Lady Matilda?" Evans asked softly.

Lady Matilda's eyes narrowed, and she looked straight at the judge as she said, "The poor girl had been viciously caned, and there were lacerations on her back. Madam Ai Lin pushed up Mei Mei's dress for me to inspect the wounds."

A loud babble broke out in the courtroom—indignant cries from the British spectators, and an uneasy murmur among the native ones.

"And who had inflicted these wounds on the accused?" Evans asked.

Lady Matilda unhesitatingly pointed her finger at Second Mistress Meisheng, who sat in the second row of native spectators, her face carved of stone.

"I now call Sergeant William Doyle to the witness stand," announced Herb Evans.

There was a gasp from the back of the court, loud enough for Mistress Meisheng to turn her head. Inspector Robert Shipley came forward to glare at his subordinate, who was making his way to the stand. Mei Mei noticed a surreptitious glance pass between Mistress Meisheng and Shipley.

"Sergeant Doyle, you were in charge of searching the bedchamber of the accused?" Evans asked.

The stocky sergeant nodded, his eyes fixed firmly on Evans and away from his superior's angry face. "Yes. Inspector Shipley asked me to search Mei Mei's bedchamber and the bathroom adjoining the bedchamber on the afternoon the murder was discovered."

"And what did you find, Sergeant?" Evans' voice was like a pistol shot.

Doyle said, "I searched the cupboards and drawers of the bedroom of the accused, as well as the adjoining bathroom. I did not find any stolen jewellery. There was a wooden box on a table in the bedroom, which contained a half-formed crab's eye seed necklace. That necklace was displayed to the court as Exhibit A."

"There was no jewellery hidden behind the cistern in the lavatory?" Evans asked, surprise lacing his tone. "I thought Inspector Shipley informed Judge Weston that you and your men had not looked behind the cistern, and so had missed the jewellery that was found later?"

William Doyle looked stolidly ahead. "I personally looked behind the toilet cistern the day after Madam Wu was killed, and there was no jewellery there. If it was found later, someone must have planted it after our search."

"No conjecture, if you please," Judge Manning snapped, and rapped his gavel on the desk in front of him, trying in vain to stem the clamour of excited talk among the spectators.

"We will now come to your movements of a week ago, if you please, Sergeant Doyle," Evans said with a smile. "Some of the jewellery was hidden behind the cistern. Did you search for the remainder of the jewellery stolen from Madam Wu's jewellery box?"

Doyle shot a quick glance at Shipley, who was gazing at him

with his mouth open. He turned back to the lawyer and said, "Yes, I did search for the jewellery. There were some distinctive pieces in Madam Wu's collection. They were described to me by Madam Wu's mother-in-law, Madam Sim. There was a pearl necklace with a silver phoenix clasp, and a gold bangle with a dragon embellished with rubies. I reckoned that whoever stole the jewellery would likely pawn the pieces to the *chettiar*s, so I talked to all the moneylenders with premises near the House of Toh."

"Did you recover the jewellery?" For the first time, Evans' voice held excitement, and there was a hiss of expectancy from the crowd.

"Yes." Doyle's face grew animated. "I located the jewellery with a *chettiar* in Chulia Lane called Pang. He told me that a Chinese woman had pawned it on the morning of the murder."

"That will be all, Sergeant." Herb Evans thanked the policeman and watched as the sergeant stepped down into the crowd, to be confronted by an angry tirade from Inspector Shipley.

Judge Manning intervened. "Stop your noise, Inspector Shipley!" he commanded. "Your next witness, if you please, Mr Evans."

"Pang, the *chettiar*, is my next witness," Evans replied.

"We will adjourn for lunch and convene again at two this afternoon," Judge Manning decided.

Mei Mei looked at Second Mistress Meisheng, who had risen stiffly from her chair. She watched as the concubine glided towards Inspector Shipley to hold a whispered conversation. Mei Mei saw the police inspector nod vehemently and walk with purposeful strides towards the courthouse door. Before he could reach it, two police constables entered, bringing with them Ai Lin's bondmaid, Li Jun, who was crying profusely. Sergeant Doyle nodded to the constables, and in front of Inspector Shipley's outraged eyes, Li Jun was taken out of a side door and into a room for witnesses who required protection due to the importance of the information they held.

The afternoon session began, and Herb Evans called Pang to the witness stand. The *chettiar* was a round, pot-bellied Chinese man with a sly smile and a shifty expression. He recited the oath and took his seat on the witness stand. Two constables led Li Jun to the front row of native spectators. She wore a faded tunic and trousers, and her long hair was in disarray. She looked petrified, her hands nervously pleating the material of her tunic. Her small eyes fixed on the *chettiar* with dread.

After going through the motions of introducing Pang, asking the witness questions on the duration of his trade and the location of his premises, Evans finally asked the court peon to show the stolen pieces of jewellery to the witness.

"Do you recognise this jewellery?" Evans asked, after Pang had taken stock of the items before him.

"Yes," Pang said, his voice deep and rough. "A young Chinese woman pawned these pieces at my shop on 26 December last year. I gave her a hundred and fifty dollars."

A collective gasp went up from the crowd, and the spectators leaned forward in anticipation of the drama about to unfold.

Herb Evans looked around the courtroom, his face tight with concentration. When he spoke, his voice was clear, the impact of his question not lost on the spectators and jury. "We have already identified this jewellery as belonging to Madam Wu Ai Lin of the House of Toh, who was murdered on 26 December of last year. Is the woman who pawned the jewellery in court today, Pang?"

Pang nodded, and unhesitatingly pointed his finger at a cowering Li Jun. "She is the girl who pawned the jewellery."

There was a strangled cry from Li Jun, who hid her head in her hands. Mei Mei was shocked to see Second Mistress Meisheng rise from her seat and make her way to the courthouse door. Two constables barred her way, and she reluctantly returned to her seat.

"I wish to call Loh Li Jun, former bondmaid to First Mistress Ai Lin of the House of Toh, to the stand," Evans said.

Herb Evans' gentle demeanour faded, and the predator emerged. His cornflower blue eyes flashed as he barked, "You are under oath, Loh Li Jun. Did you murder Wu Ai Lin and steal her jewels?" The Chinese interpreter stepped forward and translated Evans' question into Hokkien for Li Jun.

On hearing the interpreter's words, Li Jun screamed, and with tears trickling down her cheeks, she pointed a shaking finger at Second Mistress Meisheng.

"I only did Mistress Meisheng's bidding," she said loudly in Hokkien. "She told me that the *mui-tsai* would be blamed for the crime, and all I had to do was grind some crab's eye seeds and place them in the bowl of curry prepared by the *mui-tsai*. Second Mistress promised me some of my mistress's jewellery. Pawning those pieces would provide the money I needed to pay for my passage back to my village in China. It would mean I could build a house for my poor parents. Have mercy on me!" she howled, her hands clasped in prayer. "I am a poor bondmaid, with no hope of release from my contract of servitude. The *kheh-tau* made me sign a contract for my passage to the *Nanyang,* and my father is dying of tuberculosis. I needed to send money home to pay his medical bills. If my father dies, my mother and siblings will perish as well. Our farm and house in China will be sold. Oh, please have mercy on a dutiful daughter!"

Mei Mei watched Second Mistress Meisheng rise from her seat, her face contorted with icy rage. She said in Mandarin, "Loh Li Jun lies. I did not bribe her to murder First Mistress Ai Lin. Li Jun is a thief and a murderer, and we sheltered her unknowingly under our roof. She needed money, so she killed for it. Li Jun is trying to put the blame on me to escape the gallows."

Mei Mei's heartbeat filled her chest. Could it be that she would be exonerated? Would she soon be free to enjoy the outside world, free to run over carpets of frangipani flowers, free to continue her schooling? Her tears flowed, tears of happiness mingling with tears of sorrow as she recalled the terror that had been her companion for so long. From that terror, a flame of vengeance roared to life, a determination to punish the diabolical woman who had conspired to snuff out the life of the only mother she had known. For Mei Mei had no doubt that Second Mistress Meisheng had bribed Li Jun to poison Ai Lin.

The jury took only fifteen minutes to reach a unanimous verdict of 'not guilty', and a cheer went up in the courtroom.

When the babble had finally died down, Judge Manning spoke. "I concur with the jury's verdict, and I exonerate Liao Mei Mei of the crimes of murdering her aunt and stealing her jewels.

Mei Mei can leave the courtroom with no taint on her character. As for Loh Li Jun, she is to be remanded in custody, without bail. I am sure the Chief of Police will choose a worthy Inspector of Police to gather evidence, build a case and bring the prisoner to trial for the murder of Wu Ai Lin. Inspector Shipley, you will receive your just deserts from the Chief of Police after I inform him of your conduct during this case." With a brief glance of reproach at the Inspector of Police, Judge Manning rose. "Court is dismissed."

The crowd began trooping out and a loud cheer came from the boatmen on the Singapore River, who had been rooting for Mei Mei's release. Lady Matilda came to stand by Mei Mei's side, her face flushed with relief.

"Mei Mei," she said, "you cannot go back to the House of Toh. Your aunt is dead, and your uncle has left Singapore. You will be ill-treated by Madam Sim and Madam Meisheng. The Chinese Protectorate has arranged accommodation for you at the Poh Leung Kuk Shelter for abused women and children. It will only be for a short time. I need a seamstress, and I am hiring you for the job. You will come and live with me in my house. I have grown very fond of you, my child. You have borne your ordeal courageously. My major-domo will get in touch with the orphanage when the necessary arrangements have been made, and he will fetch you home to me. I will pay your school fees, and you will resume schooling."

Mei Mei's tears of joy reflected the moisture in Lady Matilda's own eyes. The two women embraced as Richard watched, smiling.

"Thank you, Richard." Mei Mei suddenly felt shy, and would

not look at the British boy. "You went to a lot of trouble on my behalf."

Richard smiled with genuine warmth, nodded, and left.

As she walked out of the jailhouse, Mei Mei revelled in the warm sunshine on her face, the mild breeze bringing with it the salt of the sea, and the delighted faces of Winnie and Poh as they waited for her outside the prison gate. She breathed deeply, and the scent of frangipani overwhelmed her. The sweet fragrance that had always delighted her was once more her companion as she ran along the carpet of red, purple and white flowers, her face tilted to the sky, and her arms wide open. She was free.

February 1932

Dressed in a new red cheongsam, and with her hair braided into a coil at the back of her head, Mei Mei entered Sago Lane on foot. The narrow alley was lined on either side by two-storey terraced houses with shops huddling together at the bottom, dilapidated awnings covering the walkway. Rickshaws were parked at the station on the far side of the street, some of the pullers eating at the roadside stalls or playing dice on tables along the walkway.

The air was heavy with the scent of incense and the stench of sickness and death. Wails of mourning rose from the death houses lining the street, accompanied by the clash of cymbals and gongs from wakes held in the open courtyards of the funeral parlours. The comforting chants of monks formed a serene background to the stabbing cries of the bereaved.

The sago factories from which the street had derived its name were long gone, replaced by death houses. Where once the aroma of sago cakes had filled its air, now death hung in mournful splendour from every nook and cranny. The industry of churning flour had been replaced by the business of providing tools to assist the bereaved in mourning their dead and giving them a good send-off on their heavenly journeys.

Mei Mei had never imagined that, at seventeen years of age, she would be the owner of an establishment profiting from death. The murder trial had taken its toll on her, and she had failed her Senior Cambridge Examinations. It was Lady Matilda who had suggested that she open a tailoring establishment, but with intense competition in the popular tailoring enclaves, Mei Mei had had little choice but to attempt to make a living out of sewing funeral headgear for bereaved relatives.

She sewed hundreds of sackcloth head coverings at her shop every month. They would be worn by the female relatives of the deceased when the wake was over, and the coffin was ready to be transported to the burial ground. Then the women would follow the male relatives to Bukit Brown Cemetery, accompanied by the mournful music of the percussion band.

For the last six months, Mei Mei had been living with Lady Matilda, darning and sewing the curtains for the household in return for a modest salary, food and lodging. Lady Matilda had decreed that Mei Mei would not take up sleeping quarters above her shop in Sago Lane, since a lone female would be a prime target for the pimps controlling the prostitution trade in nearby Sago Street. Even so, Mei Mei had been propositioned many times by pimps, and she had been lucky to win the protection of Uncle Mok, the coffin seller, and Ah Ling from the incense shop.

The latter had gone so far as to give one of the pimps a sound thrashing on Mei Mei's behalf.

A sunny smile lit up Mei Mei's face as she thought of her blossoming friendship with Richard Harrison. He was now a frequent visitor to Lady Matilda's house, regularly challenging Mei Mei to a game of carom. Mei Mei was a proficient player, having learnt it in her father's *kampong*, but Richard beat her every time. As a prize for winning, she would take him to the roadside stalls in Chinatown where she loved to eat with Winnie, introducing him to the delights of native street food.

A shadow crossed her face. Her heart beat faster every time Richard's green eyes scanned her face, but she refused to dwell on the nature of her feelings for the free-spirited British boy who loved to eat satay at the roadside. Mei Mei enjoyed nothing more than standing beside his easel as, with deft strokes of his paintbrush, he captured the satay seller sitting by his brazier, fanning the embers in the barbecue grate with his straw hat. Every now and then the question crept into her mind. What were Richard's feelings towards her? As quickly as the thought came, Mei Mei strove to bury it in the deepest recesses of her mind; but it would resurface with irritating regularity, like the stray cat who seemed to think that Mei Mei's shop was its home.

Mei Mei awoke from her reverie to see Richard seated in front of her shop, an easel before him and a street scene taking shape on the canvas. He stopped painting, stood up and yawned. Dressed in trousers and a shirt covered by a smock, his face tanned from the tropical sun and his green eyes alert, Richard cut a handsome figure.

He looked around. "I came to watch the Lunar New Year Lion dance in front of your shop. I want to capture it on canvas. Lady Matilda told me that you have asked for the lion's blessing on your shop today."

Ten minutes later, the huge red and yellow figure of the mock lion snaked its way down Sago Lane, and stopped in front of Mei Mei's shop. The top part of the creature was made of yellow fur, while the legs were made of red cloth. The men inside the costume writhed and danced, and the lion began to move in huge, swaying motions. Its huge button eyes swivelled from right to left as it rose on its haunches, accompanied by the clash of cymbals, the beating of drums and the clang of gongs from the musicians accompanying the dancers.

The lion swayed in front of Mei Mei's shop, its wide open mouth showing teeth, its long tail swishing from left to right, and its front feet tapping. Richard had his sketch pad open, and his pencil flew across the paper to capture the scene. The lion entered Mei Mei's shop, and executed an elaborate dance before re-emerging. In front of their eyes, the creature collapsed and the men inside the costume surfaced, grins plastered on their faces.

Mei Mei offered the men a red packet of money for blessing her shop, and they went on their way to the next street.

"Golly, that was capital!" Richard's eyes shone as he gazed after the lion dancers. "This was the first time I've seen the lion dance up close. I can't wait to get back to my studio and paint it."

His expression changed. "I will be sailing to England next week," Richard informed Mei Mei. "Father is building a manor in Yorkshire, and the builders need someone to sign papers before they can get on with the construction. Father is busy with the plantation and I will be going in his stead. This is an opportunity for me to visit England, and I will go on a grand tour of Europe as well." His eyes shone. "Imagine painting in Italy, Mei Mei! I cannot wait."

A curtain of depression fell over Mei Mei, but she tried to shrug it aside as she asked in a small voice, "When will you return to Singapore?"

"In a few months." Richard was packing up his gear, and Mei Mei glimpsed a black Bentley waiting at the end of the lane to take him home.

A sudden flash of jealousy stabbed at her heart. "Are you going alone, or is Clementine travelling with you?"

Richard grinned. "Clem wanted to come, but Mother cannot leave Father to his own devices, so she cannot chaperone Clem. She will have to take the grand tour of Europe another time."

Mei Mei looked away, not wanting Richard to see the relief in her eyes. She remembered the English girl's icy glances at her in the courtroom, and acknowledged that Clem would be a chilling adversary for any girl who aroused Richard's interest. Mei Mei's face fell. Richard would probably marry Clem—Lady Matilda had told her that was Eleanor Harrison's wish, and it was clear to Mei Mei that the British boy was very fond of his childhood playmate.

That night at the dinner table, Lady Matilda and Clyde Robertson talked of Clementine. Mei Mei listened shamelessly to their conversation as she served them dinner.

Clyde had recently returned from a trip to England. "I heard something unpleasant when I visited Tom Whitehead in London, Matty," he said with chagrin. "You remember he had known Clementine Arbuthnot's father, Roger? It seems that the second wife—what was her name?"

"Clara," Lady Matilda supplied impatiently.

"Yes, yes, Clara Arbuthnot." Clyde continued after he had finished his soup. Mei Mei took her time clearing the table.

"Whitehead said that Arbuthnot had extracted a promise from Clementine that she would provide Clara and her two daughters with a roof over their heads, but Clementine turned them out. Clara was living hand-to-mouth, working in a cotton factory to support her two girls. She contracted a lung disease and died."

Lady Matilda's voice was shocked. "Whatever happened to the two mites?"

Clyde Robertson's face was sombre. "When she was ill in the hospital, Clara asked to speak to Whitehead. She begged him to talk to John Harrison, and have him persuade Clem to give shelter to her two stepsisters in her house in Cornwall."

Mei Mei stood rooted to the ground. She could not have moved even if Lady Matilda had roared at her.

Clyde looked dolefully at his fish and said, "Whitehead said that John and Eleanor pleaded with Clementine to provide for her stepsisters, but they could not melt Clem's iron resolve of having nothing to do with her father's second family. That girl is as hard as nails, Matty!"

"She gives me the chills," Lady Matilda agreed.

Lying in her bed that night, Mei Mei thought of Clementine.

Intuitively, she felt that Clementine viewed Richard as her possession, at times stalking his every move. How could someone as free-spirited as Richard love a girl obsessed with owning him?

Mei Mei shook her head. It was none of her business, and she was becoming alarmed at the frequency with which the British boy popped into her thoughts. Today was the first day of the Year of the Monkey, and she resolved to think only optimistic, happy thoughts. With those good intentions, Mei Mei slid into a dreamless sleep.

10

John Harrison's fortunes plummeted along with the rest of the gentry in the wake of the Great Depression, grinding to a halt the dispatch of funds to Richard in Yorkshire for the building of the family's grand retirement home, Stamford Manor. John had vetoed Richard's offer of cutting short his grand tour of Europe, but Richard did his best to help by renting a small cottage in Italy for a paltry sum, and cancelling hotel stays in the expensive venues of France and Switzerland. Italy captured Richard's imagination with its profusion of paintings and sculptures, and he spent most of his days at galleries, or painting landscapes in his cottage.

In Singapore, without Richard's company, Clementine had begun to spend more and more time with the plantation overseer, Jeffrey Peters.

It was a fine day, and the tennis courts of the Singapore Cricket Club shone bright in the light of the tropical sun climbing over the horizon. Clementine, her blonde hair tied back and her blue eyes sparkling, laughed as the ball she had lobbed over the net failed to find Jeffrey Peters' racquet, and fell well within his side of the court.

Jeff, his sandy hair plastered to his scalp with perspiration, smiled at Clem and shook his head in mock regret. "I'm afraid I will never get the better of you in tennis, Clem. You beat me every time. Do let me win now and then." As Clem strolled to her courtside seat, he followed her graceful movements with admiration.

It had been at a dinner at the Raffles Hotel that he had first realised he was falling in love with Clementine. Shrewdly, he knew that she loved Richard, but he revelled in the knowledge that it was he, Jeffrey, to whom Clem told her innermost secrets, and to whom she turned when troubled.

"I think my mother was mad," Clem had confided to Jeff. They were dining at the Raffles Hotel after a party at the Tanglin Club. "Her eyes were wild, and the servants gossiped that she wasn't right in the head. Oh, she was physically ill as well—but my father admitted that she suffered in her mind as much as her body."

Clem laid down her knife and fork, her steak untouched. Her eyes were stormy as she looked across the table at Jeff. "From childhood, I have had fancies. I would see things that weren't there. My mind is always churning, Jeff! I so much fear that I will go the way of my mother."

Jeff listened to Clem with kind eyes. "Nonsense!" he said blithely. "You're as right as rain. How well you play the piano! All the gentry invite you to their soirees. You are becoming famous, Clementine."

Clem smiled at Jeff's bantering tone. "Thank you. Music soothes my nerves." Her brow clouded. "My mother was also a good musician."

She continued, "I feel emotions too intensely. When my dog, Jasper, was ill, I was so worried about him that I swore at the vet. My shouting attracted all the nurses! Why do I feel things so intensely?"

Jeff attacked his bread-and-butter pudding with gusto. "Some people *do* feel more than others. Well, old Jasper is as fit as a fiddle now, and I am sure the vet understood your concern."

Clem began attacking her steak. After eating in silence for a while, she looked up at him tentatively. "You do think I am all right, Jeff?"

Clem looked so vulnerable and forlorn that Jeff had an intense desire to take her in his arms and kiss away her fears forever. He said, "You are fine, Clem. I am here for you. If you feel you need a shoulder to lean on, it's there."

It was Clem's restlessness, her obsessive nature and her insecurities that aroused a strong protective instinct in Jeff. The feeling was potent enough to make him dream of asking her to be his wife.

She looked at him now across the tennis court and smiled, sipping at a glass of lemonade, carefree and happy.

"Steven Dolittle had too much to drink last week and fell into the Singapore River," she quipped. "It was a mercy he wasn't washed away with the tide."

Jeff grinned. "You know very well he fell into shallow waters. His Indian mistress screamed for help, and natives fished him out."

Clem's blue eyes sparkled. "Poor Steven. It seems he is courting a British girl in London. I hear his family are hoping that marriage will set him straight." Clem glanced flirtatiously at Jeff.

"You should settle down, too, Jeff. The vicar's daughter, Mary, would suit you nicely."

She blushed when Jeff looked deep into her eyes and said, "No, I don't think Mary will do for me. But she will make someone else a good wife."

A cloud obliterated the sun, and in the sudden gloom Clem's face changed, becoming introspective and sullen. Jeff sighed, knowing she was thinking of Richard.

* * *

The reed mats of the Harrison house were lowered over the louvered windows of the drawing room, casting a cool shade over the brocade sofas and rich upholstery, and carving a pattern of light and shadow over the pianoforte where Clementine sat. Her fingers moved lightly over the keys as she practised Mendelssohn's Second Piano Concerto in D minor. She would be playing it at her upcoming performance with an amateur British orchestra in the Botanic Gardens.

Clementine was an accomplished pianist, a partial compensation for her lack of academic skills. Like Mei Mei, she had failed the Senior Cambridge Examinations, and much to Eleanor's chagrin, had declined to re-take them, opting instead to accompany the British orchestra as their pianist.

Clementine stopped playing and sighed. Her nineteenth birthday was approaching. While she had no shortage of suitors—with both Jeff Peters and William Doyle front-runners for her affections—Richard still showed no inclination to declare romantic feelings for her. Clem frowned. Why, he had not even sent her a letter from Europe, only hastily scrawled post-cards from a few places he had visited.

Clem thought she had glimpsed admiration in his eyes when she was dressed for a ball, or poised over the piano during musical soirees in the drawing rooms of the British gentry. A warm glow lit her cheeks as she remembered his green eyes on her as she climbed out of the swimming pool at the club, dressed in a swimsuit.

But like a stray insect on a hot day, the memory of Richard's green eyes, filled with anxiety and compassion as he looked at Mei Mei in court, flitted into her head. Clem grew still. Only her hands continued to move, pressing discordantly on the piano keys and creating a cacophony that brought Eleanor running from the recesses of the kitchen, where she had been haranguing the cook on the quality of the curry served at lunch.

"Whatever is the matter, Clem?" Eleanor's face was still warm from the cook's effrontery in daring to defend her curry. "You were playing so beautifully a moment ago. Richard is arriving back from Europe today, and Cook has made a bland curry to greet him with! I am beside myself."

Before Clem could reply, Jeffrey rushed in through the French windows.

"I've just been to the harbour to collect Richard—his ship was supposed to dock an hour ago." Jeff's eyes were wide with concern. "The ship did not arrive, and the docks are abuzz with the rumour that it was seen flying the yellow flag and has docked at St John's Island."

"Cholera!" Eleanor screamed, and would have slid to the

floor if Jeff had not rushed to hold her up.

John Harrison arrived through the French windows, looking years older than his age. "I talked to the Chief Medical Officer. The captain of Richard's ship telegraphed ahead before they sailed into Singapore's waters. It seems there is a small outbreak of cholera among the sailing crew, but one or two passengers are affected as well."

He went to his wife, who was now lying on the sofa, Clem holding a bottle of smelling salts to her nose. Eleanor's eyes fluttered open and looked with dread at her husband. "My darling," John said softly, sitting beside her and taking her hand, "the ship's captain said that Richard is one of the passengers who has contracted cholera. He will be admitted to the lazaretto on St John's Island. We must hope that the doctors at the hospital there can save his life." He took his sobbing wife into his arms.

"He cannot die," Clem whispered over and over. "Richard will live. Oh, please God, let Richard live."

The household staff stood outside the French windows, talking amongst themselves in hushed whispers. They liked Richard.

There was a knock on the glass. Everyone turned to see Lady Matilda framed in the doorway, Mei Mei, dressed in black trousers and tunic, peeping from behind her.

"I came through the garden since no one answered the front door," Lady Matilda wheezed, directing a reproving glance at the hapless Sher Singh, who was hovering behind John Harrison with a whiskey decanter. "I rushed here because Clyde came to lunch with the news that Richard has cholera, and the lazaretto is short of nurses. Clyde told me that John is willing to pay a handsome sum for any native willing to go to St John's Island to nurse Richard." Her left eyebrow curved up in a query.

"Yes, yes," John said, eagerly. "I have offered generous compensation to my household staff to nurse Richard, but they are unwilling to go because of the risk of cholera to their families. We British are not allowed on the island. Have you anyone in mind, Lady Matilda?"

Lady Matilda pushed Mei Mei forward and said, "Do you remember Liao Mei Mei from the court trial? I hired her as my seamstress last year, and she lives with me. Mei Mei has taken it into her head to risk cholera to nurse Richard."

"No!" The sound came like the crack of a pistol, and everyone turned to Clementine. She stood rigidly by the piano, her face pale, and her hands clenched so hard that the knuckles showed white. "You will not go near Richard."

Ignoring Clem, John Harrison approached Mei Mei. "I will pay you handsomely for your services when you return from the island."

"*If* she returns," Lady Matilda amended. "Cholera is contagious, and Mei Mei will be at risk of contracting the disease herself."

Eleanor asked in a shaking voice, "Why do you want to nurse my son? What is he to you?"

For the first time, Mei Mei spoke. She said in a hushed tone, "It was Richard who asked Sergeant Doyle to reopen the investigation into my aunt's murder after the first trial. This is my chance to repay his kindness."

"Richard does not need your pity!" Clem cried, her features twisted with jealousy. "You will not nurse him."

Eleanor ignored her, saying warmly to Mei Mei, "Thank you, Mei Mei. Be assured that John will pay you well."

"I do not want payment," Mei Mei said. "I go to nurse Richard to pay my debt for his kindness. Please excuse me now. I must go home and pack a suitcase. The ferry leaves in an hour." She left the room, followed by Lady Matilda.

"But Aunt Eleanor—" Clem began, her eyes stormy.

Tears still streamed down Eleanor's face. "Don't be churlish, Clem, not at a time like this. We must do what is best for our son. Oh, this news has given me such a turn!"

John said, "Eleanor, we have to hope that Richard will be fine. Please go to bed now. You must protect your own health."

"No, no!" Eleanor tottered to her feet. "I have to go to Cold Storage to buy supplies to send with Mei Mei for Richard. Oh, John, I cannot fathom life without our son!"

"Now, now." John helped his wife to the door, where a maid waited to take her upstairs. "I will have Achmed bring the car to the door, Eleanor. Please take a maid with you when you go to Cold Storage. Take heart, my love. With good care, Richard will recover."

The sun began to slip towards the horizon, and the house fell silent. Eleanor left in the car, and John went with Jeff to the Chief Medical Officer to get more details of the cholera outbreak. Only Clementine stayed in the house, holed up in her room, staring bleakly at the horizon, the image of Mei Mei sitting tenderly by Richard's bedside playing havoc with her mind and heart.

11

The night was filled with the chirping of crickets, a droning hum from swarming mosquitoes and, above all, a gentle swoosh as sea waves lapped onto the shore of St John's Island. Mei Mei sat beneath a palm tree on the sandy beach, watching obscure figures on the jetty, and listening to the song of the sea. In the distance, the horizon arced into the twinkling lights of the mainland. Nearer, lantern lights bobbed from Chinese junks at sea, and from sampans banked on the shore. The wind brought with it the tangy scent of salt and seaweed, setting the leaves of the palm trees rustling softly, like a whisper of warning.

Mei Mei's long hair, drying after a shower, hung down to her waist, and her liquid eyes held a hint of worry as she sat on the sand. She remembered her first sight of Richard at the lazaretto. His eyes had been sunk into their sockets, and his pallid skin and the blue tinge to his fingers had made her fear he would not survive. He had been lying on the bed in his own faeces, breathing torturously.

She had cleaned him, not deterred by his body's stench, unafraid to undress him and view for the first time the private parts of a man's body. She decided to regard him as she had her baby brother, Wen Long, and set about towelling his cool and sweaty body with hot compresses, murmuring healing platitudes, her hands busy, her mind focussed on easing his discomfort. Diligently, she fed him salt-and-sugar water, and when he retaliated by ejecting white vomit all over her *kebaya*, she bore with it silently, and coaxed more electrolytes down his throat. She sat deep into the night on a mat by his bed, a lantern by her side, eyes trained on her patient, ears pricked for sounds of distress, her own well-being forgotten in her intense desire to heal Richard Harrison.

Mei Mei looked up. Some of the lights on the mainland had been extinguished and the boatmen were dousing their lanterns. The dark night closed around Mei Mei like a shawl. Images crowded her mind: Richard's uncomprehending green eyes staring at her from hollow sockets, the red strands of hair on his arm that she gently touched when he was asleep, the red of his hair which turned golden when the sun shone through the window. Her heart began to beat faster, and her cheeks felt warm, as she recalled sponging his naked body that morning. Interspersed with those images were the memories of his kindness to her, his compassion, and his single-minded intensity in working to set her free from gaol. The images and memories coalesced into an inebriating elixir of romance, in which Mei Mei felt she could drown.

By the second week of his stay at the lazaretto, attended by a harried, overworked British doctor, a Dutch nurse who spoke little English, and the ever-vigilant Mei Mei, Richard began to revive. His symptoms began abating as his body rehydrated with the fluids Mei Mei poured down his throat. His complexion started to lose its pallor, and the blue tinge to his fingers all but disappeared. Richard swam upward towards light and life.

On the tenth night of his stay on the island, he began to mumble incoherently. Mei Mei rushed to the bedside and anxiously felt for his pulse. Excitement coursed through her as she realised that his heart was beating more strongly than before. She felt his forehead and was relieved to find it cool. His eyes opened.

He looked at her, puzzled. "Mei Mei?" He glanced at the hospital walls, and tried to sit up before flopping back onto the bed. "Where am I?" he asked weakly.

"You are in the hospital on St John's Island," Mei Mei said, joy filling her features. "You were returning from England and cholera broke out on the ship. You caught the disease and were quarantined, but the worse seems to be over, Richard. You will recover."

"Cholera?" Richard said, his eyes filling with horror. "I have cholera?"

"You will get better," Mei Mei assured him. She thrust a tin cup at her patient. "Take this salt-sugar-water, Richard, your body needs it. Sip it slowly."

After taking a few sips, Richard looked up at Mei Mei. "But why are you here?"

"I came to nurse you," Mei Mei replied demurely. "Your family was looking for a native nurse to take care of your needs, and I volunteered. No British family is allowed on the island for fear of contracting the deadly disease."

A curious light burned in Richard's eyes that set Mei Mei's heart fluttering. "You are at risk of contracting cholera," he said.

"I take a disinfecting shower every day."

Richard's eyes began to droop and soon he was sleeping soundly. The doctor, on his nocturnal round, professed satisfaction at Richard's progress.

"He will recover," the doctor said, smiling at the relief on Mei Mei's face. "He has passed the danger period. You have helped save his life. Today I lost another patient to dehydration." The doctor continued, "I will send word to Harrison that his son is on the mend."

Next morning, Mei Mei brought pails of hot water to sponge Richard's body. The sun shone in brightly through the windows.

"What are you doing?" Richard demanded, as Mei Mei began to undress him. He sat up on the bed in agitation.

Mei Mei paused in untying the string of Richard's pyjamas. "I am going to bathe you," she said.

"No, you are not." Richard's voice was surprisingly loud, and echoed through the empty ward.

"But I have been bathing you for the past week!" Mei Mei protested. "I am your nurse." She looked at the colour flooding his face and dropped her eyes, her own face feeling warm.

"Isn't there a certified nurse in this ward?" Richard asked.

Mei Mei's eyes glistened. "Have I done anything wrong? Did I hurt you when I removed the potty from under you?"

"Dear God," Richard murmured. He looked at the tear making its way down her cheek and said gently, "You have done nothing wrong, Mei Mei. I owe you my life. You can understand that I might feel shy when you bathe and clean me? It was all right when I was unconscious, but now it is difficult for me to accept your care in that particular way."

"I am only doing a nurse's duty," Mei Mei said practically. "You are far from well, and I still need to take care of your needs. There are very few nurses at the hospital, and last night a ship docked here with coolies suffering from beriberi. The nurses have been swept off their feet. Please allow me to take care of you, Richard. It is only for a short while longer."

Richard looked at her pale face, her eyelashes dusting her cheeks like shadows, and his heart contracted with a deep emotion he had never felt in his life. He nodded and allowed her to ease off his pyjamas. He heard her gasp as she saw his hardened manhood and turned his head away. He thought she would leave, but soon he felt her cool hands on his body and the warmth of the sponge, gently massaging his tired limbs.

He looked at her as she bent over his face, feeling a thrill as her soft breath fanned the tendrils of hair on his chest. He breathed in the sweet scent of her hair and felt an urge to uncoil her plait, and thread his hands through the black strands until she trembled. His eyes swivelled away guiltily as she looked at him and brought the sponge to clean the dirt from his face.

One night, as he gently touched the hand that was feeding him his first solid meal in weeks, she reciprocated timidly, allowing her hands to trace his features wonderingly, the gruel spoon lying forgotten in its bowl. The expression of longing in his green eyes set her heart fluttering. Sighing, Mei Mei acknowledged to herself that she loved the free-spirited artist who had saved her from the gallows, and she would follow him to the ends of the earth.

January 1933

Sago Lane glistened after a morning shower. Muddy water bubbled and frothed like volcanic lava in the ditches. Street urchins played merrily in the puddles, sprinkling each other with the dirty water, laughing to see the sun dry their faces and leave behind black, grimy streaks that made them resemble chimney sweeps. Gongs sounded from the death houses, and the air was redolent with the scent of incense.

Mei Mei sat inside her shop, working slowly on her Singer machine, her hands aching from rotating the wheel of the contraption sewing chain stitches on the fabric. As she worked, Mei Mei's thoughts fluttered wildly between images of Richard, before focusing on the sweet kiss they had shared a week ago in the dilapidated Chinese opera stall of New World. While the opera singer, dressed opulently in brightly coloured clothes, her face painted in a caricature of longing, belted out a mournful melody, Richard had gazed at Mei Mei, his green eyes unfathomable, his hands clasping hers. He had leant over in the dim stall that reeked of cheap perfume and *beedi*, pressed his lips to the tic near the corner of her mouth, and sensually caressed it into nothingness, before moving to claim her lips with a ferocity that frightened and thrilled her at the same time.

Mei Mei shivered. On the fringes of her mind dwelt the continuous foreboding of doomed romance. She knew the difficulties she and Richard faced, due to the differences in their race and class. They were made worse by her having been born on the double seventh; whatever she did in her life, she would never escape the clutches of misfortune. Mei Mei sighed, closed the shop, and returned to Lady Matilda's bungalow.

Lady Matilda was feeling poorly, and for the first time in her life, she had stayed in bed all day. Mei Mei sat at her feet and began to massage her.

Lady Matilda smiled wanly. "My child, we have received news that the bondmaid, Li Jun, died in prison." She nodded at Mei Mei's gasp. "As you know, she was tried and found guilty of your aunt's murder, though we know who the real perpetrator was. The news that her penniless parents had died in China broke Li Jun's spirit. She stopped eating, and passed away last week.

"Child, I worry about you. The Chief of Police reinstated Shipley as an Inspector after sending him back to Britain for a few months. Second Mistress Meisheng is Shipley's mistress, and you have not yet turned eighteen. If anything were to happen to me, Shipley will help Meisheng take you away and sell you to a brothel."

"Nothing will happen to you, madam," Mei Mei said comfortingly. "It is full moon tonight, and that is why your body aches so."

But despite Mei Mei's reassuring words, Lady Matilda's fears proved to be well founded. Later that week, she suffered a massive stroke that robbed her of the power of movement. Clyde Robertson, Mei Mei, and a retinue of servants kept vigil at the General Hospital, but the prognosis was grim.

On the fourth day at the hospital, Lady Matilda whispered to Mei Mei to summon the rubber planter, John Harrison, to her bedside.

Matilda's eyes fluttered open when John gently pressed her

hand. Clyde sat on a chair by the window, weeping inconsolably. Lady Matilda's eyes sharpened and focused on her visitor.

"John," she whispered, "I told Liao Mei Mei, the Chinese *mui-tsai*, to contact you. She has no guardians in Singapore, and that greedy second wife of her uncle's, Meisheng, is after her again, wanting to make money by selling her to a brothel. The Office of the Chinese Protectorate can intervene in this matter, but Robert Shipley, Inspector of Police, is smitten by Meisheng and has set her up in a bungalow outside the city. The Protectorate may turn a blind eye if Meisheng fetches Mei Mei from the orphanage and sells her to a brothel. John, do you understand what I am saying?"

John Harrison had been straining his ears to catch Lady Matilda's words, and now he straightened up. He said kindly, "What do you wish me to do, Lady Matilda? I support abolishing the Chinese slavery system, and am willing to carry on your work, but I cannot intervene in individual cases. This is a matter for the Protectorate."

Lady Matilda raised her head and glared at John Harrison. "Don't be such a nincompoop, John! This is a heaven-sent opportunity for you to be the architect of the Bill abolishing the *mui-tsai* practice. Give shelter to Liao Mei Mei in your house, and you will be perceived as a benevolent protector, intent on abolishing barbaric practices.

"Please honour my last wish, John. Mei Mei is a plucky, hard-working girl, but misfortune has dogged her every step because of her *mui-tsai* status. I can't protect her any longer, but you and Eleanor can give her shelter. It will only be for a few months, John, then she will turn eighteen and Mistress Meisheng will have no claim on her."

When John Harrison hemmed and hawed, Lady Matilda glared venomously at him. She said in a deceptively casual voice, "Richard would have died of cholera on that island if Mei Mei had not nursed him back to health. Eleanor and you owe her a debt of gratitude, John. For heaven's sake, repay that debt by giving her protection."

Lady Matilda played her last card in her effort to secure Mei Mei's short-term future with the Harrisons. "Clyde's involvement in the *mui-tsai* cause is earning him a seat in the British Parliament. He played a big part in changing the law so that *mui-tsais* have to be registered. I don't see why you cannot follow in his footsteps, John. There is a great deal of work left to be done to abolish the *mui-tsai* system altogether. My successor at the Chinese Protectorate, Sandra Norbert, will help you. She and I have a plan to accelerate the passing of the *Mui-tsai* Abolition Bill in the British Parliament."

The glimmer of ambition in John Harrison's eyes brought a cynical smile to Lady Matilda's lips, and she closed her eyes wearily. The nurse entered and shook her head, and after awkwardly patting Clyde's shoulder, John Harrison left the room. Mei Mei sat silently in a corner, trembling with trepidation. Her future was uncertain yet again.

The sky lightened and the trees rustled as the birds began waking up. The lantern next to the hospital bed sputtered bravely, seeming to mimic the flickering life of the big-hearted Englishwoman who lay there. Mei Mei gently caressed the grey hair and worn face of her benefactor.

"You are in love with the Harrison boy." The whisper hung between the two women in the otherwise empty hospital room. Clyde had gone back to his house to snatch some sleep.

Mei Mei blushed and hung her head. She felt a gentle pressure from the hands that held hers. Lady Matilda's eyes were a clear grey as she looked at her.

"Overcome your emotions." Matilda's breath was falling in laboured gasps. "It will bring trouble. Eleanor Harrison is not broad-minded like me. You deserve better than a mistress's fate."

Mei Mei gasped, her eyes wide with horror.

Lady Matilda's eyes were tired but shrewd. "What else can you be, Mei Mei? Our society will not have it otherwise. We do not marry natives. Keep away from Richard, Mei Mei, that is my advice to you. Marry a nice Chinese man who can give you the love and care you deserve."

Lady Matilda's venture into consciousness was brief. Even as Mei Mei gathered her thoughts together and raised her eyes to the Englishwoman's face, she saw that her lids were closed and her face had taken on an unhealthy pallor. Lady Matilda strained to draw breath from a world she was leaving. Mei Mei clasped her benefactor's hands more tightly and offered soothing words. Soon the nurse came in, felt the patient's pulse, and silently shook her head.

PART THREE

The Book of Testimonies

Singapore 1933–1934

"Our human compassion binds us the one to the other—
not in pity or patronizingly, but as human beings
who have learnt how to turn our common suffering
into hope for the future."
Nelson Mandela

12

March 1933

Mei Mei gazed into the stream at the back of the Harrison house. Her reflection stared back at her, puzzled, anxious. She had been buffeted from one household to another in her seventeen years of life, and the sole house she had lived in without fear had been Lady Matilda's home. Now her British benefactor rested in a grave in Bukit Brown Cemetery, where Mei Mei visited every Sunday to leave fresh flowers. She had packed two suitcases, and the major-domo of the Robertson household had ordered a hackney carriage to take Mei Mei and her belongings to John Harrison's rubber plantation. Sitting inside the four-wheeled horse-drawn carriage, her suitcases on its roof, Mei Mei had taken one last look at the white bungalow that had been her home. A solitary tear trickled down her cheek as she remembered sitting at Lady Matilda's feet and listening to her tales of England.

Jamal, a tall Malay man with brilliant black moustaches who was the Harrison houseboy, had opened the carriage door, handed her out and showed her into the house. He asked her to follow him to the attic, where a small but beautifully furnished bedroom had been allocated to her.

"Madam is busy with her elevens coffee morning," Jamal

had said in halting English. "She is hosting seven British ladies."
Suddenly his teeth had flashed in an attractive smile, which Mei
Mei had tentatively returned. "She will see you before lunch."
Coughing discreetly, he had added, "Master Richard is at the
plantation with *Tuan Besar.*"

"Clementine?" Mei Mei had raised an eyebrow.

"Miss Clem is taking the grand tour of Europe and will return
in a few months."

How fortuitous that at least she would be spared Clementine's
cold dislike while she settled into the household. A blush filled
Mei Mei's face and a small smile tugged at her lips. *If the memory
of Richard's kisses is all I take with me to my grave, I will be happy,*
she thought passionately.

Last night, in the shade of a tree outside New World, with the
music of the dances reaching them faintly, Richard had taken her
in his arms and covered her face with kisses. She had trembled so
much that he had had to hold her in a tight embrace. Her heart
had raced, and she had begun to gasp for breath. He had let her
go and tenderly moved his mouth to her hair, and she had buried
her face in his chest and clutched at him, not wanting his caresses
to stop.

There was the sound of voices, and Mei Mei quickly stood up
from the bank and glanced towards the apple orchard. Richard
appeared, dressed in white trousers and a shirt, a hat covering
his head. A thin, small boy was holding on to his hand, eating an
apple. Richard waved at her, and she went to meet him.

"Hallo!" A delighted smile broke on his face. "You have
arrived."

The small boy forgot his apple to gaze at her with wide eyes. "She is pretty girl," he said in Bazaar Malay.

Richard laughed. "That she is." He pushed the boy forward. "Shake hands with Mei Mei, Ali." He looked at Mei Mei tenderly and said, "Ali is the son of one of our Malay plantation workers. He is very naughty and runs away from school every day."

Mei Mei liked the mischief lurking in the eyes of the Malay boy and warmed to him. She was about to speak when Jamal appeared.

"Master Richard, Miss Mei Mei is wanted in madam's boudoir. *Tuan Besar* and madam are waiting to speak with her. To follow me, Miss."

Mei Mei waved a farewell, and with faltering steps, followed Jamal into a small room by the rose garden where the sun streamed in. Eleanor Harrison rose from a settee and came to shake Mei Mei's hand.

"Welcome to our house, Mei Mei," she boomed, her boiled gooseberry eyes wary, her lips stretched into a reluctant smile. "I hope your bedroom is to your satisfaction."

"It is very nice, thank you." Mei Mei turned to the burly man with electric blue eyes who had come to stand next to his wife.

John Harrison's ruddy face was warm with a hospitality that was lacking in his wife's countenance. "Mei Mei, welcome, welcome. Ahem, sorry about Lady Matilda, eh? I understand you were close to her."

Mei Mei inclined her head politely, and Harrison continued, "Sit down, sit down."

"John," Eleanor Harrison intervened, "the luncheon hour is

nearly here. We will sit to lunch soon enough. Why don't you broach the matter of Mei Mei's occupation in our household to her?"

"Yes, yes, ahem." John Harrison wiped his perspiring brow with a large white handkerchief. "I understand that you were a seamstress at the Robertson house, but we already employ two seamstresses. The position of schoolteacher is vacant at my estate school. I can hire you for the job for two dollars a week." He waved aside Mei Mei's protestations. "Yes, yes, I know you own a tailoring establishment in Sago Lane. How about night school, eh? My plantation workers have very young children who need to learn the alphabet and some sums. Would you be too tired in the evening to take an hour of class?"

"Nonsense!" Eleanor Harrison's voice was outraged. "Mei Mei is a farmer's daughter and accustomed to hard work. It is settled then."

Mei Mei finally opened her mouth. "Thank you," she said.

"Tomorrow my driver will take you to meet Sandra Norbert, the secretary to the Assistant Chinese Protectorate. She and I have planned a project that will speed up the abolishment of the *mui-tsai* practice in Singapore. I am sure you want to see that happen, eh?" When Mei Mei nodded, he continued, "Yes, yes, barbaric, that's all I can say. But Sandra has a good plan and we will need your help, Mei Mei."

"We will go to lunch now," Eleanor Harrison said peremptorily. "Come, child, you must be hungry."

Mei Mei followed dolefully, wondering when she would find the time to sew sackcloth for the bereaved and pay the rental of her shop in Sago Lane with the responsibilities foisted on her by John Harrison.

Sandra Norbert was a tall, horse-faced woman with intense blue eyes and brown bobbed hair. She brimmed with activity in her office at the Protectorate, driving her poor Chinese peon to scuttle out with papers and scurry in with more, his expression becoming ever more harried.

Sandra turned a sweet smile on Mei Mei, inviting her to sit in the visitor's chair.

Her eyes were warm when she said, "It is a pleasure to meet you, young woman. Lady Matilda spoke highly of your intelligence, and we are going to need that. Here is the plan Lady Matilda and I dreamed up to speed up the Bill for the abolition of the *mui-tsai* system. The law to register bondmaids is already in force, but we need to do away with the buying and selling of young Chinese girls altogether. Do you agree, Mei Mei?"

A curious light was burning in Mei Mei's eyes. She saw again her father cringing at Grandma Sim's feet, accepting money for her services. *Selling her like a chattel.* A tremor of outrage swept across her features before her face set into blandness.

"Yes." She spoke the word with such emphasis that Sandra was satisfied.

"We have much work to do then, Mei Mei." Sandra's eyes narrowed. "Many Chinese households accept the bondmaid system as part of Chinese culture. It was imported from the mainland, and Chinese families with bondmaids will resist any attempt to whip up sentiment against the system." Sandra leaned forward, her eyes bright. "We need testimonies of abuse from Chinese bondmaids, oral testimonies that will be recorded in a book. We will send this book, with the draft Abolition Bill, to the British Parliament. You will collect the bondmaid testimonies and translate their stories into English."

Mei Mei half-rose in her seat, her eyes round. The nervous tic near her mouth began to pulsate. "But the bondmaids will not speak against their employers, Ma'am, for fear of repercussions. They will be beaten, or worse. They still have to live with their employers."

Sandra Norbert said authoritatively, "You must persuade them to steal away from their houses and meet with us to testify about their lives as bondmaids. Their employers will remain unaware of their actions, and their testimonies will remain anonymous. The book will use fictitious names for both employers and maids. John Harrison has lent us his schoolhouse to provide a meeting place on Sundays, when there are no lessons. A building in a remote rubber plantation will be a good rendezvous point, don't you agree?"

"I don't know if I can influence the bondmaids to tell their stories."

"Do you know of any bondmaid from your *kampong*?" Sandra Norbert demanded. "We can start there."

"There is Mong Li. Her sister, Mong Jen, died from breaking coal at four o'clock every morning. She is a bondmaid in an oil palm merchant's house in Beach Road." Mei Mei frowned, a tendril of hair escaping from her braid to fall on her forehead.

"We will go there tomorrow. Meet me at ten in the morning."

Next morning, Sandra and Mei Mei sat in a horse-drawn carriage rolling along Beach Road. Mei Mei alighted at a tree-lined avenue and made her way to the Lee mansion. It was an imposing three-storey building with colourful shutters. A beautiful garden could be seen through the wrought iron gates. Mei Mei stepped into an alley and skirted the house to a back lane. There she found a smaller latched gate, with a winding path leading through a vegetable garden to the kitchen door. Mei Mei lifted the latch and sidled in. Her soft knock on the kitchen door was answered by an emaciated girl in rags. Her pointed face was dirty, and her huge eyes gazed sadly at Mei Mei.

"Mong Li!" Mei Mei exclaimed in a whisper. "You are Tan Mong Li from the Bukit Ho Swee *kampong*?" she asked in Hokkien.

There was a spark of recognition in the sad eyes. "Liao Mei Mei," Mong Li said in a soft voice. "All us sisters were glad when you were acquitted of murdering your aunt. What happened when you went back to the House of Toh?" Mong Li's nose twitched with curiosity. "Come, come, sit down. It is convenient that the cook is out. We can talk in the scullery."

Mong Li led Mei Mei to a room with a small table and two rickety chairs. A mattress lay in one corner. There was a huge sink piled high with dishes and wooden draining boards. In another corner, a bucket of water had been placed on a raised platform.

"This is my room, all mine." Mong Li gave a cackle. "I sleep on the mattress on the floor, and I eat with the junior kitchen maid at the table. I wash all the utensils and dishes the family uses for cooking and meals." She pointed to the bucket. "I also wash clothes over there. Have a seat, Liao Mei Mei."

Mei Mei sat in one of the chairs and told Mong Li her story.

Mong Li's eyebrows shot into her thin, matted hair. "You are indeed lucky to gain the protection of the British gentry," she said. "Your employers would surely have sold you off to a brothel."

Mei Mei spoke in a determined voice. "Mong Li, our British masters want to abolish the *mui-tsai* system. We are slaves. We earn no wages for our labour. Many of us are abused. You must record your experiences with Mrs Norbert of the Office of the Chinese Protectorate, and help make sure no one else suffers like Mong Jen."

Mong Li was gazing at Mei Mei in horror. "Get out!" She began shepherding Mei Mei out of the scullery. "Speak against my master? Have you gone mad? They will bury me alive."

Mei Mei shook Mong Li hard. "They will not know, Mong Li. On a Sunday, you are to sneak out, and I will take you to a rubber plantation where you will be well hidden. We will record your testimony of abuse, that is all. Once all the statements have been collected, the British in England are going to pass a Bill, and after that there will be no more bondmaids. No children bought and sold for labour."

Tears trickled down Mong Li's cheeks. "I will tell my sister, Mong Jen's story, and my own."

Mei Mei entwined her thumb with Mong Li's in kinship, and both girls whispered: "For Mong Jen."

And so, on a rainy Sunday, sitting in the schoolhouse of John Harrison's plantation, the first *mui-tsai* story was recited in Hokkien by Mong Li Tan, duly translated into English by Mei Mei, and written down in an exercise book under the watchful eyes of Sandra Norbert.

Testimony of Mong Li Tan
on behalf of herself and her deceased sister, Mong Jen.

It was a rainy evening and we, seven brothers and sisters, huddled together in the main room of the hut, near the clay stove where Ma was stirring a brownish brew. Pa was away in the city, supposedly working in the shipyard, but more likely gambling. Our Pa gambled something terrible. It was in his blood, he said; our grandfather was a gambler, and surprisingly he made enough money from the habit to build the brick house we lived in. Pa wanted to be like him.

The bullfrogs groaned in the drains, and crickets chattered as darkness fell. My little sister, Mong Jen, was nine years old and I was eleven years old. It was I who saw the lurching figure by our gate and crying, "Pa!" rushed out into the small vegetable patch Ma tended with such care. My siblings followed me with welcoming cries that stopped when we realised that our father had had too much to drink.

Singing a drunken song, my father paused at the threshold of the rectangular door of light leading to our house.

"My boy!" he shouted at my seven-year-old brother, Junxiong. "Come and give Papa a hug."

"Stay outdoors, children!" Ma warned us from inside. We knew it was better to do so. My father flew into fierce rages when he was drunk.

We sat behind the hedges and murmured to each other. Suddenly there was a shout. We peeped from around the foliage.

The light from the doorway framed a giant man with a bulb filled with acid in his hands.

"Tek, you gambled away your house tonight. Now you move out with your family and allow the triad to claim what's ours—or else." The acid bulb swayed dangerously.

"Or else what?" my father jeered. "This house was built by my grandfather, and it's not going to the triad. Go away!"

We could not breathe, even if we had wanted to. The man at the door paused, but only for a second. Then he threw the bulb into my father's face, and the night was rent by an agonized cry as our own mouths opened in soundless screams. We watched our father's face dissolve in front of our eyes. The villagers took him to the hospital. It took him two days filled with agony to die.

The triad arrived to claim our home. We left with our meagre belongings to take shelter in my maternal uncle's hut at the edge of the village.

My mother had no money, so she sold her daughters as *mui-tsais* to well-to-do households. The money enabled her to apprentice my two young brothers to carpenters in the city, and she hoped that soon they would be able to earn a decent wage. It is true that we probably would have died if we had not been sold as bondmaids.

I was sold to an oil-palm merchant who lived with his wife and children in a mansion on Beach Road. Mong Jen, my little sister, was sold to a Peranakan household in Bukit Ho Swee. I missed Mong Jen most—the feel of her small, warm body as we cuddled together to sleep, her bright button eyes full of mischief as she chased me by the stream. I was miserable.

My employer's wife, Old Mistress, was a strict disciplinarian, but she did not abuse me. She made me her scullery maid, and I was put in charge of washing the household clothing and linen, and cleaning the utensils used for cooking. I slept on a mattress on the scullery floor, woke up at four in the morning, and went to sleep at midnight. I earned no wages except my food and lodging, and I had no holiday leave to visit my family.

It was through the cook of the household, a Hainanese man who was kind to us maids, that I heard that Mong Jen was in Middletown Hospital. She was physically fragile, and her employers made her wake up at four in the morning to break coal for the stoves. The Hainanese cook said that the coal dust had lodged in her lungs and she began to cough something terrible. Soon she could not breathe anymore and collapsed. It was then that her employer admitted her to a hospital. I ran to Old Mistress, begging to see my sister, but was refused leave to do so. I heard that she died two days after being admitted, and by then her whole body had turned blue. Mong Jen was only ten years old.

Old Mistress called me to her room two days ago. I will soon turn eighteen and need to be married off, she said. She was smiling when she said she had already found my groom. The Hainanese cook whom I called 'Uncle Ming' had asked for my hand. I was shocked to the core because he is old enough to be my father and, as far as I know, he has a wife in mainland China and grown-up children. Old Mistress had it all planned: I would marry Uncle Ming, and he would continue as cook and I would be housekeeper, the *samsui* woman who had been housekeeper having died a year ago. Old Mistress offered wages for my housekeeping duties, and I could see the relief on her face when I nodded my acquiescence.

Uncle Ming is kind, and he will take care of me and any children I have with him. He earns good wages and I could have done much worse, getting married to one of the rickshaw coolies. One asked for my hand, I am told, but we all know they earn a pittance for plying jinrickshaws across the city.

I fear that I cannot love Uncle Ming in the way I am supposed to love a husband, but does it matter? I am more afraid that one day he will leave me and go home to China to his first family. So I am resolved now to have children as soon as I am married—to bind Uncle Ming to me. I think I should not call him 'Uncle' anymore?

Mei Mei laboriously wrote down the last sentence of Mong Jen's testimony in English in the thick exercise book given to her by Sandra Norbert. She looked up. Dusk had fallen outside, and she had been writing in the schoolhouse by the light of a lantern. There was a soft sound in the otherwise empty building and Mei Mei stiffened.

She cried, "Who is there?"

There was a giggle, and a round face, with two button eyes, and crowned by a mop of curly hair, peeped from around the door.

"Ali!" Mei Mei cried in relief. "It is you. What are you doing here? You should be doing your homework."

"Ma and Pa are quarrelling too loudly and the baby is crying its head off," Ali said in Bazaar Malay. "I cannot study at home. But I study by candlelight in the back room here."

Mei Mei followed Ali into the small anteroom where broken furniture, cleaning utensils and other knick-knacks were kept. Ali had a candle stuck on a small desk, on top of which were his slate and chalks. He had managed to obtain a tall three-legged stool to sit on.

"Hm, very enterprising," Mei Mei said in Bazaar Malay and laughed. Ali was one of her favourite pupils, and while mischief was his chief attribute, he also possessed loyalty and a heart of gold that manifested itself in his assistance to the younger students.

Mei Mei had settled well as the teacher of the estate school, where she was the proud instructor of ten children, who varied in age from five to eleven years. The children were the progeny of the plantation workers, and most were Tamil: John Harrison had been forced to recruit workers from India after the British government had imposed restrictions on hiring from the Chinese mainland, fearing anti-imperialistic uprisings initiated by the Kuomintang Party. Mei Mei took her classes early in the morning, even managing to teach some English songs to the children before she left for her tailoring establishment at eleven. She returned from work at seven in the evening, enabling her to put in an hour helping the students with their homework. Sundays were devoted to writing *mui-tsai* testimonies and translating them into English.

Sandra Norbert had instructed Mei Mei to find other bondmaids willing to record their testimonies, but few were inclined to talk for fear of inciting their employers' displeasure. Sandra and the Chinese Protectorate did not offer any protection to the bondmaids, and many decided that the risk of their employers discovering their betrayal was too great. But on a sunny morning, as Mei Mei worked in her shop, she was given a heaven-sent opportunity to record the story of an abused bondmaid.

She was surprised to see a pimp, Ah Choy, dart inside. She knew he plied his trade in neighbouring Sago Street. Mei Mei thought he was going to force her to accompany him to the brothel he served, and prepared herself to scream loudly for help. But the pimp vigorously shook his head and put a finger on his lips.

"I do not come to harm you," Ah Choy whispered in Mandarin, his pockmarked face like a moon with a myriad of craters. "One of my girls, Mei Ren, wishes to record her story with you. She was a former bondmaid and was sold to a brothel. She is desperate, and when you hear her story, you will discover the reason. She is waiting outside."

He darted out and was soon back with a tall, slim, beautiful girl, dressed in a formal cheongsam.

"Please help me, sister," the girl said in a whisper to Mei Mei. "Word is out that the British are looking for bondmaids willing to tell their stories of ill-use at the hands of their employers. I have nothing to lose and much to gain. I will talk."

Wee Mei Ren's Testimony

I was the only child of my parents, and my father was a rickshaw coolie. When I was thirteen years old, he started taking opium in the city dens. Money was scarce, and we were starving. One day my father did not come home from the opium den. His body was recovered from the Singapore River two days later. He had no wounds and nobody knew how he died. The villagers speculated that he had fallen into the river in a stupor after consuming too much *chandu*.

My uncle, my mother's brother, had a friend who worked in a rice warehouse. This friend began courting my mother after Pa's death, and when I was fourteen, my mother married this man. My stepfather did not wish to keep me in his house and sold me as a bondmaid to a pineapple merchant who lived near Geylang Serai. My mother and I cried, but what was the use?

My master's pineapple plantation was outside the city and he had a bungalow there where he spent some of the week. My master was about sixty years old when I entered their household, but my mistress was about thirty years of age. She was beautiful and had been married to my master for ten years. Their sad story was that my mistress was barren and could not carry a child in her womb.

My duties were to tend to my mistress. She was pleasant to me, sometimes buying me good clothes and food. Since my master was sometimes away from the house in his plantation, I accompanied my mistress when she went to play mah-jong with her friends or to buy food and clothes in the city. We were driven by a chauffeur. I ate good food and my duties were not too harsh. The family employed other *mui-tsais* for cleaning and sewing.

After my sixteenth birthday, my mistress called me to her bedchamber and told me that my master was sick. She wanted me to go to the plantation bungalow and tend to my master. She said that she had to stay and look after the Geylang mansion.

The car drove me outside the city with my bundle of clothes, and soon we were in the rural countryside. The car entered through big wrought iron gates, and I saw pineapples growing as far as the eye could see. Birds were singing, and the men and women of the plantation were also singing as they tended to the pineapples. I was happy. The plantation's rustic layout brought my birth village back to me—a time before my father starting smoking *chandu*.

The plantation bungalow was big and breezy. The green shutters were open, and there was light everywhere. A dour-looking Chinese man received me, introducing himself as Lai, my master's major-domo. He took me to a nice room at the back with a big bed. I was shocked when he said this was to be my room. He told me to eat in the kitchen with the other staff, and to tend to my master at night.

The kitchen staff consisted of a male Chinese cook and two very young bondmaids who helped clean the house. They looked at me askance when I sat to eat with them and would not speak. I felt uneasy.

When dusk fell, Lai knocked on my door and took me to a small room next to a bedroom with a shut door. To my horror, I saw an opium lamp, two opium pipes and several bowls and scrapers on a table. Lai told me he would teach me how to prepare master's pipe, as he smoked opium every night. I was terrified, but what could I do?

I learnt from Lai how to make the concoction that killed Pa. Every day, I would dilute the *chandu* with water and let it set into the required consistency. Then I would take some of the brown leathery mass, a little bit at a time, at the end of the needle and heat it over the flame of the opium lamp. Then I would pat the mass and heat it some more, watching it splutter and emit golden smoke—the elixir of the gods. Then I would fill the opium bowl with the *chandu* and take the pipe in to Master, along with the opium lamp. As he reclined on a big, ornate bed, I would hold the lamp so that the opiate in the bowl sizzled and vaporised, allowing him to inhale the smoke through the stem. Some time later, he would heave a sigh and let go of the pipe. He would lie back on the bed to sleep and dream of another world.

I soon grew accustomed to my job and became quite good at preparing master's opium pipe. A month into my stay, Master asked me to massage his legs, and I did his bidding. He said he was very ill; he looked grey and waxen. His small eyes gazed at me, travelling down to rest on my breasts, before swivelling away. Master had a bulbous nose, thick lips and a thatch of white hair. The servants said he was the second wealthiest pineapple merchant in the whole of Singapore.

One night, six months into my stay, it was raining and cold. I prepared master's opium pipe and brought it to him. This time he was sitting up on the bed, and he smiled at me.

"My little Mei Ren," he said affectionately, "how dutifully you tend to me. I want to reward you, my child. Come, smoke with me."

I backed away in horror and bumped into Lai, who was waiting at the door with another opium pipe.

"No! No!" I cried. "Please, Master, do not give me *chandu*. My father died from this poison."

I felt pressure on my back as Lai propelled me forward until I was sitting on my master's lap. He clasped me to him, murmuring endearments, his hands cupping my breasts, his breath fanning my face. He was strong, and my struggles were in vain. I watched helplessly while Lai prepared two opium pipes.

"Come now, little one, have a smoke," Master cajoled while Lai giggled.

The stem of the pipe was thrust into my mouth and I inhaled. My tears dried, my struggles ceased, and I lolled like a limp doll in my master's arms. I smiled as his thick lips came closer and closer. I put my arms around him when he kissed me, his tongue exploring the depths of my mouth like a silken snake. After some more *chandu*, I allowed him to lay me down on the bed. Lai was nowhere to be seen. My thoughts were waxing and waning. I felt so calm and relaxed. My father came to me in my dream, pulling me roughly to him, placing me on his shoulders, taking me to the *pasar malam* and buying me goreng pisang. I smiled happily. My body seemed to be on fire, I tore at my clothes, I wanted them off my body. I moaned as tongues of flame began licking my entire body. What a heavenly sensation!

I must have dozed off, because when I woke, it was morning. At first, I did not know where I was. Then I saw Master snoring next to me, stark naked. I too was nude, and I knew what had happened. Master had taken me as his concubine.

Was I surprised? No. This was a bondmaid's fate, after all. I knew of many bondmaids who were their masters' concubines. My whole body was aching, and I left the bed to go to my room. I took a long time over my bath that day, but no amount of water or soap could wash his stench off me.

We shared the same bed, Master and I, for six more months, until I fell pregnant. Master treated me with tenderness, and plied me with jade bangles and earrings, and the staff of the bungalow treated me with respect. I no longer ate in the kitchen, but with Master in the oval dining room, served by Lai. I began to wear silk cheongsams and took pride in dressing well for Master. And when I fell pregnant, a tiny hope sparked in me that I would become Master's second wife, my child the heir to his fortune. I was so immersed in my dreams for the future that I spared no thought for Mistress and how she might feel.

In my fifth month of pregnancy, Master, as was his habit on the weekend, left for the Geylang Serai house; but this time, he did not return. Instead, a tall thin Chinese woman with a faint moustache came in the car and was ensconced in a bedroom of the house. Lai's insolent manner returned.

"That is the midwife. She will assist in the delivery of the child," he said dismissively, when I asked him about the visitor. "Madam Ang."

"When will Master return?" I asked anxiously.

One of the kitchen maids was laying the dining table, and she burst into giggles and had to rush off. A faint smile touched Lai's lips.

"Mistress has sent for him. Master will live in the city now."

I was not jealous, but I did feel a waning of my power

as concubine. I knew that my child would give me the status I deserved and ignored the staff, choosing to eat nutritious meals, supervised by Madam Ang, to ensure the good health of my unborn child.

My labour was long and my child, a son, they later told me, was born in the eighth lunar month. Madam Ang and the *sinsei* worked hard to bring him, healthy and bawling, into the world. When I heard his cry, I tried to sit up, but Madam Ang shook her head and made me sip some concoction she had prepared. I slid into a dreamless sleep.

When I woke up, it was dark and there was no one in the room. My insides were lacerated, and I shouted for my child. Silence greeted me. After a long time, Madam Ang appeared with soothing bandages and hot water. She gave me some medicine that put me to sleep again.

I think Madam Ang drugged me for a week, because I do not remember anything clearly after the birth of my son. When I was healed, and my mind was clear, Lai took me into the living room.

A fat woman in a tight cheongsam with painted lips was sitting on a chair. She got up at my entry and appraised me with a knowing eye.

"Hm," she said, her double chins wobbling. "Tell Master I will pay a hundred dollars for her. She is a beauty."

When the woman had left, I accosted Lai. "Where is my child? My baby?" I cried.

I saw a look of pity cross Lai's unremarkable features. In a soft voice, he said, "Mei Ren, you gave birth to a healthy son, Master's son and heir. Master and Mistress will bring him up in the lap of luxury, do not fear. They needed an heir and you have delivered one. Your son will have a mother—Mistress will be a good mother to him. You will go tomorrow to Mamasan's brothel in Sago Street. Master has sold you to her for a hundred dollars."

The walls began receding, the ceiling collapsed, everything went dark. When I came to, Madam Ang was kneeling beside me, her eyes kind for once.

"You are still recovering from the birth of your son, Mei Ren," she said in a whisper. "Do not strain yourself."

"But my son! He is my son! They cannot take him away from me like this. I am his mother. Tell me what to do, Madam Ang, to get my son back."

Madam Ang's stern face crumpled. "You can do nothing, my child. You are a bondmaid, only seventeen years old. You are a piece of your master's property, and he can do with you as he likes. Your life with Master and Mistress is over."

When my storm of tears had subsided, I asked, "So I was a vehicle to bring Master's child into the world because Mistress was barren? I have no identity other than as a surrogate mother?"

Lai had come into the room. "You are a *mui-tsai*," he said sadly.

I have been working in a brothel for five years now,

and not one day goes by that I don't yearn to see my son. The *samseng* of the brothel follows me, and I cannot sneak into Geylang Serai to see my son, even from a distance. He must be five years old by now.

One of the little sisters who visits her older sister, a whore, told me that the Chinese Protectorate was seeking bondmaids to tell their stories so that the *mui-tsai* system is abolished. The sister said they were looking for stories of abuse. To take a son from his mother without leave—is that not abuse? I am a flesh and blood woman, with a heart that beats with love for my child. I tell my story in the hope that someone reads it and unites me with my son, for I wait for him every day.

Mei Mei wiped her eyes as she translated the last sentence of Mei Ren's testimony into English. The lantern light was dimming; it was dark outside. Ali lay sleeping on one of the school benches, his face peaceful. Mei Mei closed the exercise book and placed it in a small cupboard in the corner. A few more stories and Sandra Norbert would send the papers for printing at the press, and then on to the Parliament in London.

13

The ship approached the quay and the shouts of traders and coolies filled her ears. Clementine patted her hair into place and eagerly climbed on to the deck crowded with the ship's passengers. She could identify Tessa Fanshaw by the red hat perched rakishly on her dark curls. Clementine pushed past passengers to stand at the rail beside Tessa, watching the shoreline of Singapore slowly approaching. She thought back to the time when she had arrived at the dock as a child, and how mystified she had been by the dark, menacing vegetation of the island. She had missed Singapore, Clementine realised with a jolt. The familiar shoreline, the shouts in Mandarin, the raucous laughter of the coolies, the faint scent of frying lard, the sweet breath of the dank, tropical air, the cloudy January skies threatening rain, all coalesced into one word—home, the place where Richard lived.

She looked at Tessa, whose mouth was slightly open as she absorbed the colour and brightness of the tropics, and the heat that shimmered in waves of undulating intensity around them. Clem had taken the grand tour of Europe with Tessa Fanshaw, who had been introduced to her by her father's friend, Tom Whitehead. At twenty-three, Tessa would ordinarily have been considered a little too old for the expedition, but an aunt had recently died and left her a small fortune, and Tessa had quickly booked a tour of the Continent. Tom Whitehead had solved the need for a companion by suggesting Clementine, who had ample funds to take the tour from leasing out her manor in Cornwall.

Tessa was slim, with deep-set blue eyes and jet-black hair. She had become engaged to Stephen Dolittle, a rubber planter in Singapore, a year earlier. With the tour of Europe concluded, she had set sail to marry him and assume control of his household. Clem had been useful not only as a companion in Europe, but also as a source of information on the tropical island that was going to be Tessa's new home.

As the ship threw down its anchor, Clem shaded her eyes and eagerly scanned the dock. She was disappointed to see Jeff waiting to receive her. After perfunctory introductions, Clem turned impatiently towards the crowd at the quayside.

"Where is Richard?" Her voice was petulant. "I thought he would be here to receive me. I have been away for more than seven months."

"A lot has happened in those months," Jeff said enigmatically, before inviting Tessa to climb into the Bentley. "Miss Fanshaw, we will drop you at your plantation. Stephen will be waiting for you at the gate."

After Tessa had alighted from the car to be swept into Stephen's arms, and the car had started the five-minute drive to the Harrison plantation, Clem asked, "What changes in the plantation are you talking about?"

"Eleanor will tell you herself." Jeff said hurriedly, and turned to the chauffeur. "Achmed, drop me off here. I will take the short-cut to the plantation. Drive Miss Clem to the front door and look after the luggage, man."

Eleanor was pleased with her gifts from Milan and Paris. She exclaimed over them, her face flushed with pleasure and anticipation. She was jolted back to reality when Clem asked her for news from the plantation.

"Oh, it's very good, very good." Eleanor's bulbous eyes swivelled away from Clem's penetrating blue gaze. "John needs evidence of *mui-tsai* abuse to draft the Abolition Bill, and he and Sandra Norbert have come up with an astonishing plan. You remember the bondmaid, Mei Mei, who was tried for her aunt's murder? She is recruiting abused bondmaids and writing down their stories. Most of them are illiterate, and Mei Mei is invaluable as a translator and recorder. Sandra Norbert is using the plantation schoolhouse as a headquarters, and that's where all the writing and recording go on. I hear that after another five testimonies, the book will be ready to be sent to England with the draft Abolition Bill." Excitement crept into Eleanor's voice, and she failed to see the hard glint in Clem's eyes.

"Mei Mei." Clementine said the words with care, before asking casually, "I was wondering what happened to her after Lady Matilda died? Does she live at the orphanage then?"

A red flush crept into Eleanor's round face and she lowered her eyes as she said, "Lady Matilda requested that John take care of Mei Mei until she turns eighteen, which is next year. She implored him on her deathbed, so John had no choice but to honour her wish. He hired Mei Mei seven months ago as a teacher for the estate school on the plantation, but she spends most of her time preparing the book of bondmaid testimonies." In a low voice, Eleanor said, "We have arranged for her to sleep in one of the attic bedrooms."

"She stays here." The cold voice cut into Eleanor's speech as sharply as a knife into butter.

"Yes, yes. She is out of the house for most of the day and only shelters here at night." Eleanor was anxious to change the subject. "How did you find Tessa Fanshaw? Will she suit our Stephen? They will be married at the Cathedral of the Good Shepherd in a fortnight."

"Mei Mei nursed Richard back to health, Aunt Eleanor. He is grateful to her for his life. Do they go out together?"

"Oh, tosh!" Eleanor cried. "Listen to you, prattling on about Mei Mei. No, why should they go out together? She is a native! You must be mad to even suggest it. He will be your escort again, don't you fear. I am positive that an English rose will smell sweeter to Richard than the native Flame of the Forest. John is only using Mei Mei's services to get into Parliament. Come now, tell me about Tessa."

August 1934

Clementine sat under an apple tree in the Harrison orchard, deep in thought, Jasper, her spaniel, curled into a ball at her feet. She had followed Mei Mei and Richard without their knowledge, and seen them planting frangipani seeds by the stream at the back of the house. A month ago, she had discovered that Mei Mei was posing as Richard's model in his studio at the top of the house, helping him to perfect his portraiture techniques. Clem bit her lip so hard that a drop of blood trickled out and hung from her lips, as though she were a vampire. Sometimes she climbed the staircase to Richard's studio, and pressed her ear to the door; but the door was made of sturdy oak, and soundproof.

Clem returned to the house to dress for dinner. She looked at her face critically in the mirror. She could not have looked more beautiful in her life. Her soft hair curled alluringly over her forehead and hung over her shoulders like fine golden mist. The scent of incense and a smell of burning drifted in through the windows of her bedroom and, frowning, Clem rose to look out into the back garden. To her surprise, she spied Mei Mei with incense sticks in her hands, bowing low before an urn where paper still burnt, dark sooty smoke rising into the evening air. Clem climbed down the stairs and went out into the back garden.

"What on earth are you doing?" she asked Mei Mei in a voice laced with surprise and distaste.

Slowly Mei Mei turned, and Clementine stepped back with shock. Mei Mei looked even more beautiful when her liquid eyes swam with tears.

"We celebrate the feast of the hungry ghosts this month," Mei Mei said in her soft, musical voice. "We have to pray for the souls of our departed ancestors. Only our prayers will release them from the courts of hell. I am praying for my father's soul."

"And why is your father in hell, may I ask?" Clem's voice was derisive.

Mei Mei raised her eyes to Clem's. "He sold his daughter for gold coins," she replied.

The fire had burned out and Mei Mei stoked the ashes with a stick, her long black braids swinging to and fro, her face covered with a sheen of moisture from the heat. She looked intensely desirable, Clem thought, and she could imagine men being attracted to her. A hard light burned in Clem's eyes.

"Mei Mei, why are you playing with Richard's affections?" Clem's voice was rough and rasping. "You are a native girl and he is a British gentleman. You have no future together. Why are you encouraging him to love you, when you two can never be married?"

Clem saw with satisfaction the colour fly from Mei Mei's face. Driving home her advantage, she continued, "I see the way you look at him—like a puppy looking at its master. It's disgusting. Rein in your emotions, Mei Mei. Do not be too ambitious, like the moth who burns in the flame, and don't take advantage of the trust that Uncle John and Aunt Eleanor have placed in you. If they had not given you shelter, you would be in a brothel now."

Clem pursed her lips in a moue of disdain. She was surprised when Mei Mei looked at her out of fearless eyes.

"I don't know what you are talking about, Clem," she said, her voice soft. "I am employed as a teacher at the estate school, and I am friends with Richard."

Clem burst out laughing, her eyes as sharp as blue splinters. She came close to the Chinese girl and whispered, "Don't take me for a fool, Mei Mei. You think I don't know of your trysts at New World, and that Richard makes love to you in his studio?"

Mei Mei's eyes widened. "You are mad!" she cried. "We have never made love."

Clementine said sagely, "You know I am perfectly sane, Mei Mei. I know what you are up to, and I am warning you to stop making eyes at Richard. He and I are to be married in the future, and the last thing I need in my life is a mistress hanging around in the slums of Chinatown!"

She was unprepared for the rage in the Chinese girl's eyes. "You think a British boy and a Chinese girl cannot love each other like a British boy and a British girl?"

"Don't delude yourself, dear Mei Mei." Now the mirth playing on her lips reached Clem's eyes. "Richard will marry me and do his duty by his parents. Tell me, have you seen any British gentleman here with a native wife?"

Mei Mei turned her face away from the other girl's triumphant eyes and began walking towards the kitchen door. Halfway there she turned, and said in a deceptively sweet voice, "We would not be having this conversation if you were so certain of your marriage plans, Clementine."

Clem stood rooted to the ground and impotently watched Mei Mei disappear around the corner of the house. The smoke from the dead fire in the urn attacked her eyes and with tears streaming down her face, Clementine stormed into the kitchen, startling the cook into burning the onions she was frying.

September 1934

It was nearly dark, and some plantation workers were untying the tin cups tied around the bark of trees that held that precious commodity—rubber sap. They paid scant attention as Clementine walked by on the winding path, silent as a shadow beneath the trees. She paused when she sighted the schoolhouse, a dark silhouette away from the plantation, with a single lantern shining in the window. Skirting the path to the schoolhouse door, Clem kept to the bushes, creeping up silently to peep in through the window.

Mei Mei sat by the lantern, her face frowning in concentration, her eyes on the thick exercise book in which she was writing laboriously. Clem crept back the way she had come. As she neared the house, the dinner gong clanged, slicing through the silence of the night.

John Harrison looked at the roast beef he was carving with satisfaction. He glanced at his wife and said, "One more bondmaid's story, and the book of testimonies will be sent off to the press for printing." He ladled pieces of meat on to the plates for Sher Singh to take to the table. "My word, I am impressed with Mei Mei. Her ability as a translator at such a young age is commendable; but how hard she works at the book! She really burns the midnight oil. I will be sure to mention this to my friends in Parliament when I show them the Bill."

Clementine looked at Richard and froze. His face held a red tinge and his green eyes were wide, shining with a light that left Clem in little doubt of his feelings for Mei Mei. The food stuck in her throat and she felt nauseous.

There was a knock on the front door, and Sher Singh hurried out to see who was calling at such a late hour. He came back and whispered some words to John Harrison.

"The head of the Chinese Chamber of Commerce, Lee Chup

Yew, is here to see me. Carry on with your dinner while I see what he wants."

When John came back to the dining room, his face was flushed and his eyes were blazing. He began to splutter with indignation, and it was quite some time before he could bring himself to speak clearly.

"The Chinese Chamber of Commerce has voted against the *Mui-tsai* Abolition Bill, and Lee has expressed deep dissatisfaction with our interviewing bondmaids and recording their stories. News of what we've been doing has got out to the Chinese employers of bondmaids. They are all up in arms, and Lee spoke on their behalf—said that the *mui-tsai* system was part of Chinese culture and had to be treated with respect. The Chinese Chamber of Commerce takes a dim view of invading the privacy of Chinese households by interviewing bondmaids. Lee said that the Chamber will vote on lodging a complaint against Sandra and me with the Superintendent of Police.

"The effrontery of these natives! They treat human beings like chattels and talk about privacy! Lee said that we cannot publish our book of testimonies. He threatened to take me to court. I assured him that the testimonies would be anonymised, but to no avail."

Eleanor hastened to comfort her husband while Richard and Jeff began to argue about the validity of Lee's concern. Clem quietly got up and left the dining room. It was time to act and put a stop to this charade once and for all, she thought viciously.

She shut her bedroom door and sat on the chaise lounge near the window. She gazed out mesmerized, her blue eyes focussed on the pinprick of light in the otherwise dark plantation—the light that was spilling from the schoolhouse. As she watched, biting her lower lip, the light went off and there was uniform darkness. Fifteen minutes later, she heard the back gate creak open and soft footfalls approach the kitchen door. Clem gazed out from her darkened bedroom, and in the pool of light from the kitchen window, she made out Mei Mei's silhouette knocking softly on the door. The cook let her in and the door shut behind her, erasing the snatch of conversation and laughter from the staff.

Clem remembered the look in Richard's eyes, and imagined what those eyes would hold when the book of testimonies was published, and Mei Mei's name was celebrated as the fearless bondmaid who had been instrumental in abolishing a system that abused young girls. Her hands clenched into tight fists. She could not allow that to happen.

An hour later, a dark figure made its way along the winding path of the plantation towards the schoolhouse. The door was unlocked, and Clem entered easily. She went to the table and looked long and hard at the thick exercise book lying there. Then she took out a box of matches from the pocket of her frock and struck a match. Eyes shining with a curious light, she held it to the cover of the exercise book. When the match burnt out, she exclaimed in annoyance and lit another one. This time the cover caught fire. Clem stepped back, and with parted lips watched the fire kiss the book, crackling merrily as the pages burnt to cinders. Suddenly, the tongues of flame spread to the cheap wood of the table.

Clem stepped back with an exclamation. The table burnt

steadily, before the flames began to glide down the legs on to the wooden floor. With a scream, Clem rushed to the door and ran outside. The fire was out of control now. Like a deranged monster, it attacked the floor, licked the net curtains at the window, and spread to the wooden benches the children used for studying. Clem watched in horror, her blue eyes wide, her mouth opened in a silent scream.

There was a shout in the distance, and galvanized into action, Clem ran away. She skirted the schoolhouse to the winding path at the back. This would take her on a circuitous route back to the house, without passing the *kampong* where the workers lived. Clem raced down the track, her golden hair flying in the wind that had sprung up, her back to the burning schoolhouse, her mind in chaos, every instinct on alert to reach the bungalow undetected. Under the cover of darkness, she walked through the flower garden to the front door. Fortunately, Sher Singh had not locked up for the night and, with dishevelled hair and a grimy face, Clem climbed the stairs to her bedroom. From the window there she watched Richard, John and a retinue of servants running to the burning schoolhouse with pails of water.

She closed her window and sat on the bed, drained. *At least that darned book has been burnt to cinders,* she thought. Her hands trembled; she had not expected the whole schoolhouse to burn down. Her eyes grew heavy and, fully dressed, she lay on her bed and slid into a dreamless sleep.

Clem awoke to the sound of knocking on the door. The sun was streaming in through the window, and she got up from the bed and looked outside. The charred remains of the schoolhouse were still smoking. She went to open the door.

Eleanor was in her dressing gown, and her face was white with shock.

"A terrible thing has happened, Clem! There was a fire in the schoolhouse last night. Mei Mei said she had doused the lantern when she returned to the house, and we don't know how it started. The book of testimonies is burnt to cinders. Poor John will now not have the evidence needed to pass that Bill. But there is a greater tragedy. A little boy called Ali was in the schoolhouse at the time of the fire and he ...he's dead. His charred remains have been found." Eleanor burst into sobs.

Clem stood turned into stone. "A little boy died in the fire," she whispered. "Why was he there?"

"Dear child, don't take on so. Why, you are as white as a ghost! It seems that Ali, the little boy, used to sometimes sleep in the back room of the schoolhouse and do his homework there. His family is large and noisy, and he escaped there often to spend the night. The police are coming to investigate the death.

"What a terrible thing to happen! I am going down to John. He is beside himself, berating himself for agreeing to Sandra's foolhardy way of gaining evidence of abuse from vulnerable bondmaids. He says this is the end of any political ambitions he harboured. He will give up working for the Bill, he said. I have never seen him so distraught! He even suggested that Lee and the Chamber of Commerce hired hoodlums to set fire to the schoolhouse to destroy the book. I must go, dear child."

Clementine watched the police arrive at the distant schoolhouse and her heart thumped with dread. Her trembling hands covered her face and she burst into racking sobs. Her action had killed an innocent child. She was a monster. But how could she have known there was someone in the back room? She had only wanted to destroy the book, and the Chinese Chamber of Commerce had wanted to do that too.

Lunch was a sombre meal. Mei Mei was at the *kampong*, comforting Ali's family. Richard's green eyes held a sheen of tears and his voice was soft as he said, "I loved Ali. He was a scamp— mischievous and lazy, but with a heart of gold. He was only eleven years old. He was coming along nicely with his studies. His family is one of the poorest in the plantation. The father is always gambling, and there are too many mouths to feed. Ali used the schoolhouse as his special place, his sanctuary."

Like Roche Rock, Clem thought, horrified. Poor Ali had been like her. If only she had known that he was there. A solitary tear trickled down her cheek.

Jeffrey Peters, the overseer, came into the dining room, and a melancholy Sher Singh served him a plate of hot roast beef and potatoes.

"The police think it was arson," Jeff said, after taking a few mouthfuls of beef. "There were matches on the floor. The little boy had died of smoke inhalation. The police think that the book was the target of the arson, and the arsonist did not know that the boy was in the schoolhouse. John is debating whether to press charges against the Chinese Chamber of Commerce."

"It won't bring back the dead," Richard said softly, before rising from his chair and leaving the room. His food remained untouched.

The ruins of the schoolhouse had stopped smoking by the next morning, but the stench of burning remained in the air for a week, and the burden of remorse continued to burn brightly in Clem's heart.

John Harrison was surprised to see her knock and enter his study a fortnight after the fire.

"Uncle John, I have a favour to ask of you." Clem's eyes were downcast, her face white and pinched. She looked ill. "I understand that my stepsisters are at an orphanage or workhouse. Is it possible for you to track them down? And if you do find them, would you have them admitted to St. Peter's boarding school in Devon? The school fees are to be paid from the lease dividends of my Cornwall house."

And so it was, that in 1934, Clementine Arbuthnot finally did the right thing by her stepsisters. What no one knew was that it was atonement for the dark deed she had committed one night, a deed that had robbed the world of a small boy's innocent smile.

PART FOUR

Love and Duty

Singapore 1934–1941

"Happiness and moral duty are inseparably connected."
George Washington

14

November 1934

Queen Street resounded with noise and chatter as Richard sat with Mei Mei and Winnie at a roadside hawker stall, eating lunch. The scent of frying lard was strong, mixing with the fragrance of coconut from the chicken curry boiling in a huge wok at an Indian stall nearby. Richard laughed with delight as he watched the stallholder toss the noodles into the air. A small shaft of flame spiralled out of the wok, lighting up the leathery face of the chef. Richard's hands itched for his drawing pencil and pad, but he knew that would be rude: he was Mei Mei's guest, and was expected to make conversation with Winnie.

All Winnie could talk about was Dan Long. "I have not heard from Dan Long in three years," she said in a teary voice. "He was teaching in a school and had savings. He even told me that in another year he would be back in Singapore. Then silence. He did say that he was attending some rallies, so I believe he is mixed up in Chinese politics."

"I wonder if he is taking part in the Long March?" Richard looked hungrily at the noodles on his plate and began to eat with gusto.

"What is the Long March?" Mei Mei asked, daintily nibbling

at dim sum from a steaming wooden basket.

"I say, this noodle dish is delicious." Richard smiled, before continuing, "There is a chap called Mao leading the Red Army against the government in China. Chiang Kai-shek of the Kuomintang Party is chasing the Red Army, and I heard that the communists are fleeing from the southern provinces to the north and west. But Dan Long's sympathies are with the Kuomintang, so he should be all right."

"Oh, I don't know," Mei Mei frowned. "Dan Long's leanings were always leftist. It is probable that he's shifted his sympathies to the Red Army."

"Then he is in trouble." Richard gazed outside where it was getting dark. "It's going to rain again. I will be off. Thank you for the very tasty meal, Mei Mei. Can I give you a lift to your shop?"

Winnie went into a paroxysm of coughing, and Richard looked at her with concern. "I say, you need to have that cough seen to. It does not sound like the cough one gets with a cold."

Winnie nodded while Mei Mei said, "I will come back to the house later. You go ahead, Richard."

Alone with Winnie, Mei Mei looked up, her eyes shining with a strange light. "Clementine is jealous of me, Winnie. She warned me off Richard."

"And are you in love with each other?" Winnie asked, eating the last of her fried noodles with gusto.

"We've kissed," Mei Mei whispered.

Winnie sighed impatiently. "Mei Mei, you are a native. Richard will never marry you. Do you want to be his mistress?"

Mei Mei blushed and lowered her eyes. "I don't know."

Winnie stood up, her eyes angry. "Liao Mei Mei, what would Dan Long say if he saw you mooning after an *angmoh* and wanting to be kept by him? Shame on you."

Mei Mei protested, "I love him, Winnie. I think of him day and night. I dream of him making love to me."

"Control your emotions," Winnie said in a loud voice which set her coughing again. After she had recovered, she said softly, "Richard will be married to Clementine in due time, and then you will regret tarnishing your reputation. No Chinese man will marry a British man's native mistress." Winnie continued, "You want to be a mother, Mei Mei. What kind of life will you give your child if you are bound to a man outside matrimony? Your child will always be called a bastard."

The colour fled from Mei Mei's face. Winnie nodded and said, "Yes, think carefully of the future, dear friend. If Richard really loves you, he will propose marriage. Otherwise, don't give him any thought."

Mei Mei rose from the chair, shaken. With tearful eyes, she said, "You talk sense, Winnie, you always do. I will not be ruled by emotion. If Clementine marries him, she will make sure that Richard never sees me again."

* * *

The rains came early that year, sweeping the land with a vengeance, uprooting young trees, overflowing monsoon drains, pummelling the rubber trees in the plantations and halting work. The rubber latex was useless diluted with rainwater, and there were no tin cups to be seen tied to the tree trunks as rain obliterated the land. The workers sat idle in their houses with no food on the table; their wages were paid daily, and without rubber tapping, there were no wages to be had. Some of the workers came to the Harrison bungalow to beg for work cutting the plantation grass—they needed to feed their families. A few used their savings and free time to frequent gambling dens and brothels in the city, leaving their wives weeping at home. While John Harrison and his foreman, Jeffrey Peters, were busy implementing plans and projects to keep the workers occupied spraying the drains and cutting grass to prevent the scourge of malaria, Richard paid scant attention to his father's livelihood, immersed in his art and his model.

Richard's studio, a cheerful room stacked high with easels, oils, brushes, palettes and unfinished pictures, had a sloping roof broken by two huge skylights filtering in the scattered light of a cloudy day. Mei Mei, wearing a Chinese wedding dress, sat on a chair at one end of the room with sunlight illuminating the contours of her face.

Richard stood in the middle of the room at his easel, where Mei Mei's umpteenth likeness was taking shape. As he studied the shapeliness of her head and the proud lift to her chin, he tried to commit these attributes to memory so that he could work on the portrait without the model.

"I need you to wear different clothes for the next sitting," he murmured, his brush slowly etching her forehead on the canvas.

Mei Mei asked haltingly, "What should I wear?"

Richard blushed. His imagination ran riot, conjuring up

Mei Mei in the nude, and he came back to earth on seeing her perplexed and apprehensive face.

"Oh, dress up in trousers and tunic. I want to portray you as a Chinese beauty gazing at a frangipani flower. In a few years' time, I hope to have an exhibition of my paintings at the Raffles Hotel promenade. Your portrait will be shown too."

Mei Mei smiled at Richard, innocently wondering why he was so red in the face.

"Why a frangipani flower?" She was intrigued.

He envisaged her holding a flower in her hand, gazing at the five white petals with yellow edges, and murmured tenderly, "You are like the scent of frangipani, sweet and lingering." He frowned as a tendril of fine hair fell over Mei Mei's alabaster forehead, and he strode to her chair to push it back into place with infinite tenderness.

She blushed when he gently stroked her hair. When he uncoiled her plaits and ran his fingers through the silken strands, she uttered a small cry and moved away to the wall.

"No, Richard," she said, her voice firm. "No more kisses and fondling. What are your intentions towards me?"

Richard looked at Mei Mei, his mouth open. "What do you mean?"

"Do you love me enough to marry me?" Mei Mei asked in a loud voice, fearlessly meeting his puzzled eyes.

After an eternity, he spoke. "Mei Mei, I love you with all my heart. I can never love another. But I cannot offer you marriage now. My parents will disinherit me. I must wait until I am financially independent and then I will marry you. Be patient,

Mei Mei."

Mei Mei nodded. "We will stop the art sessions, Richard. We will not go out together or meet at the cinema or opera. When you are financially independent, court me, Richard. I will have it no other way. My reputation is at stake. People are talking."

Richard sighed but said stoically, "All right, my love. I do not want you seen as my mistress, because I know that is the way British people think. I admire your courage, your endurance, and your optimism. I want to make you my own."

A red flush spread over Mei Mei's face like the setting sun streaking the sky. Richard's heart beat with joy when she lowered her face and coyly whispered, "I hope your paintings will soon fetch a lot of money, and then we can be together."

As Richard returned to his easel, all Mei Mei could think of were his words: *I want to make you my own*. Her eyes unconsciously reflected the singing of her heart. She gazed at Richard with the flush of first love in her expressive eyes. And great artist that he was, he captured the expression on canvas for the last time.

May 1935

It was a blisteringly hot day. The reed mats drawn halfway over the windows of the Long Bar at Raffles Hotel, and the fans whirring frantically high in the ceiling, were insufficient to cool the brows of the customers sitting at the tables surrounding the bar, who insouciantly refreshed themselves with make-shift paper fans or newspapers. There was a pleasant hum of lunchtime conversation as waiters hurried from behind the bar with trays laden with food. The air was thick with cigar smoke as the British gentry puffed away over their beers and Singapore Slings.

Tessa Dolittle wrinkled her nose as the smoke from the cigar of a rotund man at the next table wafted over her. Married to Stephen Dolittle for three years, to her chagrin, their union had failed to produce any offspring, making Tessa wear a perpetually irritated expression on her face. Where she had been slim with long, dark hair when taking the grand tour with Clementine, now she was plump with cropped hair. She looked unhappy as she sipped her vodka.

"I consulted a doctor in Harley Street when I went home for Christmas," she confided to Clementine, who was sitting opposite her sipping a lemonade. "He said I had to make love many more times if I hoped to conceive a child. There's little chance of that when Stephen spends most nights at his mistress's place. They have two little girls too."

The colour faded from Clementine's face. Tessa was living what Clementine perceived would be her future nightmare married to Richard.

"Why does Stephen go to his mistress every night?" she asked faintly, an expression of distaste spreading over her white face.

"These natives are wily with their ministrations." Tessa's mouth twisted into a frown of disdain. "They are very good in bed, let me tell you, Clem." She tossed her head. "I don't care. He had a mistress before our marriage, but was it wrong of me to expect him to give her up after we had wed? One child was born before our marriage, one after. I will give our marriage another year, but if no baby comes along, I will return to England without Stephen."

Clem looked away from the film of tears in Tessa's eyes. After her friend had recovered, Clem leaned forward.

"You must help me, Tess. I love Richard, but there is a native girl tagging after him. Unfortunately, she is not only beautiful, but she saved his life. Of course, Richard will marry me, but I don't want to be burdened with a mistress."

Tessa laughed mirthlessly. "Mei Mei is her name, I think. Yes, there is talk about her and Richard. I am surprised that John and Eleanor have not disciplined him yet." She wiped the beads of perspiration from her round face with a hot towel that the waiter had solicitously placed near her place mat, and sipped the Singapore Sling from a frosted glass.

"You are becoming an alcoholic, Tess. You downed that vodka, and now you're having a cocktail." Clem frowned. "Richard is not a child who can be disciplined. He is a grown man. I see how he looks at her at the dining table," she muttered. "He sees himself as her knight in shining armour."

Tessa looked with discernment at the steak and kidney pie in front of her. "I daresay that the portions in this hotel diminish by the day. Pity that the prices escalate at the same time. Well, what do you want me to do, Clem?"

"Speak to Aunt Eleanor," Clem said promptly. "She scoffs at me when I suggest Richard loves Mei Mei. I am certain she will listen to you."

Tessa looked at Clem, who flinched at the pity she saw directed towards her. "Even if Eleanor and John speak their minds about his interest in Mei Mei, they cannot stop Richard from keeping her as his mistress when you are married. It is quite an accepted practice."

Clem's eyes were blue shards of ice. "I will never share Richard with another woman," she said, her voice hard.

"What choice will you have? Look at Stephen."

Clem's mouth was a hard line. "There are always choices." She said abruptly, "Jeffrey Peters wishes to court me. He is a dear friend, but I don't love him."

Tessa's knife and fork clattered to the floor and she gave a nervous laugh as the waiter placed a new, shining set of cutlery by her plate. When he had left the table, Tessa said in a cold voice, "I rather thought Jeff was interested in me. He comes over to our house quite often."

A spark of pleasure lit Clem's eyes. "You are married, Tess. I love Richard with a passion that scares me. I will say no to Jeff, don't worry. I hope that he and I can remain friends. You will help me with Eleanor?"

Tessa sighed. "Yes." She looked shrewdly at Clem and said, "If I were you, I would allow Jeff to court you, and I would marry him. Jeff is a good man, without a mean bone in his body. And most importantly, he is not in love with another woman."

"Richard is like the air I breathe," Clem said. "I cannot visualize a future without him."

Tessa looked nonplussed. "Too much emotion is not a good thing, Clem. You sound obsessed. Does Richard love you?"

"He kissed me and courted me before Mei Mei came along," Clem said, her face black.

Tessa waited until the waiter, who had arrived with dishes of custard and jelly, had left the table. She shook her head at Clem.

"Richard is not like other Englishmen. I would not be surprised at all if he decided to marry a native. He is bohemian and free-spirited." Tessa rose, and her chair grated against the wooden floor. "I will see what I can do, Clem. Thanks for lunch."

Clementine watched Tessa leave through the swing doors into the bright sunlight outside. Her eyes smouldered with a deep emotion as she thought of Richard and Mei Mei. Would Tessa be successful in her mission?

* * *

Eleanor Harrison looked uneasily at her visitor, Tessa Dolittle.

"It's one thing to give shelter to a Chinese *mui-tsai*, Eleanor," Tessa said in a conversational tone, "but when this girl plays with your son's affections, your husband's reputation is at stake. Mei Mei and Richard were seen cavorting around in public."

Eleanor's face went purple. "C…c…cavorting around?" she asked in a whisper. Her eyes goggled. "Where?"

"At the Padang," Tessa said with satisfaction. "Richard had set up his easel underneath a tree and was painting Mei Mei, who was posing for him seated on a bench. Preposterous!"

"Richard was painting Mei Mei?" Eleanor heaved a sigh of relief. "Well, that can hardly be called cavorting, Tessa! Really! My son is a painter and Mei Mei is his friend. What's the harm in him painting her?"

Tessa narrowed her eyes into slits. "The British gentry here do not cross lines, Eleanor. Richard and this Chinese girl were seen eating at one of the wayside hawker stalls and laughing together.

A friend of mine saw them together at New World. Mei Mei is not our equal, Eleanor. What you seem to forget is that Richard is twenty-two years old, and this girl is only about three years younger than he is. They have their places in society to keep, Eleanor. I'm sure Richard is not thinking of marrying Mei Mei, is he?"

Eleanor's bosom heaved, and her face reddened. "Marry her, Tessa? How can you say such a thing?"

"Well then." Tessa's face was triumphant. She looked sagely at Eleanor. "John's reputation has taken a beating after the little Malay boy was killed in the fire at your schoolhouse. The natives despise him for prying into their lives, and the Chinese Protectorate has cut off ties with him. His political ambitions are in shambles. The last thing he needs now, Eleanor, is a scandal involving his son and a bondmaid. Take heed."

* * *

John Harrison found his son sitting on a bench in the orchard, eating a ripe apple while twilight folded the landscape in a misty hue.

He sat next to his son and said, "Richard, you are our only child and Eleanor and I have many expectations of you. What are your feelings for Mei Mei?"

John watched the colour flee from his son's face and sighed.

"Your face tells me that you are in love with her. This won't do, Son. We don't marry natives, you know that. People are talking about the two of you, and it will be hard for me to show my face at the Singapore Club. I don't like being ridiculed. After the tragedy at the schoolhouse, I need to extricate myself from associations with bondmaids, and focus on rubber planting, and you must help me. Mei Mei is nineteen years old, and Mistress Meisheng no longer has any claim on her. She is now free to leave our house and make her home elsewhere. I have hired a new Eurasian teacher for the school, and Eleanor has suggested that Mei Mei goes to live with her friend, Winnie. This is all for the best, Son."

Observing the obstinate curl to Richard's lip, his father hastened on. "Wait for three years, Richard, and know your own heart. In the meantime, try to stay away from Mei Mei." John Harrison hesitated. "After three years, if you feel that you can't overcome your feelings for her, I'll purchase the apartment over her tailoring shop, and you can keep her there as your mistress."

Richard jumped angrily to his feet. "Mei Mei will never be my mistress, Father! If she cannot be my wife, I will stay away from her and not see her again." He looked at his father candidly. "Very well. I will do nothing for three years and then we will talk again. Be warned, Father, that if after this period I realise that Mei Mei is the love of my life, I will marry her, no matter what you say."

"We will see about that." John's eyes glinted with anger and determination. "If you marry a native, you can kiss the plantation goodbye. I will sell it rather than hand the reins to you. You had better hope that your paintings fetch enough money for you to support a family, if you are intent on marrying Mei Mei. Eleanor and I will leave Singapore if you marry a native. We will never be able to hold our heads up in British society again! To think we raised you to bring shame and scandal upon us."

John Harrison strode away, leaving his son white-faced on the bench. Richard understood the distress and shame his parents would feel if he married Mei Mei. He remembered his father arriving home late, tired and dirty from the Malaya plantation, at the beck and call of an unkind employer; his mother spending months shivering with malaria; and his own experiences of tuberculosis, when taking a breath was a commendable feat. His parents had worked hard for their status in society, and one action on his part would denigrate the reputation they had built for themselves. Richard doubted whether his mother would survive the shame of becoming a pariah—the mother-in-law of a native girl. Richard's full and sensual lips trembled, and his eyes grew moist. It was as if Fate had placed a weighing scale before him, on which balanced love and duty. Which would be the heavier weight?

Richard sighed. He shut his heart away for good, in a wooden box with a sturdy lock, guarding his dreams—dreams of lying in Mei Mei's arms, laughing at her fears of an early death, kissing away her worries until she melted into him; of painting her with his child at her breast, wiping away the sorrows she had endured in her young life by giving her happiness, marking her with the accolade of an Englishman's wife to drown forever the stigma of being a slave. But could the phoenix of a life with Mei Mei rise from the ashes of his parents' devastation? Shaking his head, Richard slowly made his way home. There really was no choice, after all.

January 1936

It was dusk, her favourite time in the tropics, as Clementine walked in the cooling air towards the *kampong* where the plantation workers lived. In her hands, she carried baskets of food and medicine. Since Ali's death, Clementine had formed the habit of visiting his family with gifts every week. While this did not remove the look of sadness from Ali's mother's face, it somewhat alleviated the suffering caused to the family by his father's gambling habit.

The tappers were humming tunes as they wound up for the night, but happiness eluded Clem. She had been elated after Tessa's conversation with Eleanor: the painting trysts in the attic had miraculously stopped, as had Richard and Mei Mei's sojourns into the city to sample local cuisine or visit the cinema. After a decent interval to allow Richard to overcome his depression, Clem had tentatively asked him to escort her to the Governor's Ball.

"I am not going," he had said tersely, turning his face away from her. "Ask Jeff to escort you."

"What about a picnic then?" Clem had tried to infuse cheeriness into her voice. "A moonlit picnic at the Botanic Gardens? I hear the new symphony orchestra will be playing there next week."

Richard had turned a ravaged face to her, and Clem had flinched at the unhappiness on his face. "Clem, I may as well tell you now as later. I intend to remain a bachelor all my life. Painting and taking care of my parents are my priorities."

The colour fled from Clem's face and her voice trembled as

she asked, "Why, Richard? Can you never love me?"

Tears had sprung to her eyes on seeing the pity on his face. "No, Clementine. I am sorry."

Eleanor had found her in a flood of tears in her bedroom later, and had counselled her wisely.

"You need to give Richard time to overcome his infatuation with Mei Mei," she had soothed. "Arouse jealousy in my son, Clem," she had continued, a smile tugging at her mouth. "Jeffrey pays enough attention to you, God knows. Why not flirt with him? It will rouse Richard, I promise. Your twenty-third birthday is coming. I will ask John to hold a dance in your honour. Your own ball, Clem! Think of that."

Smiling serenely, Eleanor had sailed out of Clem's bedroom, leaving a doubtful girl behind.

July 1936

The Harrisons celebrated Clementine's birthday with pomp and style by throwing a lavish ball in her honour at their bungalow. Cleared of tables and chairs, the drawing room became a makeshift dance floor, and a musical band, hired specially for the occasion, played popular tunes. A white tent on the lawns housed a resplendent buffet supper, and the guest list included the cream of Singapore's British gentry, a reflection of John Harrison's prominent social position. Clementine looked lovely in a sequined sky blue silk gown, the colour matching her eyes as they sparkled with joy and anticipation. Her golden curls, mastered and dressed high on her head, revealed the swan-like quality of her throat.

Jeff appeared at the door in a crumpled dinner jacket, his

straw-coloured hair brushed hastily back, and the tiredness in his eyes reflecting a hard day at the plantation. Clementine swept imperiously towards him.

"Where is Richard?" she demanded, a shrill edge to her voice, her eyes straying beyond Jeff to the street filled with people.

"I don't know." He looked at her curiously, noting the angry sparkle in her eyes. "I went to my bungalow straight from the plantation. The studio lights were on in the house. Richard must be so busy finishing a painting that he forgot the time."

Clem rushed to the staircase, oblivious to the curious stares from her guests, and climbed to the attic. The door of Richard's studio stood ajar, and Clem peeped in cautiously. At first, she thought there was no one in the studio, but as her eyes adjusted to the gloom, she saw Richard seated by the easel where Mei Mei's portrait held pride of place. As she watched, Richard leaned over and kissed the lips of the portrait.

A sob caught in Clem's throat and, gasping, she fled down the stairs, wiping angry tears from her eyes before entering the drawing room. She skirted the dancing guests and made for the veranda.

When Jeff found her, she was pale but composed.

"What is wrong, Clem?" he asked, his heart turning over on seeing her desperately unhappy face. "Life can be good, but only if you search for happiness in the right places."

Colour returned to Clem's face. She blinked back tears and smiled tremulously at him. "You are right, of course. I don't know why I chase a fantasy, Jeff."

Awkwardly, Jeff took a satin box out of his pocket and

presented Clem with a sapphire ring belonging to his grandmother.

"I am not Richard, Clem," he said softly, "but I do love you with all my heart. Wouldn't you rather have a man like me, than someone whose heart belongs to another? We both know the score, Clem. I will take care of you, and our friendship will blossom into love. Please, Clem, consider my proposal seriously."

Clem's eyes brimmed with tears. She looked at the ring and said, "Jeff, you are sweet."

"Will you marry me?" he asked. "I am not a wealthy man, but my salary and savings are enough to build a cottage in Yorkshire, and a small bungalow here in Singapore." Jeff's voice choked, and his thin lips trembled.

All Clementine saw was Richard tenderly kissing Mei Mei's likeness, and before her throat closed up, she muttered, "Yes, Jeff, I will be your wife. You are as good as any other suitor I am likely to have. I don't bring a large fortune with me, but I do own a house in Cornwall. You're right; it is fruitless to hanker after a man who doesn't love me. I have always treasured our friendship, and I will do my best to love you."

After a minute, she said softly, "Jeff, you must give me time to change Aunt Eleanor's mind. She has set her heart on my marriage to Richard. I will not wear the engagement ring now."

Jeff smiled wryly. "In Eleanor's eyes, I am the hired help and no better than Sher Singh as a son-in-law." He said softly, "Richard has not been able to overcome his emotions for Mei Mei. But please do not accept my proposal because you can't have Richard, Clem. Do so out of regard for me, and with the conviction that once we are married you will be able to love me.

Shall we dance?"

The cloying scent of frangipani was overpowering, and Clem quickly nodded and took Jeff's arm to go into the drawing room.

March 1937

The chandelier in the ballroom sparkled and shone, throwing its illumination on scores of landscape paintings on the walls, lighting up a fiery sunset here and a serene green field there. As she walked slowly around, Clementine noted that Richard's first solo exhibition at the Raffles Hotel had been well attended by the British gentry and upper-class Chinese residents. Mei Mei's portrait stood on a pedestal in the centre of the room. Unknowingly, Richard had captured the enthrallment of first love in Mei Mei's eyes. Clementine was turning her face away when she froze.

A young Chinese man in his late twenties, dressed in a Mandarin tunic, was gazing so fixedly at Mei Mei's portrait that his absorption in the painting had become noticeable to the other visitors. Clementine saw a frown crease Richard's smooth forehead as he noted the intent contemplation of the young admirer.

Richard turned at his father's voice. John and Eleanor Harrison were striding towards him with an old Chinese man dressed in rich robes by their side.

"Richard, I want you to meet Mr Gan. He is the head of one of Singapore's most illustrious Chinese families, and our neighbour at Boat Quay, where he has a rice warehouse." John Harrison made the introductions with flare, and his face glowed with paternal pride as he continued, "His son, Shiwei, is smitten with Mei Mei's portrait, and Mr Gan wants to purchase the painting for his son."

"Is that your son?" Richard wagged his finger at the young man gazing at Mei Mei's portrait, and his green eyes smouldered with jealousy.

Old Master Gan smiled, showing two gold-capped teeth. He was in his early sixties, short in stature, with bright eyes and a long, thin beard hovering uncertainly above his waistcoat.

"Yes, Mr Richard, that is my son, Shiwei. He has met many beautiful Chinese maidens in his young life, but I have never seen him so captivated by a maid's beauty before. I'm willing to offer you a hundred dollars for the portrait."

Staring at the young man gazing at Mei Mei's image, Richard's eyes lit up with an alien primitive rage. He was barely civil as he said, "That portrait is not for sale."

He turned away from his parents' bewildered eyes and stumbled blindly out of the ballroom. In the corridor, he paused, his hands trembling with emotion. When would his paintings sell, allowing him to be financially independent? Would it be too late? For he had discovered from the young Chinese man's rapturous gaze that Mei Mei was ripe for the picking.

Clementine stood by Mei Mei's portrait, her shoulders hunched, her face white. Only her eyes, fixed on the painting and burning with intense emotion, suggested the turmoil within her.

Why could Richard not forget this native girl?

15

December 1937

Mei Mei would never be able to forget that day. The wet market had been filled with noise and colour, as women in bright sarongs bargained loudly with the fishmongers. Mei Mei had purchased some fish and walked slowly back to Winnie's quarters. Entering the sitting room of the flat they shared, she had been surprised not to see the familiar sight of her friend hunched over the table, marking student homework. It was then that she had heard Winnie coughing loudly, and she rushed to the bathroom, where she watched, horrified, as her friend regurgitated blood-red spittle into the basin.

After that, events had unfolded with such speed that Mei Mei had felt she was on a spinning carousel, unable to disembark. Winnie had been diagnosed with tuberculosis, had temporarily relinquished her teaching post, and left to live with her stepmother, Mona Ma, in her *kampong*. Winnie's father had died in Australia, leaving Mona Ma and her stepsisters as Winnie's only surviving relatives. The school's principal kindly allowed Mei Mei accommodation in the teachers' quarters, in exchange for light teaching duties and child-minding the younger students. The doctor had said that a lung operation was necessary to save

Winnie's life. That operation cost a thousand dollars, and the sale of Mei Mei's floundering tailoring business would not be sufficient to raise such a huge sum. Mona Ma and her family lived from hand to mouth and could not contribute, and Winnie was sinking fast.

On a rainy day, Mei Mei walked to the wet market to do the day's shopping. A student stuffed a pamphlet into her hand, and Mei Mei read that the Malayan Communist Party was asking for money to feed refugees in China. In July of 1937 the Japanese had captured Pei-p'ing and were advancing remorselessly towards Shanghai and Nanking.

The nervous tic near Mei Mei's mouth pulsated as her thoughts dwelt on Dan Long. Her brother was unaware of Winnie's affliction, and she wondered if he was alive, for there had been no word from him for years. Mei Mei thought of the days when Winnie, Dan Long, *Kor* Poh and she had gone to New World, happy with life and optimistic about their futures. What had happened to them? All their dreams had been shattered by the cruel blows of poverty and disease. She had heard that Poh was living in a Chinatown hovel, and the Chinese girl he loved had grown tired of waiting for him to propose and had married someone else. And here she was, foolishly having given her heart to an *angmoh* who would never have the courage to marry her. Richard's love was the breeze that had set sail her boat for the shores of the future; without his passion, she was bereft. She was now that same inauspicious girl, born on the double seventh day, destined to lose all whom she loved. Her only support as she railed against her destiny had been the soft, loving words of Winnie, and Mei Mei shuddered to think that her friend would soon become as much of a memory as her father, her aunt and Dan Long. Her lips thinned into a hard line. She was determined to save Winnie's life at all costs.

After eating lunch, Mei Mei took a trolley bus to Sago Lane. The air reeked of the scent of frying lard, prawn paste and incense. Passing a death house, Mei Mei paused. The scent of incense was familiar; it was the joss-stick brand Grandma Sim had favoured. Mei Mei glanced curiously into the courtyard of the death house and froze.

His appearance had changed, but Mei Mei had no difficulty recognising Towkay Toh, as he bowed with lit joss-sticks in front of a photograph of Grandma Sim. Mei Mei stood by the courtyard door, her eyes scanning the interior for Second Mistress Meisheng, but the former call-girl was nowhere to be seen. A young boy standing behind Uncle Toh, about thirteen years of age and with a prominent squint, caught her eye.

"Chu Meng, go and fetch your mother. It is her turn to pray," Uncle Toh ordered in Hokkien, looking askance at the young boy. As the boy ran off into one of the houses around the courtyard, Towkay Toh spied Mei Mei at the door. He rushed to her and they embraced.

"Little one, I was going to visit your shop this evening," Uncle Toh said affectionately. He was thin and gaunt, and his once bright and intelligent eyes were sad and dull. His clothes, though of good quality, hung around him like a shroud. He sighed and nodded towards his mother's photo.

"Ma breathed her last four days ago. I have businesses in Calcutta, and I was informed by my associates that she was at death's door, but when I arrived, she was already gone. Her liver was shot with cirrhosis. It seems she had taken to drink." Uncle Toh's eyes were angry. "She was in Meisheng's power, and that hussy coerced Ma to sign over the House of Toh to her. I met the lawyer yesterday, and Meisheng is the legal owner of our house in Waterloo Street." He avoided Mei Mei's eyes. "Let her have it. After all, she killed for it. Come little one, let us go to your shop."

Seated on a low stool in Mei Mei's dingy tailoring shop, Uncle Toh told his story from the time of his flight from Singapore. He had spied Meisheng's former *samseng* near his warehouse at the time of Mei Mei's trial, and had known that his days were numbered.

"I knew the *samseng* because I had been one of Meisheng's clients." Towkay Toh's dark face glimmered again with a sheen of fear. He continued in Hokkien, "I understood that Meisheng had contrived Ai Lin's murder and I was the next target, so I escaped from Singapore. I struggled to make a living in Calcutta in India. I spent years kicking my opium habit. Oh, it was a wretched time, little one!" His face twitched, and he said dismally, "I have done many wrong deeds in my life, but bringing Meisheng to our house was the worst mistake of all, and I am paying dearly for it. I will leave soon for Calcutta. My atonement now lies in asking you to make your home with me. I am poor, but we will be wealthy in love, eh? What is it, Mei Mei?"

Mei Mei was shaking her head, and when she looked up into her uncle's face, he was startled to see tears swimming in her eyes.

She apprised her uncle of Winnie's condition and started to weep softly. Towkay Toh rose and took her in his arms.

After he had dried her tears, he looked at her speculatively. "On the day I reached Singapore, I visited some of my friends in the rice trade. One of them is Gan Niu—we call him Old Master Gan. He told me that his son, Shiwei Gan, is smitten with you after viewing the portrait of you painted by Richard Harrison. Shiwei desires to court you with marriage in mind, and Old Master asked me for my permission. I told him I needed to talk to you first, and Old Master agreed. He has promised a very generous dowry if his son's courtship culminates in marriage."

The joy in Mei Mei's eyes was enough to illuminate the dark shop and the whole of Sago Lane. "Will the dowry be enough to pay for Winnie's lung operation? It will cost a thousand dollars, Uncle."

Towkay Toh gave a worried smile. "More than enough," he assured her before continuing, "but you must think about this, carefully. Your whole life is before you, and you must choose your partner wisely." He stroked his face thoughtfully. "Old Master Gan is industrious and wealthy. He made his money from scratch, arriving from China on a boat with a few pennies in his pocket. Now he is one of the wealthiest rice merchants in Singapore. He is a little eccentric, immersed in ancestral worship and prayers, but what's the harm in that? I have heard his son helps him run his rice business, though they don't always see eye to eye. Shiwei Gan finished school, is educated, and is a fine musician, playing the Chinese lute."

Mei Mei's mind was made up. "I give permission for Shiwei

Gan to court me, Uncle. I have to raise money for Winnie's operation." Her voice was soft with love. "Winnie is the sister I never had, and she is my brother's betrothed. In his absence, it is my duty to take care of her. It is settled then. Please talk to Old Master. I am willing to be courted."

Towkay Toh nodded reluctantly. His eyes brightened as he said, "Little one, I have business friends who come and go from Calcutta to cities in China. Two of them told me that Dan Long is alive. He is in Nanking and embroiled in politics. I told my friends to give him my address in Calcutta. There is always a job for him in my business." He smiled at Mei Mei's radiant face. "I think Dan Long will flee Nanking soon. It is dangerous there, with the Japanese looting and pillaging. I will inform you as soon as I hear from your brother."

When Towkay Toh had left the shop, Mei Mei seated herself behind her sewing machine and thought of Winnie and Dan Long. She shivered when Chinese gongs marked the time for Grandma Sim's departure for Bukit Brown Cemetery.

From the door of her shop, Mei Mei watched Uncle Toh, Second Mistress Meisheng and Chu Meng walking in their funeral garb, Uncle Toh holding aloft the photo of his mother as the musical band led the coffin bearers along the street. As Grandma Sim left on her last earthly journey, all Mei Mei could think of was the old woman's gloating face as she sat in her chair in the hall of the House of Toh, paying her father gold coins for Mei Mei's services as a *mui-tsai*.

January 1938

Mei Mei sat on the bench in the children's playground adjoining Winnie's quarters and waited for Richard. Twilight lent a gentle and hazy hue to the landscape—the world waited for night to spread its umbra. A twig cracked, and she turned sharply to see Richard standing under an *angsana* tree, with the flame-coloured flowers above his head seeming an extension of his hair.

"You're going to be married to Shiwei Gan," Richard stated, his face white and pinched.

Tears stained Mei Mei's cheeks. "You cannot unlock the doors to my world, just as surely as I cannot enter your society, Richard. We're unsuited for marriage. Besides, Winnie has contracted tuberculosis and will die if she does not have an operation soon. The operation costs a thousand dollars, and my marriage dowry will pay to save her life. I cannot wait for you to be financially independent and marry me, Richard."

Richard strove hard to imprison a future rushing away from his grasp. "Once Winnie is on the road to recovery, you will be unhappy with your life as you did not marry for love, Mei Mei," he pleaded. "Please allow me to raise money for Winnie's operation. I will talk to Jeff and some of my other friends. It is obvious you are marrying Gan because of Winnie's ill-health, but you are throwing your happiness away, Mei Mei. Please let me help."

"No." Mei Mei's voice was sharp. "Winnie is betrothed to my brother and it is my duty to take care of her. I have made up my mind, Richard."

He turned on his heel and walked away, his shoes making no

sound on the grass.

Tears welled up in Mei Mei's eyes and streamed down her cheeks. Her breaking heart could not be restrained anymore. She flung herself on the ground. "Gods, forgive me for making Richard unhappy. I can bring him nothing but misery, and I love him too much to do that. I cannot see a future without Winnie. What else can I do, dear gods, what else can I do?" As darkness cloaked the earth, the crickets started their sudden metallic cranking, sympathizing with Mei Mei as she wept inconsolably. The scent of frangipani remained as strong as ever, enveloping Mei Mei in its sweet fragrance.

March 1938

Thunder burst across a sky punctuated by blinding lightning flashes, but the chaos outside found no echo in Mei Mei's empty heart as she sat in the bridal chamber of the House of Gan, a figure carved in stone. The house stood at the back of Beach Road, glowering over a winding lane, dwarfing smaller buildings on either side, a green-mossed giant with turrets rising out of its roof. It was rumoured that Old Master had visited London before building his legacy, and that he had been influenced by British architecture. The house was a monstrosity, the confused architect unable to elicit either a British essence or a traditional Chinese stamp from the edifice. When the sun set, the turrets gleamed orange while darkness spread over the lower storeys, and pedestrians in the lane paused to stare at the brooding structure. To one side, a forest stretched away, and huge trees swayed over the roof terrace. Behind, a disused field meandered into a busy thoroughfare.

The events of the past few weeks were like a dream in Mei Mei's mind, the residue of which remained as flitting thoughts that arrived and left, one on the tail of another, bringing no excitement or comfort, merely a nagging anxiety as to whether Winnie would be fully cured.

Shiwei Gan had courted Mei Mei for some weeks before their marriage. He was thin and angular with an effeminate face and a shock of thick black hair. There was a hint of petulance around his mouth, and a trace of wildness in his eyes. He spoke good English, but his unseemly habit of occasionally picking at a mole on his nose in public made Mei Mei cringe.

Her heart leapt with joy as she remembered the betrothal gifts the Gan family had sent a week ago, carried by a retinue of servants arriving at the small house by the sea which Uncle Toh had rented for her wedding. The red packets containing over a thousand dollars for her dowry, and the basket of pig trotters for Uncle Toh as a token of appreciation from the groom's family for raising her, were duly delivered. Mei Mei had immediately dispatched the money to Mona Ma, and five days ago word had arrived that the operation on Winnie's lung had been successful. She was on the road to recovery.

"Have some chicken and ginseng soup, Young Mistress."

Mei Mei awoke from her reverie, turned and smiled at the old bondmaid, Li Li, who stood behind her chair. Li Li had bright eyes, a thatch of white hair, and a round moon face. Mei Mei was grateful for Li Li's guidance and kindness in the alien household.

The mistress of the wedding ceremony, a distant aunt of the

groom, entered the chamber with a pair of white silk pyjamas embroidered with golden dragons. Thrusting the apparel at Li Li, she said in Hokkien, "Your mistress is to wear these pyjamas tonight before Young Master Gan snatches her virginity. Tomorrow morning, I will inspect them to check for the blood. Get the bride ready for the tea ceremony."

A clap of thunder drowned the woman's words and reverberated through the cavernous mansion like a bell of doom, the echoes ringing softly like the ghostly sound of faraway firecrackers on Lunar New Year. The wind howled angrily, and the rain pounded like fists on the mansion walls.

The Gan patriarch, a white-bearded man with piercing black eyes, sat at the far end of the huge hall of the Gan mansion. Maids stood at appointed places with urns of tea and small cups in their hands. Mei Mei bowed low with Shiwei, her new husband, in front of Old Master, before presenting a cup of tea to him.

"What grace and perfection!" The patriarch cried in Hokkien, as he beheld the beauty of his daughter-in-law. "May you bear healthy sons, who will make the name of Gan resound through Singapore. My grandfather served the Qing king in China, and it is imperative for us to carry on our line in the traditions of our revered motherland. Be a good daughter-in-law to the House of Gan and you will know happiness. Li Li!"

The elderly bondmaid hurried forward with a satin box. Old Master opened it up, and a green jade pendant held at the end of a thick gold chain shone in the light of the chandeliers.

"Young Mistress Mei Mei, my mother gave my wife this piece of jewellery when she entered the Gan house as a bride, and I am passing the gemstone to you in the hope that you expand my family tree."

As Li Li placed the necklace around Mei Mei's neck, Old Master said, "Wait in your chamber. Some of my female relatives and friends, who are making merry in the dining room, want to see you. We will have a large banquet celebrating your wedding in a week's time at the Raffles Hotel." Old Master gave a dismissive nod.

Mei Mei sat with her back straight, her hands clasped demurely in her lap, as the first flurry of Old Master's female relatives and friends came through the door.

"Well! Well! I hear the bride's beauty surpasses that of all other maidens in the country!"

Mei Mei's head jerked up at the familiar coarse voice. Her eyes wide with surprise and apprehension, she gazed directly into the kohl-lined stare of Second Mistress Meisheng of the House of Toh.

Meisheng jerked her hands from under Mei Mei's chin, recoiling sharply. "You…" Second Mistress Meisheng whispered, horrified. "It is you. I would recognise your face anywhere."

Before Mei Mei could frame a reply, Meisheng stumbled out of the room, bumping into Li Li, who was entering with a bowl of tea.

"Young Mistress?" Li Li's eyes held a calculating gleam as she gazed after Meisheng's retreating form. "Do you know Mistress Meisheng?"

Mei Mei, who had recovered her equilibrium, wiped the sweat from above her upper lip daintily with her handkerchief, before saying nonchalantly in Hokkien, "She was my Uncle Toh's concubine. How is she known to this household?"

Li Li towelled Mei Mei's sweating forehead. "Old Master and Master Toh are good friends, and Old Master retained his friendship with Mistress Meisheng after Master Toh left Singapore." Li Li's lips twisted in contempt. "The British police inspector, Robert Shipley, set up Mistress Meisheng in a nice bungalow outside the city. She was happy there with her son, Chu Meng, but the inspector's wife, Nora Shipley, would have none of that. She threatened to divorce her husband if he insisted on keeping a mistress. A few years after your trial, Mistress Meisheng was shut out of Shipley's bungalow, and had no choice but to return to your uncle's house. Old Master helps her run the rice business for old times' sake, but my sources tell me the business is on its last legs. Young Mistress, please put on your white pyjamas. Young Master will soon be here." The bondmaid glanced outside the window at the dark garden.

Lying in her pyjama suit on the canopied bed with its silken red sheet of embroidered flowers, Mei Mei allowed her mind to transgress into the familiar realm of fantasy. The memory of Richard's eyes made her want to lose herself in their murky depths, forgetting the harsh reality of her wedding day. She had dreamt innumerable times of a night laden with the scent of frangipani flowers and promise, with Richard by her side. She whimpered with the realisation that the man her heart desired would not be the one to explore her body, to lift her to unknown hillocks of ecstasy, and travel with her through an endless vista of pleasure. The scent of frangipani wafted in through the windows, as sweet as ever.

Later, when her husband was asleep, Mei Mei cried into her pillow, her insides less lacerated than her broken heart. Shiwei Gan had been tender and patient, but as he made love to her, all she could see was Richard's face, the light in his green eyes, the red tint to his hair, and the freckles on his face. She whimpered with the realisation that Richard would always hold her heart.

July 1939

Mei Mei opened her eyes and listened to the dawn birdsong from the huge flame tree outside her bedroom window. She glanced at her husband—he was in deep slumber next to her with his head buried in the pillow. More than a year had passed since her marriage, and Shiwei and Mei Mei had discovered that they were pleasant bedfellows. While Mei Mei was not in love with her husband, she felt affection for him. Lately, Shiwei had abandoned his lute and instead spent his evenings taking singing lessons with a Chinese tenor in Chinatown.

Mei Mei rose from the bed and peeped out from behind the heavy brocade curtains that hung across the window. The sun was beginning its leisurely ascent in the blue sky, and the city lay shimmering in pristine nakedness, the streets bare of traffic. Mei Mei loved this time of the morning, when the world waited with bated breath for the day to begin. She remembered such mornings in the Harrison house. Richard would sometimes stand at his easel in the back garden, trying to capture dawn in its myriad of colours. A wave of love and nostalgia swept over Mei Mei before she pushed the past firmly back to the recesses of her mind. The

Harrison houseboy, Jamal, visited her occasionally, and she had been worried to learn that Richard had taken to drink.

Mei Mei glided down the corridor and found Li Li in the laundry room, dispatching the household's soiled linen to the huge wash tubs in the back courtyard. Mei Mei took Li Li to an anteroom where they would not be overheard, and shyly informed her that she was pregnant.

Old Li Li's face broke in joy, and she gave a toothless grin. "My prayers have been answered, Young Mistress. May you deliver the heir to the House of Gan and fulfil Old Master's wishes."

The two women went along the corridor to the laundry room, where the washed household linen awaited inspection. Mei Mei quickly flicked her eyes over the sheets and clothing and nodded.

Li Li began folding the linen and Mei Mei observed conversationally, "If my aunt had not died by another's hand, she would have died of a broken heart. Her world fell apart the day Second Mistress Meisheng entered the House of Toh."

Li Li sidled closer to Mei Mei, her face reflecting sympathy and fear. "These *Karayuki-san*! They are encouraged to ply their trade in Singapore by our British masters, but they are full of coquetry and treachery, mark my words."

Mei Mei started. She rose, her hands gripping the old bondmaid tightly. "What, do you mean she is a Japanese prostitute, Li Li? Mistress Meisheng is of Chinese and not Japanese descent."

Old Li Li's garrulity overflowed the banks of discretion. "Mistress Meisheng wants people to believe that she is Chinese, but I have a cousin who lives in the crowded tenements of Chinatown, and her room-mate is a former Japanese prostitute called Osaki-san. According to Osaki, Mistress Meisheng was born in a village in Kyushu. She hid her ancestry from Towkay Toh knowing he would only marry a Chinese girl. If you look at her carefully, Young Mistress, you will notice that her nose is too sharp and her complexion too white for her to be Chinese."

"Can you take me to meet Osaki-san, Li Li?" Mei Mei asked eagerly. "It is very important for me to know Mistress Meisheng's true background. I have an old score to settle with her. I will reward you by bequeathing you some of my wedding jewellery. I hear that your great-niece in China is to be married."

Li Li's eyes gleamed with greed and pleasure. She nodded her head and hobbled away, leaving an animated Mei Mei sitting on the bed.

October 1939

On a dark, cloudy evening, Li Li, the old bondmaid, entered Mei Mei's bedchamber, her face full of apprehension. "Mistress Meisheng of the House of Toh has called on Old Master, Young Mistress! She stayed away from this house after your wedding, but now the rumour goes that her rice business is on its last legs. I thought she came to consult Old Master about business matters, but when I passed the drawing room where they were conversing, I heard her mention your name." Li Li's eyes were round with conjecture.

Mei Mei's face paled and she rose from her bed with a graceful movement to go to her dressing table. She combed her hair and applied lavender scented powder to her face. "Li Li, when Mistress Meisheng takes her leave, ask her to meet me in the small room on the ground floor next to the kitchen entrance. I wish to speak privately with her." She turned to the bondmaid, her face triumphant. "I owe you a debt, Li Li, for taking me to the blind prostitute, Osaki-San, who knew Mistress Meisheng as a Japanese prostitute. I have power over Meisheng now. She won't dare try to manipulate my life."

Second Mistress Meisheng's face was still beautiful, though applying constant make-up had coarsened the skin. Her slanted black eyes blinked in anticipation as she faced her adversary across the room.

"Little Mei Mei." Her voice was soft, the smile on her lips not touching her eyes. She spoke as usual in halting Mandarin. "We meet after an eternity. You have made a good match by marrying into one of the most illustrious families in the country. What is your business with me?"

Belligerently Mei Mei thrust out her chin and said, "Second Mistress, you have been whispering malicious gossip into my father-in-law's ears. I am sure of it! A leopard never changes its spots. Old Master may not be aware of your bad character, but I want to make sure that you won't make trouble at the House of Gan."

Mistress Meisheng drew herself up to her full height. Her lips twitched with laughter as she said, "What are you going to do, Mei Mei—tell your in-laws that I engineered your aunt's murder?" She laughed harshly. "Li Jun was sentenced for committing the murder and she is dead. I keep my ears open. Do not forget that your position at the House of Gan is tenuous since you have been unable to bear a Gan heir. There was bad gossip about you and the *angmoh* boy, Richard Harrison. I don't believe Old Master knows you kept a lover before your marriage. Your character leaves a lot to be desired."

Mei Mei stroked her stomach, protectively. Meisheng's eyes widened and the colour faded from her face.

Mei Mei's voice throbbed with anger as she cried, "You have inherited the House of Toh and become successful in your endeavour to gain respectability. You have chased my uncle away from Singapore and yet still you choose to create trouble for me. Why?"

"The British police placed me on their blacklist for suspected *mui-tsai* abuse, and kept a strict eye on my movements. Lady Matilda Robertson had influential connections at Government House. After her death, with Grandma Sim's help, I attempted to trace your whereabouts, since you were still contracted to domestic labour at our home, and had not turned eighteen. But a British police inspector visited the House of Toh and threatened to put me in jail if I ever attempted to go near you or sell you to a brothel. It was only later that I discovered you had taken shelter with a rubber planter. My movements were monitored, and all because I was trying to uphold our traditions." Meisheng's face twisted with hate.

"The *mui-tsai* system is open to abuse by people like you," Mei Mei said spiritedly. "My aunt and uncle desired to adopt me as their child, and they would have done so if you had not entered our house. My aunt was my mother's flesh and blood and she never intended for me to end up in a brothel. The slavery system is on its way to oblivion, and people like you can no longer take advantage of vulnerable girls. You have desecrated many lives. Remember Li Jun and Osaki-san? You deserve to pay for your crimes."

Meisheng's face became as white as paper. "Whose name did you speak?"

"Osaki-san," Mei Mei replied, her eyes fixed on the former prostitute's wild ones. "Do you remember her? You recruited her from Japan with the promise that she would work in a rubber plantation. Instead, you sold her to a brothel, like you were going to do with me."

Mei Mei continued quietly, "You are a Japanese woman who arrived here from Kyushu province in 1905. My father-in-law is a patriotic Chinese man, who donates money for the welfare of Chinese refugees of the Sino-Japanese war. Your country is at war with China—Old Master will be appalled if he learns that he's entertaining the enemy in his house."

Meisheng backed away from Mei Mei, her eyes wide with a terrible fear. Her mouth opened, and a strangled cry issued from her dry lips. She turned and stumbled blindly out of the room.

Mei Mei bit her lips and her eyes filled with such a fire of vengeance that Li Li, peeping in from around the door, quaked in fear.

*　*　*

Dawn was breaking over Singapore, the November skies cloudy, the breeze bringing with it a hint of rain, the earth smelling dank and musky. Mei Mei awoke, performed her toilette, dressed herself in a gold tunic and trousers, glided along the corridor, and tripped down the stairs to the back door. Li Li was already seated on the doorstep and smiling, Mei Mei joined her. Both women looked at the road.

A speck in the distance assumed shape and soon Jaffar, the *nasi-lemak* seller, appeared like a shimmering mirage. Two wicker baskets bounced jauntily up and down from a pole balanced over his shoulder. He stopped and grinned as he drew abreast of the two women. Without speaking, he dug out two banana leaf-wrapped packets from a wicker basket and offered them to Li Li.

Mei Mei smiled and handed him some coins. "Thank you, Jaffar Uncle. See you tomorrow."

After the *nasi-lemak* seller had gone on his way, Mei Mei and Li Li unwrapped the packets and dug into the breakfast fare with gusto. On the banana leaf was a white mound of coconut rice with fried *ikan bilis*, pickles, a piece of fried chicken and a fried egg. Mei Mei quickly spread the red mound of chilli paste over the rice. Allergic to anchovies, Mei Mei ladled the *ikan bilis* from her leaf to that of Li Li.

"I have not heard from Shiwei in two weeks," Mei Mei said to Li Li. "He is touring Sichuan province with his opera troupe, but he usually sends letters every week. No letter has come for two weeks. Daily I pray to the Goddess Kuan-Yin for his safe deliverance. China is fighting Japan, and I am afraid that Shiwei is caught in the crossfire and hurt. I told him not to go this time, what with the baby arriving, but you know your young master, Li Li. Music and singing are his passions."

When the postman knocked on the main door that afternoon

with a telegram, Mei Mei knew that it was bad news concerning Shiwei. Old Master opened the telegram in his study, and the rest of the household froze when they heard his agonized scream. There had been a skirmish near where the opera troupe was performing in China, and a single bullet had killed Shiwei.

A tear trickled down Mei Mei's cheek. What an end to her gentle, mellow husband, who had been such a fine musician. She had thought to grow closer to him through their baby, but now she had lost him forever. He would never see his child. The thought made her whimper into Li Li's breast.

Shiwei's ashes arrived a month later in an urn carried by the head of the opera troupe with which Shiwei had performed with such enthusiasm. Old Master locked himself up with the urn for a day in the ancestral hall, praying for Shiwei's soul. When he emerged, his face was drawn and haggard, his eyes swimming with tears.

"Shiwei is gone," he quavered as Mei Mei rushed to him. "Young Mistress, our line can only be propagated by a male heir, and you are my only hope. I await eagerly the birth of your son, who will pray for Shiwei's soul in the seventh lunar month and prevent him from being a hungry ghost."

Mei Mei felt a twinge of unease. Her father-in-law was obsessed with myth and ritual. What would he do if she presented him with a granddaughter?

February 1940
The cool night breeze floated in through the windows of Mei Mei's bedchamber, relieving the oppressive heat of the

confinement room, where in one corner a hot cauldron of water boiled vigorously over a spirit lamp. The crickets were silent on the moonless, starlit night in the first lunar month of a year when war raged like a roaring fire over Europe.

Periodically the chant of street peddlers coercing pedestrians to purchase their wares echoed out of the silent night. The *sinseh*, midwife, and Li Li hovered around Mei Mei's immobile form, and all waited avidly for the birth of the Gan heir. Thankfully, it was an auspicious day by the Chinese almanac.

"Richard!" Mei Mei murmured as a contraction hit her with force, springing fresh sweat from her brow. "Oh, my God, Richard!"

"Whose name does she speak?" Li Li bent her rather deaf ears to Mei Mei's moving lips.

The midwife hurried away with basins of cooling water to replenish them from the hot cauldron in the corner. Li Li, seated near Mei Mei's head, mopped her moist forehead with a cool towel. Chinese lanterns hanging from the ceiling of the bedchamber cast their dim light over the twisting, writhing form on the bed, as the *sinseh* glanced worriedly at the clock on the wall ticking away ominously.

"The baby is taking a long time to emerge," he muttered in irritation, fussing by the bedside. He glanced at the clock again. "Twelve hours in labour—I will say that the Gan bride has fortitude. I have to deliver another child at Bukit Ho Swee, and I will be late."

Mei Mei thrust out her legs with renewed vigour, gripping Li Li's gnarled hands for support, her eyes wide with suppressed pain. She screamed as the baby pushed itself out of her body, the excruciating agony tearing her private parts. She dimly heard Li Li cry, "It's a girl," before sinking into a tired slumber.

It was morning, and the sun streamed in through the Venetian blinds, flooding the bedchamber with warmth and hope. There was a crib by her bed, and smiling in wonder, Mei Mei rose to look at her baby daughter. She was sleeping peacefully, her head covered with a down of night-black hair, her pale skin translucent like papyrus. The little nose was as sharp as her mother's, and the lips were half-open lotus buds.

Li Li came into the bedchamber with blankets and towels, her face shining with joy. "Isn't she beautiful, Young Mistress?" Li Li cooed softly to the baby. "What name will you give her?"

"Hong Ling," Mei Mei said without hesitation. "She is the rainbow that came after the deluge of misfortune blighting my life. I am a daughter of the hungry ghosts, Li Li. Calamity is my companion, and the stars foretold that I would die young. If that be so, I bless Hong Ling to be what I will never be, and I gain comfort from the fact that she will live my life for me."

There was a peremptory knock on the door and Old Master Gan entered the confinement room. He looked at the baby with chagrin. "A girl—when I was praying every day for a boy-child. You are truly cursed, daughter-in-law, and a fitting daughter of the hungry ghosts." The disappointment on his face was intense.

Mei Mei said laconically, "A girl can always wed a man willing to take the Gan name. We should rejoice that a Gan child has been born, and I am positive that, through her, the Gan line will be preserved."

After Old Master had left in a huff, Mei Mei lay back on the bed, Hong Ling's chubby fingers imprisoned in her own, feeling uneasy about Old Master's reaction to the birth of a granddaughter. She could only hope that with time, the old man would grow to love the child, and not feel bitterly about the lack of a male heir.

16

March 1940

Clementine stood quietly in the sweltering heat of the Harrison back garden and watched Richard from behind a tree. He sat patiently at his easel, painting a portrait of Mei Mei standing by a stream and feeding ducks and geese on the water. No images, other than Mei Mei's likenesses, flowed from Richard's brush. Clementine had watched helplessly as picture after picture of Mei Mei took shape on his canvas. Why, he could exhibit a whole collection of paintings of Mei Mei, Clem thought derisively. His essence was so entwined with his art, that his grief at Mei Mei's marriage found expression there. He could possess her artistically, when denied her emotionally and physically.

News of Mei Mei's husband's death had reached Clementine like a bad omen, filling her with the fear that now Richard would leave his parents to court Mei Mei. When Eleanor had suggested that she accompany her to bless Mei Mei's baby, Clem had agreed with alacrity; she needed to know Mei Mei's plans. She had been relieved to see Mei Mei happily ensconced in her marital home, taking care of her baby and father-in-law. In their conversation, there had been no hint that Mei Mei would want to remarry.

She had expected it to be so easy to snare Richard once Mei

Mei was married off to Shiwei Gan, Clem reminisced. She had been sure that all she would have to do was to rupture her engagement to Jeffrey Peters, and Richard would be hers. A sob caught in her throat. She had reckoned without the strong honourable streak in Richard's nature, and his deep friendship with Jeffrey.

Clementine frowned, her eyes narrowed with speculation. *I must find a way to break off my engagement to Jeff, now that Richard is free from Mei Mei's clutches*, she thought. Jeff loved her too much to break off their engagement, however angry she could make him; but Richard would be unhappy with her and refuse to court her if *she* broke off her engagement to Jeff. He was Jeff's best friend and loved him like a brother. No, she had to devise a plot to discredit Jeff so that she would not be blamed for the rupture of the engagement.

* * *

"It is easy to do when you know how," Tessa Dolittle said, delicately nibbling at a cucumber and watercress sandwich in her beautifully decorated drawing room. She smiled at Clem, who was munching a scone. "Get Jeff in a compromising situation with a girl tapper, and no one will blame you for breaking off your engagement to him." She leaned forward conspiratorially and began to whisper instructions, watching Clem's eyes widen with apprehension and excitement.

When she had finished, Tessa leaned back on the sofa and gazed around the room. Her eyes grew soft as they rested on the baby's crib by the window.

"How simple everything becomes when someone dies," she said softly, her blue eyes narrowed with memories. "When Stephen's mistress contracted smallpox, she was gone within a week and those brats ...well, with her gone, Stephen had no time for them. Now he is all mine. You, on the other hand, have much to do before Richard can be all yours." She looked at Clem's speculative eyes and gave a tinkling laugh. "I don't mean that Mei Mei has to die. Mei Mei is devoted to her daughter and does not give Richard a second thought. Now is the time to act, Clem, to remove the thorn that is Jeffrey Peters."

They both laughed, though uneasily.

* * *

Clementine sat on the bed and an unfamiliar, uneasy feeling stole over her. All her life she had pursued her goals ruthlessly, with no thought of the pain or distress she caused others, friend or foe. Yet the thought of hurting Jeff made her pause. Fond memories of their tennis games together, of dinners filled with laughter, floated to the surface of her consciousness, momentarily making her feel guilty. But like a wave gaining strength, the overwhelming tide of her desire to possess Richard soon submerged her compassion for Jeff, wiping the pensiveness off her face and hardening her resolve. She got up, dressed in outdoor clothes and slunk out of the house.

Clementine stole into the garden like a common thief. The trees huddled together under a new moon, and only a shaft of light from the kitchen window threw into dim focus the winding garden path. When Lim Soon Lai, John Harrison's assistant overseer, stepped out before her, Clem jumped.

"Is it to be tonight?" His oily voice was a whisper above the sounds of the night.

Clementine looked intently at the assistant overseer's face. "You told me that the girl tapper, Zainab, is willing to trick Jeffrey for 200 dollars. Why?"

A soft giggle escaped the overseer's thin lips. "There are two reasons, Ma'am. One, her father lost his fortune at the Malaya casinos and the family is destitute. Two, Zainab is attracted to Master Jeff, and believes he will eventually fall in love with her."

"I daresay that Jeff, with his liberal ways, may welcome the notion of a native wife when the dust settles." Clem's mutterings came on the tail of a tired sigh. "I hope you don't want more money than I've already given you, Lim."

"Your payment was satisfactory," Lim hid the cunning in his eyes behind a curtain of humble respect.

Clem nodded. "It is to be tonight. I do not want scandal, so use an aphrodisiac which will achieve our purpose without bringing complications."

"Don't worry, Mistress. I will use *chan su*, a medicinal herb well known to us Chinese. Since it is quite potent, a small dose will achieve your purpose. The herb is made from the skin of the toad."

Clementine gave an elaborate shudder before walking away, a niggling unease filling her being. The die was cast, and Jeff would have to deal with the results.

* * *

Jeffrey Peters sat on the porch outside his small bungalow, drinking whiskey in great gulps, allowing the warm liquid to fire its way through his throat, inducing welcome lethargy after a hard day's work at the plantation. Frustrated anger enveloped him whenever he thought of Eleanor's obdurate refusal to acknowledge his love for Clementine. He knew she was waiting for her son to forget Mei Mei, and then she would arrange his marriage to Clem.

Jeff frowned. While Clem remained pleasant enough with him, their secret engagement had placed a strain on their friendship, and she did not talk to him as freely as she had before. He had hoped that Clem had developed stronger feelings for him and was now shy to confide in him as she had done in the past; but common sense told him that she remained infatuated with Richard. At dinner, she still followed his every word and move.

The mild breeze stirred the leaves of the nearby *rambutan* tree and hissed past his ear with a whisper of warning. The earth smelt dank, and he breathed in his fill, the scent of the tropics lulling his fevered brain. There was the sound of a twig snapping, and a beautiful apparition, dressed in silken robes, appeared. With his senses dulled by the alcohol in his stomach, Jeff failed to recognise the Malay woman until she spoke.

"*Tuan* Peters, I work in the rubber factory under Lim Soon Lai. We make crepe rubber for *Tuan Besar*. I also tap the trees twice a week. Do you remember me?" The woman spoke in Bazaar Malay, and her voice was lilting and sweet.

Jeffrey cast his mind back and recollected her. She was one of the new women recruits hired due to the labour shortage in the rubber industry. She had attracted his attention with her sharp intelligence and dedicated work ethic.

He smiled groggily and replied in the colloquial tongue, "Zainab is your name, right? What can I do for you?" He dragged himself up to a half-lounging position and peered at her hands encircling an enamel cup. "What have you got there?"

"This herbal tea will ease your tension after a gruelling day's work," the girl said, her eyes enormous in her round face. The silk scarf covering her head blew in the gentle breeze. "I saw you looking very tired at work and I prepared this brew for you. It is a medicine for fatigue, and the ingredients remain a secret within my family. If you like it and benefit from its therapeutic powers, I can teach you how to make it."

Soporific from the alcohol, the Malay girl's gesture assumed false proportions of tenderness, inducing Jeff to take a sip of the brew. It had an invigorating taste that lingered pleasurably on his tongue, and he finished it in a gulp.

The girl's face appeared close, and a thrill of desire rippled through his groin. He felt embarrassed when he became hard, but then he found a hand on his arm, urging him to a supine position on the grass. The night exploded around him as desire held him imprisoned in its slippery net. His all-consuming urge combined with the pleasures her touches aroused in his body, and they grappled on the grass in a frenzy of wild mating.

A stifled scream penetrated the drugged recesses of his brain, making him glance up blearily from the ground. Clementine stood at the gate, her eyes pools of horror, and her mouth trembling with a denial she could not utter.

Jeff's dreams of happiness crashed around him in the balmy night, visions nurtured over years crushed to a pulp in one insane moment. An owl screeched piercingly like a town crier announcing a tragic event, as Jeffrey stumbled into his bungalow to face a lonely, uncertain future.

* * *

The sun was rising in the east, a red ball of fire creeping over the horizon, flooding the grey sky with a promise of hope. The leaves of the rubber trees glinted in the sunlight like fireflies, joining in the song of daybreak with their mild music. A farmer on his bullock cart laboriously made his way down the dirt road, the wheels clanking against the gravel. Beyond the plantation, the *kampong* lay sleeping, its grim poverty accentuated by the harsh light of morning, bringing into sharp focus the bleak wooden huts and tiny overgrown plots where weeds and tendrils reigned in dubious glory.

Clementine walked along the plantation searching for Jeff. Her blonde hair blew in a soft breeze that kissed her pale, drawn face. Her affection for Jeff was genuine, and the task of breaking off their engagement was unpleasant and guilt-ridden. She saw him in the distance, supervising the tapping of the rubber trees, his face lost and tired.

"Jeff," Clementine said in a hushed voice. "I have no choice but to break off our engagement. The British community looks at me disdainfully, and the native community leers at me because of your indiscretion. You can understand how difficult it is to go on this way. People don't suffer fools gladly, and now they think I'm one. The only way out is to make my own way in life, without you by my side."

She clasped his hands in sudden intimacy. "Dear Jeff, you have given me innumerable moments of pleasure and offered protection from the often-cruel world. I am intensely grateful for your love and comradeship. I do not blame you in any way, and I hope that we can remain friends. I will do my utmost to dissuade Uncle John from terminating your employment."

Sudden tears blinded her eyes, and Clementine rushed away down the dirt road. Jeff watched her fade like a mirage, his heart beating with sorrow, his mind numb to the reality that his misdemeanour could cost him his job. With heavy steps, he shuffled towards the Harrison bungalow for an interview with his employer. Jeffrey tilted his head towards the sun so that the warm rays could dry his tears.

April 1940

Richard sat on an ornate chair, looking around him. He had knocked on the door of the House of Gan and asked to see Mei Mei. The maid had shown him into the study as Old Master Gan had been entertaining his Chinese Chamber of Commerce friends in the drawing room. The study was gloomy, even with the windows open. Bookshelves crowded into the room from all four walls, and the space was dimly lit by old Chinese lanterns hanging from the ceiling.

On hearing of Shiwei's death, the lock of the rusty box that housed Richard's heart had broken and he had felt reborn, his ardour for Mei Mei undimmed. Now, at last, he was free to court her. With no thought in his mind other than reuniting with Mei Mei, he had allowed an appropriate time to pass after Shiwei's death, before making his way to the House of Gan.

There was a sound by the door and Mei Mei entered. She looked beautiful in a blue cheongsam, motherhood lending maturity to her face and form. She shook hands with Richard and smiled pleasantly.

Her smile faded when he poured out his heart to her, and asked her permission to court her.

"To what end?" Mei Mei asked sharply.

Richard blinked, his mouth open.

"Are you asking me to marry you, Richard?" Mei Mei asked softly.

"Eventually, of course," Richard stammered.

Mei Mei sighed. "Richard, are you making money from your paintings?"

Richard shook his head, eyes downcast, disappointment written on his face. "After you got married, I lost the inspiration to paint. When I do, I only paint portraits of you. I cannot paint landscapes. It is almost as if you took away with you my painting abilities and motivation."

Mei Mei looked at him sadly. "I am a mother now, Richard. I must think of my daughter. If I were to allow you to court me for marriage, you must have the means to take care of not only me, but also my daughter." Mei Mei's eyes erupted with liquid fire. "Are you asking me to be your mistress, Richard?"

Words poured out of Richard, born of desperation and longing. "We would live together for a short time, without being man and wife," he said. "When you are with me, I am positive I will be able to paint. As soon as my paintings make money, we will marry, Mei Mei."

Mei Mei rose from her chair with a swift movement. Her face white, she said, "Do you think I will allow my reputation to be tarnished by being a kept woman? The scandal and sordidness will affect my daughter's future, and I won't have that. Hong Ling was born in an illustrious family, and here she will remain." A solitary tear trickled down Mei Mei's cheek. "Nothing has changed for you, Richard. You are not financially independent, and therefore you cannot marry me. And I will never be your mistress!" Before emotion overcame her, Mei Mei quickly left the room.

* * *

Clementine was dressed in an elegant white linen frock, cutting flowers in the garden. While the idea of breaking off her engagement to Jeff had brought her distress and guilt, once the deed was done, she was her usual sunny self, scheming how to instigate intimacy with Richard. He had been shocked and disconcerted at the news of the broken engagement, and had urged Clementine to forgive Jeff's indiscretion. With equal zeal, he had prevailed on his father not to terminate Jeff's employment and for once, father and son had seen eye to eye.

The garden gate flew open and Clem was startled to see Richard entering the house, his green eyes blazing with anger and his face flushed.

"Whatever is the matter, Richard?" Clem asked.

"Mei Mei would rather remain a widow and live in that stifling House of Gan raising her daughter than be with me," Richard said, his voice shaking with agitation. He rushed into the house and Clementine knew that he was going to his studio to get drunk.

When darkness had fallen, Clementine, her golden hair fanning her face in a halo, stood in front of the couch where Richard lay, an empty bottle of whiskey rolling on the floor nearby.

"What're you doing here?" Richard mumbled.

"Why do you need Mei Mei?" Clementine's voice was like a soft breeze and her breath fanned Richard's face. She sat beside him on the couch and began stroking his arm. "You have me, the English Rose." Her lips twisted bitterly, though her eyes remained alert.

Richard peered at her and muttered thickly, "A beautiful rose."

Clementine started to softly kiss Richard's neck and her lips moved to his ears to nibble affectionately. He lay still, his eyes dull and his mouth stupid, an easy target for Clem's seduction. As she bent to him, the triumphant power in Clem's blue eyes impaled Richard, who gazed at her through a haze of alcohol, not only powerless but unwilling to ask her to stop.

He made love to her with a savagery whose intensity matched the hunger in her cloudy, blue eyes. His desire satiated, he even murmured terms of endearment into her golden hair so that she would restart her tender ministrations.

Slowly but surely, Clementine made Richard her sexual prisoner until, of his own volition, he was regularly sneaking into her bedroom at night. He despised himself for his weakness, but not as much as he hated Clem for taking advantage of his vulnerability—but even after hours of making love to Clementine, Richard still could not paint his beautiful landscapes. It was as though his art was a direct expression of his finest and darkest emotions, flowering during good times and withering away in bad.

PART FIVE

The War Years

1941–1942

"What difference does it make to the dead, the orphans
and the homeless, whether the mad destruction
is wrought under the name of totalitarianism,
or in the holy name of liberty or democracy?"
Mahatma Gandhi

17

Old Master Gan sat on the terrace, his mind awash with chaotic, fear-filled images, watching twilight embrace the city. The shout of street peddlers reached his ears dimly from another world, and he was lost to the rhythms and sounds of dusk.

There was a soft footstep and Mistress Meisheng was by his side. "Old Master," she said coarsely in Mandarin, "you are unhappy, my friend. I marked you absent downstairs and the bondmaid said I would find you here."

"Meisheng, my friend, I am desperate!" Old Master cried in a desolate voice. "It is written in our scriptures that only a male heir can pray for our tormented souls in the ghost month, and I have a granddaughter. I have failed my ancestors!"

Meisheng's kohl-lined eyes flashed. "True, true. If there is no one to carry on our name, we will be punished by being made to roam the earth endlessly as hungry ghosts, and made to suffer until the end of time."

"Time is endless," whispered Old Master. "I will suffer forever!"

Mei Mei, coming up the stairs to retrieve the day's washing from the clothesline, was happy. While Japan's war on China had escalated, leading to Singapore's Chinese merchants forgoing trade with their Japanese counterparts, word had reached Mei Mei and Winnie that Dan Long had escaped the Nanking Massacre and sailed to Calcutta, where he was working for Uncle Toh. Mei Mei paused behind the terrace door on hearing voices.

"I look on my granddaughter with bitterness," Old Master Gan was saying angrily. "I cannot help it. She should have been male. My daughter-in-law refuses to marry a young man willing to assume our Gan name and beget a male heir. What shall I do?"

Mistress Meisheng raised her voice. "There is a remedy, Old Master. In our village in China, a widowed young bride would become the wife of the patriarch, be it a brother-in-law or father-in-law. That was the custom. Bring forth a marriage proposal to Mei Mei. How can she refuse you, Old Master, when she eats your salt? And beget a male heir with her, my friend."

Mei Mei gasped, and peeping around the corner she saw Old Master's eyes widen and his mouth fall open. A multicoloured butterfly alighted on the terrace balustrade and with a lightning swoop, a *mynah* bird impaled it and sat chewing impassively. Moving to the balustrade, Old Master turned his face towards the moon, rising from behind the forest bordering the house. He watched as the white globe rose higher in the sky, surrounded by pinpricks of light from the stars and planets. A curious stillness filled the air, and the world waited.

Mei Mei trembled behind the terrace door, her teeth chattering so hard that she thought Old Master and Meisheng would hear her. The moon sailed behind a cloud, throwing the terrace into shadow. A hungry lizard clucked in anticipation of its nocturnal feast, and from far away came the sound of waves thundering to the shore. Peering around the door, Mei Mei was horrified to see Old Master look at Meisheng and nod his head in acquiescence.

Her heart thumping like an engine, Mei Mei raced down the stairs, burst into her bedchamber and dressed in outdoor clothes. She knew what she had to do.

Mei Mei hailed a rickshaw for Collyer Quay. She alighted in front of an alley and paid the puller. She turned into a twisting, cobbled lane where the smaller rice businesses were located. Most of the godowns were in darkness, a solitary light here and there casting golden shafts on the dirt and garbage of the alley. Mei Mei peered at the names of the businesses emblazoned in faded letters on square plates hanging from door hinges. *Yeo Brothers Trading* warehouse was in darkness, though the door stood open invitingly.

Mei Mei entered the cool interior of the Yeo warehouse, and when her eyes adjusted to the gloom, she saw that, save for a tiny, lit office at the end of the storage area, the warehouse was in darkness. Mei Mei surreptitiously moved towards the shaft of light, her senses on the alert for danger. Even so, when strong arms captured her from behind, she uttered a petrified scream.

"What are you doing here?"

Mei Mei felt weak-kneed with relief when she recognised the gruff tones of *Kor* Poh's voice. She twisted around in the sinewy arms until she saw his leathery face. "*Kor* Poh! Don't you recognise me? I am Liao Mei Mei, your former pupil at the House of Toh."

The bespectacled man relinquished her arms so abruptly that Mei Mei nearly dropped to the floor. He pulled Mei Mei to the lit room at the end of the warehouse and examined her features slowly and carefully under the overhead light.

His face broke into a delighted smile. "Little Mei Mei," he said, "how could I ever forget you and Dan Long?" He continued in fluent Hokkien, "Oh, what carefree days we spent together, going to New World operas and films, and eating noodles. Where is your brother, Mei Mei? And Winifred? I had heard that Dan Long was in China. Oh, it was difficult to make ends meet when the British clamped down on the KMT youth movement."

Mei Mei smiled. "Dan Long is working for my Uncle Toh in Calcutta, and Winnie is teaching in a school. She contracted tuberculosis but is fully recovered now." Mei Mei quickly told Poh of her marriage, daughter and widowhood.

Poh lowered his skeletal frame into a chair. His lips twisted into a wry smile. "I was betrothed to Yiu Lin, a Chinese girl, daughter of a rice merchant. But I had no money. I could not offer her marriage. That was more than five years ago. She did well. Married a well-to-do tin merchant's son and is the mother of two boys."

Mei Mei touched Poh's hand sympathetically. "I am sorry, *Kor* Poh, you deserve better. Maybe one day you will marry the love of your life."

Poh laughed and the bitter sound grated on Mei Mei's ears. "If I had enough money, I would return to China. That is my dearest wish. My parents are old, and I wish to take care of them. My little sister got married to a farmer, but they live far from my parents' home." Poh flicked a glance at Mei Mei. "How is Second Mistress Meisheng? I remember how her triad put me in hospital when I was planning to complain to the Protectorate about her treatment of you."

"That is what I came to talk about." Mei Mei lowered her voice. "I need your advice, *Kor* Poh. Mistress Meisheng is causing mischief in my life again." She told Poh of Meisheng's conversation with Old Master and saw Poh flinch with anger. She proceeded to inform Poh of Meisheng's Japanese heritage and history.

Mei Mei said crisply, "I must stop Meisheng from encouraging Old Master to marry me. Meisheng is an evil woman; she duped my uncle and killed my aunt. Oh, if only I could prove that she is a Japanese spy! Then I would go straight to the Chinese National Emancipation Volunteer Corps and denounce her. I hear that this organisation is holding rallies and whipping up anti-Japanese sentiment in Singapore."

Poh stroked his face thoughtfully and said, "You don't need to prove she is a spy for her to experience jail." He smirked. "A source in the Malayan Communist Party gave me information that there is a shop in Beach Road where Japanese spies are known to meet. If I can get Mistress Meisheng to visit the shop, and have the authorities raid it while she is there, they will arrest everyone as spies. Even if she can later prove that she is not a spy, it will be some time before the authorities release her from jail. Mistress Meisheng will enjoy the claustrophobia of her tiny cell for enough time to break her spirit. My head still aches from the blows her thugs inflicted. I have an old score to settle with Second Mistress."

Poh's bitter face touched Mei Mei's heart. "You have experienced enough pain through that woman, Mei Mei. I will denounce her as a spy." Poh hesitated. "I don't have much money, and I will need to flee Singapore for China as soon as the deed is done, or Meisheng's triad will get me."

Mei Mei took off the gold necklace with the jade pendant that Old Master Gan had presented to her on her wedding day and offered it to her former tutor. "*Kor* Poh," she said, her voice soft, "please take this ornament. Selling it will earn you enough money to take a boat to China. I have no regrets," she continued in a hard voice, tears glistening in her eyes, "for I am sure that Mistress Meisheng engineered my aunt's murder. And I will not marry my father-in-law. With Meisheng out of the way, the old man will see sense."

When Mei Mei stepped outside the warehouse, a cool wind from the sea was whipping across the road. Mei Mei shivered as a cold hand gripped her heart. She looked back into the past, saw a stricken child gazing at her beloved aunt's immobile face, and strode with determination along Collyer Quay.

October 1941

The claustrophobic prison cell, reeking of stale air and illuminated by a bar of sunlight, resounded with a harsh sobbing that rose above the chatter of women prisoners.

Mistress Meisheng sat on the stinking floor, her body shuddering with the pent-up emotions of a lifetime. She saw in front of her not the dark, grimy walls of a prison cell, but the lush green fields of Japan, ablaze with pink cherry blossom that promised a bountiful spring. She saw six little girls playing by a stream where water bubbled in white spray, and she heard the laughter of children dreaming of an innocent future.

Her dreams had shattered—the shards of her life lay around her in the airless cell, pieces she had striven to knit into the kaleidoscope of a meaningful life. She had escaped the squalor of prostitution only to be branded a Japanese spy.

Meisheng gazed blankly at the opposite wall. She had gone to such lengths to garner a good life for her son, Chu Meng; she had even resorted to murder. First Mistress Ai Lin's face swam into her mind's eye, and she turned her face to the window. The sun's dim rays lit up the hatred in her eyes.

She should have poisoned that vicious little girl, Mei Mei, when she had the opportunity, for she had little doubt that Ai Lin's niece was avenging her aunt's murder by sending her to jail as a Japanese spy.

Was she sorry to have murdered First Mistress? Second Mistress Meisheng laughed derisively. Yes, she was sorry to have poisoned the wrong person. With Mei Mei dead, Ai Lin and Toh would have had no choice but to accept Chu Meng as the Toh heir. Why had she killed Ai Lin? At the time, the plan had seemed elementary: murder Ai Lin and blame Mei Mei. With Mei Mei safe in a juvenile home, Meisheng would have prevailed on Toh to will his money to Chu Meng.

She had reckoned without Mei Mei's courage and Toh's foresight in escaping with his wealth. That opium-ridden fool had developed clarity when it was least desired, she thought. Her eyes glittered as she recalled Li Jun's murder trial, and how she had nearly been arrested for Ai Lin's murder after the defence attorney had hinted at her complicity. Robert Shipley had saved her by lying on oath about the crab's eye seeds he had found in her dressing table drawer. From beneath the umbrella of his protection, she had continued hounding Mei Mei, but had reckoned without Lady Matilda Robertson's philanthropy and John Harrison's ambitions to be elected to the British parliament.

At least she had got the house. Meisheng giggled. Old Ma Sim had taken to drink like a duck to water. It had been easy to guide her hand to sign a will in her favour. Her eyes darkened. That accursed witch, Mei Mei, born on the double seventh, had not left her alone. Her only solace lay in the fact that Mei Mei would soon be forced to marry a half-senile old man to beget a male heir.

"Mei Mei, may you die young!"

The curse resounded eerily around the prison walls. Suddenly, the tempest of rage was over and black depression settled on Meisheng. Who knew how long her country would be at war with China? She was in the wrong place at the wrong time. She refused to languish in jail.

Slowly, she raised herself from the ground and detached her kimono sash from her dress. She moved, puppet-like, to the ventilator to tie the sash to the window bars, committing her last act of indignity, and leaving the world that had always denied her respectability.

18

Richard walked desultorily through the rubber plantation, hands in the pockets of his khaki shorts, his mind meandering through past images of Mei Mei, his attention distracted from the rubber tappers under his supervision. His mother had pressured him to announce his engagement to Clementine, and he had finally yielded. He had once resolved to stay a bachelor, but his parents' dreams of a retirement playing with their grandchildren in England after a hard life in the tropics had swayed Richard, his soft heart sacrificing his love for Mei Mei for a marriage of convenience to please his parents.

John Harrison had grown apprehensive about Singapore's vulnerability to a Japanese attack, and had refused to hold a grand celebration of his son's marriage. Eleanor had reluctantly agreed to a civil ceremony between Richard and Clementine, as war raged in the world.

Richard sighed. His thoughts were bound to Mei Mei, and he was limited by his great fear that he would not be able to love Clementine. The wooden box where he kept his heart lodged a secret belief that Mei Mei and he would one day be reunited. Wisdom told him that a physically satisfying relationship without emotional attachment spelt disaster for any marriage, and Richard could not emotionally engage with Clem. Instead, his thoughts flew on ardent wings to that slim, Chinese girl with doe-like eyes who had captured his heart on a remote island.

Richard pushed his thoughts away and turned to the houseboy Jamal, who was standing respectfully to attention in front of him.

Jamal said in a hushed voice, "Master Richard, Mistress Mei Mei wishes to meet you."

Colour washed over Richard's face and his eyes glittered. "Mei Mei? Is she ill?"

"She did not look sick, *Tuan.* There is trouble at her house, and she sent word to meet her in the fields at the back of the House of Gan after nightfall, at eight or so. She is hoping to see you tonight, *Tuan.* What message shall I take back?"

"I will be there," Richard said shortly, and watched Jamal disappear into the wooded area of the *kampong.*

His heart stirred to life, hammering away at the rusty lock on the wooden box. Forgotten was his engagement to Clementine— all he desired at that moment was to look deep into Mei Mei's lustrous eyes, to trace the dusky shadow her eyelashes made on her smooth cheeks. Throwing discretion to the winds, and with a bemused smile on his face, Richard strode towards his house.

* * *

The House of Gan stood like a black sentinel, guarding the myths and beliefs of a culture that was in danger of being extinguished by the war looming over the Asian horizon. Not a light shone in any of its windows. No one observed the shrouded figure that crept out of the back door to melt into the anonymity of the kitchen garden, only to appear again as a silhouette in the green field stretching behind the Gan mansion.

The field of trees and shrubs, bordering a normally busy thoroughfare, was quiet at night. Distant lampposts on the road, and a pale sickle moon hanging like an ornament from the inky sky, dimly lit the dark field. Mosquitoes buzzed vengefully in the grass that was as tall as man's waist, fattening on Richard's blood as he stood in the middle of the field, contemplating the night. He did not see the apparition that rose noiselessly behind him.

"Richard," Mei Mei whispered.

The world exploded around Richard at the sight of her, and emotions long suppressed strove to find liberty. He cried, "Mei Mei!"

Mei Mei looked at Richard's gaunt face, his jaw a sharp ridge above the thin neck where his Adam's apple throbbed palpably. Her heart turned over in love. This was the boy she had nursed back to health when he was hovering on the precipice of life and death. Now it was she who was helpless, facing an old man intent on making her his bride, irrespective of her wishes and desires.

She had thought that once Mistress Meisheng was gone, Old Master Gan would see sense and not pursue his plan to wed her to beget a male heir. But she had reckoned without the old man's fanatical beliefs. The fear of hungry ghosts was deeply rooted in his psyche. It seemed that the seed planted by Mistress Meisheng in the old man's mind had rapidly flowered into a steadfast determination to marry her.

Mei Mei moved towards Richard, bereft of the shackles of decorum. He saw that her eyes were glistening with tears.

"Richard, there is no one else I can turn to. You must help me escape from the House of Gan." She quickly told Richard of Old Master's plan. "The only way out is to escape to my Uncle Toh in India with Hong Ling, my baby. My father-in-law looks on Hong Ling with bitterness. What if he were to harm her?

"Once Hong Ling is older, we will come back to the House of Gan. Maybe my father-in-law will not be so stubborn and obsessed then. But war is at our shores, and Dan Long cannot come here at short notice. I need an escort on our voyage to Calcutta, and you are the only one I could think of turning to. I did try to find my former tutor, Poh, but he has disappeared. Maybe he has left for China. Please help me, Richard."

"My God!" Richard's eyes glittered with horror. "What a family you have married into, Mei Mei." He grasped her hands and a bolt of electricity shot through them at the physical contact. The lock on the wooden box housing Richard's heart sprang open.

"I loved you then, and I love you now, Liao Mei Mei," Richard said softly, holding her hands tightly in his. An idea was crystallising in his mind, and colour suffused his face. "Mei Mei, I could not offer you marriage before, because I could not take care of you in Singapore. Father would have disinherited me, and it would have been difficult for my parents to continue living in Singapore if I married a native. But now there is a way out. If we elope to Calcutta together, my absence will be mourned, but my parents will not have to live in the same place as their native daughter-in-law. They will say madness has seized me. I will return in time, but their reputation will not be tarnished too much. In Calcutta, I can start painting and try to sell my work." He rushed on. "You said your uncle has businesses in Calcutta. You may be sure that while I paint, I will work for my keep. I will work night and day for your uncle, and when I have enough savings, I will propose marriage to you. Mei Mei, my love," he cried, "I cannot live without you."

Mei Mei blushed deeply and a small smile tugged at her lips. "Yes," she said demurely. "We can get married in Calcutta." Her brows furrowed. "But Jamal told me that you are engaged to be married to Clementine?"

Richard said, softly "I have been miserable engaged to Clementine to please my parents. I am afraid if I marry her, I will soon leave her. You know me, Mei Mei, I beat my own drum."

Mei Mei lowered her eyes and said, "They say war is imminent. I read the *Singapore Herald* and the Japanese editor, Tatsuki Fuji, gives no hint of a Japanese attack."

"Fuji is pulling the wool over everyone's eyes. War is coming to Singapore." Richard's voice was sober.

Mei Mei looked at him and the past washed over her like a waterfall, images of their closeness and love cascading over each other. When he took her in his arms, enveloping her in a crushing embrace, they forgot their long separation in the sweetness of physical contact.

Languorous in his arms, Mei Mei allowed Richard's words of endearment to wash over her, cleansing her of the dark thoughts that had been her companions on desperate nights, and bringing her the happiness that had eluded her. As his lips finally found hers after long years of separation, the lovers gave themselves up to the moment, their dreams and desires mingling together in the night.

After a long moment, Richard drew away, his hunger temporarily satiated.

He said, "Japan is sure to attack us by the South China Sea. Thank God the naval base is ready. It is unlikely that the Japanese will strike during the monsoon season, so we must run away in January before war starts in earnest. We must plan our escape. It will be difficult for you to leave the house with the baby. She may cry and raise the alarm," Richard suggested tentatively.

"I have spent much time thinking about my escape from the House of Gan." Mei Mei's eyes looked far away into a delightful future. "I will send Li Li and Hong Ling to Winnie and Mona Ma an hour or two before I leave the house. Ma has relatives who will row them over to St John's Island, and later that night, I will leave the House of Gan and meet you on the beach. Jamal can row us over to the island to collect Hong Ling. We can hide out there for a day or two before we take a ferry to Tanjong Priok, the Batavia port. From there it will be easy to board a ship for India."

A light shone in the depths of Richard's green eyes as he observed, "We may be poor in our lives elsewhere, but your child shall not want for love."

Mei Mei kissed him. "You have made me so happy, Richard. Please come to meet me here whenever you can, so that we can plan the details of our escape. Jamal will be our messenger." She added tentatively, "You will break off your engagement to Clem? It will break her heart."

Richard said coldly, "Clem will get over it. I don't love her, Mei Mei. Our union would not be happy. I yielded to Mother's wishes, but I was wrong to do it." He said ruminatively, "I won't break off our engagement. There is no need raise the alarm. We will elope in January without anyone's knowledge, Mei Mei. That is the best way."

The starry night enclosed the lovers in a private world, their union sweeter due to their time apart. For the first time in her life, Mei Mei dared to dream of a future where the hungry ghosts did not lurk like menacing shadows to cut short her life.

19

December 1941

At eight o'clock on a dark, tropical night, Clementine stood at her window staring into the inky blackness. Crickets chirped, and frogs croaked loudly from the monsoon drains that brimmed with water after a heavy downpour. To one side of the house stretched the plantation, a deeper shade of ink than the surroundings, primordial and menacing. The streetlamps glowed in the misty air like hesitant beacons.

Clementine shivered in the cold wind whipping through the garden, and an icy hand gripped her heart as she saw Richard at the gate, glancing furtively over his shoulder at the house. She stepped back behind the brocade curtains and observed him through the gap in the folds as he quickly walked towards the road. Clem switched off the lamp by her bed, rushed down the stairs and trailed behind him, taking care to keep to the shadows.

The streets were slick with rainwater, and in the dim light of the lamps, Clementine saw Richard hail a rickshaw. She did the same, whispering to the puller to follow Richard's transport. She was surprised when the rickshaw stopped in an alley off Beach Road, and Richard alighted. Clem quickly paid off her puller and kept to the shadows thrown by the *rambutan* and tamarind trees growing in the back gardens of the affluent Chinese homes lining the street. Her brows drew together in a frown. She had been observing Richard leave the house at eight every other night, and had become suspicious. Today she would find out his destination.

Richard walked through the alley and stopped at a low stile separating the road from a field of *lallang*, the ends of the long grass glittering in the dim light of streetlamps. Calmly, he climbed over the stile and made his way through the tall grass, with Clem following at a distance. Vengeful mosquitoes hummed in her ears, and she stifled a scream when an insect landed on the back of her neck and began crawling towards her golden hair. Impatiently, she slapped it away and squished forward, her elegant shoes ill-suited to the muddy path.

The moon came out from behind a cloud and flooded the field in a cold glow. Clem stepped quickly behind a tree. In the moonlight, she attempted to get her bearings. She could see a familiar silhouette in the distance, a dark mansion rising out of the land like a primeval beast. A wave of memory flooded through her, leaving her heart fluttering with panic and her senses alert with apprehension. Why, this was the back of the House of Gan— Mei Mei's home. She could not mistake the peculiar turret at the end of the roof terrace that housed the old man's calligraphic paintings. She had been taken there to admire them when she and Eleanor had visited to bless Mei Mei's baby.

Keeping behind the trees, Clementine crept forward, pausing when she heard the soft murmur of voices. She inched closer and ducked down into the *lallang*, wincing as the grass tickled her face. She ran a few feet under the cover of the grass and slid behind a huge banyan tree near the House of Gan. Slowly, she poked her head around the trunk—and turned to stone at the sight of Mei Mei in Richard's arms, the moonlight encasing the lovers in a protective glow. Blue eyes wide with anger, her nostrils flaring with indignation, sandy brows drawn together in an ugly frown, Clem watched Mei Mei ardently kiss the man she was going to marry in two weeks' time.

* * *

A sombre Harrison family sat drinking coffee after dinner in the drawing room of their mansion.

Jeff broke the uneasy silence. "Well, that was a spectacular sight we saw today, the *Prince of Wales* and *Repulse* sailing into the naval base. Those mighty ships will offer us protection from a Japanese attack."

"I don't know what to think after the debacle of Dunkirk," Richard said.

"Gross mismanagement!" John Harrison opined.

"So many British soldiers dead! And some were saved by civilian boats. It almost seems that Britain is on the losing side." Eleanor's voice was tearful. "Do you think the bombs will reach Yorkshire? Our manor, John!"

"We cannot underestimate the Japanese," Richard said, "even with the warships that sailed in."

"I fear it is not safe for you here anymore, Eleanor. You, Richard and Clementine need to sail back to England and hole up in Yorkshire." John's tone was decisive.

"What about you, John?" Eleanor asked in a frightened voice.

John Harrison's face was determined. "I cannot desert my plantation. Jeff and I will remain here."

"I will remain here as well," Richard said, and the hard light in his eyes convinced his father that further attempts at persuasion would be useless. "War is at our door," Richard continued soberly, looking directly at his father. "This is no time to get married."

Richard refused to meet Clem's narrowed eyes. He continued, "We will all meet again in Yorkshire, when the world is safe once more. That will be the right time for nuptials and celebrations."

A derisive snort escaped from Clem, and she rose haughtily. "Of course," she said coldly. "There is no question of our getting married now—if ever." She muttered the last words under her breath and walked out of the room.

When dawn finally streaked across the sky, Eleanor reluctantly accepted her husband's recommendation of evacuation, agreeing to return to Yorkshire with Clementine and wait for the rest of her family to join her there. She looked around the bungalow dazedly, loath to exchange the pedestal of a rich planter's wife for the anonymity of daily life in Britain. Here, servants did her bidding, and she entertained on a lavish scale. Back in England, she would be one of many, with nothing to distinguish herself from her fellow matrons.

In her bedroom, Clementine sat on the window seat watching Stephen and Tessa Dolittle pack their belongings into a van that would make its way to the harbour, from where they would sail for Britain. The British were deserting the tropical isle as war loomed on the horizon. Her mind began to plot ways and means of staying on in Singapore, for she had no intention of leaving Richard in Mei Mei's clutches.

Clementine had continued spying on Mei Mei and Richard when they met at the disused field behind the Gan mansion. Attuned to the subtlest changes in Richard's routines, Clementine was convinced that he was about to flee Singapore with Mei Mei. Clem felt she could not care less if the whole world was at war; all she cared about was dogging Richard's footsteps. If he were not leaving Singapore, well then, neither would she. If he were fleeing to another destination, she would do the same. She would not be separated from Richard.

A week later, in the dead of night, Clem packed her bags and made her way to Jeffrey Peters' bungalow at the edge of the plantation. She'd had to escape from the Harrison house and take refuge with Jeff, as Eleanor was expecting her to accompany her on the ship sailing the next day for Liverpool.

Jeff tried in vain to plead with Clementine to leave Singapore.

"Our people have started to flee, Clementine," he said. "I have obtained two tickets for you and Eleanor on *The Orion,* sailing for Fremantle. From Australia, I have booked your passages on a ship to England. It will be a herculean feat to get another ticket out of Singapore at short notice."

Without a word, Clementine left Jeff's drawing room and disappeared into the inner sanctums of the house. Jeff sighed. He knew that Clementine could never love him, but the memory of her from their younger days, her carefree laughter, her friendship before his indiscretion with the Malay tapper, her increasing unhappiness regarding Richard, kept his protective instinct for Clem burning bright. He was determined to persuade her to leave Singapore.

* * *

Clementine, wrapped in a voluminous cloak, a black scarf hiding her blonde hair, her dark clothes blending with the night, followed Richard to his rendezvous with Mei Mei. Her cheeks were gaunt and hollow, a wild light burning in the depths of her eyes. She had lost her parents and her spaniel, Jasper; was Richard going to be next?

Clem gritted her teeth and clenched her fists. Not if she could help it. There had to be a way of separating Mei Mei and Richard. The depth of her dislike for Mei Mei frightened her—a native girl dogging her footsteps for a lifetime, like the hangman's noose waiting for a prisoner condemned to death. A sob caught in her throat as she watched Richard bend his head to Mei Mei, his hands holding her so close that they appeared as one figure under a raintree.

The Japanese navy had sunk *The Prince of Wales* and the *Repulse* off the coast of Malaya, Kota Bahru Airfield had fallen into Japanese hands, and bombs had started dropping over Singapore. When the British troops began withdrawing from the Malayan peninsula, Jeff had sat Clementine down and told her that she needed to leave for England, as war was now at Singapore's shores. Clementine frowned. But where were Richard and Mei Mei going to flee? She had to know.

There was a rustle in the *lallang* and Clem froze. Slowly, a figure rose out of the tall grass and stood silhouetted for a moment against the light of the distant lamps before crouching low behind a flame tree. Clem inched back behind her tree and, unseen by anyone and stooping low in the *lallang*, crawled back into the road beyond the stile. There, under an *angsana* tree, she waited quietly for the other watcher to emerge from the shadows of the field behind the House of Gan.

20

At around eight, sirens shattered the tranquillity of dusk. Singapore lay open and vulnerable to yet another gruelling Japanese air raid. Bombs rained down vengefully on that January night of 1942, and while the Japanese fought their war from the skies, the land wrote another story of vendetta.

The Singapore port teemed with frightened British men and women fleeing their tropical dreamland, battling each other for the few places left on the ships sailing for home. Some of the boats had been bombed, and their fiery skeletons and blackened shells stood as stark reminders of the peril at hand. British convoy escorts led some outbound ships off the harbour into safer waters, like mighty swans leading their cygnets. The streets of Singapore were empty that January night.

Mei Mei stood shivering in the long veranda of the House of Gan, senses alert, hands tightly gripping the handles of her old suitcase. Dressed for travel, she wore a black tunic and trousers. A moth circling the Chinese lantern that swung pendulum-like above Mei Mei's head, began to climb the lit stairway to heaven, impervious of its impending doom. Like the moth, would the clear, cold light of morning find her burnt to ashes for daring to touch the sun? The wail of the all-clear siren sounded.

Once on the empty road, Mei Mei glanced back fearfully. The moon hung like a jewel over the silent, brooding House of Gan. The master's desires and plans had spun a treacherous web from which Mei Mei now had to extricate herself and her daughter.

With a shiver, she remembered her stepmother's curse—*may you die an early death.* Buffeted by the winds of misfortune from early childhood, she had believed in the unlucky prophecy written in her stars. Her reunion with Richard, and the delightful promise of a future with him and Hong Ling in Calcutta, made her dare to dream that she would be spared the curse of the hungry ghosts.

An acrid smell assailed her nostrils as she turned into the desolation of Beach Road. A trolleybus burned furiously, overturned cars littered the road, and the pavement had splintered into angry pieces of jagged debris. The sickening stench of burnt timber and explosives scorched her lungs and she coughed and stumbled. A hand steadied her, and she looked into the weary, grimy face of a British soldier, his eyes black with defeat and frustration. She mentally saluted the lone keeper of the dying flames of an empire, even as an ominous hum in the distance heralded the bombers' return.

She hurried into a dark lane and at last could see the sea, shimmering and sparkling in the moonlight, untouched by the ravages of war. In the distance, she spied several sampans tied to the shore and knew that Richard waited for her in one of them, ready to row her over to St John's Island from where, with Hong Ling, they would sail to India and freedom.

Footsteps. Her heart leapt, and a small dread, ever present

in her, burgeoned and strained to escape the cage of reason and logic. Bombs had ceased to fall over Singapore and a pregnant, uneasy silence hung over the wounded city. History drew a deep breath before writing the next bloody chapter.

Stealthy footfalls were coming from the maze of warehouses huddling together on the waterfront, and she started to run. Boat Quay, a familiar, colourful haunt by day, assumed a sinister hue by night. Her breath came in gasps as the footsteps thundered closer and closer.

Suddenly, a siren wailed, heralding another swarm of bombers. She ran as fast as the wind whipping across the sea. The sound of footsteps had stopped, but looking up, she saw the horizon filled with Japanese aeroplanes. She stumbled into a ramshackle hut as the planes roared overhead.

Trembling with exhaustion, she huddled fearfully at the door of the hut to wait out the air-raid. The warehouses of Boat Quay tilted away, the sound of the sea was a gentle murmur, and there was a roar in the distance. Mei Mei fainted quietly away, as Singapore festered like a sore on the earth's face.

When she regained consciousness, the sirens had stopped. Hurriedly, she got up, only to sink back down on the dirty floor with a moan. She had twisted her ankle when falling to the ground. She would rest a while before crawling to the river's edge and Richard. Mei Mei felt for the jade bangle her father had given her, but her wrist was bare. As she put out her hand to search for the ornament, glass cut into her fingers. With dismay, she realised that the bangle must have broken when she'd fallen to the floor. Mei Mei shivered—it was inauspicious to have lost her parents' protection. The shadow of the curse fell over her once more.

Memories floated around the broken-down hut like cobwebs from the past. The murder trial had changed her life forever, for it had been in the courtroom that she had first met Richard Harrison. Mei Mei's eyes shone. As surely as death defined life and evil defined good, so did premature darkness craft the forthcoming light into a precious and brilliant gift. The light of Richard's love had followed the darkness of her aunt's murder, a love that had lingered over time like the sweet scent of the frangipani flower.

Dreaming of Richard and her future life with him, she did not see the figure looming in the doorway of the hut until it was too late.

21

An oil dump burning on a nearby island across the sea threw incendiary sparks into the night sky, lighting up the wounded city of Singapore with a glow of ironic merriment. Richard waited tensely near the water's edge for Mei Mei. A sampan bobbed up and down in the waters nearby, manned by the Harrison handyman, Jamal, his face lined with apprehension. A shrill cry rent the air, sending shivers down Richard's spine.

A hum in the distance grew louder, and pinpricks of light dotted the sky. "Quick, Jamal! Make for the nearest warehouse. We are going to be bombed!"

The wail of a siren drowned Richard's words, and both men ran as fast as they could towards a warehouse near the sea. A plane swooped overhead with a deafening sound, and an orange ball of fire dropped near their feet. The blast sent mud soaring upwards, the shockwaves driving the running men to the ground. Machine gun fire peppered the open beach, forcing them to remain where they had fallen.

When the gunfire ceased, Richard and Jamal crawled snail-like along the ground to the shelter of a warehouse. An hour later, the two men crept out of their shelter and lumbered cautiously towards the water's edge, their eyes trained warily on the sky. All was in darkness; even the oil dump had burnt out, like the British resistance. The sampan continued to bob forlornly up and down on the water, and there was no sign of Mei Mei.

"I hope my family is safe in the village," Jamal said in Bazaar Malay. "What will happen to us? My Chinese friends speak of horrendous atrocities committed on their relatives in China by the Japanese. How will we survive under the Japanese? The British were supposed to fight for us and save us from them, Master! The British are deserting us."

"Yes, I know." Richard shook his head. "We are fighting a big war, Jamal, and the British are on the losing end. We should have planned better to protect Singapore from a Japanese attack. But who would have thought that the Japanese would arrive in Singapore by land? We were unprepared, Jamal." He continued urgently, "We need to find Mei Mei. Please go to the House of Gan and see if she is there."

Richard knew that Jamal was friendly with the cook of the House of Gan. After sending him to find out if Mei Mei had been delayed, Richard began to feverishly comb the beach in case she had been injured in the air-raid. Jamal turned towards the city, looking back once at the lone man on the sandy shore, his eyes raking the crevices of the palm trees that swayed in the gentle breeze. Far out at sea, a burning *tongkang* loomed into view like a ghost ship, faint anguished cries of souls in torment coming from its depths. As the flaming sails crashed on to the decks, the cries grew fainter. Soon there was silence.

Jamal trudged along an ill-lit lane leading to bomb-torn

Beach Road. Stealing into the back garden of the House of Gan, he saw the building blazing with lights, an easy target for Japanese bombers. Knowing something was amiss, Jamal knocked very softly on the kitchen door. The dishevelled cook appeared and informed him that Mei Mei, Li Li and Hong Ling were missing, and Old Master had sent his henchman out into the streets to search for them.

Jamal sped away to inform Richard that Old Master Gan's servants were on the prowl.

"Master, you cannot go back to the house. Master Gan Niu's men will track you there. We go to Mistress Winnie's *kampong* in the jungle?"

Richard nodded. "It will be safe for me to hide out at Winnie's. Please tell my father that I am spending time with my friend, Tom, before he sets sail for Britain."

Together, Jamal and Richard trudged to the pig-farm where Winnie was sheltering with Mona Ma, away from the city and the rampant bombing.

The darkness was intense in this isolated part of the island, vegetation and forests stretching as far as the eye could see, with scattered pig farms lying miles apart. As he waited quietly by the door of Mona's hut, Richard mused that the menace of the jungle, with the occasional cry of a wild animal or the hiss of snakes, was preferable to the city, where death now rained down from the sky.

The door creaked open cautiously, and Winnie, dressed in a housecoat over her nightgown, peered out, her face filled with apprehension. She burst into tears when she heard of the bombing and that Mei Mei was missing. She informed Richard that her stepfather had rowed Li Li and Hong Ling to St John's Island three hours earlier. Winnie rushed to an altar, where a cross was hanging, to pray for her friend's safety.

Mona Ma, waiting in the shadows, spoke quietly. "Someone ought to row over to St John's Island and inform my husband of developments. He is waiting at the jetty for Mei Mei and Richard."

"I will row over myself," Jamal said reassuringly.

Mona Ma nodded at Jamal. "My brother-in-law, Ng, has a pig farm right in the middle of the jungle, where rumour has it that communists are hiding. It will be some time before the Japanese arrive in our remote part of the world, so Ng can hide the baby and Li Li away from the bombings. And away from Old Master Gan's thugs. Jamal, my husband's bicycle is outside. Use it as transport. It will take you to your sampan faster. Bring Hong Ling back to us."

Jamal nodded and left the house. They could see him wobbling on Winnie's stepfather's rusty bicycle along the dirt road. Soon the dark night swallowed him up.

* * *

Richard walked along the dirt road to the village where Mei Mei had spent her early childhood. As the *kampong* came into sight, he froze. The scene in front of him sprung out of the serene landscape like a horrible nightmare—a mass of tangled structures silhouetted harshly against the fire of a setting sun. Gone were the wooden huts floating on the river or stacked around a circular grassy field. The tin roofs of the houses lay on the grass in mangled scraps along with blackened wood, the only evidence of homes built over generations with the sweat and toil of farmers, labourers and hawkers. The village had been bombed.

Grimy children sat on the black wooden planks, tears dried into streaks on their cheeks, scrabbling among the ruins for their paltry toys. Their parents sat beside them with sunken eyes, gazing miserably into space, the hunger in their stomachs rumbling on without relief. A mongrel sniffed disdainfully among the rubbish before ejecting hot steamy urine to mark its displeasure at the lack of edible scraps. Only the stream flowed on with its sweet gurgle, winding and disappearing behind trees with trunks charred by the fire that had razed the *kampong*.

Shu Lan's house was still standing, a blackened shell staring with blind eyes at the road. The vegetable plots were a tangled mess of trodden earth and trampled plants. Fire had gutted the left half of the house, and as Richard made his way down the path, he slipped on mud and fell over plants that twined parasitically around his shoes in a desperate attempt at life. He looked in through the window and observed a man sitting on a mattress on the floor, staring helplessly into space. The man looked up with vacant eyes as Richard came in through what had once been a door.

Richard spoke in Bazaar Malay, asking the man if he knew of Liao Mei Mei's whereabouts.

The man spat on the ground, his face twisting into a grimace. "My wife hated the sound of her stepdaughter's name," he said. "She blamed Mei Mei for her son's death. Anyway, my Shu Lan is united with her Wen Long now. She was injured when the Japanese bomb hit the house. She had multiple burns and lingered on in the hospital for four days. She died a painful death. We have not seen or heard from Liao Mei Mei since our marriage. She never graced our door."

Richard thanked him, and wiping the perspiration from his face with a tired hand, he slowly left the village of Mei Mei's birth.

22

February 1942, Singapore

John Harrison walked restlessly through his plantation, a haunted look in his eyes. General Tomoyuki Yamashita's Japanese forces had rapidly advanced through the Malay peninsula and had established headquarters at the Sultan of Johor's palace, just across from Singapore's shores. His forward party had landed on the north shores of Singapore and were inexorably making their way to Bukit Timah, overcoming the last vestiges of brave British resistance. Richard had disappeared on a night in January, and there had been no word from him.

John felt bewildered; he had planted rubber seeds with his own hands, and watched the plants grow into trees that kissed the skies. The rubber latex from his trees had given him great wealth and status in Singapore. Now Governor Shenton Thomas had ordered a scorched earth policy preparatory to an unconditional surrender, and John had to burn his rubber trees and stocks, watch them turn to cinders in front of his eyes. The very fabric of his life was tied to his beloved plantation. The prospect of setting his trees alight pierced his soul cleanly like a dagger, and comprehension faded slowly from his broken mind, like hot blood trickling out of a wound.

"Shall we start burning the trees, sir?" Jeff looked at his employer compassionately. It broke his own heart to set fire to the trees that were not only his livelihood but his very essence. "You should have left on the ship with the other planters. I could have continued searching for Richard. Sir, I can still arrange a passage for you to Indonesia. Shall I go ahead?"

"I cannot leave my plantation." John Harrison looked around him like a lost child.

As machine gun fire sounded nearby, the rubber planter nodded his head dejectedly, giving the signal for the destruction of his life's work, turning away sharply when Jeff torched the first tree. John Harrison stumbled away from the pillage of his plantation, his confused mind meandering through the mists of the past. Behind him, smoke billowed up from orange flames hungrily licking the bark of the trees.

He walked on, his head bare, his shirt tattered, and his heart broken. He heard gunfire nearby, his ears registering the sound but his mind a swirling kaleidoscope of beloved images: Clem sitting at the piano, playing music in the drawing room of the bungalow; Richard playing sweet notes on the violin; Eleanor presiding regally over a dinner table laden with delectable food; and after-dinner conversation with Jeff about the day's affairs at the plantation.

He stopped and peered at a monsoon drain. Torsos with heads and legs severed by Japanese sabres lay still, the blood running down the drain like a monsoon flood. He looked up and saw British soldiers hanging from trees, their hands tied behind their backs, their faces displaying the same surprise he felt. He walked on among the dead bodies, whistling quietly to himself as the sound of shelling intensified. He would buy some more acres with the profit he had made last year, he thought, his eyes dreamy. In the distance, he heard Jeffrey's warning shout.

He smiled with childlike gratitude at the tropical sun that had nurtured his land. The force of the blast lifted him off his feet and flung him against the bark of a tree, splitting his head open. As he lay amidst tattered bodies, the life easing slowly out of him, John Harrison saw the sunburned face and heard the deep voice of the merchant who had inspired him to seek his fortune in the tropics:

"Johnny, old boy, you have no idea of the riches that can be harvested from the tropical soil. Huge rubber trees grow in a paradise of clear skies and brilliant sunshine. The milky liquid from these trees coagulates to form the rubber that you see on bicycles and cars. You earn a pittance as a bank clerk in England. Why don't you try your luck in Singapore? You will be wealthy in no time. The land is like a virgin maiden, waiting for you ..."

His sightless blue eyes gazed at the sun while his precious plantation burned savagely and surely. John Harrison's tropical dream was over.

23

Winnie was sitting in a tiny bedroom at the back of Mona Ma's house. She looked out of the window and watched twilight enfolding the land. There was no breeze, but the air resounded with the song of birds flying to their nests. Her window overlooked the back garden, unkempt and filled with odds and ends. Beyond were the pig pens, but the population of pigs had dwindled in the hard times. This was the hour in the evening when she and Mei Mei had once walked in the school playground, watching the children play, reciting to each other their deeds of the day. Winnie whimpered.

"Mei Mei, where are you?" she whispered brokenly.

She remembered her friend's sacrifice in marrying Shiwei Gan to save her life, and Winnie's tears flowed freely. She turned her head as the bead curtains over the door tinkled alarmingly. The colour fled from her face leaving it paper-white, and she could only whisper, "Dan Long!"

The man in the doorway strode into the room, and in a moment Winnie was in his arms. It was then that she collapsed, sobbing loudly.

"Oh, Dan Long, I thought I'd never see you again." She cried into Dan Long's thin shirt. "You never wrote from China, and

I thought you had died. And all the time you were mixed up in politics again!"

Winnie broke free from Dan Long and glared at him. "You hadn't learnt your lesson? You were nearly killed at Kreta Ayer, for heaven's sake! Yet you joined the communists in China, and if it had not been for Mei Mei, I would be dead."

Dan Long took off his spectacles and wiped the tears from his own eyes. "I have been irresponsible, Winnie. You don't know what heartbreak I suffered when I heard that you had contracted tuberculosis and had had a lung operation. I was fearful for your health, but what could I do, Winnie? The British were still hunting for me. I can only come over now because the police are too busy with the Japanese to think of me.

"Where is Mei Mei?" His face went white when Winnie mutely shook her head. "What, Winnie? Why are you shaking your head? Mei Mei and Richard have sailed for India, surely?"

Dan Long was disconcerted when Winnie burst into fresh tears.

"Mei Mei escaped from the House of Gan the night we kidnapped Hong Ling, but failed to meet Richard at their rendezvous," Winnie sobbed. "Hong Ling and Li Li are staying at Uncle Ng's farm, right in the middle of the jungle. They must stay hidden, as Old Master Gan's servants are searching for the baby. Mei Mei has disappeared, Dan Long!" She hesitated and then blurted out, "There were multiple bomb raids the night she disappeared."

"The hospitals?" Dan Long cried.

Winnie nodded. "Richard has visited all the hospitals, but

there is no sign of Mei Mei. He is still searching for her all over the island. Mona Ma has rented him a room in the neighbouring hut, since he must hide from Old Master Gan's retainers. Old Master may be aware that Mei Mei and Richard were lovers. Mistress Meisheng may have told him before she died."

Dan Long sighed. "When the ship docked here, my heart swelled with joy. My breathing was uneven. I strained to catch the first glimpse of my land of birth. Winnie, you do not know how I have missed Singapore, my home! It is only when you leave and travel far away that you realise the worth of your homeland. So many nights I dreamt of the hawker stalls with the men cooking *char kway teow*; of your kind brown eyes; of the bustle of Queen Street, our colourful harbour, and the sea, glistening in the sun. Calcutta is on the banks of a river and the waters are grey and murky. Oh, Winnie, I have missed home, and I have missed you, my darling!"

He took Winnie in his arms and embraced her long and hard.

That night, Dan Long met a gaunt and haggard Richard.

"I have searched the central part of the island," Richard said, his voice tired. "I've taken my father's handyman, Jamal, with me since I cannot speak the lingo so well. It will be good if you accompany me tomorrow, Dan Long." Richard wiped his face with a towel, and in the lantern light, Dan Long saw that he looked old and dispirited.

"What about the ship that you were to escape on? Did you go to the docks at all? You were to sail from Singapore and not Batavia, Winnie tells me." Dan Long asked, worry creasing his forehead.

"Yes, the *Aorangi* left Singapore's harbour on the 16th," Richard replied. "I did go down to the docks, and no one of Mei Mei's name or description boarded the ship—the harbourmaster showed me his log."

In Winnie's room, Dan Long voiced his anxiety. "Did Old Master's men find Mei Mei? If so, they may have killed her in an honour slaying. Oh, my poor sister, she was, after all, born on the double seventh!"

Winnie snorted so derisively that Dan Long hurriedly went to the veranda, where Mona Ma had provided him with a makeshift rope bed for the night.

* * *

For days, Richard and Dan Long searched all over the island for Mei Mei, scouring the hospitals, scanning the faces of the dead and wounded women brought in daily from Singapore's streets. The air in Singapore tingled with panic as people prepared themselves for an unwelcome, uncertain future.

In the second week of their quest, Richard and Dan Long reached the Bukit Timah jungles with the march of Japanese feet ringing in their ears. Distressed cries filled the air and a soldier staggered out of the forest, his hands clutching his bloodied chest, trying to stem the blood pouring out of a deep wound.

"Help me!" he cried. "The Japs are hanging us from trees. Help!"

Richard and Dan Long strode on, impervious to the soldier's

piteous cries, both intent on finding their loved one. Artillery fired nearby, and the smell of gunpowder mixed with the noxious odour of smoke as thousands of rubber trees burned to the ground.

"My father's plantation! Where is it?" Richard sobbed, gazing at the incandescent trees in bewildered horror.

A blast rocked the land, sweeping Richard off his feet and sending him crashing to the ground two metres away. The earth cracked open in front of Dan Long's horrified eyes, and he threw himself down, covering his head with his hands. As the dust settled, the noise of the machine guns began to recede towards Holland Road. Dan Long found Richard lying very still among the debris, an ugly red gash on his forehead. But he was still breathing.

Dan Long ran to a nearby shed in the hope of finding manpower to help him carry Richard home. There was no sign of human life; only miscellaneous items lay cluttered in the small rectangular room—fishing nets, tools of various sizes, a wheelbarrow and fishing tackle.

Dan Long's mind worked furiously, and he pushed the wheelbarrow to where Richard lay. Sweat poured from his face as he struggled to lift Richard's inert body into the wheelbarrow. He fought a rising tide of nausea as he wheeled the barrow slowly along, among burning trees and drains filled with bloodied remains. Death and decay hung all around, with British soldiers hanging from trees, their hands tied behind their backs, and flies buzzing around rotting human flesh.

When Richard was safely inside Mona Ma's house, lying on a makeshift bed of mattresses, Dan Long turned to Winnie, who had washed Richard's wound with tearful fortitude.

"The wound on his head doesn't look good, and he's burning up with fever. We need a doctor. We should take him to John Harrison. Richard is his son, after all. What if he were to die without seeing his father?"

"Don't be silly," Winnie snapped. "He cannot be moved in his condition. Mona Ma's brother is a *sinseh*. I will go and get him. When Richard is a bit better, we will inform his father." She gripped Dan Long's hand. "Mei Mei would want us to take care of Richard."

Tears came into Dan Long's eyes as he thought of his sister, and he nodded.

"Remember, Dan Long, we have to rescue Hong Ling." Winnie's face was frightened. "Jamal came today in the afternoon. Old Master has redoubled the search for Hong Ling with a larger retinue of hoodlums and servants. We must set sail for India soon with Hong Ling. Mei Mei had told me that if anything happened to her, I was to take Hong Ling to India to Uncle Toh and you. She did not trust Old Master to take care of his granddaughter, as he was always bitter that she was not a boy."

Dan Long made up his mind. "My little niece is my priority," he said. "We cannot be burdened with Richard. You do understand that, don't you, Winnie?"

"He can stay here one week," Winnie agreed. "We will take him to John Harrison after that."

Winnie and Dan Long looked sadly at Richard's sleeping face.

24

On Singapore's streets, residents hurried along, stocking up on rations. Some women sat in front of their houses, sewing Japanese flags, while a shopkeeper busily erected a poster of welcome to the Japanese on the walls of his shop. Life had to continue; that precious commodity called allegiance had to switch sides, for civilization is but a jungle, where survival is the only command that is obeyed.

The soft breeze blew Jeffrey's blonde hair and cooled his burning face as he sat in an armchair on his porch, thinking sadly of his dead employer. He had buried John in the back garden of John's bungalow, and marked his resting place with a simple, wooden cross, thousands of which would sprout over the green fields of the world, fertilized by the bombs of death and cultivated by the hatred of men.

A shadow detached itself from behind the oak tree.

"Clem!" He gazed at the wild blonde hair blowing in the breeze, and the blue eyes sparkling like jewels. "Your ship sails in two days—are you sick?"

"I cannot leave without Richard," Clem said dully. "He has disappeared. This was not supposed to happen."

"Clem, the Japanese are going to capture British civilians

and imprison them. You need to leave on the *SS Devonshire* for Fremantle, and then on to Liverpool. You will be safe—that ship has convoy escorts to guide her away from Singapore's waters without harm. Who is there?"

Dan Long came forward from the shadows of the garden and breathlessly informed Jeff of Richard's condition.

"Why is Richard with you?" Clem asked sharply.

Dan Long averted his eyes from Clem's blazing ones and murmured, "Mei Mei and Richard were eloping to India, but Mei Mei did not turn up to meet Richard. There were bomb raids that night. We fear my sister may be dead. Richard and I were searching for Mei Mei when shrapnel hit Richard." Dan Long added, "The doctor said that, other than his memory loss, Richard will recover. The wound was not too deep."

"Richard has amnesia?" Clementine's soft voice held a glimmer of hope and a thrill of joy. She turned peremptorily to Dan Long. "We will remove Richard from your quarters, and I will sail with him to England. I will not let him be interned in prison here. Jeff, please purchase another ticket on the *Devonshire*. Hurry!"

* * *

Clem entered Mona Ma's hut, her lips twisted into a moue of disdain on observing the poverty-stricken quarters. She rushed to the cot bed that stood in one corner of the living room and looked down on the emaciated form lying there.

Richard turned blank green eyes upon her. "I don't remember

anything or anyone," he cried piteously.

"You will regain your memory." Jeff took Richard's hand gently. "I am your friend, Jeff. You need to be with your mother in England. We are at war with Japan, and the Orientals have the upper hand. If you stay here, you will be interned. The ships are taking only women and children on board, but they will take you on account of your poor health. The ship for England leaves at daybreak tomorrow. Do not worry, Clementine will take care of you. You have to evacuate from Singapore, or you may lose your life."

Clementine smiled, her eyes warm and loving. "We are engaged to be married, Richard. I was so worried about you and I am so happy to have found you."

"I don't remember," Richard said, with panic in his eyes.

"This picture that you painted may refresh your memory," Winnie said, angry that Clem was taking advantage of Richard's amnesia by claiming him as her own when Richard had been eloping with Mei Mei. She dragged the huge portrait of Mei Mei that Richard had been keen on taking with him to India. Richard looked at the painting of a beautiful Chinese girl smiling at him, but his face remained devoid of emotion. Clem snatched the portrait from Winnie, her face blazing with hatred.

"How dare you?" she cried. She turned on her heel and marched out of the hut with the portrait in her hands. Jeff followed, supporting Richard and carrying his suitcase.

Midnight. Clementine stood silhouetted against a bonfire that burnt ferociously in Jeff's garden. As the sound of crackling intensified and the scent of burning permeated the bungalow, Jeff rushed out.

He ran to her side and looked down at the fire. Richard's portrait of Mei Mei burned slowly—even the flames were loath to destroy such a priceless piece of art. Patiently, the flames licked Mei Mei's hair and spread to her expressive eyes.

As the fire kissed her red lips, Jeff cried out: "What kind of a monster are you, Clem, to destroy a picture painted with a lifetime of love? You're inhuman!"

Clementine said with a face carved of stone, "I'm making sure that he never remembers her. That is the only way he can ever love me."

The orange tongues of flame killed Mei Mei's likeness on the canvas, and obliterated forever the loving touches of the artist.

Under the cover of darkness, Jeff drove Richard and Clem with their luggage to Keppel Harbour in John Harrison's battered Bentley. Richard looked dazed and soon slid into a dreamless sleep, slumped in the back seat of the car. Clem looked out of the car window. The pavements were littered with rubbish and dead bodies, fires still burning quietly in some of the bombed buildings.

She swallowed the lump in her throat. They had heard that the harbour was a minefield and ships were being blown up. Would the *SS Devonshire* survive the voyage out of Singapore? The troopship would form part of a convoy, but there was little comfort in that. The *SS Norah Moller* had recently been shelled and set on fire by the Japanese, and many on board had died. There was a rumour that the Japanese were going to capture the

Dutch East Indies, and escape from Java and Sumatra by ship would soon be unsafe.

The sky was a pale pink, the landscape was lightening, and Clem could see the masts and funnels of ships anchored at Keppel Harbour. Jeff stopped the car in the shadow of a warehouse and cautiously went to confer with the crew of the SS *Devonshire*.

Soon Jeff materialized out of the soft mist of the quayside with a thick-set man in a sailor's cap.

"We are evacuating many women and children on the *Devonshire*, Miss," the man said, touching his cap to Clem. "On account of the ill-health of the male passenger, the captain is willing to take him aboard, but we have only one free cabin, with a single berth."

The mist swirled around Clem's golden head and a cold wind whipped across the harbour. "Thank you for taking my husband, Richard, aboard," she said, crisply. "We are married and only need one cabin. I will sleep on the floor."

The man's eyes widened but all he said was, "'Tis all right then, madam. Didn't reckon you were married. Right as rain now. We are sailing in an hour. 'Twould be a good idea to board the ship now. On account of the minefields around the harbour, boats that know how to dodge them will row you over to the ship. 'Tis the blue and grey beauty in the convoy, madam, you can't miss it. I will add your names to the captain's list of passengers. Richard and Clementine Harrison, then?"

The man disappeared into the mist and only then did Clem turn to Jeff. Her face paled on seeing his stern countenance.

"Richard and I would have been married if not for the war,"

Clem said in a cold voice. "It is easier to travel as a married couple in wartime—dangerous times need stern measures."

Jeff's pale blue eyes were cool as he said, "As long as you inform Richard in England that you are not his wife, no harm done. While eventually you may marry him, Clem, a fake marriage built on a lie is not a foundation for a life together. Richard does not remember you, or his affection for you, and he was eloping with Mei Mei last month. Wait for his regard to return, that is my advice."

Without waiting for her reply, he took two suitcases in each hand, and the holdall over his shoulder, and trudged towards the boats bobbing at the jetty. Clem helped Richard out of the car and followed at a distance.

Two Chinese men helped Clem and Richard onto their boat.

"This is where I leave you," Jeff said. "Look up Quentin Goodfellow in London. You have his address. He is John's lawyer, and he will take you to Eleanor in Yorkshire. Fare you well." Jeff embraced Richard warmly, and the boat took off. Clem looked at Jeff's diminishing figure in the distance and felt a twinge of regret in her heart.

The boat reached the huge ship, and Clementine helped Richard aboard and into the cabin they were to share. She then went back onto the deck, where the captain had asked passengers to assemble before sailing.

The captain had a deep voice, and his tanned face was creased with worry.

"We were to sail to Tanjong Priok in Batavia, and from there on the open seas for Fremantle, but the Japs are manning the waters around Java and Sumatra. They already hold the Malacca Straits and have a strong naval presence in the Indian Ocean. We are afraid that we will be torpedoed by subs or bombed from the air if we sail to Australia. We have decided, therefore, to take the less dangerous route towards Colombo, via the Sunda Straits between Java and Sumatra, and then the Banka Straits. We should be all right once we clear those waters and leave the Far East behind.

"We will be sailing in a convoy with troopships and sister ships *Felix Roussel* and *City of Canterbury*, so we have protection. But please stay below deck until we have cleared the Indonesian straits. This ship will dock at Colombo in a week's time and from there sail to Bombay. Those who wish to sail to Liverpool can sail with us to Bombay, from where ships will be leaving for England. Those bound for Australia, it is better to leave us at Colombo, as there are Fremantle-bound ships sailing from there. Ladies and gentlemen, the ship will set sail now. Please stay below deck."

Clem went into the cabin she shared with Richard, her brows drawn together in a frown. Jeffrey had booked them on a ship from Fremantle to Liverpool a week after the *Devonshire* berthed there, but now, with the amended route, she would have to fend for herself and Richard in Bombay until they found a ship that could take them to Liverpool.

There was a lurch and the ship moved forward. Clem went to the porthole and peered out. Green vegetation swirled by, and even during the war, the frangipani trees were in full bloom. In a flash, Clem remembered her inbound journey to Singapore, her exile from England because of Clara, and how she had hoped that she would find happiness in an exotic and alien land. A glimmer of tears touched her eyes. In the end, she had done right by her two stepsisters. They were being schooled in Devon, with the fees paid out of their elder stepsister's English bank account.

Tenderly, Clem glanced at Richard's peacefully sleeping form on the berth and smiled. She had found her happiness. She turned away from the porthole. She did not regret leaving a land where a beautiful native girl had held the man she loved prisoner. It was good to go.

About fifty miles from Singapore, there was a loud report, and Clementine rushed to the porthole and looked out. The silhouette of an island lay in the distance with a red cliff glinting in the morning sun, waves lashing on to the thin strip of sand. Peering further out, Clem froze. Over the red rock, a formation of Japanese aeroplanes was approaching, already so near that Clem could discern the writing on a plane flying overhead. They were going to be bombed by the Japanese.

Clem rushed to the sleeping Richard, shielded his body with hers, and shut her eyes tight. There were loud reports, and the big ship shuddered alarmingly. Richard woke with a jump, and Clementine cajoled him to lie down on the berth to wait out the Japanese attack. They could hear shouts and the sound of feet running to and fro on deck. When the shouting had died down, and the ship appeared to be sailing onwards once more, Clem rushed to the porthole and looked out. The ship had cleared the island with the red cliff and was now out in the open sea. She could see the hull of one of the other ships in the convoy and heaved a sigh of relief, just as a knock sounded on the door.

The sailor who had met them at the dock opened the cabin door and peered in. "All fine here, madam?"

"Yes, what happened?" Clem asked, and Richard sat up on the berth with interest.

"The Japs bombed us, but our escort ships opened fire on the bombers, and we suffered only slight damage. We were off Berhala Island, and now we are sailing towards the open sea. We ought to be safe now, though you never can tell. Food is rationed, madam. Only corned beef and bread, I am afraid. You will find your rations in the dining cabin."

* * *

On 16 February 1942, the SS Devonshire docked at the colourful harbour of Colombo. There Richard and Clementine, with their belongings, transferred to the SS Plancius which would take them on the short journey to Bombay, since the SS Devonshire had suffered minor damages during the Japanese bombing and needed repairs.

The Bombay docks were dirty and littered with garbage and beggars. Clem pinched her nose to ward off the stench of rot and decay, as she and Richard followed a coolie, on whose head their luggage rested, to a small alley off the wharf.

The coolie stopped in front of a building and gesticulated eagerly. A small hotel, cleaner than neighbouring dwellings, boasted the name of London Hotel. Clem and Richard followed their coolie through a swing door into a cool interior where, behind a wooden counter, stood a thin Indian man with brilliant black moustaches and well-oiled, curly hair.

"Oh, please to come," he rushed forth ingratiatingly. "Welcome, madam and sir." He turned to the coolie and said some rude words in Hindi, which made him deposit the luggage on to the floor and scamper out.

"But we have not paid him," Clem said.

The man smiled showing two gold-capped teeth. "No need. He receives commission for bringing the British to my hotel. A generous commission. Besides, he is a thief of the highest order. Another few minutes and your handbag would have gone, madam." The man bowed to Clem and said, "My name is Mathur and I am general manager here. I give you a nice big bedroom overlooking sea, yes?"

Richard spoke up. "Can we have two bedrooms? One each, if you please?"

Mathur's bushy eyebrows shot up, but otherwise he kept his cool, his eyes swivelling away from a furiously blushing Clem.

"Not a problem, sir." Mathur peered at a register on the counter. "One face sea and one face back alley, bad smell." He looked sad.

"I will take the one facing the alley," Richard said hurriedly.

Mathur shouted, and a youth in white clothing came from the inner sanctums of the hotel.

"This is Patel, my nephew, sister's son. He will take you to your rooms." Mathur bowed sycophantically.

"Wait," Clementine said. "Do you know if there is a ship sailing for England in the next few days? We are bound for Liverpool."

"Ah, going home to England," Mathur grinned amiably. "Yes, ship sail in a week from Bombay docks for Liverpool. You need tickets, I cut for you."

"That would be nice." Clem looked relieved. "We will go up now."

"Not to go out in the streets, Memsahib," Mathur admonished, following them to the dirty stairs. "India in shambles. Some want British to quit, you know? Fellow called Gandhi, should have his head examined. We eat British salt for many years. And another fellow called Bose in Calcutta, ingratiating himself with the Japanese. Processions in the streets and Memsahib, so many thieves about. Must keep money safe. You stay my hotel, you safe and sound." Mathur gave a high-pitched giggle.

Two days later, to his chagrin, Richard found that he had been robbed. Plagued by mosquitoes and lying under a ragged mosquito net with glaring holes, Richard had left the first storey window of his room wide open to allow the breeze to enter and remove the stench from the garbage dump in the back alley. An agile thief had taken this golden opportunity to clamber up the mango tree outside Richard's window, enter his room and remove his luggage. Mathur wrung his hands and bleated piteously on the bad morals of his race, but Clem found it interesting that his nephew, Patel, went missing from that day.

Clem's luggage was intact, and since she held the purse strings, their money had not been touched. Clem ventured out one day to buy Richard some clothes, and soon they boarded a ship from Bombay's docks sailing for England's shores. Relief washed over Clem in waves. The dirt and stench of India, coupled with the dishonesty she had witnessed, made Clem determined to leave Asia forever.

Five days out at sea, and rounding the Cape of Good Hope, Richard came down with a bad bout of malaria. The holes in the mosquito net at the seedy Bombay hotel had allowed deadly mosquitoes to feed on his blood.

The rain lashed against the porthole of the airless cabin like stinging slaps, and the wind howled with the fury of an untamed beast fighting to be let into the ship. The lantern hanging from the ceiling of the tiny cabin swung precariously, like a fallacious pendulum, in the wake of the ocean storm, lurching so dangerously that Clementine grabbed at a candle and matchsticks, expecting that at any moment the lantern would crash to the ground and break, plunging them into darkness. The Cape of Good Hope was well known for its squalls.

She bent down to Richard, who was trembling uncontrollably. She fed him more quinine and piled her blankets as well as his on top of his shaking body. His body became so hot that tears sprang to Clem's eyes. She remembered Richard's stories of Mei Mei nursing him through cholera on St John's Island and gritted her teeth. She could match Mei Mei's love and care. She had not come all this way to lose Richard now.

"There is no more quinine left in my stock," the ship's doctor told Clem. "One of the ship's passengers, Mathew Sinclair, a wealthy American, has many phials of quinine, though. He brought his own supply from Bombay."

That night, Clem feared she would lose Richard. The fever refused to abate, and he suffered convulsions, his eyes rolling, his limbs thrusting out, his teeth clamping down on his tongue. Clem held on to his arms and legs, and when the attack had passed, sat on the floor, weeping. After a while, eyes blue and stormy, hair wild and face pale, she sought out Mathew Sinclair in his large cabin suite.

"A lovely girl like you must give me something in return for my quinine, eh?" Sinclair, a short, fat man with sparse hair and beetling brows, smiled, showing yellowing teeth. He had an ugly birthmark on his neck.

"What do you want?" Clem asked harshly.

It was daybreak when Clem returned to Richard's cabin. Her matted golden hair, the hunted look in her eyes, her swollen lips, the red marks on her pale face, and her torn bodice were lost to Richard as he lay on the berth, burning up. Clem looked at herself in the small mirror she carried, and a sob escaped her throat. Then she slowly opened her fist. A large phial of quinine reposed in her hand.

On the tenth day after being struck with malaria, Richard's fever broke, and perspiration covered his body. Clem undressed him, lovingly sponged off the sweat, and gently gave him a massage until he slept. She cleaned and bathed him for three days, and on the fourth day, fed him gruel and soup. By the time the ship approached the motherland, Richard was weak but able to eat solid food.

"Your wife has saved your life," the ship's doctor said, after examining Richard before the ship docked at Liverpool. He wondered at the tight smile on the patient's face and the blank look in his green eyes.

Clementine had forgotten the cold of England. As the Liverpool docks came into sight, she rushed below deck to wrap herself in a shawl, and checked to see whether Richard was wearing his coat. When she emerged again and leaned on the rails of the ship, the silhouette of Liverpool lay before her, stark buildings outlined against a dark sky, cranes piercing the mist swirling on the horizon. The gentle rain brought Clem's childhood back to her in a flash.

Reverentially, she breathed in the salty air of England. *Freedom*, she thought exultantly, *freedom from Mei Mei and her world*. Finally, it was her time in the sun, away from the shadow of the beautiful Chinese girl.

25

History wrote a bloody chapter when British troops surrendered in Singapore. Japan assumed its reign as conqueror of the tiny tropical isle, renamed Syonan-to. The Japanese *kempetai* dwelt harshly with the Chinese population of Syonan, establishing their principles of law and order by savagely punishing any perceived disobedience. Slight offences resulted in decapitated heads decorating the vantage points of the city, in order to force a recalcitrant population into grudging subservience.

On a day in February 1942, Japanese soldiers began marching through Singapore's streets with loudspeakers, their rough voices urging men between the ages of eighteen and fifty to report to concentration camps for *sook ching*, a purge of misplaced ideals. Anyone failing to report would face certain death.

Dan Long found himself in a crowd of people that snaked its way to the Jalan Besar concentration camp, fear written on the faces around him. Hundreds of men were crammed in the courtyard of the camp, cringing collectively when the *kempetai* poked them with their bayonets as they watchfully patrolled the grounds.

Dan Long stood in line with other men, dirty and unshaven, his eyes shifty like that of a trapped lizard searching for a crack to slither through. "Why are we here? Who are the soldiers looking for?" he whispered to the man next to him, a barber who was clicking his tongue annoyingly every five minutes.

"The Japanese are weeding out former members of the Kuomintang and the Malayan Communist Party, purging them of their misplaced ideals by segregating them to be taken to an undisclosed destination for punishment." The barber said in Hokkien, giving a vicious click of his tongue. "I am positive these people are being butchered at a slaughtering place somewhere on the island."

Dan Long swallowed the lump in his throat. "How do the Japanese know the identity of former members of the Kuomintang Party?" he asked.

The barber jerked his head towards several hooded men talking to Japanese officers. "Those men are informers, cowardly traitors of our race, turning against us to profit during these troubled times, ingratiating themselves like fawning curs smelling a joint of meat." He spat viciously. "Those who are free from contamination of misplaced ideals will be given a piece of paper saying 'EXAMINED', which they are to wear on the lapel of their shirts daily. Then they can freely roam the streets of Singapore. The chit of paper is your passport in Syonan-to, my friend."

The hooded figures began making their way through the assembled line of people, inspecting the cowering mass of humanity through the slits in the headgear, their cruel eyes assessing, their rough hands prodding faces into position for better viewing. One informer crooked his finger, prompting a Japanese soldier to drag a Chinese man out of the line to stand alone in a corner, where he sank to his knees, whimpering for mercy. Soon other civilians joined him, as informers weeded out 'traitors' and segregated them. The informers approached like harbingers of doom. A slim, hooded man looked long and hard at Dan Long before crooking his finger. The Japanese soldier accompanying him dragged Dan Long out of the line.

"What is your name?" the informer asked in a silky voice.

"Liao Dan Long." The name came on a whisper.

"Are you Liao Mei Mei's brother?" Dan Long glimpsed the mean eyes behind the slits in the hood and shivered. "Liao Mei Mei, the bride of the House of Gan?"

Dan Long nodded eagerly. After all, the Gan men were respected in the business community and had no connection to the Kuomintang Party. Linking himself to the House of Gan would allow him a safe passport, he thought.

The informer looked at the Japanese soldier and said, "He is a former KMT member." He watched as the soldier dragged Dan Long out of the line and pushed him into the rapidly growing segregated group.

After several hours, Japanese soldiers pushed Dan Long into a truck transporting a legion of humanity from the Jalan Besar concentration camp to Changi Beach. At the beach, sharp bayonets pricking their backs herded the prisoners into the sandy dunes, where soldiers provided them with spades to dig trenches. Pillboxes with machine guns jutting out of slits stood on the beach.

Tears glistened in Dan Long's eyes. He had escaped slaughter at Kreta Ayer and survived the Nanking Massacre, only to come home years later to be murdered by the Japanese. He had spent so many years without his Winnie, always dreaming of her honest, laughing brown eyes, and how soft they became when they looked upon him. Now, when happiness was within his grasp, he was going to lose it.

A wave of distress washed over him. He had deserted Winnie when she was gravely ill. This had been his chance to protect her during wartime, but instead she would be on her own again, taking up the cudgels of responsibility towards his family by removing Hong Ling to safety. Could a woman and a small baby survive the war? Dan Long whimpered.

When the trenches were dug, the prisoners stood in front of them with their backs to the pillboxes. Lethargy, generated by fear of losing his loved ones, swept over Dan Long, producing hallucinatory images which waxed and waned in his mind. The sea was sparkling with blood from the rays of the setting sun, the waves lapping the shore in froths of white foam. Dan Long was soothed by the gentle sound. His father had sung the boatmen song to him in his childhood, and he began to hum it deliriously.

The almighty river guide our path
Through night and day be our mace
For we have left our families at home
To master the great Hwang-Ho!

The sea tilted away from Dan Long, and the sky came to meet him with bursting stars, as fear overcame his senses. He fell to the ground a split second before the machine guns opened fire. When Japanese soldiers stopped by to inspect the men lying in the trenches, they saw Dan Long prostrated on the ground, his eyes closed, the body of a fellow prisoner covering his in a grotesque mimicry of intimacy. The Japanese soldiers glanced cursorily at him before moving away.

When Dan Long regained consciousness, it was night. The sea had merged with the sky and the stars were out, shining on lacerated bodies in the massive graveyard on the beach. Like an animal with its instincts on high alert, Dan Long staggered to his feet and crawled slowly along the edge of the beach towards civilization.

When he came to the rusty gate of Mona Ma's compound, he found Winnie standing there, a forlorn figure with anxious eyes. On seeing him, she rushed to him and was enveloped in his arms.

"Dan Long, I thought the Japanese had butchered you!" she cried, tears streaming down her face. "I never thought I would see you again. Our island is rife with rumours that the Japanese are killing Kuomintang Party members, and I was afraid they had found you out."

"They did," Dan Long said grimly. "Someone informed on me, and I was taken to Changi Beach to be butchered." He related to Winnie the circumstances of his escape.

"We have to leave Singapore," Winnie whispered, holding Dan Long in a tight embrace, her tears falling on his white hair. "You are in danger again, Dan Long. The *Khota Gede* sails from Java, bound for Colombo, and from there, it will be easy to book a passage to Madras, and from Madras take a train to Calcutta. We will fetch Hong Ling from Uncle Ng's farm, and the three of us will leave this war-torn island. KMT members have fled to

Indonesia, hiding out in the islands, and the communists are holed up in the jungles here. They all fear the *kempetai*. Jamal will row us over to the Java port. It is time to bid goodbye to Singapore, my love."

Under the cover of the inky shawl of night, Jamal rowed Winnie, Dan Long and Hong Ling in a sampan to the Java port. As they rounded Keppel Harbour, the moon shone brightly on the burnt hulks of ships listing in the water, lighting up the grim devastation of war. A mild breeze blew across the sea, bringing with it the scent of damp earth; the sky was tinged a silvery white from the moon's glow, the clouds accentuated with silver edges. Would he see Singapore again? Dan Long sighed.

Dawn was breaking when the sampan reached Java. Unlike Keppel Harbour, the Javanese port had ships at anchor, their funnels and masts silhouetted against a pink sky. After alighting from the sampan, Winnie and Dan Long stretched their legs. Hong Ling decided she was hungry and let out a loud wail. While Winnie fed her from a bottle, Jamal helped Dan Long carry their suitcases and holdalls to the huge ship. *Khota Gede* was written on the stern in white paint. The gangplank was already in place, and before boarding the ship, Dan Long thanked Jamal for all his help. The two men embraced. Winnie and Dan Long watched as Jamal's figure diminished in the distance. Men and women were slowly climbing the gangplank, weariness, fear and sorrow written on their faces. Many had lost their homes and were escaping the war.

"Come, Winifred, the baby is asleep, and this will give us time to locate our cabin and berths and settle in. The ship sails soon for Colombo. We will arrive in Ceylon in a week's time, if all goes well."

The tiny cabin of the huge ship chugging its way to Colombo was stuffy and claustrophobic, but Winnie remained impervious to her surroundings. She gazed with love and enchantment at Hong Ling in her arms. The baby grinned at her toothlessly, and tears came to Winnie's eyes. Singapore was already becoming a mere memory, and Winnie felt sad. Her grandmother was buried there, and she had grown up on the tropical isle. It was the only home she had known. India would be a different and alien country—but with Dan Long and Hong Ling by her side, she could be happy anywhere.

Dan Long leaned over the deck railing to watch the foamy waves the ship left in its wake and thought of his sister. If Mei Mei were dead, why had they not discovered her body? Richard and he had scoured all the roads and hospitals, to no avail. A tiny hope burgeoned in his heart that they would clatter into Calcutta's train station, to find Uncle Toh receiving them with Mei Mei on his arm. Dan Long shivered as the images of burning ships and injured civilians dragging their bodies along the streets of Singapore crowded his mind. How could a single woman survive such devastation? Mei Mei had been in the eye of the war storm.

* * *

The voyage from Java to Colombo, and then to Madras on ships, had been long, dirty and tiring. Hong Ling had developed a fever and been churlish. It was a relief when the ship's doctor proclaimed that she was suffering from the common cold, and she would recover with hot compresses and medicines. The doctor prescribed good doses of quinine for all of them as a prophylaxis, before entering mosquito-ridden India.

Dan Long marvelled at the speed and dexterity with which Winnie assumed her maternal duties towards Hong Ling. He loved watching her sitting on the bunk with the baby in her lap, crooning an English lullaby or bathing her in the small sink of the dirty bathroom they shared with the other passengers on their deck. A small flame of hope began to quietly burn in Dan Long's heart, that one day, he would give Winnie her dearest wish and become her child's father.

At long last, the tired man of thirty-five with hair going grey, berated himself for his selfishness. What had he achieved in going to China? China was not his homeland. The wars he had fought had not saved his family from disaster. And while he was fighting another country's war in Nanking, Winnie was desperately ill with tuberculosis in Singapore, and Mei Mei was in danger of being shackled to an old man in marriage. The realisation hit him with such ferocity that Dan Long found himself reeling with regret, thoroughly ashamed of himself. He had promised his dying mother never to leave his sister's side, but he had not only broken that promise, he had left two women to fend for themselves in the melting pot of violence and lawlessness that Singapore had become.

Dan Long sighed and looked out of the window of the carriage. They had disembarked from the ship at Madras and stayed at a cheap hotel for two nights, before embarking on a train bound for Calcutta. Paddy fields, and farmers driving ploughs pulled by water buffaloes, had given way to the pale blue waters of the Godavari River, and canoe-shaped wooden boats banked on the silty land. The train clattered along a long bridge over the river— the Havelock Bridge. A long whistle heralded the approach of the township of Rajahmundry.

A blind man playing a harmonium strapped to his chest, and accompanied by a young girl holding his hand singing a poignant song in Hindi, made their way along the train corridor, the man encouragingly thrusting out a tin cup containing coins. *What a beautiful voice,* Dan Long thought. Rich in timbre, sweet and lilting, it reminded him of the waterfalls in China, cascading down with a tinkle that echoed from the surrounding mountains. The voice rose in cadence, and he was back in Singapore, in a stall at New World with Winnie, Mei Mei and Poh, mesmerised by the Chinese opera singer, singing of opportunities lost. Tears sprang to his eyes.

Dan Long awoke from his reverie as the train grinded to a stop at Rajahmundry. Yelling urchins, carrying aluminium kettles of steaming tea and small clay cups, shouted enthusiastically through the window. India was such a large country with a multitude of resources, different from Singapore where trading was the primary means of earning income. Dan Long tilted his head proudly—owning an eatery and a carpentry shop in his own name, and assisting Uncle Toh in his leather shop at Hogg's Market in Calcutta, would enable him to rent a small flat in Calcutta's Chinatown for Winnie and Hong Ling.

On a bright morning, the air sharp with a winter nip, the train clattered into Howrah Junction in Calcutta. Indian porters, wearing red kurtas and white dhotis, began running along the sides of the platform, peering into the windows, hollering for custom. Dan Long crooked one finger, and an old porter jumped nimbly into the train. While Winnie settled Hong Ling against her shoulder, the porter placed their two suitcases and a holdall on a red turban coiled around his head. Balancing expertly, the porter ran down the train steps and into the station, followed by Winnie and Dan Long.

Dan Long had sent word through one of Uncle Toh's business acquaintances that he would be arriving with Winnie and Hong Ling. While not expecting a welcome, given his uncle's busy schedule, Dan Long still glanced down the length of the platform. He froze, and an inarticulate sound escaped his lips. Winnie turned around to look at him, and all he could do was point down the platform, tears coursing down his cheeks, fogging his spectacles. Winnie looked to where Dan Long pointed, and the sun broke out on her face, making it radiant.

For there she was, dressed in red tunic and trousers, her braided hair coiled around her head, her doe-like eyes wide with unbridled joy and shining with tears as they gazed on Hong Ling. She stretched out her arms, as she used to do long ago, when Dan Long returned from farming his father's land, his steps quickening as he approached the portico, where his sister waited with a pitcher of water for him to wash his face.

PART SIX

The Girl in the Portrait

1948–1963

"If only there could be an invention that bottled up
a memory like scent. And it never faded, never got stale.
And then when one wanted it, the bottle could be uncorked,
and it would be like living the moment all over again."
Daphne du Maurier

26

January 1948, England

Angry waves pounded the unyielding Cornish shore, and a thunderous roar resounded from the surrounding cliffs. The majesty of Nature's fury reminded the lone red-haired man on the shore of his puny existence, and the timeless landscape mocked his feeble attempts to achieve immortality through his art. After some time, the waves grew silent from the tale of woe and tragedy it muttered to those inclined to hear it. The sun ruled supreme, shining brilliantly, bringing into focus the figure on the headland, facing the beauty of Nature and yet unheeding of it, eyes instead fixed on the easel on which a beautiful Chinese face was taking shape. The fingers on the brush were tense and moved slowly, exploring every drawn line before repainting, the red brows frowning in concentration, as consciousness explored the deep recesses of a flawed memory. The green eyes grew mesmerized at the creation taking shape, the mouth opened in wonder, and at last, the fingers on the brush trembled to a stop.

A stubborn instinct, odd and incomprehensible, had prevented Richard from asking Clementine for details of his past life, though he knew the younger version of him lived on in her memories. Richard felt that he could survive in the present if he lived with the hope that the mists of amnesia would clear on their own, and he would regain his memory. He had thought to ask his mother about his past, but Eleanor Harrison had died two months after Richard's arrival in England, of a broken heart. She had not been able to overcome the shock of John's loss.

Lost, alone and frightened, the memory of his past life a void, Richard was seized with a desire to be remembered for generations to come, to live forever in the embroidery of his work. The loss of his past, he thought, could somehow be compensated by permanence in the future. From 1943, he had started again to paint, at first slowly and laboriously, later with a frenzy that amazed even himself. He had not forgotten his trade, although he had forgotten everything else.

John Harrison had failed to transfer his fortune from the Singapore banks to England before World War II, and money had run out of the Harrison coffers, making it difficult to continue the upkeep of Stamford Manor, the house the rubber planter had built as his retirement home in Yorkshire. On the advice of his lawyer, Quentin Goodfellow, Richard had leased Stamford Manor in 1945 to tenants, and relocated his family to Clem's manor house in Newquay, which she had elected to run as an inn with some of the staff from Stamford Manor. Richard had joined the St Ives artists' community in 1946, and was busy re-learning his trade.

Suddenly, there was a whisper in the breeze. *"Richard, should we sail to Calcutta?"*

Richard jumped violently and looked wildly around. The gulls continued squawking, scarcely disturbed. The sun was overhead now, beaming down on him with mild benevolence. He recollected suddenly and vividly the fierce ruthlessness of another sun in another world, one that beat down relentlessly on scores of rubber trees and on a tennis court, scorching the earth with a vengeance.

He heard again the lilting musical voice, *"Richard, it is hard for me to stay here any longer. You must take me away."* A girl. A Chinese girl.

Richard's heartbeat quickened, and his mind searched frantically for a familiar face in the dark caverns of his lost memory; but there was nothing.

"That is a beautiful portrait, Harrison." Nathan Langley, a fellow artist from St Ives, had come to relieve the monotony of the lonely landscape. He gazed admiringly over the artist's shoulder at the painting. "With more work, yes, a lot more work, it could be a masterpiece." The tone of wonder bordered now on the casual. "Who is she? Someone you knew in the tropics?"

Richard turned pain-filled eyes and a face drained of colour to his friend. "I have no idea as to the woman's identity. My memory hasn't come back, Nathan, but I can remember faces without their names. I must dig very deep into my memory, concentrate hard in peaceful surroundings, and then a face is conjured up. The identity of the person remains a mystery. I've heard that people can imagine the faces of folks they don't know and have never met, so it's conceivable that I didn't even know this Chinese woman."

"You knew her," Nathan Langley said with conviction.

"How do you know that?" Richard asked sharply, swivelling on his seat to face his friend.

"You've captured an expression in her eyes." Nathan traced the eyes on the portrait with a reverent finger. "An artist rarely captures an expression this thoroughly if he hasn't met the model in real life."

Richard squinted against the sun, shading his eyes to look better at his creation. "What is the expression you see?" he asked curiously.

"Come, Richard, you can't be that naïve," Nathan smiled. "The expression is the intimate loving look a woman gives a man when he means the world to her. It could be that you caught her gazing this way at another man, but I doubt it. The eyes are looking straight at the painter."

When Nathan had left, and with black clouds darkening the sky, the lone man on the headland bundled up his gear preparatory to departure; but he still lingered, gazing long and hard at the darkly muttering waves to decipher their mysterious message, in the same way he strove vainly to sieve his reluctant memory for enlightenment. A dog can pick at a bone, but the meat may have long since disappeared, and only the essence remains.

There was a yelp of delighted laughter. A girl of six appeared on the road on the headland, her black hair escaping from pigtails, her elfin face alive and laughing, her dark eyes bright with joy. She ran towards Richard and was enveloped in his arms as a dour-faced woman panted towards the headland.

"Emily!" Richard cried. "You should not be here. You will catch a cold. Where's your coat, child? Nanny, wrap her up, please." Richard looked at the nanny anxiously.

"I cannot stop the child from wanting to be with her father," the nanny said virtuously, while enveloping the little girl in a voluminous black coat. "Missus says to come to lunch, and little Emily wanted to give you the message, Mr Harrison."

"I lose track of time when painting." Richard smiled.

Emily entwined her fingers in Richard's, and father and daughter started walking, silhouettes on the headland, soon lost from view.

27

Summer, 1959, Cornwall, England

Clementine was weeding in the front garden of her house in Cornwall. It was a beautiful place, with roses, pansies and poppies flowering in abundance, lending a riot of colour to the landscape, providing a contrast to the blue of the sea, thundering not far away to the shore. The sun shone down mildly, but Clementine had protected her head with a wide-brimmed straw hat.

She paused in her weeding and sat back looking at her house. A green creeper covered most of the facade and draped around the upstairs windows, lending the house a pleasing allure. Clementine shaded her eyes and smiled, before a frown marred her features. She had Richard, Emily and her Cornwall house. She had promised herself she would be happy in England with her own family. Why did peace continue to elude her?

Emily. The sun was obscured by a cloud and Clem's face was in shadow. But the trembling of her hands on the spade spoke of her intense emotion regarding her daughter.

At eighteen, Emily was tall and slim, with black hair cut in a pageboy style, shining black eyes in a pointed face, a pudgy nose, and thin lips. She refused to hide the ugly birthmark on her neck with a cluster of pearls. At best, her well-wishers said that she had an interesting face. Clem's eyes flashed. She was tired of telling Richard's friends that her father, Roger, had had black hair and dark looks, and that Emily took after her maternal grandfather. What choice did she have but to lie about her daughter?

The sun sailed out, and Clem swept back her blonde hair, which she still wore long, and which still shone like golden mist. She had aged well, the skin of her face retaining its elasticity, her slim form remaining, and her eyes still the clear blue of the sea. That was the problem. She, with her beauty, provided a stark contrast to her dark, ugly daughter. But did Emily care how she looked?

No. Clem frowned heavily. All Emily cared about was Richard's love and company. The two of them were inseparable. A sudden sob escaped Clem's throat. It almost seemed that, after losing his memory, Richard had transferred the warmth and affection he had had for Mei Mei to Emily. Clem clenched her fists. How she had hoped that when she told Richard that they had made love on the ship bound for England and that she had fallen pregnant, he would finally return the full measure of her regard. Instead, he had calmly arranged for them to get married in a poky registrar's office in Truro. And when Emily had been born in a hospital in the same town, it seemed that Richard had been reborn. He had loved little Emily with the same intensity he had loved Mei Mei. He only had time for painting and the girl. Clem had been unceremoniously pushed to the background, the two of them only paying attention to her when they needed a meal.

Clem seethed. Richard had taught Emily painting from a young age, and he had been delighted when he found she had a gift for watercolours. Emily had held her first exhibition in Truro and had managed to sell her paintings at good prices. The fact that she was the daughter of one of Britain's topmost landscape and portrait painters, Richard Harrison, opened doors for her in the art world—she was making quite a name for herself.

Instead of being proud, Clem was intensely jealous of her daughter. Painting was yet another bond that shackled Emily to Richard, and Clem was full of resentment. From the moment Emily had been put in her arms after her birth, Clem had felt revulsion for the dark-haired, ugly baby, and as quickly as possible had hired nannies to take care of her. Her lack of maternal feelings had affected Richard, who had tried to compensate by giving Emily more and more affection. Clem had tolerated Emily, but little Emily had fought back by ignoring her mother and doting on Richard. When Clem had suggested boarding school for her daughter, Richard had agreed, as painting took him to different parts of Europe, and he could not pay heed to her studies. What Clem had discovered was that, previously unknown to her, Richard had frequently visited Emily at boarding school, taking her out for lunches and to the cinema. She had fumed when she had found out, but what could she do?

Clem stood up and sighed. Now that he earned a lot of money from his paintings, Richard had renovated Stamford Manor and lived in Yorkshire. He had not invited Clem to live with him, but she knew that Emily, fresh out of boarding school, had made her home with Richard. Clem's eyes narrowed. She did not crave Emily's affection, but she had to get Richard back, and she knew how to do it.

Smiling, Clem went indoors. Shortly afterwards, Richard and Emily arrived from Truro, where Emily had been talking to an art gallery owner interested in exhibiting her paintings.

"Hello, Mother!" Emily said, her voice bland. "How are you?"

Clementine rose from the sofa, a cool smile on her lips. "I am well, thank you, Emily. What brings you to Newquay?"

Richard, looking thin but tanned, his hair salt and pepper now, his face lined, said cheerfully, "Emily is going to take the grand tour of Europe. I have rented a villa in Tuscany and we cannot wait to paint landscapes." He suddenly looked boyish and full of fun.

Emily smiled, and when she did so, she lit up the room and people forgot that she was not beautiful. "Dad is coming with me. He will be my companion and escort on this grand tour. We will take Europe by storm and come back with many paintings between the two of us. I came to pack some clothes. I will go up to my bedroom now."

The colour had fled from Clem's face at Richard's words, and when she turned to him, her eyes were blue shards of ice. "I take it that I am not to accompany you to Europe?"

Richard, in the act of pouring wine into a glass, paused. He turned a nonplussed face to Clem. "Oh," he said. "I assumed that you would not want to come. It is a working holiday, really, for us." He tried to infuse cheeriness into his tone as he said, "You can come with us, of course, Clem. But would you not be bored?" His voice was worried. "The doctor in Truro said that you needed peace and quiet. Should you be gallivanting around Europe with us?"

Clem had moved to the French windows, from where she could see the sea thundering to the shore. Her nostrils flared at Richard's words, and she thought of her stepsister, Lily, berating her after she had made the effort to educate her and her twin sister, Rose. Rose had died in childbirth. How could that be her fault, Clementine fumed. But Lily had admonished her for her lack of care towards her stepsisters, and blamed her for their mother's death. Lily had said that if Clara had continued living in the Cornwall house, she would not have died. When Lily had left the house after looking at Clem with accusing eyes, stating that their father would have been ashamed of her, lying to him on his deathbed, Clem had collapsed and had a nervous breakdown. The image of a dying Clara Higgins coming into her dreams had haunted her, and she had screamed in agony.

Now she turned to Richard, and her eyes were shining with an odd light.

"Richard, you and Emily can go to Europe. I will stay here in Cornwall." She tossed her head. "Emily is lucky to be so loved and pampered by a man who is not her father."

Richard went white and dropped the glass of wine he was holding. It fell to the floor, the liquid spreading insidiously over the grey carpet like a murderous bloodstain. With incredulous eyes, Richard looked at Clem.

"What do you mean, Clementine?"

Clem shrugged her shoulders. "I had hoped that I would never have to tell you this sordid and sad story, but I think it best you know that Emily is not your child. You were burning up with malaria on the ship when we were fleeing Singapore. The ship's doctor had no more quinine, and you were at death's door. One of the ship's passengers, a wealthy American businessman, had a large stock of phials for his own use. To save your life, I went to beg him for quinine. His price for a phial was outraging my modesty. Emily is the product of that hateful night when that American raped me."

Richard had tottered to a chair and sat on it, his head in his hands. When he looked up, his green eyes were horrified. "Why did you lie to me, Clementine? If you had told me the truth about Emily's parentage, I would have understood. I am grateful to you for saving my life, but you should have told me the truth. Can you imagine how I feel knowing I am not Emily's biological father?"

Clementine looked at Richard, her eyes hopeful. Maybe now, with the knowledge that he was not Emily's biological father and that she, Clementine, had saved his life, finally Richard would give her the love she deserved.

Emily entered with a suitcase packed to the brim. "Dad, you should buy some summer clothes. Italy is going to be hot!"

Clementine watched Richard's eyes light up with love as he looked at Emily, and her own eyes lost hope, became lacklustre. She should have told Richard the truth before Emily's birth. Maybe then he would not have become so attached to her. It was too late now.

When Emily had gone down to the village to buy some necessities for the journey, Richard accosted Clem in the garden.

"I don't know why you told me of Emily's parentage," he

said, his voice throbbing with emotion, "but you will not mention a word of it to Emily."

Clem looked up from her weeding, her face sulky. "You must have wondered why she did not look like either of us," she said.

"No, I took your word for what happened. My mind is not as devious as yours, Clementine. My past is shrouded in a mist, and you took advantage of that. But if anything, after today, I will love Emily even more. She captured my heart from the moment she was born, and she will always be my daughter."

"I mean nothing to you, Richard?" There was a shrill edge to Clem's voice as the gardening shears dropped from her hands. "Why can Emily claim your heart and I cannot?"

"I would not tell Emily about her parentage if I were you, Clementine," Richard warned her again. "I don't want Emily to be unhappy. If you ever tell her the truth, I will cut off all ties with you, I promise. I will leave you now."

Clementine watched Richard stride confidently back to the house, his shoulders straight. Tears glittered in her eyes and fell silently onto her cheeks. Richard loved Mei Mei, and he loved Emily, but he had never loved her and never could.

"Why?" Clementine shrieked, and the birds on the trees in the garden flew away hastily, with surprised chirps. The sun began setting over the land and Clementine's heart.

28

March 1963, UK and Singapore

In the United Kingdom, people in buses and on the tube, and over their morning breakfasts and coffees in their homes, read about the scandalous news of the Duke and Duchess of Argyll's divorce case, about the six men sentenced to death in France for conspiring to assassinate President Charles de Gaulle, about a musical band called the *Beatles* releasing their first album, *Please Please Me*, and about the portrait of a Chinese girl painted by Britain's famed painter, Richard Harrison.

THE TIMES
Tuesday, 26 March 1963

Painting Exhibition at Tate Best in a Decade

A new painting exhibition unveiled at the Tate Gallery includes a painting that is causing a stir in art circles. The painting, by Sir Richard Harrison, is a portrait of a young Chinese girl. Other paintings of note are the portraits, *Girl in the Woods*, by Nathan Langley, and *A Chimney Sweep*, by Robert Gorman. According to art experts, the exhibition at the Tate heralds a revolution in portrait painting. The Louvre has asked for a loan of *The Chinese*

Girl for a year-long display in Paris.

"The painting of *The Chinese Girl* is exquisite in detail and execution," Sir Norman Thomas, the highly acclaimed painter from Durham said, in an exclusive interview. "I strongly recommend that it continue being exhibited, and not be put up for sale."

The exhibition at the Tate Gallery will end by the middle of May.

THE DAILY MIRROR
Wednesday, 24 April 1963

WHO IS THE GIRL IN THE PORTRAIT?

The portrait of a Chinese girl painted by Sir Richard Harrison is continuing to create ripples in the art world. Artists who have seen the painting insist that they have never seen such a lively portrait before.

"It's the eyes," Robert Gorman, the painter from Manchester, said in an interview, "They are flushed with love and looking directly at the painter. Draw your own conclusions."

Sir Richard Harrison first rose to fame in the early 1950s with his landscape paintings, homed in the technique of the St Ives artist colony. His portrait paintings carry his own original stamp, their uniqueness unrivalled through the years.

Sir Richard was born in Malaya and raised in Singapore during colonial rule. Tragically, he was hit by shrapnel during the Japanese bombing of Singapore and was brought back to England by his fiancée and childhood sweetheart, Clementine Arbuthnot, who nursed and later married him. The head wound caused Sir Richard to lose his memory, and he has not regained it.

In 1960, Harrison was knighted, and Sir Richard, with his daughter, Emily Harrison, herself a famed watercolour artist, travelled extensively in Europe. Some of the artist's later paintings of European landscapes fetched millions of pounds. Now in his fifties, Sir Richard lives in his native Yorkshire, in a rambling manor in Grassington.

When questioned on the paucity of South-East Asian landscapes in his portfolio, especially from the country of his upbringing, Sir Richard said, "I have no memory of my childhood and adulthood before the Second World War. If one must see a country through new eyes when one has seen it already through forgotten eyes, one would be lying when painting that country. I'm sure that I would paint Singapore as a stranger now, and I don't want to do that." Yet, Sir Richard has painted a Chinese girl, and the painting took fifteen years to complete.

Did Sir Richard meet the young Chinese girl in his youth in Singapore? Did he reciprocate the love of the girl in the portrait? Who is she? Is Sir Richard's memory returning? When approached, Lady Clementine Harrison and her daughter, Emily, declined to comment on the identity of the girl in the portrait.

THE STRAITS TIMES
Saturday, 18 May 1963

THE GIRL IN THE PORTRAIT IDENTIFIED!

The worldwide speculation on the identity of the Chinese girl painted by renowned British painter, Sir Richard Harrison, is finally at an end. In an exclusive interview to *The Straits Times*, 50-year-old widow, Mong Li Tan, identified the mystery girl in the Harrison portrait as her friend, Liao Mei Mei. According to Madam Tan, Madam Liao was a *mui-tsai*, sold at a young age to an affluent Chinese family. Unlike other bondmaids, she was treated well by her wealthy aunt and uncle, until the arrival of her uncle's second wife. Madam Tan claims that Madam Liao was arrested by the police at the age of fifteen on charges of murdering her aunt. After a trial, she was acquitted, and her aunt's bondmaid was arrested for the crime. Madam Tan claims that it was at this trial that Madam Liao met Richard Harrison, who was the court artist.

Madam Tan says, "Richard Harrison fell in love with Mei Mei when she nursed him back to health from cholera on St John's Island. Mei Mei was aware of her cultural and social differences with Richard Harrison, and rebutted his advances. Madam Liao went on to marry an affluent Chinese merchant and gave birth to his daughter, Gan Hong Ling."

According to Madam Tan, Madam Liao Mei Mei disappeared during the Japanese bombing of Singapore and is presumed dead. But according to our reporters, who visited Madam Liao Mei Mei's marital home, she lives there with her daughter, brother and his family.

The Girl in the Portrait is alive!

29

The Tate Gallery was busy mid-morning, flocks of visitors gathering in front of paintings, admiring the artwork and chatting with each other. A long queue moved slowly towards a large painting framed in gilt, the latest Harrison original, *The Chinese Girl*.

Clementine craned her neck to glimpse the painting, but at least twenty men and women were in front of her in the queue. After an hour, she was close enough to discern the slim figure of the painted Chinese woman within the frame, and to distinguish the red cheongsam that Mei Mei had worn when she had sat for Richard as his model. Clem's heartbeat quickened, and her chest felt tight. She still could not see the face in the picture. She rudely pushed the woman in front of her, who left the queue with an indignant squeak. Clem sailed forth and stood in front of the painting. Her mouth trembled with a denial she could not utter, and her whole body began shaking uncontrollably.

From the frame, Mei Mei smiled serenely, her eyes filled with the light of love that was so familiar to Clem, and which so incensed her. The past rushed back with a frightening intensity— Clementine was back in the tropics, looking through the keyhole into Richard's studio, where Mei Mei sat in the same red dress she wore in the portrait. Richard approached her to smooth away a tendril of hair from her forehead with a tender hand.

But she had destroyed that painting, Jeff was witness to that! How could Richard have painted the same portrait he had painted thirty years ago? It was uncanny and unbelievable. She must be dreaming.

Then she saw his signature at the bottom left hand corner of the portrait. She knew then that Richard had painted Mei Mei recently from a flawed memory, but as lovingly as he had painted her long ago.

A strangled cry came from Clem. "He has painted a ghost! This girl is dead, you hear me! She is dead."

There were uneasy murmurings around her, and the pain in Clem's chest intensified. Hammers drummed away inside her head, and her mouth opened, but no sound came. The drumming increased, the world swam away and exploded in one searing flash of pain, before a merciful darkness descended.

Cornwall

Richard paced the corridor outside Clementine's room at a private hospital in Truro. The doctor, a dark-haired Welshman with clear grey eyes, came out of the room followed by a dour-faced nurse, whose uniform crackled as she walked.

"It was a mild stroke," Dr Bevan assured Richard, "and your wife was lucky that there was a doctor at the Tate Gallery, and she received immediate medical attention." Dr Bevan's gaze sharpened. "You need to be careful, though. Lady Harrison's heart is weak, and she suffers from high blood pressure. I have prescribed pills, and Nurse here will administer them. You need to be aware that Lady Harrison is also highly strung, and she should not be exposed to undue excitement or stress. Otherwise, I am afraid she may suffer a breakdown. Again, I have prescribed some pills for her nervous condition. It will be good if Nurse Tallman accompanies you when Lady Harrison is discharged, and stays at least a week in your home, until Lady Harrison is settled into a routine of taking her medications."

Richard went into a paroxysm of coughing. When he recovered, he said, "Clementine lives with her old nanny, Mrs Morton, in her house in Newquay. Mrs Morton will give her the best of care. There is no need for Nurse Tallman's services."

Dr Bevan nodded. "If you say so, Sir Richard. You should have that cough of yours seen to, eh? Make an appointment with my nurse for a consultation. It does not sound good."

* * *

On a bleak morning, when dark clouds rode across the sky like stallions, Clementine left the hospital in a car to make the journey back to her home in Newquay. The shock of seeing Mei Mei staring at her out of a gilt frame had sapped her energy, leaving her a caricature of her former self. Her hollow cheeks, matted hair and lacklustre eyes elicited an abundance of sympathetic clicks from kind Mrs Beresford, the cook.

"Nothing that nourishing soups and good bits of meat won't put right, my lady." Mrs Beresford smiled reassuringly, before bustling off to the kitchen.

A week later, Clementine was sitting by the hearth in the front room of her house, watching the fire crackle merrily. It was evening and Hungerford, the butler, had driven down to the station to fetch Richard from the London train. She wished she could go to Roche Rock, but everyone would think it strange if she went to sit in a ruined chapel when convalescing from a stroke. Clem's fists clenched, and her lips hardened. She refused to become an invalid like her mother, lying on a bed day and night, immersed in another world.

There was a knock on the door and Richard entered. He looked tired, and Hungerford poured him a tumbler of whisky.

"That will be all, Hungerford," Richard said. After the door had closed behind the butler, Richard turned to Clem. "I am sorry, Emily had some engagements in Scotland and could not come with me. She will come to see you later. I will stay a week and then return to Yorkshire. I see that Nanny is taking good care of you."

"You need not offer excuses for Emily," Clementine said in an icy voice, her blue eyes pinpricks of dislike. "There is no love lost between that girl and me. She might not be your flesh and blood, but she's more your daughter than she is mine." She directed a penetrating blue gaze at Richard. "Has your memory returned? You painted that Chinese girl."

Richard shook his head. His eyes entreating, he leaned towards Clem. "Please tell me who she is, Clem. She must have meant something for me to paint her out of a flawed memory."

"She is dead." Clementine's voice was devoid of emotion. "She died during the war."

343

Richard was pacing the floor, his brows puckered, his hands running through his untidy salt-and-pepper hair. He coughed from time to time. He took a crumpled newspaper out of his pocket and proffered it to Clem.

"This is the official English newspaper from Singapore, and there is an article on the girl in my portrait. According to the reporter, the girl I painted is alive and lives in a house on Beach Road with her daughter." He went to stand near the window to look out at the darkening landscape. "I have decided to visit Singapore. I need to see this woman. Maybe then my memory will return."

The walls began to oscillate in front of Clementine's eyes, the ceiling tilted dangerously towards her, and she could hear concerned voices coming from a great distance. Sighing, Clementine allowed the darkness to swallow her.

Night had fallen, and Richard sat by his bedroom window in Clem's house, overlooking the Cornish sea. Moonlight slanted across the waters and crested the waves thundering onto the strip of sandy shore. Rocks and cliffs bordered the coast, and he stiffened when he saw a figure make its way down the road to the bus-stop. He recognised Clementine by the anorak she wore.

She had refused to see him after he told her of his plans to visit Singapore and had taken to her bed. She would only see Nanny, and whenever he crept up the stairs towards her room, he would hear a keening cry and moaning, like an animal in pain.

He felt uneasy as he saw Clementine waiting for the bus to Bodmin. Why, she was going to Roche Rock at this hour! She had told him of her childhood sanctuary and her hours spent there alone, trying to come to terms with her mother's death and her father's intention to remarry. What was she going to do at Roche Rock?

Filled with foreboding, Richard dressed in warm clothes, went down to the hall, eased into his anorak, and hurried to the bus stop. But all he saw were the taillights of the bus. Sighing, he sat on the bench in the cold, waiting for the next one.

* * *

Clementine stood framed in the window of the ruined chapel on Roche Rock, silhouetted against the Cornish sky under which she had been born, gazing at the dark landscape. As she stood with the wind blowing in her face, she remembered Governess Clara. She had been exiled as a child, but her mother's mantra had propelled her on, and she had transferred her obsessive love for Muriel to Richard.

What had she achieved? She seethed as she thought of Richard's portrait of Mei Mei. Why had she been unsuccessful in making Richard forget that girl? He loved Emily more than life itself. Why could he not love Clem? Would she have been happier married to Jeffrey Peters?

Clem laughed. No, from the minute he had shaken her hand in that colourful harbour of Singapore, taken her under his wing, taught her tennis, accompanied her on the violin while she played the piano, she had loved Richard with an overpowering love. That was the way she was made. She had chosen to love and to possess, and now she faced the consequences of those choices. In the bleak chapel on the rock, in the dead of night, Clementine embraced the only path that was open to her. She moved towards the hollow of the window and stood poised there, like a giant vulture.

"I have nothing more to live for," she said to the wind howling into the chamber. "Richard will leave for Singapore and be reunited with Mei Mei. But surely, Mei Mei is dead, and it is a question of mistaken identity? But the house in Beach Road? That is Mei Mei's marital home. So she escaped!" A sob caught in Clem's throat.

Her eyes darkened. She had told Richard that he had not fathered Emily, and she bitterly regretted her choice in disclosing that information. Since then, Richard had devoted himself to Emily even more than before.

"But I am still married to Richard, and I will never grant him a divorce so that he can gallivant off to Singapore and marry Mei Mei." Triumph momentarily gleamed in Clem's blue eyes before they dulled again. "Oh, I am so tired of fighting for Richard. Even if I remain married to him, he will love Mei Mei, and for all I know, he will set up a home with her in Singapore. She is such a shameless native hussy!" Anger shone from Clem's eyes.

There was a sound in the chamber and Clem turned. There was someone in the room with her and her heart began to beat erratically. The moon sailed out from behind a cloud, and its silver light flooded the chamber. Clementine saw a small boy with a blackened face gazing at her with sorrowful eyes.

"Ali!" she whispered, then screamed, "No! No! Don't come near me, you hear? I did not know you were in the schoolhouse. I only wanted to burn the book of testimonies. Please forgive me! I did not mean for you to die." Clem buried her face in her hands, and when she looked up, she was alone.

Sobs wracked her body. Why did she have such passions? She had hated Governess Clara, and because she had not given her shelter, Clara had died a pauper working in a cotton factory. She was a murderer, according to her stepsister, Lily.

"You are totally self-absorbed," Lily had said scathingly. "You don't have a compassionate bone in your body."

Clementine whimpered. She saw herself stealing into the garden to hatch a plot to compromise Jeff, a man who had loved her with all his heart. And all for someone who had never loved her and never would. Clementine saw her life in a flash, a life lived on one hope and one hope only—to be loved by Richard. She took stock of the havoc she had wreaked to meet her goal.

She had killed Ali in order to dim Richard's regard and admiration for Mei Mei and her work with the bondmaids. She had portrayed Jeff as a lustful adulterer to break off an engagement. She had turned Clara and her two very small children out of her house into the cruel world, after promising a dying man that she would give them shelter. She had participated in a plot to kill Mei Mei, and what had she achieved? The last humiliation of all— Richard choosing to love Clementine's daughter over Clementine, knowing that Emily was not his child.

There was a sound again, and Clementine looked with drooping shoulders and resigned eyes at the small blackened figure moving towards her. Its hand was raised, and its finger pointed towards the open window.

"Yes, Ali," Clem whispered. "I know where salvation and atonement lie. I could not make Richard love me, although I love him more than life itself. And I brought death and destruction in the wake of my love. Goodbye, Richard!" Her heartbroken lament was carried away by the wind.

Clementine perched on the windowsill, a shadow against the moonlit sky, before vanishing from view. An owl gave a heart-wrenching cry.

When Richard arrived at Roche Rock, he ran to the black figure lying on the rocks below the chapel, lit up by bright moonlight. Clementine lay still, curiously at peace, as she had lain so many times on the quilt at the Botanic Gardens of Singapore, gazing at the moon while orchestral music swirled around them. Her blonde hair fanned out over the misshapen black rock, and he choked with emotion, remembering the girl who had been exiled to Singapore, who had disembarked from the ship at a colourful harbour, surly and taciturn, and who had smiled for the first time when presented with a golden spaniel puppy.

Richard knelt by his childhood friend and held her lifeless hand. The tear-laden moonlight fell over her half-closed blue eyes, even as the wound on her head seeped blood, staining the bodice of her dress a deep crimson. Maybe Clem's end was merciful, Richard mused. With her mind gone and dwelling in the darkest of places, her obsession with him directing her every action, she would never have been happy.

He raised her hand and put it next to his heart, before placing his handkerchief over her dead face. He would rather remember her as the laughing girl in a white dress, running across the tennis court at the Goodwood Park Hotel in Singapore, chasing after a ball, carefree, happy. Her fingers had played beautiful music, and he remembered attending her concerts when her music would speak of pain, longing and heartbreak, leaving her audience enthralled.

Slowly, he rose and took a last look at the woman who had not found the right soil to flower into a happy person, knowing already that he would bury her where she had marked her resting place—the bleak and solitary rock, the only place she had found sanctuary during her tumultuous life.

It was only when he was on his way to alert the police, that Richard realised that his past with its childhood memories of Clementine had come into his mind of their own accord, without effort, without strain. He knew for certain then, that with time, he would remember the Chinese girl, Mei Mei. He would not have been able to finish her portrait if his memory had not been on the mend.

While waiting at the police station, a fragment of his past flitted enticingly into his mind.

He was lying on the narrow bed with light from a tropical sun streaming in through the huge windows. She came towards him, her doe-like eyes cast down, a basin and a jug of hot water in her hands, white towels hanging over her shoulders. As she reached out to unbutton his shirt, he put his hands over hers and looked at her face. Her imprisoned fingers fluttered in his big ones, like small birds in cages. A blush filled her cheeks, and when she raised her eyes to his, they were shy and luminous. Yes, it was in the lazaretto of St John's Island that he had fallen in love with

Mei Mei, while she was nursing him back to health from cholera.

The shifting sands of his memory were settling, the clouds were parting, and gladness filled his heart as he saw her clearly, giving him a sponge bath all those years ago, in a hospital he had never thought he would leave alive.

30

Mei Mei walked briskly along Beach Road towards the Gan mansion, carrying two bags of groceries in her hands. A voice from a loudspeaker rent the air. Mei Mei glanced up to see a small truck making its way slowly along the road, with men shouting slogans. The General Elections would be held in September, and parties had started campaigning for seats in the Legislative Assembly, as Singapore chugged towards independence.

Mei Mei frowned. Even in his mid-fifties, her brother, Dan Long, had not given up his political aspirations. Paying scant heed to Winnie's admonitions, he was a strident member of the leftist leaning Barisan Socialis Party.

Poor Winnie, Mei Mei thought. She was in constant dread that her husband would be detained in jail via the Internal Securities Act, as most members of the Party had been, including its head, Lim Chin Siong.

Uncle Toh had died peacefully in his sleep in Calcutta two years after Hong Ling's arrival. Their sorrow at his death had been replaced by joy when Winnie gave birth to Dan Long's daughter, Rose. Mei Mei worked in Dan Long's businesses in Calcutta, but when they learnt that Old Master was on his deathbed, they had returned to Singapore. Old Master's lawyer had produced a document in which the old man left the House of Gan and his assets to Hong Ling. Dan Long had decided to relocate back to Singapore with his family and Mei Mei, and started opening businesses there.

Dan Long had done well for himself as a businessman. He was a rubber distributor and had provision shops and leather goods shops all over Singapore. The businesses generated the income that allowed him, Winnie, Mei Mei, Hong Ling and Rose to live in comfort at the House of Gan. Mei Mei smiled as she thought of Rose. She was a vivacious young woman, with Winnie's smile and complexion and Dan Long's stubbornness. She and Hong Ling, who had grown up to be Mei Mei's spitting image, were inseparable, like the true sisters she and Winnie had been.

Winnie was waiting for Mei Mei in the hall of the House of Gan. Her hair was grey, and she was overweight, a result of overindulgence in cooking and eating Eurasian dishes learnt from Gran. She had a newspaper in her hands.

She pointed excitedly at an item and said, "Second Mistress Meisheng's son, Chu Meng, died a week ago. The House of Toh is to be auctioned off. Some household treasures and artefacts are being sold by his estate at the Raffles Hotel ballroom today."

A myriad of emotions chased each other over Mei Mei's face. "The House of Toh. Oh, had Uncle been alive today, he surely would have bought back the house he had been born in."

"Uncle Toh died a serene and dignified death," Winnie assured her. "He did not suffer at all. He went to sleep in our house in Calcutta one night and passed away in his sleep. That is the best way to leave this world, Mei Mei. Believe me, he would not have wanted to buy back a house which held a multitude of bad memories for him." Winnie pointed to the article. "It says here that Chu Meng had been residing in Japan after the Occupation ended. He only recently returned to Singapore because of ill-health."

Mei Mei said, "Chu Meng died young. Let us go to the auction. I may see some of the Toh heirlooms from my childhood."

A dark, swarthy Japanese man stood next to the auctioneer in one of the smaller ballrooms of Raffles Hotel, his eyes sad and pensive. His gaze never left the belongings of his late master, the jade figurines of great value, Ming vases, and silken robes. He stood there like a recalcitrant sentinel.

"Now we come to a very valuable piece of jewellery," boomed the auctioneer, his face shiny with sweat, even with the overhead fans whirring madly. "This is a jade pendant belonging to the Ming dynasty. Its value is immeasurable. We will start bidding at one thousand dollars, but it is worth at least three times more!" He held out the sparkling pendant on a chain that twinkled in the light of the ballroom chandeliers. "Yes, mistress, do you want to buy this piece? Please wait at your seat, and let the auction begin."

But Mei Mei was making her way to the front of the ballroom, and the auctioneer reluctantly handed over the jade necklace to her for examination. There was a gasp from the Japanese retainer, who was looking at Mei Mei in horror. He turned and ran away.

Mei Mei's eyes were luminous, perspiration beaded her nose, but her voice was strong as she said, "I will bid a thousand dollars for this jade necklace, even though it belonged to me." She turned to the auctioneer. "Who was the Japanese man standing next to you?"

"His name is Obuchi, and he was the retainer of Toh Chu Meng of the House of Toh."

When Mei Mei came out onto the road, the sun had elected to hide behind dark, rolling clouds. There was no rustle in the trees, and the birds waited for the storm to break.

Mei Mei looked at the jade necklace in her hands, and tears clouded her eyes. "Old Master gave me this necklace as a gift on my wedding day. I gave this heirloom to *Kor* Poh to help him escape to China after he denounced Second Mistress Meisheng as a Japanese spy. I never heard from Poh again," Mei Mei murmured softly.

Back at the House of Gan, Winnie rushed into the drawing room, where Dan Long sat reading a newspaper, and articulated her riotous thoughts. "Chu Meng killed Poh? It is true that if Chu Meng had ever discovered that Poh was responsible for Meisheng's suicide, he would take revenge." In a breathless voice, she told Dan Long about the jade necklace found in Chu Meng's possession.

"Poor *Kor* Poh." Mei Mei began to cry softly for her childhood tutor and friend. "If I had not incited him to denounce Second Mistress, he would still be alive."

Hong Ling came into the sitting room with a crumpled newspaper in her hands. Mei Mei never ceased to marvel at how kind and gentle her daughter was. Her eyes were reflective, and her thick lips, her father's legacy, never pouted or showed ill-humour. She was a dear thing to have in the house. She had fulfilled her mother's ambitions, passed the Senior Cambridge examinations, trained successfully as a teacher, and was teaching in a primary school. Rose would soon follow in her footsteps.

"Ma," she said to Mei Mei. "I was at the National Library researching history for my notes in class. I came across this British newspaper from June of this year, a report of a suicide in Cornwall. Ma, we have heard so much from you of Richard Harrison and Clementine. This is a newspaper report of Clementine's suicide. She killed herself in June, Ma."

Mei Mei snatched the newspaper and read the article, her eyes burning, Winnie and Dan Long leaning over her shoulders.

"Why did Clementine commit suicide?" Mei Mei sat down on the sofa.

"Because Richard painted your portrait? The portrait was exhibited in April in London," Dan Long said, his eyes bright behind his spectacles. He was ageing well, his hair, thick and grey, his body muscular, and very few wrinkles on his face. "Clementine had thought that Richard had forgotten you, but he had not, and she could not take that blow."

Mei Mei's eyes were bright with unshed tears. "No, it was probably because Clementine discovered that I was alive from the newspaper reports on the identity of the girl in Richard's portrait. She believed me to be dead."

"Why?" Winnie demanded. She looked shrewdly at Mei Mei and asked, "What happened to you that night in 1942 when you went to meet Richard, Mei Mei? You have never spoken of it, and you never told us why you decided not to elope with Richard. We didn't pry, because Dan Long told me that we needed to move forward in life, and if you did not choose to tell us what happened, we should not bother you about it."

"Yes, maybe now is the time to tell you of my nightmare during the war." Mei Mei motioned Hong Ling to sit beside her and leaned back on the sofa. "Richard and I were going to elope to India. This was in 1942, when Japanese bombs were falling over Singapore. Our rendezvous was at Boat Quay where Jamal, Richard's house-boy, was to be waiting with him in a sampan.

"I left the House of Gan at eight. It had been decided that Winnie's stepfather would take Hong Ling to St John's Island in his boat. Richard and I would meet him there late at night, stay there a day or two, and then Hong Ling, Richard and I would sail for India.

"I was walking towards Boat Quay when I heard footsteps. I thought my father-in-law's men were after me, and I began to run. There was the sound of a siren and I saw Japanese bombers dotting the sky. I ran into a hut and took shelter. I fainted from fear and fell and twisted my ankle. I rested for a while, and then suddenly a shadow darkened the door of the hut and a torch shone in. It was Jeffrey Peters, John Harrison's overseer in the rubber plantation."

Winnie gave a gasp. "Jeff was in love with Clementine."

"Yes, but he was Richard's best friend and my well-wisher." Mei Mei nodded. "Jeff told me that Clem was sheltering with him and had refused to leave for England with Eleanor. He understood that she was waiting for Richard. One evening, he overheard her talking to two men in his garden. He eavesdropped on their conversation and heard her informing them that I was going to elope with Richard. The two men said that they would 'take care' of me. Jeff knew of Clem's obsessive love for Richard, but he would not allow her to become a murderer.

"He began to follow her to my rendezvous with Richard at the back of the House of Gan. And then the night I ran away, Jeff followed me. The footsteps I had heard belonged to one of those two men who had conspired with Clem to kill me. It was fortuitous that Jeff was tailing me. He got to me in that hut before the two men did.

"Jeff reasoned with me. He told me that I was a mother, and that Hong Ling was my priority. If I chose to elope with Richard, Clementine would follow us wherever we went, he said. I was afraid for Hong Ling, and when Jeff gave me a ticket on a ship carrying Japanese women and children to Bombay via Singapore, I decided that I would escape on that ship to India. I knew that everyone would think I had been killed by Japanese bombs, and I also knew that Dan Long would soon arrive in Singapore to escort Winnie to Calcutta. I had told Winnie that if anything happened to me, she was to hide Hong Ling with her, and wait for Dan Long to take them both to Calcutta. All the plans had been laid, so I decided to take Jeff's advice, fled on the ship, and took a train from Bombay to Calcutta. I then waited for Hong Ling to join me, and she did so in March of 1942."

Mei Mei stopped her tale and looked at Hong Ling, her eyes narrowed in pain. It had cost her a great deal to tell everyone the truth of that night, which would remain as a nightmare in her memory. Her daughter took Mei Mei's hands in hers and gave them a tight squeeze.

Dan Long turned to Mei Mei, his eyes excited. "Second Mistress Meisheng's son, Chu Meng, had your jade necklace, which he snatched from Poh when he killed my comrade. If Chu Meng knew that Poh had denounced his mother to the authorities as a spy, he also knew that you had a part to play. The two men Jeffrey Peters saw with Clementine in his garden could have been Chu Meng and Obuchi. I would not be surprised if Chu Meng wanted to kill you to avenge his mother. Clementine was a willing collaborator but not the instigator of your planned murder. Perhaps Chu Meng was the informer who denounced me to the Japanese. The informer asked me if I was your brother. I hear that he lived in Japan after the Occupation, his mother's homeland. Chu Meng and his retainer followed you that night and would have killed you if you had not taken shelter from the Japanese bombing, and if Jeffrey Peters had not found you, Mei Mei."

Dan Long shuffled over to his sister. He tenderly smoothed his sister's hair and said, "I will call at the police station to track down the servant, Obuchi, and the police will make him confess, for I am sure he was his master's shadow. What an ordeal you went through, Mei Mei. Richard would not have married Clementine if he had not lost his memory. Clementine took advantage of his amnesia to spin lies about the past in order to marry him."

"What is done is done," Mei Mei said practically. "I chose my destiny. I chose maternal love over romantic love, and I have no regrets." She rose and folded Hong Ling into her arms.

Silence fell between them, and they heard a hawker loudly selling his wares on the street outside.

* * *

Mei Mei was on her way back from supervising the workers of Dan Long's leather goods factory. She spied Hong Ling through the wrought iron gates of the House of Gan, feeding 'Bank of Hell' notes into an urn in the garden. The corners of her lips lifted in a satisfied smile. Hong Ling was a dutiful child, praying for the souls of her father and grandfather every seventh lunar month. Winnie, who had been trimming her roses in the garden, straightened up as the gate creaked open.

"We have a visitor," Winnie said. Her brown eyes narrowed and the creases around them deepened. "Emily Harrison, Richard and Clementine's daughter, is here. I have shown her into the study and Rose is talking to her. I have settled Emily with *sugee* cake, devilled eggs and, of course, Darjeeling tea." Winnie was shepherding her friend towards the front door, Hong Ling following. "Emily seems a very nice young woman, not much older than Hong Ling and a famous painter, as well. Takes after her father, no doubt. But not in looks. She looks nothing like either Richard or Clementine."

The interior of Old Master Gan's study was lit with Chinese lanterns hanging from the ceiling, with rosewood shelves of dusty books crowding the walls. Emily rose from a chair as Mei Mei came to the door. She exclaimed softly on seeing Mei Mei, her hand going to her mouth, her elfin eyes wide open in excitement, her black hair falling across her forehead.

She brushed back the strands with an impatient hand and said, "Why, Dad painted your likeness so exquisitely! I cannot believe he has not regained his memory. Madam Mei Mei, I have come to take you to my father. He has begun to remember parts of his past, the fact that you nursed him back to health from cholera. If he sees you in person, I am certain his memory will return in its entirety."

"I cannot go with you," Mei Mei said softly.

Emily said, "Madam Mei Mei, my father is gravely ill. He had consumption in his childhood when he lived in Malaya. Now, the tuberculosis bacteria have again reared their ugly heads. His doctor says Dad needs warmth, sunshine and care from a loved one at home. Dad very much wants to live in Italy, a country he first visited when he lived in Singapore. The climate is warm, and he loves painting there.

"Madam Mei Mei, I can look after him, but he needs you, both physically and emotionally, if he is to recover. My mother's death hit him hard. They led separate lives, Dad and Mum, he in Yorkshire and she in Cornwall, but he has begun to remember parts of his childhood when Mum and he were teenagers, and they shared a great friendship."

Tears were trickling down Mei Mei's cheeks and she sobbed, "Richard is ill!"

Winnie said in a comforting voice, "I recovered from TB and so will Richard. Look at the medical treatments we have now! Penicillin and other medicines will cure his disease."

Mei Mei stood up. "I cannot go to Richard, but I will pray every day for his good health."

Emily got to her feet. "Please do reconsider your decision, Madam Mei Mei. I will be staying at Raffles Hotel for a few more days. If you change your mind about coming to England, please inform me and I will book your ticket for the plane."

"But why won't you go to Richard, Mei Mei?" Winnie asked, her eyes round. "There is no barrier to your union now. Richard had nothing to do with the night you set sail from Singapore to India. Why blame him?"

Mei Mei's face was white, and her eyes looked haunted. "Winnie, Richard has lost his memory, and he does not remember me. I would rather carry the memories of my time with him when we loved each other, than go to him now and try to make him fall in love with me. He may not, you know. We do not share any history together. While he did not love Clementine, he was fond of her in their childhood and growing up years. Yet, he could never fall in love with her while he was married to her, and it is because he could not remember his friendship with her. I could not bear it if he remains indifferent towards me when I love him with all my heart."

Winnie lost her temper. "Liao Mei Mei!" she cried. "You dare to compare yourself with Clementine? She was very different from you! Her love for Richard was obsessive, and she was a very self-absorbed woman. That is not who you are. According to Emily, Richard has remembered that you nursed him at the lazaretto and saved his life from cholera. It is only a matter of time before he remembers the rest of his life in the tropics. Seeing you in the flesh may bring back his memory in a flash. Richard is ill with tuberculosis. If you love him, how can you not go to him now? Don't be such a coward, my friend!"

Winnie's voice became soft and distressed. "Don't mount more guilt upon me, Mei Mei. You were waiting to marry Richard all those years ago when I contracted tuberculosis. You entered a marriage of convenience so that your dowry could pay for my lung operation. Can you imagine the burden of guilt I have carried over the years? You and Richard would have been married, had it not been for my illness. You are getting a second chance at love, my friend. Take it!"

A blush filled Mei Mei's cheeks and when she looked up, her eyes were luminous. "I want Richard to love me like he did before."

Dan Long, who had been standing at the door, now came in and said, "Richard's love never died. Think about it, Mei Mei. If he did not love you deeply, he could not have painted you. Some part of him has remembered you, for him to paint you in such detail. That beautiful portrait is the strongest testimony of his love for you. And you love him, too. It has been twenty years, Sister, and you were widowed young. You never remarried, never allowed any man to court you. There comes only one great love in one's life, Sister, and you have remained true to that love. Emily told me that Richard had decided to come to Singapore to meet you before Clem's suicide. The suicide and his own illness have stopped him from coming to meet you, and that is why he sent Emily."

A frisson of joy lit up Mei Mei's face, and a smile tugged at her lips. She imagined Richard, with his memory gone, sitting frowning before his easel, drawing her features slowly over the years, and knew that his love was intact. All she needed to do was remind him of his life in the tropics.

Dan Long was still speaking. "It is time, dear sister, for you to continue the journey you undertook on that fateful night in 1942. Hong Ling is grown now, and Richard is waiting for you as ardently as he was twenty years ago. It is time to find your happiness with the love of your life. Your feelings for each other were a melody of love, interrupted many times. Now that he is ill, go to Richard, Mei Mei, nurse him back to health and allow the melody to play on without interruption. Your place is by Richard's side. Our mother entrusted you to my care, Sister, and I advise you to go to him and be his wife."

Nodding at Dan Long and a radiant Winnie, Mei Mei made her way outside to hail a trishaw to take her to the nearby hotel, where Emily Harrison was spending the last few nights of her sojourn in Singapore.

Outside, a new Singapore was being born, the People's Action Party holding victory processions after winning the general elections of a Singapore rushing towards independence. Mei Mei smiled. A new era was opening up for her, too. An era away from the shadow of the hungry ghosts. A time of love.

After raising their children to be bright and kind human beings, it was time for her and Richard to slip away unnoticed from the busy world, to continue in solitude and peace the journey they had started twenty years ago. Her eyes lit up with love for him; she ached to be by his side, and to nurse him as she had at the lazaretto of St John's Island, all those years ago. It was there that their melody of love had first begun.

The breeze brought with it the sweet scent of frangipani. Mei Mei lifted her face to the sky, finally free to possess the man she loved.

Acknowledgements

Other than noted historical figures, all characters have emerged from my imagination and have no resemblance to actual people. This is a work of fiction. However, care has been taken to depict colonial Singapore and to accurately bring to readers a world that existed long ago and for that, I need to thank several sources.

My thanks to the National Library Board of Singapore, for having a multitude of books for research. One such book is *A History of Modern Singapore: 1819-2005*, by C. M. Turnbull. My thanks to journal articles on bondmaids and *The Straits Times* archives from the 1930s. My sincere thanks to the Singapore Law Archive and academic articles of true crime stories and court trials of 1930s Singapore. I deeply appreciate Singapore's National Archives and its section on Oral History Interviews. Listening to people recollecting the past helped me craft the world of colonial Singapore. Finally, thanks to the Internet and many articles online, especially records of ships leaving Singapore for Great Britain when Japanese bombs were dropping over Singapore.

My thanks to Philippa Donovan of Smart Quill Editorial who guided the manuscript in the early stages. My thanks to the publishing team at Monsoon Books and my editor,

Claire Cooper, who worked hard with me on the final product. She gave me insightful feedback, encouraged me, throughout, and was a joy to work with. I thank my husband, Royston Hogan, without whom this book would never have been written. He is my warmest critic, and strong and loyal support.

Fiction set in Singapore

Titles published by Monsoon Books
under the *Dollarbird* and *monsoon* imprints.

And The Rain My Drink by Han Suyin

A Yellow House by Karien van Ditzhuijzen

Circumstance by Rosie Milne

*Detective Hawksworth Trilogy (Vol.1: Singapore Black,
Vol.2: Singapore Yellow, Vol.3: Singapore Red)* by William L. Gibson

Finding Maria by Dawn Farnham

Olivia & Sophia by Rosie Milne

Singapore Girl by James Eckardt

Singapore Love Stories edited by Verena Tay

Singapore Noir edited by Cheryl Lu-Lien Tan

*Singapore Saga (Vol.1: Forbidden Hill, Vol.2: Chasing the Dragon,
Vol.3: Hungry Ghosts)* by John D. Greenwood

The Devil's Garden by Nigel Barley

The Eight Curious Cases of Inspector Zhang by Stephen Leather

The Expat by Patricia Snel

The Man Who Wore His Wife's Sarong by Suchen Christine Lim

*The Straits Quartet (Vol.1: The Red Thread, Vol.2: The Shallow Seas,
Vol.3: The Hills of Singapore, Vol.4: The English Concubine)*
by Dawn Farnham